"If we decided to get married, how soon do you think…"

Dana didn't need to finish the sentence. Jared had already thought through their marriage of convenience.

"As soon as possible," he said firmly. "I don't receive the money from the trust fund until I have a marriage certificate."

"Of course, it wouldn't be a real marriage." Dana gave him a questioning look. "I mean, you can't expect me…us…"

Jared bit back a groan. Oh, he wanted her all right, and if she were honest, she'd admit she wanted him, too. The two times they'd kissed diminished any doubt of that. They'd been nothing less than explosive. "To consummate the marriage," he finished for her.

She nodded as a blush covered her cheeks.

"Dana, if you're worried I'm going to jump you, I'm not. If you want to take the relationship further, I'll leave that up to you."

HOME ON THE RANCH:
A TEXAN COWBOY'S CLAIM

———— ⚔ ————

PATRICIA THAYER

Previously published as *Jared's Texas Homecoming*
and *Wyatt's Ready-Made Family*

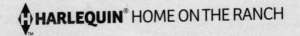 **HARLEQUIN**® HOME ON THE RANCH

Recycling programs for this product may not exist in your area.

ISBN-13: 978-1-335-00799-5

Home on the Ranch: A Texan Cowboy's Claim

Copyright © 2020 by Harlequin Books S.A.

Jared's Texas Homecoming
First published in 2003. This edition published in 2020.
Copyright © 2003 by Patricia Wright

Wyatt's Ready-Made Family
First published in 2004. This edition published in 2020.
Copyright © 2004 by Patricia Wright

For questions and comments about the quality of this book, please contact us at CustomerService@Harlequin.com.

HARLEQUIN®
™ www.Harlequin.com

Printed in U.S.A.

CONTENTS

Patricia Thayer was born and raised in Muncie, Indiana. She attended Ball State University before heading west, where she has called Southern California home for many years.

When not working on a story, she might be found traveling the United States and Europe, taking in the scenery and doing story research while enjoying time with her husband, Steve. Together, they have three grown sons and four grandsons and one granddaughter, whom Patricia calls her own true-life heroes.

Books by Patricia Thayer

Harlequin Western Romance

Count on a Cowboy
Second Chance Rancher
Her Colorado Sheriff

Harlequin Romance

Tall, Dark, Texas Ranger
Once a Cowboy...
The Cowboy Comes Home
Single Dad's Holiday Wedding
Her Rocky Mountain Protector
The Cowboy She Couldn't Forget
Proposal at the Lazy S Ranch

Visit the Author Profile page at Harlequin.com for more titles.

JARED'S TEXAS
HOMECOMING

To Tyler.
My buddy, I'll miss sharing my office with you.

To Hence.
Your knowledge is invaluable to me; so is your friendship.

Prologue

He only came back because of his brother.

Jared Trager Hastings stepped into his father's office. The musty-smelling room looked dull and gloomy with its dark-stained paneling and opaque drapes. The heavy oak desk and chairs were the same pieces his grandfather had used years ago.

With his brother, Marshall's, death, Jared knew that he had just moved to the head of the line to take over the family business, Hastings Development. That was never going to happen. Jared had always been a major disappointment to his father, unable to live up to Graham Hastings's high standards. Marsh had been the perfect son. Now he was gone, dead at thirty-one from leukemia.

A strange numbness claimed Jared. Two brothers couldn't have been more different—one doing everything to please his father, the other doing whatever possible to alienate the man, including running off at twenty. The one regret Jared had was that he'd missed knowing his brother. Now it was too late.

Jared checked his watch. He needed to get on the road. It was a long drive to Nevada. Suddenly the door opened and Graham walked in, along with Marsh's wife, Jocelyn. She was slender to the point of looking frail. Her dark brown hair was pulled back in a bun and her eyes seemed too big for her face, but she appeared to be the one helping GH into the room.

"I thought you'd be gone by now," his father said.

Graham had aged rapidly. At fifty-nine, he easily looked an extra ten years older with his deeply lined face and thinning gray hair. Today, his back was bent and his gait shaky.

Jared refused to let the man rile him. "You asked me to stay so we could talk."

"Since when did you care what I wanted?"

"Like you ever wanted me around," Jared threw back.

"Please, no fighting today," Jocelyn pleaded. "Marsh wouldn't have wanted this."

Jared felt ashamed. "I'm sorry, Jocelyn."

She nodded her appreciation. "I'm the one who wanted you to stay, Jared. To tell you how grateful I am you could be here today. If we could have gotten word to you sooner—"

"Hell, boy," Graham snapped. "Your own brother was dying and no one knew where the hell you were."

Jared clenched his fists to keep from saying anything. He turned to his brother's widow. "You were saying, Jocelyn?"

She looked at her father-in-law. "If you'll excuse us, Graham…"

"As if anyone here cares what I want…." the older man grumbled as he walked around his desk and collapsed into the chair.

Jocelyn went to a far corner of the room and Jared followed. "I need to give you something." She spoke in a hushed voice as she reached inside her purse and drew out an envelope. "Marsh wrote you a letter just days ago." Her dark eyes filled with tears. "Jared, your brother struggled with himself for a long time, but he felt you deserved to know some things."

Jared tensed. "Know what?" He took the envelope from her and began to open it.

Jocelyn stopped him and glanced at his father. "Not here. When you're alone, read it." She released a long breath as if a weight had been lifted off her. "Marsh wasn't perfect. He made mistakes like all of us, but I loved him." She brushed the tears from her cheek. "And I know it gave him comfort to be able to say what he had in his heart. He did love you, Jared."

Jared took the letter, then he pulled his sister-in-law into a tight parting embrace. Unable to speak, he nodded his goodbye and left.

Later, sitting in his truck, Jared opened the envelope. There were several papers clipped together. On top was Marsh's letter.

Jared,

I know it has to be strange to hear from me like this. It's been a long time, and no one is sorrier than I that we lost touch. I used to think if things were different, maybe if Mother had lived, you wouldn't have left home.

I've always envied you, Jared. You never felt the

need to live up to the rigid Hastings standards. You set your own. Of course it's easy now to look back and see our mistakes. And I've made many, which leads me to what I have to say.

Nearly six years ago, while going through Mother's things, I discovered a picture and an old letter that led me to San Angelo, Texas, searching for a man named Jack Randell. A man that our mother once loved. I never found Randell. I located his family, but decided not to pursue it any further. I regret that, because in my search I discovered things…many things you have a right to know. Please, Jared, read the letter.

There's more to the story. While I was in Texas, I fell in love with Dana Shayne. I didn't stay because I was to marry Jocelyn, a choice I've never regretted. But I recently learned I'd fathered a child. I'm thrilled, but I regret that I'll never be able to see my son, Evan. So I'm asking you to go in my place. I've set up a trust for the boy so he'll be taken care of. But he needs to know his family.

I know it's a lot to ask, but please, Jared, don't let Father in Evan's life. I'm afraid of what he might try to do if he learns about him. You can't let GH ruin another Hastings.

Also, San Angelo just may have some answers for you, too. I'm sorry I'm not around to help, but read Mother's letter. It explains a lot of things.
Always,
Your brother,
Marsh

Jared couldn't believe what he'd read. He ran his hand over his face, not surprised to find tears. Marsh had a son. A child he would never know. With a shaky hand, he reached for the yellowed envelope addressed to Audrey Trager, opened the flap and took out the single sheet of stationery along with a picture. It was a younger version of his mother.

Dressed in brightly colored Western clothes, Audrey Trager wore a rhinestone crown on top of her blond hair. The white ribbon draped across her had the bold lettering, Western Days Rodeo Queen 1971. Next to her stood a tall man dressed in jeans and a Western-tooled shirt. He had dark hair, partly covered by a large black Stetson. Grinning at the camera, he had Audrey pressed against his side.

On the back of the photo, was written, "Audrey Trager, Western Days Rodeo Queen, and Jack Randell, bull-riding champion." Jared then unfolded the single piece of paper that had only one paragraph.

Audrey,
    I'm sorry to hear your news, but I told you from the beginning that all I could give you was a few good times. Now it's time I move on. As for the baby, you're on your own. Guess I forgot to mention I'm already married. So you might want to get rid of the kid.
Jack Randell

Jared's heart pounded in his chest as he reread the paragraph that suddenly changed everything. He checked the postmark, six months before his birth date. Damn, he wasn't Graham Hastings's son. That explained so much. The man's anger, the resentment...the hatred.

Jared glanced down at his fisted hand and the crumpled letter inside it.

So he'd been passed off to one bastard by another. To another man who didn't want him. As if he had a choice about who his father was. It didn't sound like Jack Randell was any better at the job.

But that didn't stop Jared from wanting to find out the truth.

Chapter 1

She was doing this for Evan's sake.

Dana Shayne dreaded the trip into town, but it had to be done. She closed the door to the house and walked down the porch steps with her four-year-old son in tow. Evan's dark, wavy hair was neatly combed for a change, and his best jeans and striped T-shirt had been freshly laundered. On his quickly growing feet, he wore his black-tooled cowboy boots that Bert had taught him—to her dismay—to spit-shine.

Her son looked up at her. "I saved my 'lowance, Mom. Can we get ice cream?" he asked, using his best, how-can-you-resist-my-face? look. Then he added a few blinks over his chocolate-brown eyes.

Dana doubted they'd have anything to celebrate today, but she wouldn't deny him the simple pleasure of an ice-cream cone. "Sure we can, honey. That sounds good."

She opened the door to her daddy's old 1970 Ford crew cab truck and helped Evan into the safety seat in the back, then went around to the other side. She checked her gathered print skirt and white short-sleeve cotton top. Already the late-spring weather caused her to perspire, and today of all days she needed to look cool and confident. The last thing she wanted was for Mr. Wilson at the bank to see her sweat.

Dana started up the truck and headed toward San Angelo. Passing the Lazy S Ranch sign that her granddaddy had put up years ago when he'd settled in West Texas, she suddenly felt sad. How much longer would a Shayne own this land? This had been her and Evan's only home. How could she leave it? But since her father's death, she and the sixty-five-year-old foreman, Bert, couldn't handle the place alone, and not many ranch hands would work for what she could afford to pay.

Dana had hoped to expand the cattle operation. Maybe if she had done it a year ago, she'd be able to pay the upcoming balloon mortgage payment. But there wasn't enough money. As if on cue, the truck hit a rut in the road and she groaned. So many things around the ranch needed fixing, not just the road, but the roof on the house and barn, along with most of the fencing.

Dana sighed. Somehow she had to convince the bank that if they lent her more money, she could make a go of it.

"Hey, Mom," Evan called from the back seat. "I'm gonna get pep'mint."

Dana smiled and turned to her son. "Peppermint sounds good. I think I'll have that, too." She couldn't believe how fast her baby had grown. He'd soon turn five, and this fall he'd be heading off to kindergarten. No doubt the separation would be tougher on her than her son.

A horn sounded and Dana turned back to the road only to discover she had wandered into the path of another vehicle. With a gasp, she jerked the wheel to pull the truck back on her side. Overcompensating, she ended up going off the shoulder and into the high grass. The truck bumped and bounced but she managed to keep it under control until it finally stopped. That's when she heard the screech of tires, followed by a crash.

With her heart beating like a drum, Dana managed to put the truck in Park and unbuckle her seat belt. She turned around to Evan. "Are you okay?" Her hands were shaking as she reached for him. She caressed his face, trying to soothe his fears.

"Mom, that was scary."

She saw the fear in his eyes and his trembling lip. She stroked his arm soothingly. "I know, honey, but we're okay." She didn't want to remove him from his safety seat, not until she checked on the other vehicle. "Mom needs to check on the people in the other truck. So you have to stay here."

The child nodded. "Hurry, Mom."

"I will," she promised as she climbed out of the cab. Her legs were weak, threatening to give out, but she gathered her strength, knowing someone could be seriously hurt. She raced across the deserted two-lane road to the late-model Chevy extended cab with Nevada plates. With the new highway, hardly anyone used this road, not unless they were coming to the Lazy S. Seeing the bent hood and hearing the sound of steam from the radiator, she knew there could be serious injuries.

"Oh, God, please, don't let anyone be hurt," she

chanted as she ran to the driver's door and found a man slumped against the wheel. When she jerked the door open, he started to lift his head and groaned. That was a good sign, wasn't it?

"Wait! Don't move, you could be hurt."

"If a devil of a headache counts, I'm dying."

Dana watched as the man raised his head all the way and turned toward her. He had thick, raven-black hair and deep blue eyes. He had at least a day's growth of beard, but not enough to hide the cleft in his chin. She didn't see any sign of injury or blood.

"Do you hurt anywhere other than your head?" She examined his broad shoulders and his chest covered by a denim shirt. Her gaze moved down over long, muscular legs encased in faded jeans. On his feet he wore crepe-soled work shoes, instead of the area's standard cowboy boots.

"No, and if the air bag hadn't gone off, I'd have been fine."

Somewhat relieved, she finally noticed the evidence of the deflated bag hanging from the steering wheel. "It probably saved your life."

The man looked toward the front of his truck. "At least I'm better off than Blackie."

"Blackie. Who's Blackie?"

He did it then. He smiled. "Blackie is my truck." He started to climb down.

"Wait, you shouldn't move."

"I'm just going to stretch my legs and try to clear my head." He managed to get out of the truck and stood. She reached out to assist him, gripped his large forearms, then quickly released him when she realized he was doing better without her help.

"I think you should sit down." When he ignored her suggestion, she watched vigilantly for any sign that he might pass out. He seemed pale, but that could be the powder from the air bag. He didn't appear to have any visible bumps or bruises on his head, but she couldn't take any chances. "Do you want me to drive you to the doctor?"

He stared at her. "Why?"

"Because, you could be hurt and… I was the one who ran you off the road."

"You did kind of take your half out of the middle."

"I only glanced at my son, and when I turned back there you were. This is the main road to my ranch. No one comes this way, unless they have business at the Lazy S." She paused, knowing she caused the accident and couldn't afford to upset this man. "I know that's no excuse…." She brushed her hair from her face. "I'm sorry. I'm Dana Shayne. My ranch is the Lazy S and it's just over the rise."

He hesitated as he looked her over. "I'm Jared Trager."

She didn't recognize the name and she'd lived all her life outside San Angelo. No doubt he was a drifter. "Are you sure you're okay, Mr. Trager?"

He nodded. "It's Jared. I could use something for this headache."

"Then let me take you back to the house. You can also call for a tow truck from there."

"If it's not too much trouble."

"No, of course not," she said. She watched as he took a duffel bag from behind the seat then reached into the bed of the truck and took out a toolbox.

"You can leave that."

"Not on your life. These tools are my livelihood."

She'd known men who felt that way, but usually about their horses and saddles.

They started to walk across the road. At about six-two, with a sturdy build, Jared Trager didn't have any trouble carrying his belongings. When they reached her truck, he dropped his things in the bed then went around to the passenger side and climbed in. Dana hurried to her side and got in her seat.

"Mom, who is he?"

Dana twisted around toward her son. "This is Mr. Trager, Evan. Mr. Trager, this is my son, Evan."

Dana couldn't help but notice the close scrutiny the stranger was giving Evan. Then the man grinned.

"It's nice to meet you, Evan. Just call me Jared," he said as he reached back to shake the boy's hand.

Her son's eyes lit up. "Your truck got smashed up."

"Yeah, Blackie is a little banged up."

His eyes widened. "You call your truck... Blackie? I got to pick a name for my pony. Sammy."

"That's a good name."

"But I want a real horse. Mom says I'm too little. But when I'm six, I'll be big enough."

Jared Trager gave Evan the once-over. "I'd say by then you'll be about the right size for a horse. But your mom is the one who decides that."

Dana started the engine, before her son talked the man to death. "You didn't tell me why you're on this road."

He gave her a sideways glance. "I was coming to see you."

Jared wasn't prepared for this. He'd only arrived in San Angelo yesterday. After discovering the Shaynes and the Randells were conveniently neighbors, he'd asked around for directions to both ranches. Not sure yet if he was ready, if ever, to conquer the Randells, he'd decided to come to the Lazy S first.

More than likely this was how Marsh had first met Dana Shayne. Jared stole another look at her. Damn, she sure wasn't what he'd expected. Tall and willowy, she had a head full of wild auburn hair, green eyes that drew you in, while hinting at secrets. He had to admit that she'd taken him by surprise. Although pretty, Ms. Shayne didn't seem his brother's type. Hell, he didn't even know Marsh's type, or why he should care. He was here to fulfill a dying request, and that was all.

Jared blew out a tired breath. All the way from town he'd been rehearsing his speech to Ms. Shayne. How to relay Marsh's wishes for her and the boy. His strategy had been just to walk up to her door, say what he needed to say as he handed her the information about the boy's trust, then with a quick goodbye, he'd hit the road. What did he know about playing uncle? Family had never been his thing.

Now his plans had to change. How could he predict that Dana Shayne would run into him…literally? He gripped the edge of the torn bench seat as the truck bounced over a pothole. Hell, later he'd tell her who he was.

As they drove through the ranch's gate, Jared got a good look at the place. The Lazy S had obviously once been a showcase, but it had seen better days. The faded red barn and the once-white two-story house were both in need of paint. The corral fencing needed repair, as did the barn doors. He could spend weeks here and have plenty to keep him busy.

Wait, what was he thinking? He didn't need a job. He had one waiting for him in Nevada.

Dana drove up to the back door and turned off the engine. She climbed out and went to assist her son.

"You want to come see my pony?" the boy asked, his dark eyes wide. Jared hadn't missed the strong resemblance to Marsh. The same features and coloring. Surprisingly, finding this little version of his brother didn't make him sad.

"Not now, Evan," his mother said. "Mr. Trager's head hurts."

Jared noted the boy's disappointment. "Maybe later, son."

Dana and Evan led the way up the steps to the door. The wooden slats needed to be replaced, as did many of the boards in the porch. Inside, there was a mudroom with a washer and dryer and several pairs of boots lined against one wall. The temperature dropped when they entered a big peach-colored kitchen with floral curtains at the windows. An oval table surrounded by six chairs was the center focus, and on top, a big bowl of fruit. The place was so homey, it caused an ache in his gut for what he'd never had.

"You sure you're okay?" she asked.

He nodded as he leaned against the counter.

Looking unconvinced, Dana went to the phone on the wall and dialed a number. She walked into the other room and talked in muffled tones. In a few minutes she returned.

"Can I get you something cool to drink?" she asked.

"If you have some iced tea, that would be nice."

"I do." She went to the refrigerator where several

pieces of artwork were on display. No doubt the boy's handiwork.

Evan pointed out one of the pictures, an abstract figure. "See, that's my pony. That's Sammy."

"He looks like a fine animal."

The boy nodded. "My grandpa got him for me for my birthday. I was three years old." He held up five chubby little fingers. "I'm almost five."

Jared frowned, finding he was curious about Dana's father. "Did he teach you to ride?"

Again the child nodded. "Then he got sick and went to live in heaven." He looked so sad. "I miss him."

Jared was happy the kid had been loved. "I bet you do."

Dana returned to the table with a glass of tea and one of lemonade. She handed the tea to Jared and set the lemonade on the table for her son. After the boy took a long drink, she said, "Evan, go change out of your good clothes."

"We're not going into town?" he asked. "What about my ice cream?"

"We'll go get some another time. We need to take care of Mr. Trager."

"Oh." That seemed to interest Evan more. "Is he gonna stay until he gets all better?"

"For a little while," his mother said. "Stop asking so many questions and go change."

"'Kay." Evan shot off, his footsteps sounding as he scurried down the hall and up the stairs.

"Sorry, my son is very inquisitive."

"He's not a bother," Jared assured her. Which was true. "Besides, I'm the one who's intruding on you."

"And I'm the one who ran you off the road."

He shrugged. "No one was hurt."

"Your truck didn't fare too well. And I'm not convinced you're completely all right. Your face is all red."

"It does itch. It's the air bag." He tried to make light of the situation. "I should have ducked to get out of the way."

She went to a drawer and took out a kitchen towel, wet it, then brought it to him. "Sit down."

When he did, she pressed the cooling cloth to his face. He was taken aback by her casual manner. But it wasn't so casual for him. Her gentle touch definitely was causing a reaction.

"You could have been seriously hurt," she said.

"But I wasn't. So no need to worry." He took the cloth from her, but she didn't pull away. She was close. So close he breathed in her scent, a freshness he couldn't describe, but knew he could quickly become addicted to it. He raised his gaze to hers. Her eyes were a liquid green with tiny golden flecks in the center. His body began to heat up and he'd be lying if he told himself it had anything to do with the Texas weather. Finally he diverted his gaze.

She also pulled back. "I—I called Doc Turner anyway. He's going to stop by just to check you out."

Before Jared could argue that a doctor's visit wasn't necessary, he heard the door open and an older man walked into the kitchen. "Hey, you're back from the bank already? They give you the loan?" Just then the man noticed they weren't alone and his face reddened. "Sorry, Dana, I didn't know you had company."

"Bert, this is Jared Trager. Jared Trager, Bert Marley. We nearly collided on old Parker Road. I managed to get out of the way, but Jared's truck hit a tree."

Bert winced. "Well, jumpin' jackrabbits. Ain't that all we need. How bad?"

"His truck isn't drivable," Dana said. "But I'm more worried about Mr. Trager. The air bag went off."

Bert limped over and examined Jared through his wire-rimmed glasses. "Looks like you got a nasty rash."

"I heard that's one of the drawbacks," Jared said. "I was hoping I'd never find out, but I'll survive."

"Doc Turner's coming out," Dana said.

"What were you doin' out on our road?" Bert scrutinized him. "Take a wrong turn?"

Jared didn't miss the hostility in the man's eyes. This was the opening he needed. *But how do you just blurt out that you're the brother of the man who left you pregnant?* "No. I was headed this way."

"Why?"

Jared felt the beads of sweat on his forehead. "I wanted to talk with Ms. Shayne."

A grin spread across the old man's weathered face. "So you come about the job."

Jared was caught off guard by the question. He meant to say no, and tell the truth, but his answer didn't come out that way. "I guess I could use the work."

Later after supper, Dana went to her father's office. What a day it had been. She hadn't gotten to the bank to talk to Mr. Wilson about the mortgage. Instead, she ended up causing bodily injury to a stranger.

She was so grateful when Doc examined Jared and declared the man fit, then gave him cream for the rash. And by mealtime his headache was gone, too. All she had to do was send the drifter on his way. But something stopped her. Being a woman alone, she didn't like hiring somebody she didn't know. But thanks to her, the man was stranded. His truck would take nearly two weeks to repair so Trager couldn't leave for the time being. She knew that he might get work somewhere else, but she owed him.

It felt like she owed everyone, including the bank. Dana shook the worrisome thought from her head. Not tonight. Nighttime was for Evan. She walked into the living room and found Jared sitting in her father's chair with her son next to him as he read a story.

Dana's chest tightened. The picture of the two seemed so perfect. Father and son. But in an imperfect world, Dana knew she couldn't give Evan what he wanted the most. A father.

Jared raised his head and smiled at her.

Her son looked happy, too. "Jared was reading me a story, Mom. He's good, and he don't even have kids."

Jared shrugged, looking a little uncomfortable.

"I guess it's just a talent," Dana said. The man probably had many other talents. "I think it's time for you to go to bed, Evan."

Evan started to argue but looked at Jared, who nodded. To her surprise her son said, "'Kay, Mom." Then he climbed out of the big chair and came to her, giving her a hug and kiss.

Dana called to her son as he climbed the stairs. "I'll be up in a few minutes to say good-night." She then turned her attention back to Jared.

"I appreciate you spending time with Evan. He really misses his grandfather and…his father isn't in the picture." Why did she tell him all that? "About the job, if you're serious about working for me, you need to know I can't afford to pay you much." She quoted him the wages. "But I'll cook all your meals and you can stay in the bunkhouse."

"Are you saying you want to hire me? I'm not an experienced ranch hand. I'm a carpenter by trade, but I can ride pretty well and I've spent time on a ranch."

Dana hesitated, not needing any complications in her life...or her heart. But she had no choice. She did need a man. "That's what I'm saying."

He stood. "Thank you."

"Don't thank me just yet. Around here our day starts at five-thirty. Breakfast is at six-thirty and you'll be in the saddle by seven. And the day doesn't end until everything gets done. Think you can handle that, Mr. Trager?"

He reached out his hand and took hers. "The name is Jared. And yes, I can handle it."

Dana placed her hand into his callused one. Immediately she felt heat shoot up her arm, warming her entire body. Maybe he could handle the work but suddenly she had doubts about her ability to handle Jared Trager.

Chapter 2

He had to be crazy.

Jared tossed his duffel bag on the first bed in the bunk-house. He'd had the perfect opening to tell her who he was, and he blew it. He puffed out a tired breath. Now what? He'd hang around a few days, help her out a lit-tle, make a few repairs. Maybe spend some time with the boy, then hand over the trust fund information and leave for Las Vegas.

"Damn." Pulling his cell phone from his pocket, he punched in Stan Burke's number. With the time differ-ence, it was still early enough to catch him at the office.

The familiar voice came over the line. "Burke Con-struction."

"Stan, it's Jared."

"Hey, Jared. Where the hell are you?"

"I'm afraid I'm not in Nevada. And I won't be there for a while."

"What's the problem?"

"A couple of things," Jared began. "I need to do some things for my brother and it's going to take a little longer than I expected. Especially since my new truck met up with a tree."

"Are you okay?" The sound of concern in Stan's voice touched Jared.

"Just a headache and a little air-bag rash. I'll be fine."

There was a long pause. "How long will you be there? We have a tight deadline on the Black Knight Casino."

"A few weeks. I'll call a friend of mine—Nate Peterson. We've worked together before. He's a good guy and a top-notch carpenter. He can be there late tomorrow and help out until I get out of there."

"Sounds good."

"Thanks, Stan. I'll make it up to you when I get back."

"All I want is my best carpenter back."

Jared laughed. He'd been working for Burke Construction for the past three years. He liked Stan a lot. His friend was getting older and wanted to retire soon. Stan had offered to sell him the business. And Jared wanted to buy the profitable company. He'd have the money, but not until he'd receive his inheritance from his mother when he turned thirty-five or married. He doubted he'd ever marry, so that meant two more years of waiting.

"It's nice to know I'm missed."

"Always," Stan said. "Besides, you're going to help me reach those golden years of retirement." There was laughter, then a long pause. "Is everything okay with you, Jared?"

No, everything wasn't okay, but Jared had never been

one to share his problems. "Yeah, just some family business. I need to be in Texas for a while."

"Well, take the all time you need. Family is important."

Too bad Jared didn't know who his family was. He gave Stan the phone number of the ranch. Next, Jared dialed Nate. Luckily the carpenter was in between jobs, and was excited about spending time in Vegas.

After a quick goodbye, Jared hung up and turned to find Dana standing in the doorway. She had on the same print skirt and white top as earlier. Her hair was down, curls brushed against her shoulders. She looked wholesome and sexy at the same time.

"Sorry to disturb you. I just came out to make up your bed." She walked inside, set sheets and blankets on the chair next to the single bunk, then began to make up the bed.

"You don't have to do that," he said. "I'm capable of making my bed."

When she didn't stop the task, Jared joined in. Accidentally their hands collided and Dana jerked back. Jared, too, felt the jolt, but continued to fit the pristine-white sheets and blanket over the lumpy mattress.

When finished, Dana glanced around the long room with five other empty bunks. "I think that's everything. I put towels in the bathroom down the hall." Her gaze shifted to his. "I'm sorry, but I couldn't help but overhear. Did you just turn down a job? I thought you came here for a job."

Jared froze. He could end this now if he told her the truth. *Tell her the truth, then you can leave.* "I couldn't make it to Nevada in time. Had a family emergency." He shrugged. "So I decided to stay in Texas for a few weeks. It's okay. I can catch another job when I get there. There's plenty of work in Las Vegas, especially in the construction business."

Dana seemed relieved. "It's not like that here. The small ranchers have been struggling for a while. I'm not going to lie to you. Most ranch hands want to work for the larger operations. They pay better."

"You trying to get rid of me?"

"No. I need an extra hand now. I just wanted you to know that I can't pay the kind of money you're used to."

"Let's not worry about that. I don't need much right now." He raised an eyebrow, wondering how she could manage with only Bert. "How large is the Lazy S?"

"Ten sections now. Landwise I can handle more cattle, but we're in a drought and it costs a lot for feed. And I had to sell off quite a few head last year...."

"Sounds like it's been rough on you and Evan."

"That's what it's like for most ranchers. Feast or famine."

"Why stay in?"

Dana smiled and his heart tripped in his chest. "Ranching is all I know, and the Lazy S is the only home I've ever known. I don't know if I could handle city life." Those green eyes rose to meet his. "What about you?"

He hesitated. He hadn't been ready for her question. "I've lived a lot a places over the last dozen years. Mostly large cities. Working in construction, I haven't spent much time in the country."

"We move at a pretty slow pace here," she said. "After Las Vegas, think you can handle it?"

At the moment Jared couldn't think of anywhere else he wanted to be. "Yeah, I can handle it," he assured her.

"And I'm used to getting an early start. Like in Nevada. It's wise to start work before the sun gets too hot."

Dana checked her watch. "We both should be getting to bed...." Color flamed in her cheeks. "Well... I should leave and let you get some sleep."

He nodded, trying to distract himself from the picture she had alluded to. No, he couldn't think about her that way—about wanting her. "You're right. I'll see you in the morning. Good night."

"Good night." Dana turned around and Jared couldn't ignore the soft sway of her rounded hips. Desire shot through him. He knew the last thing he could do was get involved with Dana. She was off-limits, in more ways than one.

Jared sat on the bed, unlaced his work boots and pulled them off. Stretching out on the mattress, he stared up at the wooden slats in the ceiling. What had possessed him to take the job? He had no business being here. Well, what business he had wouldn't take more than an hour. He needed to forget what Marsh told him about their mother and just get the hell out of Dodge.

Reaching into his back pocket, he pulled out the crumpled letter from Jack Randell. Hell, why couldn't he just let it go? The last thing he wanted to do was find out he didn't fit in somewhere else. He doubted the three Randell brothers wanted a bastard brother showing up.

But, damn, he had to know where he belonged.

Dana walked through the back door of the house. She couldn't believe she had flirted with Jared Trager. And worse, she knew better. There was danger written all over the man, from his slow, easy saunter to his sexy grin. Besides, he had a home in Las Vegas. And probably a woman waiting for him.

As her father used to say, drifters come and go as fast as the seasons. If only she'd heeded those words when she'd met Marshall Hastings.

At twenty-three, Dana had had yet to experience love...until she'd met Marsh. A good-looking stranger who had come to the ranch, asking for directions. He gave her the attention she craved, but in the end he took off. Marsh hadn't cared that he'd taken her innocence. But he'd left her a gift. Evan. Because of her son she would never regret what had happened between them.

Now, at twenty-eight, Dana had given up on finding what her parents had. Although their time together had been short, Kathryn and Drew Shayne had truly loved each other. But their daughter would never risk her heart again. Dana never wanted to feel that kind of pain for the second time.

If she ever got married, she was definitely going to play it safe. Look for a nice, safe guy...like Hal Parks. The local deputy sheriff was nice enough, not bad-looking, either. She'd known him all her life. He still came around to the ranch and it was easy to see that, with some encouragement, the shy deputy might ask her out. Was that what she wanted?

Maybe. She had Evan to think about. He was getting older, and he needed a father figure. Hal liked kids, even coached Little League.

"If there were just a few sparks," she murmured, wishing she could get up some enthusiasm.

A warm shiver slid down her spine as her attention turned to her new ranch hand. Jared Trager sent off sparks with just a look from those bedroom eyes. What would his touch be like?

"Stop it," she chided herself, shutting off lights as she walked through the quiet house. On the stairs, not wanting to wake Evan, Dana skipped the fifth step to avoid the squeaky loose board.

Once in her bedroom, she closed the door and turned on the lamp on the night table. A soft glow illuminated the room she'd slept in all her life. It was still painted a light pink, but she had exchanged the twin bed for a double. After her father's death, she hadn't seen any reason to move into the master suite.

She went to the window and glanced down at the barn. Everything looked peaceful. Just the way she liked it. But for how long? How long could she hold on? How long would this ranch belong to a Shayne? The place was mortgaged and the payment was due soon.

A mortgage that her father had taken out when his only child had developed complications in her pregnancy and had delivered his grandson, Evan Andrew, six weeks early. At less than four pounds, her infant son had had to remain in the hospital for weeks. That had cost money, a lot of money.

When she'd told him of her pregnancy, not once had her father complained or lectured her. He'd never judged her when she said that her baby's father was not in the picture. And from the day she'd brought Evan home from the hospital, he'd loved the boy.

Now, it was just her and Evan. And as a legacy to her father and her son, she couldn't lose the Lazy S. She might not know what the future of the ranch would be, but she wasn't going to give up easily. She would do whatever it took.

* * *

The next morning, Dana was putting breakfast on the table when Bert walked in the back door, Jared behind him. His chambray shirt and jeans looked as if they'd already seen plenty of work and it was only 7:00 a.m. If Bert had had anything to do about it, they'd been up well before the sun.

"I hope you're hungry," Dana said as she tore her gaze away from her good-looking new employee. "Have a seat."

"Yeah, Mom made biscuits and her special gravy," Evan said from his chair at the kitchen table.

Bert hung his hat by the door. Jared also placed a hat on the hook next to the foreman's. She recognized the familiar battered straw that always hung in the barn. So her new ranch hand didn't even own a cowboy hat.

"Is it someone's birthday?" Bert asked as he walked to the table.

"I just felt like making biscuits and gravy," Dana replied, a little too quickly. "Of course, I'm not going to force you to eat them."

Bert grinned as he raised his arthritic hands in surrender. "Hey, I'm pleased as a calf in clover. Just surprised." The older man glanced at Jared. "This girl here is the best cook around these parts." He patted his rounded stomach. "I should know—been eating it for years. That alone should be enough pay to work here."

Dana returned to the table with a plate of eggs and a basket of her butter biscuits. "Yeah, too bad that isn't true. If it were, I'd have ranch hands lined up outside my door."

"Mom, I'll work for you," Evan volunteered as he reached for a biscuit.

She ruffled her son's dark head. "Thanks, but I'd be

happy for you to pick up your room and give me a few kisses."

He puckered up and Dana leaned down and took his offering. "Bert and Jared need to give you a kiss, too."

Dana fought the heat flaming in her cheeks. She lost. "Oh, I'm pretty stingy with my kisses. I save them for my best guy. You." She tickled his ribs, making him giggle.

Jared sat back and watched the exchange between mother and son. Marsh would be happy to see how good they were together. Once again he reminded himself he should leave. It had been a lot of years since he'd worked on a ranch. Just that short time right after he'd left Graham Hastings's house some dozen years ago. He smiled to himself, recalling another time when he and Marsh were twelve and thirteen and attended a summer ranch camp for wannabe cowboys.

Maybe he'd just finish the week, then go and stay in town until his truck was repaired. While he was here he could replace some of the stall gates in the barn. How long could that take? He knew that Bert was limited to the amount of work he could do. Just feeding stock and keeping the fences repaired and upright was a full-time job.

That's what they'd been doing since five this morning when Bert had come to get him. Having had a restless night he'd already been awake. He'd been thinking about Dana, and the direction of his thoughts were dangerous. That's the reason he needed to finish this job and get going. His pretty boss was trouble.

"What ya doin'?" Evan asked.

Jared stopped his hammering and turned to find the boy standing behind him in the wide concrete aisle inside the barn.

"I'm fixing Sammy's stall. Some of the boards rotted out and I thought I'd replace them. You don't want your pony to get hurt, do you?"

The boy shook his head. "No, I love Sammy." He glanced around the barn. "Where's my pony?"

"I took him outside so the noise wouldn't scare him."

Evan gave the situation some thought. "Do you have a horse?"

"No, I don't."

"Do you want one?"

He pulled another rusted nail from the rotted wood. "I probably did when I was your age."

"Do you know how to ride?"

Jared bit back a smile at the artillery of questions. "Probably not as good as you, but I manage."

"I bet Mom will let you ride Scout. He's gentle and doesn't bite or kick."

"That's good to know in case, but I'm busy for a while repairing the stall." Jared replaced his hammer in his tool belt.

"Wow, what's that?"

"My tool belt." Jared crouched down to show the boy his different tools and the pouches for nails and screws.

"That's cool."

"I'm a carpenter. I need to have a lot of different tools so I can do my work."

"Can I help you? I know how to use a hammer. Bert showed me one time."

Jared scratched his head as if thinking about it. "I guess I could use a helper. Maybe you can hand me nails and tools."

The boy's dark eyes lit up. "Really?"

"As long as it's okay with your mother."

"She went into town. Bert's watchin' me."

"I guess we should ask him. Then maybe you can help me carry some more wood from the side of the barn."

"I'm strong, I can do it. Come on," Evan called as he took off to the corral to ask Bert. A smiling Jared walked after him as the boy eagerly chattered with the older man, selling his case. Bert looked toward him. Jared nodded his approval and the foreman gave the child permission. He found he was looking forward to spending time with Evan. He was a great kid.

The next two hours flew by. Surprisingly, Evan didn't get tired or complain about the work. The boy held tools, handed Jared nails and did just about anything Jared asked of him.

They were working on the third horse stall and Evan was still talking nonstop. The current subject was about some wild mustangs.

"Are there mustangs on the Lazy S?" Jared asked.

Evan shook his head. "They live in Mustang Valley, but that's really close to here." He pointed off to the west. "Over by the Circle B that Hank owns. He's Bert's friend. But Bert says Hank turned the ranch into a sissy dude ranch."

Jared couldn't help but laugh.

"They got a whole bunch of people who go there just to look at the mustangs. They pretend to be cowboys and cowgirls. Bert says it's plumb crazy. That city people are loco."

"How big is this place?"

"Real big." There was a pause as Jared hammered in another nail. Evan handed him another one. "They want Mom to sell them some of her land." The boy picked up the conversation. "But Mom never will 'cause when I'm growed up, the Lazy S is gonna be mine."

"So Hank has been after her to sell?"

Evan shook his head. "No. She says it's Hank's boys. They aren't really his boys, they just lived with him."

Was someone pressuring Dana into selling? "How do you know they aren't his kids?" Jared asked.

"'Cause Bert said they have a good-for-nothing daddy. Hank took them in and saved them from a life of crime."

"Who are these boys?"

"The Randells."

Dana finally had made it back into town. A lot of good it had done her. The bank hadn't been interested in listening to her idea to expand the cattle operation. Worse, they refused her the additional money she needed, only allowing her a sixty-day extension on her current mortgage. Things didn't look good. She turned off the highway and headed down the road to the Lazy S.

Why not just give up? She could sell part of the ranch to the Randells. Cade had talked with her several times about wanting the section that was attached to the valley and their property.

Dana wiped way her tears. She didn't want to think about it now. There was still an outside chance that she could scrape up enough money when she sold off her yearlings. But what would she and Evan live on for the next six months? She could get a job in San Angelo. But what was she qualified to do? Work as a waitress? And besides, Evan would only be in school half days. Bert would probably be able to watch him. But how could she ask her dear sweet godfather to do more?

She pulled the truck up to the back door, disappointed

when Evan didn't come running to greet her. She climbed out and started for the barn, wondering what her son was up to. She was surprised to hear the sound of hammering greet her as she walked into the cool structure. She followed the noise and found her son...and Jared Trager.

The two had their dark heads together as they measured the piece of wood that was going to be a slat for the stall. Dana glanced around and discovered that several of the stalls had new boards and shiny new hinges. So this was what her new hand had been doing all day.

"Evan," she called.

The boy turned and grinned at her. "Mom, you're home." He ran to her and hugged her. Dana relished having her son in her arms. It made her lousy day suddenly brighten.

Evan pulled back. "Look what me and Jared are doing."

She glanced around at the three stalls with the new wooden boards and gates. "By the looks of things, you both have been busy." What was Evan doing in here?

Jared stood. "I checked with Bert before I let Evan help me."

The boy pointed to Jared. "Look at Jared's tool belt, Mom. It's cool."

Dana's gaze went to the area that had her son so fascinated. There were several kinds of tools that hung from a wide strip of honey-colored leather around Jared's narrow waist and hips. But her attention lowered to his fitted jeans over long muscular legs. A sudden awareness rushed through her body, catching her off guard with the sensual direction of her thoughts. Her gaze shot upward to catch a knowing look in the man's eyes.

"Yes it is," she agreed, a little perturbed that he'd discovered her bold appraisal. "But you shouldn't have bothered Jared, honey. He has chores to do."

"I finished everything Bert asked me to do," Jared assured her. "I don't like to sit around. So I found a few things to fix."

Dana stiffened. She didn't needed him pointing out that the Lazy S was badly in need of work.

"Evan, why don't you go to the truck and take the bag of groceries into the house?"

"But, Mom, I'm helping Jared."

Before Dana could say anything, Jared spoke up. "Remember what I said, Evan. You have to do your other chores before you can work for me."

The child frowned, but he nodded. "Okay. But I'll be back." He shot out of the barn, leaving the two alone.

Dana watched him go, then turned back to Jared. "I'd appreciate it if you talked to me before recruiting my son. Besides, I hired you to feed the stock and repair the fences."

Jared stood there for a long time, then finally spoke. "I checked with Bert. He didn't have a problem with Evan helping me. I wouldn't let the boy get hurt. I only let him hand me some nails and help carry wood. I didn't mean any harm, Dana." He took a step closer and she fought the urge to back away. "What's really bothering you? If you don't want me around your son, just say so and I'll leave."

His gaze locked with hers and a warmth erupted in her stomach. She had overreacted. "It's not that. It's just… I can't afford to pay you any extra."

A smile spread across his face. "I don't believe I asked. As I said, I finished the jobs you assigned me, and thought I could fix a few things."

Dana blinked back threatening tears. She was acting

silly. Was she jealous of this man because her son was drawn to him?

For so long, it had always been just her and Evan. He'd had a close relationship with his grandfather, but that was different. It wasn't a secret Evan wanted a father. And as his mother, Dana was terrified her son would get hurt attaching himself to every man who he met. In walked Jared Trager and he was getting the brunt of her wrath just because Evan longed to spend time with him.

"You're right. I apologize. I appreciate what you've done here." She brushed back her hair. "I guess I just had a bad day."

He cocked an eyebrow. "Any way I can help?"

She released a tired breath and shook her head. "This is something I have to handle on my own. The worst part is, it looks like there's only one answer."

Chapter 3

That evening, Jared walked toward the house for supper. Bert had gone up earlier and Jared had thought about skipping the meal and just staying in the bunkhouse. He figured if Dana hadn't wanted him around the boy, she surely wouldn't want him at her supper table.

It had been hours since she'd stopped by the barn and more or less told him to stay clear of her son. Normally, he'd never given a second thought to kids. But little Evan was starting to get to him. No doubt the boy was aching for a father. "He needed you, Marsh. You should have been here for him."

Emotions tightened Jared's throat and he stopped on the porch to pull himself together. Damn, he didn't want to do this. He didn't want to feel anything. Years ago he'd learned how to cover all the hurt his father dished out—he'd learned to turn off emotions. After he'd left home, he'd avoided any and all attachments. Whenever he'd hooked up with women, he told them up front not to expect anything permanent, nothing that would put him in danger of getting hurt. Now, he was smack-dab in the middle of this…mess. A fatherless boy who was his nephew. If that wasn't enough, about ten miles down the road, there was a whole other situation.

Jared looked off toward the west in the direction where supposedly the Randells lived. The last thing he wanted—or needed—was more family. He'd never fit into that cozy scene. An anxiousness rushed through him. This was usually when he'd pack up and move on. Too late. After turning up a hero to a little boy, and wanting to help out the pretty mother, he was already involved.

Besides, he owed Marsh this. He'd never been much of an older brother, so he had to stick it out. He could do this one last thing for probably the only person who had ever loved him.

"Jared?"

Jared recognized the child's voice and turned to see Evan coming out of the house.

He smiled at him. "Hi, Evan."

"Are you mad at me?"

Jared crouched down to the boy's level. "Of course I'm not mad at you. Why would you think that?"

"Mom wouldn't let me help you anymore. She said I had to clean my room."

"And that is what you needed to do. You should always mind your mother. Besides, I didn't do much more work on the stalls after you left. I had other chores to finish myself."

The boy's eyes rounded. "Did Mom get mad at you, too?"

"No. She's just worried that you might get hurt."

"She always gets afraid." He pouted. "I'm not a baby."

"Sorry, partner, that's just a fact of life. You never stop being *her* baby. And it's only because she loves you so much that she worries."

"But I'm gonna have a birthday. In July." He held up his hand, his fingers spread wide. "I'll be five. I'm gonna go to school, too."

"You are getting big. But we still have to listen to our mothers."

"I bet you don't."

A sadness spread through him as he thought about the fragile woman who'd stood in the shadows as Graham Hastings ruled the family like he did his corporation. Then one day Audrey Trager had gotten sick. She'd died when Jared was only ten, taking so many secrets with her. "No, but I'm a lot older than you."

Evan looked thoughtful. "You old enough to be a dad?"

Dana stood at the screen door, shocked by her son's question, and surprised to find Jared Trager there. She had figured he'd be gone by now. Which was unrealistic since he didn't have a vehicle to drive off in.

"I guess I'm old enough," Jared began. "I've just never settled down and married."

"My mom isn't married. She's pretty and you could—"

Hearing enough, Dana called out to her son. "Evan."

Both males turned in surprise.

"It's time for supper." She glanced quickly at Jared, fighting to keep the heat from her cheeks. "You both need to wash up." She headed back to the kitchen, knowing she had to have a long talk with her son. She didn't want him trying to marry her off, especially to a drifter.

All through the meal, Jared felt invisible as the conversation centered around the next day's chores and Dana directed her orders to Bert. Evan was quietly eating his supper, obviously sensing his mother's sullen mood, and remained on his best behavior.

Smart boy.

Jared knew that he, too, better watch how far he went without checking with Dana. She wasn't a helpless female by any means. She had run the ranch and raised her child pretty much on her own. But something had happened today, something related to her trip into town that seemed to take away her fight. Did it have anything to do with her business at the bank? Bert had let it slip earlier that Dana was having trouble financing the ranch. Even Dana herself had admitted this past year had been a rough one.

Mind your own business, he told himself. Stay the two weeks as agreed, then just give Dana Marsh's letter and walk away. There was probably some money for her along with Evan's trust fund.

"Jared." Dana spoke his name, surprising him. "I want to thank you for repairing the stalls. I didn't get a chance to see everything, but Bert said you did a great job."

"You're welcome. I had a good helper." He winked at Evan.

"That's me, Mom." The boy puffed out his chest. "Can I help Jared tomorrow? There's lots of things broke."

Dana felt a sting of battered pride. Even though the condition of the ranch was evident to everyone, she hated to think even her son saw it, too. "I know, Evan, but you can't keep expecting to tag along after Jared. It's not his responsibility to—"

"The boy isn't a bother," Jared blurted out, then quickly took another bite of food.

Dana couldn't hide her irritation. "That's not what I meant. I just don't want you to think that I expect you to repair everything around here."

"Unless you have a problem with me replacing the wood in the stalls or corral, I don't mind doing it, and there is plenty of wood stacked behind the barn."

"Yeah, Mom," Evan said. "Jared's real good at fixin' stuff and Sammy likes his new gate. And I'm a good helper."

Dana and Jared exchanged a look. Jared smiled, then said, "Evan is the best helper I ever had."

"See, Mom. Jared wants me to. Please…can we?"

Once again Dana looked at Jared. Big mistake. Those bedroom eyes were lethal. "I guess it's not a problem if your other chores are done."

"Oh, boy!" Evan cheered, then jumped up from his chair and hugged his mother. "I love you."

Dana enjoyed the moment. Just as quickly her son released her and went back to his seat and began eating his least favorite vegetable, green beans. So there were miracles.

"Who wants dessert?" Dana stood and picked her still-warm Dutch apple pie up off the counter.

Bert's eyes lit up. "Hot diggity! Jared, you haven't lived until you've had a taste of Dana's apple pie. Won a blue ribbon at the fair four years in a row."

"I guess I have to try it." Jared carried his and Bert's plates to the sink; Evan followed with his. Then Jared walked to the coffeemaker. "Would anyone like a cup?"

"I wouldn't mind at all," Bert said, "since you're up." He glanced at Dana. "How about you?"

"Coffee would be nice."

Dana turned back to her task of serving up dessert, allowing Jared to enjoy the view of how her jeans fit over her nicely curved bottom and long shapely legs. His body began to stir and he finally turned back to the counter and busied himself with the coffee.

"Jared, you want ice cream with your pie?"

He could only nod. Oh, yes, he definitely needed something to cool him off.

Around midnight, Dana couldn't sleep and, finally giving up, she made her way to the porch. So many times she would go sit on the old glider swing and enjoy the peaceful night. The sound of the crickets and faint scent of jasmine in the air was a quick cure to lull away the day's troubles. The ranch had always been her sanctuary. She loved it and wanted desperately to raise Evan here. But for the first time it appeared that might not be a possibility, and she had to face it.

Dana tucked her feet under her and tugged her robe tighter around her body. Where would she and Evan go? What would she do? Never in her life had she thought about doing anything else but ranching. She hadn't finished college. So what was she qualified to do to support herself and her child? There were so many things she had to think about.

She was desperate enough, she'd even thought about finding Evan's father, Marsh Hastings. The last thing she wanted was to drag a man into her son's life who didn't want to be there. Marsh had made his choice nearly six years ago. If he'd cared, he would have checked to see if something happened after their one night together. When he'd never called, that pretty much told Dana what he thought about her, and his child. A tear found its way down her cheek. It didn't bother her anymore, but for her son, it made her sad.

Evan needed a father.

A scuffing noise drew her attention and she looked up to see Jared walk by. "Sorry, I didn't mean to disturb you," he apologized as he stopped at the porch, then rested his foot on the bottom step.

The man had only to be around to unsettle her. "It's all right."

"Too warm to sleep?" he asked.

"And a little restless," she said. "I sometimes come out here when I can't sleep."

"I guess we're both plagued with the same problem. Walking sometimes helps clear my head." He stared out into the moonlit night. "It's pretty quiet here."

"Not like Las Vegas."

He shook his head. "Hard to tell day from night in that town." He was quiet for a while, then said, "I guess I better head back to the bunkhouse. The day starts pretty early around here."

A familiar loneliness erupted inside Dana as she watched Jared start to walk off. There had been so many nights when she'd lie awake, aching to share a conversation or a touch with another person.

"Jared?" She called out his name.

He turned around and looked up at her. When her throat suddenly felt sand dry, she swallowed. "You… got a minute?"

"Sure."

He took the three steps in one climb and swiftly he was standing in front of her, so big and intimidating. For a second she thought he was going to sit next to her; instead, he perched on the railing across from her. Still he was close, so close she could tell he'd taken a shower. She could smell a combination of soap and shaving cream.

"I wanted to apologize for earlier today," she finally said.

"It's forgotten."

"I had no right to snap at you like I did. I'm not used to people helping me."

"I was only working for my pay," he said. "I can understand about Evan. I shouldn't have let him get near tools without checking with you first. You barely know me…."

"I'm sure you were careful," she conceded. "It's just that… I know things are run-down…. Since my father took sick, it's been hard to keep up with everything." Darn, she didn't want to make excuses.

"So, you're going through a rough time. All of us have been there. I'm happy to help. If I have a little extra time, I hope you don't mind if I work on a few things around here. It's not a big deal."

"It's a big deal to my son." She had to make him understand. Jared Trager was the kind of man you didn't forget easily. "Evan is getting attached to you."

"I think he's a great kid, too."

She smiled. "Thank you," she said, trying to get the words out. "Soon you'll be moving on, and… I just don't want him hurt."

Jared studied her a while, then spoke. "Do you think that's wise, Dana?"

This was the first time he had spoken her name, at least, in that deep husky tone.

"You can't protect the boy from life," he went on.

She gritted her teeth. "I'm sure going to try. He's only four."

"He's nearly five," he offered. "And people have to say goodbye all the time. If I'm honest with Evan, he'll understand that I have to leave when my truck is fixed. Haven't there been other ranch hands that have left?"

Dana sighed. "Yeah, I guess you're right. It's just that since his grandfather died, there haven't been many men around...."

Jared knew he should get up right now and leave but something prevented him. Maybe it was seeing her with the moonlight dancing off her hair, or hearing the loneliness in her voice. Dressed in an old-fashioned white cotton gown and robe, her auburn hair hanging loose and wild, Dana Shayne resembled nothing like the bossy woman who'd hired him. Tonight she just looked vulnerable...and too damn tempting.

"What about you, Dana? Is there someone in your life?" He told himself that he wanted to know for Evan's sake.

She looked away. "No, not for a long time."

"Evan's father?"

She shook her head.

"He hurt you, so you're not going to allow another man in your life?"

Dana looked startled at his words. "As you can see, men aren't exactly pounding on my door."

That made them both smile. "Then the men in this town are crazy."

"No, they're smart. Not many guys want to raise another man's child, and take on a stubborn woman with a failing ranch."

Dana paused as if she'd said too much. "I think I should go inside."

She moved to stand up, when her foot caught in her

robe and she began to fall forward. Jared's reaction was quick and he caught her. He grabbed her around the waist and helped her to stand.

Dressed in her thin layers of clothing, there was little left to the imagination. Dana's body was slim and lush all at the same time. Desire, like he'd never known, shot through him. It only grew worse when she raised her head and their eyes locked in a heated gaze. He told himself it was because he'd hadn't been with a woman in a while. Whatever the reason, he had to put a halt to it. He didn't need any entanglements, not with this woman. He released her and stepped back.

"I take it things didn't go well at the bank today," he said brusquely.

She tugged nervously at her robe, then brushed her hair back. "They don't think a woman can handle things on her own."

From what he'd seen, Dana Shayne was more capable than most men. He wanted to ask her how much she needed. "Can you survive?"

"Maybe. If I get a good price for my calves in September. But it'll be rough going for the next six months."

He hated to ask the next question. "Could you lose the ranch?"

She sighed. "There's a chance. There's one other thing I could do...."

"What?"

"I could sell a section of my land to the Randells."

Jared was tired of hearing about the Randells. They had haunted him since he'd read Marsh's letter and found out that there was a distinct possibility that Jack Randell could be his biological father.

A cold shiver went through him as he tightened the cinch against Scout's belly. The horse shifted restlessly as Jared checked the length of the stirrups. He hoped he hadn't forgotten anything. It had been a long time since he'd saddled a horse, but Bert had expressed confidence in him when the foreman asked him to ride out to check fence in the north pasture.

Jared took the reins and walked the horse out of the barn. Pushing his straw cowboy hat down on his head, Jared placed his foot in the stirrup, grabbed the horn and swung his leg over the horse. Surprisingly, it didn't feel that strange sitting in a saddle. He'd ridden horses during the brief time he'd done ranch work years ago, and luckily he remembered how.

Bert strolled up to him, wearing a big grin. "Lookin' like a natural up there."

"Hope I feel the same by the time I return. *If* I return."

"All you have to do is follow the fence line. Check for any sections that are down. There's a supply shack under a group of trees about a mile out. Can't miss it. You'll find everything you need inside. If you see Romeo, chase him back on the east side of the fence."

Jared shifted in the saddle, wondering how to make Romeo, the huge Brahma bull, do anything he didn't want to do. "You sure this is the best way?"

"This is a job you need to do on horseback. Besides, Dana took the truck. And you got the fancy little phone in your pocket if you get lost." Mischief danced in the old man's eyes. "If all else fails, wrap the reins around the horn and tell Scout to take you home." Bert then smacked the horse on the rump sending the horse and rider on their way.

Thirty minutes into the ride, the Texas sun got a little

hot, but Jared enjoyed the easy motion of the horse. Following the fence line, he found a section that had been trampled down, but no sign of Romeo. He located the shed and materials. He spent the next two hours digging a new posthole, then stringing barbed wire. About noon, he took a break and sat under a tree, enjoying the shade and the two sandwiches that Dana had packed him. Drinking thirstily from the water jug, he stripped off his shirt and poured some water over his chest, hoping for a bit of relief.

Jared's thoughts turned to last night, and Dana. When he'd tried to sleep, her face kept reappearing in his head. He wanted to help her. But how? Making repairs wasn't going to stop the bank from foreclosing. She needed to find the money somewhere. Marsh. His brother had arranged child support for Evan's care. Jared made a mental note to call the lawyer. Could she use part of the trust money to help save the ranch? Or would Dana have to go to the Randells? And how much of the Lazy S did they want to buy? One would think it might be better to lose a small part of the ranch than all of it.

Jared released a long sigh into the hot still air. "Thank you, brother, for getting me tangled up in all this."

Deciding it was time to go back to work, Jared climbed to his feet. After putting away his tools, he climbed back on Scout and continued down the trail. After another mile the terrain began to change. Scout started down a steep slope toward a grove of trees and large shrubs. Under the ancient oaks, little sun filtered through the heavy branches, causing the temperature to be a good ten degrees cooler. It seemed like an oasis in the middle of a desert. Scout continued on toward a winding stream rushing over a colorful rock-lined bottom. The animal stopped and drank the cool water.

Jared dismounted and bent down to sample the inviting liquid himself. When he had his fill, he stood to see the horses. About fifty yards away a herd of ponies were grazing in the tall grass. Jared searched the area, realizing he might not be on Shayne property. Across the stream in the distance, he discovered the cabins dotting the landscape.

Mustang Valley. Was he in Mustang Valley?

He turned and continued to search the area. That's when he saw a man on horseback riding toward him. He was older, probably in his sixties. When he was close, he tipped his hat in greeting, then leaned his arm against the saddle horn. "You lost?"

"Could be. I'm Jared Trager, I work for the Lazy S. I was repairing a strip of fence. I think I might have wandered off course. I didn't mean to trespass."

"You didn't. You're still on Shayne land, but barely. Did that old coot Bert send you here to irritate me?" The man climbed down off his horse and walked up to Jared. He peeled off his cowboy hat, revealing thick white hair and friendly hazel eyes. "I'm Hank Barrett. This here is Mustang Valley."

Hank Barrett couldn't help but stare at the stranger. He knew two things right away. Jared Trager wasn't from around here, and he wasn't a ranch hand. But there was something about him that seemed familiar.

"Where you from, Trager?"

"Originally, Colorado, but now Las Vegas. I've been working there for the past three years."

"What ranch?"

"I didn't work for a ranch. I'm a carpenter by trade. I'm working for the Lazy S until my truck is repaired. I had a little accident a few days back and I need to stick around a while."

"I didn't realize that Dana had hired anyone."

"Does she check out everything with you?"

Hank cocked an eyebrow. Seemed like the boy was mighty defensive. "No, but we look out for one another. Her daddy and I were friends."

"Is that why you want to buy her land?"

Hank was surprised. *So Dana had confided in this Trager fellow.*

"That you'll have to take up with my boys. I'm retired." He sighed. "I come out here often for a few hours to enjoy the peace and quiet."

"Would your boys be named Randell?"

Hank studied Trager again. He had brooding looks: black hair and deep-set eyes, reminding him of three others—Chance, Cade and Travis. "Could be."

"Would I be able to get in touch with them?"

"Depends. What do you need to talk to them about?"

"Jack Randell."

That evening, Jared drove his newly rented vehicle in the direction of the Circle B. After returning that afternoon to the ranch, he'd asked Bert to take him into town so he could get transportation. He came back with a Jeep Cherokee. He also could have used a brain transplant.

He was actually going to confront the Randells. Hank had invited him to the house to speak with Chance, Cade and Travis. His brothers. Half brothers, he should say.

He turned off the main highway, then continued down a gravel road. When he was under the sign that read Circle B Ranch, a large two-story house came into view. Further down were several outer buildings painted a pristine white all lined up next to one another and all surrounded by a lattice of fencing.

He pulled into the circular drive and turned off the engine. Hesitating to get out of the vehicle, Jared took the envelope from his pocket and looked it over once again.

So many feelings rushed through him. Everything would change when he shared the secret. He didn't have proof outside the letter, but he knew. He knew now why Graham Hastings had resented him all his life. Why he'd never fit in. He didn't expect to instantly find a family. Hell…he didn't know what he expected.

He puffed out a long breath and climbed out of the car. He walked up the front steps, but before he could ring the bell, the door opened and a tall brown-haired man appeared.

"I take you're Jared Trager," the unsmiling man said.

Jared nodded. "That's right. I came to talk to Chance, Cade and Travis Randell."

"Look, I don't know what you want, but if it concerns Jack Randell, it can't be good, so my brothers and I don't want any part of it."

A pretty blonde appeared. "Chance, where are your manners? Let the man come inside. Then maybe he'll tell us what he wants." She turned and greeted Jared with a smile. "Hello, I'm Joy Randell and this is my husband, Chance."

Jared shook her hand. "I'm Jared Trager."

"Come in, Mr. Trager," she said, and moved aside.

"Please, call me Jared." He followed her and stepped into a huge living room. A soft, inviting golden color covered the walls along with shelves of books. A pair of honey-leather sofas were arranged in front of a tall fireplace where two more men stood. No doubt Randells.

"These two other brooding guys are my brothers-in-law, Cade and Travis. Their wives, Abby and Josie, are in the kitchen making coffee. Would you like a cup?"

Jared shook his head. "No, thank you." He wasn't sure if he'd be staying that long.

"I'll leave you *gentlemen* alone to talk." She kissed her husband's cheek. "Behave, Chance. Just listen to what Jared has to say before you throw him out."

Once she'd left, Chance spoke. "So, Trager, what do you want to talk to us about?"

Jared's throat dried up. "About two weeks ago, my brother died. He left me an old letter from our mother." He pulled the envelope out of his pocket and handed it to Chance. "It's from Jack Randell."

Chance opened the envelope and first pulled out the picture of Audrey and Jack. He studied it a while, passed it on to his brothers, then unfolded the one-page letter.

Jared could hear his heart pounding in his ears as an eternity seemed to pass. Finally, Chance handed the letter off to his brothers and looked at Jared.

"What the hell you trying to take from us?"

What did Jared expect? A loving hug and welcome to the family? "Not a damn thing."

Jared grabbed the letter and headed for the door. Once outside, he jumped into the Jeep and turned on the engine, then pressed down on the gas pedal and shot off, kicking up gravel along the way. He had trouble seeing the road as his anger, mixed with his emotions, nearly blinded him. Jared hated feeling this way. He gripped the wheel tighter. For years, he'd controlled the loneliness of always being an outsider, but tonight was the worst yet.

Back at the Lazy S, the Jeep skidded to a stop in front of the barn and Jared climbed out and slammed the door. He went straight to the bunkhouse and threw the letter on the bed. He wanted to hit something in the worst way—anything to burn off his anger and frustration. That was when he heard Dana's voice.

"Jared..." She spoke softly.

He looked up and saw her just inside the doorway. She was wearing a long skirt and pink blouse. Her hair was curled around her pretty face, her eyes were a brilliant green. From the first Dana had stirred something in him he didn't want to feel. He had to resist her. "This is not a good time." He worked to control his voice.

"You drove in here like the devil himself was after you." She came toward the bunk...toward him. "I don't know where you went or what happened tonight," she began, "and maybe it's none of my business..."

Hell, she didn't want to know what he was thinking right now, or what he wanted to do right now.

"That's right—it's none of your business."

Pain flashed across her face and it tore at his heart. "I think it's best if you leave, Dana."

She stood there for a long time, but started to turn, and that's when he broke and reached for her. Jared caught a whiff of her fragrance and was lost. He needed her—badly. When she didn't move away, he pulled her into his arms.

She looked surprised, excited, and came willingly.

"We're playing with fire," he breathed right before his mouth covered hers.

Jared didn't want to think right now. He'd save his regrets for tomorrow. All he wanted was the taste of her. To feel her body against his. When she opened her mouth, he delved deep to savor her sweetness, pushing all rational thoughts away.

Right now he needed what Dana Shayne could give him. For a little while, he wanted to pretend that someone cared for him.

Someone wanted him.

Chapter 4

Dana had never experienced anything like Jared's kiss.

His mouth was strong, but gentle against hers. Demanding and coaxing at the same time. She surrendered without resistance, opening willingly as his tongue swept inside like a thief. A hunger, like nothing she'd ever felt before, coursed through her. She moved in closer against him, aching for more. It had been so long since anyone had held her, kissed her…wanted her…

With a groan, his arms tightened around her, pressing her body against his evident desire. Her breasts tingled, begging for his touch and he didn't make her wait. When his hand moved under her blouse and covered her heated flesh, she was the one who whimpered. He pulled back and rained kisses down her jaw to her neck as his fingers teased her nipple.

"Oh, Jared," she breathed as she arched against his touch.

He raised his head to meet her gaze and a shiver went through her. Without a word, he took her mouth again. The hunger only intensified and Dana didn't want to think, just feel. Those glorious hands of his found their way to her skirt. Cupping her bottom, he moved her against him, causing agonizing pleasure.

A sudden noise brought Jared back to reality. He pulled back and, ignoring the stunned look on Dana's face, moved to the other side of the room.

Soon the door opened and Bert poked his head inside. "Hey, Jared—" he called, then caught sight of Dana. The old man's gaze moved back and forth between them. "Dana, I didn't know you were out here."

Somewhat recovered, Jared turned around and looked at Dana. Mistake. Her face was flushed. She looked as if she'd been thoroughly kissed. He shifted his attention to Bert. The old man wasn't a fool. "Dana...just came by to tell me the schedule tomorrow."

Bert removed his hat and scratched his head. "Funny, I thought that was my job."

"Ah... Jared—" Dana spoke up "—just wanted to know if it was okay if Evan helps him tomorrow. I let him know that he doesn't have to feel responsible for my son." She headed for the door. "I'm going in. See you both at breakfast."

Jared wanted to follow her to explain what had just happened. But what the hell had happened between them? He glanced at Bert. The man looked as if he was expecting an explanation. Well, he wasn't going to get one. Jared took off after Dana.

There were patches of light on the way from the barn to the house. Jared saw Dana in the shadows just off the porch. He ran and caught up to her.

"Dana, I need to talk to you."

She stopped but didn't turn around. "I don't think there's anything to say."

"I think there's plenty," Jared insisted. "About what happened in the bunkhouse... It shouldn't have happened. I apologize."

"That's what every woman wants to hear—that a man is sorry he's kissed her."

Jared's frustration hadn't lessened. "That wasn't a kiss, that was an all-out assault."

Dana finally turned around. He could see the leftover desire in her beautiful eyes. "Was I complaining?"

He shook his head. "You deserve more, Dana. A lot more."

"Well, we don't always get what we deserve, do we?"

Damn. Marsh had really done a number on her. If she knew who he was, it would only make things worse. "I'm not someone you should depend on. I'm only around for a while. I have to get to Las Vegas."

He saw her fighting back tears. "Why don't we forget this night ever happened?"

Jared thought back to the scene at the Randells and wished the same thing. He knew it was going to be impossible on two counts, especially with what had happened in the bunkhouse. But if was what Dana wanted... He nodded. "Good night, Dana. I'll see you in the morning."

He watched as she walked up the steps. He wanted to follow her, to tell her everything, about Marsh, about the Randells. But he knew she would toss him off the Lazy S so fast. Funny thing was he didn't want to go. He wanted to hang around. She needed him. And surprisingly, he needed her...and Evan.

The next morning, Dana didn't have to worry about facing Jared. He hadn't come to breakfast. Bert said he had something to finish up before he rode out with him to the south pasture.

"Mom, can I be Jared's helper today?" Evan asked as he walked into the kitchen, dressed in his jeans and long-sleeve shirt to protect himself from the hot Texas sun.

Dana knew her son would push this issue as far as he could. "Honey, Jared has other things to do this morning."

"But you're the boss of him. You can tell him to work in the barn."

"I made Bert the boss and he needs Jared to help him. They're going to need to move some of the herd today."

"Can't they do that another day?"

"The cows and calves have to eat. And there's fresh grass in another pasture."

"So they get fat."

She nodded. "And we make more money at market."

"So...can I go ride with them?"

"Evan, we've talked about this. You have to wait until you're older." The boy looked dejected. He'd been alone for so long without anyone to play with. Hopefully when school started in the fall he would make friends.

If we still own the Lazy S, Dana thought.

"You know what?" Dana said. "Joy is coming by today and she's bringing Katie Rose with her."

Evan looked in pain. "But... Mom, she's a baby... and a girl."

Dana had to smile. She knew one day his distaste for

girls would change. "I know she's only three and a half. But she likes you, a lot." Little Katie had toddled after Evan since the day she'd taken her first steps.

"She bothers me. She always wants to hug me, and she plays with dolls."

"Maybe today you can show her your Hot Wheels?"

"But, Mom," the boy complained. "I want to be with Jared. He needs me."

"Evan." A familiar man's voice drew their attention. Dana looked up to see the tall handsome man who'd suddenly turned into a cowboy. He had on a Western shirt, jeans and boots and all. He already had the long lanky build with all the muscles.

"Jared." Evan jumped down from the chair and ran to him. "Mom says I can't help you."

Jared crouched down. "Hey, buddy, I'm going to be pretty busy this morning. Maybe when I get back we can get in some work later."

Dana saw her son's eyes light up. "Can I, Mom?"

"If everything else gets done."

The boy's smile quickly faded as he looked back at Jared. "I have to play with a girl today."

Jared's jaw twitched. "Well, sometimes cowboys have to do things that aren't much fun. But remember, you always treat a lady with respect."

"What does respect mean?"

"That means you are nice to them."

The boy hung his head. "'Kay. I'll do it."

"And finish your chores without complaining."

He nodded. "'Kay, I will."

Jared stood up and ruffled Evan's hair. "Good. I'll see you when I get back." He looked at Dana. His dark blue eyes locked with hers, causing her body to warm.

She couldn't stop the flood of memories. The feel of his hands, of his mouth…

She shook her head. "Did you need something else?"

He smiled. "I was just wondering if you had any left-over biscuits?"

"Maybe a few." Dana picked up the lunch sacks off the counter. Inside were two ham sandwiches apiece along with slices of peach pie and biscuits. "Here. This should keep you and Bert going for a few hours."

"Thanks," he said, then drew a breath as if he wanted to say more. But after a moment he turned and walked out the door.

Dana wanted to call him back, but nixed the idea. It was better to leave things alone. He was leaving in about a week. And she and Evan would be alone again.

Jared found he was getting comfortable with Scout. The buckskin was easy to ride. Even though the Texas heat had the temperature climbing into the nineties, it didn't bother him. Just Bert's sullenness. The older man wasn't about to come out and say what was on his mind. He could just ask Jared about last night. But no. He had to grunt all morning and refuse to talk. Well, that was fine. He didn't need to talk.

Hell, wait until Bert discovered that Jared could be a Randell.

They were nearly to the pasture and the foreman suggested they take a break next to the creek. They delved into the sandwiches hungrily and then Bert finally spoke. "Heard you drove over to the Circle B last night."

Surprised that the news got around so fast, Jared was caught off guard. Had Hank Barrett said something?

"Didn't know you had business with them," Bert said.

"I don't." Jared frowned. "I just had something they needed to see."

"So you're not doing business with them."

"No, I'm not."

"Good, because if you're here to try and get Dana to sell... That would upset her a lot." The old man's leathered face showed love and concern. "She talks tough, but when it comes to some things... She may have a child, but she hasn't had much experience...."

"You don't have to warn me off," Jared said. "I'm not planning on doing anything to hurt Dana."

"That's not what it looked like last night."

"What happened between us is our business, but if it matters to you, I've already apologized to her. It won't happen again."

"Good." Bert got up slowly, put his sack in his saddle-bag and mounted his horse. "We better get back to work."

Jared gathered his things and followed Bert. Hell, the man was as grumpy as an old bear. But he was loyal to Dana and he obviously loved her and Evan. She needed someone to look after her. Jared just wasn't the man for the job.

He climbed onto Scout and tugged the reins toward the fence. They continued to ride about another mile until they found the downed fence. In the mass of tangled barbed wire there were two calves.

Two *dead* calves.

With orders from Bert, Jared was to move the bawling mama cows away from their babies. It wasn't as easy as it looked; the cows wouldn't leave the calves. With Bert's help, they managed to shoo them off, then Bert dragged the carcasses away as Jared started with the fence repair.

After about an hour, they were back on the horses.

They had to round up the rest of the herd. That took a while. By late afternoon, they had the rest of the cows and calves accounted for and moved to the new pasture.

Now they only had to go back and tell Dana the bad news.

"I'm pregnant."

Dana gasped at Joy Randell's declaration.

She got up and hugged her friend. "Oh, Joy, I'm so happy for you. I bet Chance is over the moon."

The pretty blonde smiled. "He's been strutting around like one of his stallions for the past week." She sighed. "It's going to be a long seven months." Then she smiled. "I did make him promise that this time we'll make it to the hospital."

Dana was happy and jealous at the same time. Her friend had a loving husband and child, with another on the way. "You mean you don't want Chance delivering the baby in the barn this time?"

"Bite your tongue." Joy suddenly looked dreamy-eyed. "Of course that's one way to get familiar—real fast. When a man sees you at your worst, you know right away if he's willing to hang around. Maybe you should try it."

"Oh, once is enough. I'm plenty happy with just Evan."

"Are you? You don't get lonely?" her friend asked. "The right man can make all the difference. It did for Katie and me."

Dana couldn't deny that Joy was one of the lucky ones. She found a guy who loved and adored her. But memories of Marsh Hastings had made Dana bitter. "The wrong man can make a lot of trouble."

Just then the back door opened and Jared appeared. She had to bite back a gasp at his formidable presence.

His shirt and jeans were covered with dust and mud as if he'd been wrestling a calf and lost. The day's growth of beard covering his square jaw only added to his appeal, as did his indigo-colored eyes and black hair.

Dana decided to act nonchalant, especially with her friend watching her. "Did everything go all right?"

Jared hesitated, then his gaze moved to Joy.

"So we meet again, Mr. Trager," Joy said, surprising Dana.

Jared nodded. "Mrs. Randell."

"I wish you could have stayed longer last night. I didn't get a chance to offer you some pie and coffee. And you probably could have used a little hospitality along with that."

"I got about what I expected," he said.

Jared turned back to Dana. "We found some fence down along with two calves who'd gotten tangled in the barbed wire. The calves didn't make it. Bert took care of them."

"Damn," she cursed under her breath. She needed anger to keep her from breaking down and bawling her eyes out. What else could happen?

"Sorry," Jared said.

She drew a calming breath. "It's not your fault. I knew those posts were rotted out. I should have replaced them weeks ago and this wouldn't have happened."

"They're replaced now."

"Good. Did you get the herd moved?"

"Yes. We took care of it. I need to get back and cool down Scout." He walked out.

"I'm sorry about the calves, Dana," Joy said. "I know how much you're depending on the sale…."

"Yeah, it's going to be close," Dana admitted. She

couldn't afford to lose any—at all. "That's ranching. Chance, Cade and Travis were wise to branch out, to help with the lean years. How is the Mustang Valley Campground doing?" she asked, wanting to take the focus off her.

"With the lake stocked with fish, it's booked for the entire summer." Joy smiled, then her smile slowly faded. "As much as I love the campground, it's a lot of work. And since I'm pregnant now, Chance is going to hire someone for the season." Her friend's eyes sparkled. "Dana, why don't you take the job?"

"I can't do that," Dana said. "I have the ranch to run."

"Oh, you have Bert to deal with the work here. If a problem comes up, you'll be close by. We already have a couple of college kids who work for us who could handle things. You can even bring Evan along with you. I know it's only until October, but the money is pretty good."

With the bank loan hanging over her head, Dana liked the idea of making extra money. "I don't think Bert can handle things on his own."

Joy smiled. "As if you hadn't noticed, you have a good-looking cowboy working for you." She leaned forward. "Tell me more about your Jared Trager."

Dana looked puzzled. "He's not *my* anything. Besides, I think you should be telling me. You seem to know more about him than I do."

"I don't know the entire story myself. Chance and his brothers are keeping quiet on this one. I only know it has something to do with Jack Randell." Joy looked at Dana. "And that can only mean one thing. Trouble."

That night after a long shower, Jared felt like a new man. Almost. It hadn't changed what was going on in his head. He knew he had to tell Dana the truth, and soon. How much longer could he go on like this? Not long. Not when she was so friendly with the Randells.

Jared walked out of the bunkhouse and took a stroll along the fence to eye his handiwork. With Evan's assistance, he'd managed to replace several boards in the corral. Maybe later on this week, he could get some paint on it. Yeah, right. He kept talking about doing things like he was staying here. He knew for a fact that any day, as soon as Dana Shayne discovered who he was, she would throw him off the property. Didn't matter that he was bringing her money for Evan. Even if it were a million dollars, she'd still toss him just on principle alone.

A cool breeze touched his face and Jared sighed as peace settled over him. He smiled. It probably had to do with the fact he'd been so busy working, he hadn't had time to think. A warning went off in his head. He was getting attached to this place. Over and over in the last few days, he'd fought those feelings for the Lazy S. He couldn't stay here.

Besides, the Randells didn't want him, and for sure, Dana wouldn't when she found out the truth. She was turned off of men, and Marsh's brother had to be the last man she'd want. He could leave and go into town and get a lawyer to do the job.

He turned to place his foot on the bottom rung of the fence and rested his arms on the top as he peered out into the dark night. He'd spent the afternoon with Evan as they worked on repairs. Dana was a good mother, but the kid was starved for male attention. And he was the boy's uncle. His blood. At the very least he wanted to stay around a while for Evan. Jared knew he wasn't father ma-

terial, but he cared about the child. A few more days…
maybe a week. What would it hurt to stay that long?

He started to head back to the bunkhouse when he
looked toward the house and saw the flicker of the insect
repellent candle on the porch. He heard the faint sound
of the old swing creaking, then the outline of a small figure. Dana. As much as he told himself to keep walking,
he knew he was going to stop. He was drawn to her. He
had been since he'd arrived here. The kiss last night ignited so much more. Usually, whenever he found himself getting too involved, he was more than ready to take
off. But here he was, ignoring all the warning signs and
headed right into danger.

Jared stopped at the bottom step. "Looks like it's cooling down some."

"It will only help if we get rain." He heard her sigh.
"We could really use it."

There was a long silence. Finally Jared spoke. "I'm
sorry about the calves."

"It happens. I wish I'd been able to hire a hand sooner.
Then I could have kept up with the work. It might have
been prevented. I hate to think of those calves suffering."

Jake walked up the steps, then leaned against the porch
post. "I can ride out again tomorrow and check the rest
of the fences."

She shook her head. "You've already got the herd
moved into a secure pasture—the section you repaired
the other day. They should be fine."

"Will you be?" he asked. "I know you're depending
on the sale from this herd. Can you make it?"

"I always get through." She looked at him. "I have
a child—I have to. This is our home." Her voice broke.
"We can't lose it."

Jared didn't want to think about Dana and Evan not living on the Lazy S. "Isn't that going to be difficult?"

She shrugged. "Why? Do you think I should sell to your friends the Randells?"

Jared was caught off guard by the question. "Who says they're my friends?"

"You drove over to their place last night."

How much should he tell her? "A long time ago, my mother knew Jack Randell."

She stared at him as if expecting him to say more.

"My mother died years ago, but I found an old letter…."

"How convenient, they're my neighbors." She raised those large green eyes to his and all he could think about was how she felt in his arms, the sweet taste of her mouth.

He shook away the thought. "There are things I can't talk about…yet, but believe me, Dana, I'm not trying to help the Randells get your ranch."

"That's a little hard to swallow when you show up here and then rush off to the Circle B. Chance, Cade and Travis have wanted a piece of my land for a long time. And you seem really interested in my business."

"If it's just a small piece of your land, why don't you sell it to them? No doubt the money would help you out."

He saw the anger flare in her eyes. "You know nothing about it. My grandfather worked hard to obtain this land—Shayne land. And it stays in the family. All of it. And before my father died, I promised him I'd never sell. So tell your friends the Randells no deal."

She stood and started to go inside when Jared grabbed her arm. "I'm not hooked up with the Randells. I'm just not ready to talk about my business yet. Now, you can believe me or not. Say the word and I'll pack up and leave right now."

"Don't threaten me, Trager. You show up here and get friendly with my son…and kiss me."

His grip tightened. "I like Evan—he's a nice kid. As for the kiss, okay, I overstepped on that. I already said I was sorry."

He saw her eyes flame. "And I told you a woman doesn't want to hear a man say he's sorry for kissing her," she snapped.

His own anger rose. "Fine, so I'm not sorry. Hell, woman, do you want me to admit that I wanted to kiss you? That I want to kiss you again. Well, you got it. Hell, yes, I want to." He jerked her against him. "But all you have to do is tell me no, and I'll leave."

When Dana didn't move, Jared cupped her face. "Lady, you've been warned." His mouth covered hers. His hunger only grew when her mouth opened and his tongue swept inside. Her taste was a mixture of mint and coffee and it acted like an aphrodisiac. He felt his body tense and his need for her grew. He pulled her even closer against him and the kiss escalated, threatening his control and so much more. He didn't want to think about how deep he was in. He didn't want to think about things he couldn't have. Right now, with Dana in his arms, he felt he could have it all.

He finally broke off the kiss, then leaned down again and pressed his forehead against her. He forced a smile. "I promise you'll never hear me say I'm sorry again." He turned away and walked down the steps before he made her more promises he couldn't keep.

The next morning, Dana woke up with a smile. After her shower, she hurried downstairs to the quiet kitchen and saw the sunlight streaming through the windows. She shivered, knowing she'd be seeing Jared in a little while.

She hurried through her routine, making a stack of pancakes and frying a whole pound of bacon, knowing the extra could be used for sandwiches at lunch. She sipped her second cup of coffee while waiting for Bert and Jared to come in. They should be finished with their chores by now. She checked her watch, then heard the door. With her heart racing, she looked up to see Bert come in. Alone.

"Morning, Dana," he said, and went to wash up in the sink. Then he took a cup of coffee to the table. "You might as well dig in because Jared isn't coming up. He decided to finish some repairs in the barn. Said he'd eat some biscuits later."

"I didn't make biscuits this morning."

Bert grinned. "I can see that." He poured syrup over the stack of pancakes.

Evan walked into the kitchen and took his usual seat. "Where's Jared?" he asked.

"What is it with all the questions about Jared?" Bert said. "Can't a grown man decide if he wants to eat or not? Besides, he'll be gone in a few days."

Evan looked panicky. "Mom, I don't want Jared to go away."

She fixed her son a plate. "He's not going anywhere right now, Evan. But next week he has to go to Las Vegas. He has a job there."

"But we need him here," Evan said. "A whole bunch of stuff is broke."

"Evan, eat your breakfast. We'll talk about it later."

"No, Mom. Don't let Jared leave."

Her son had inherited too much Irish stubbornness.

"Evan, you know Jared only planned to work here until his truck was fixed."

"But he can change his mind."

"Evan, we're not going to talk about this anymore. Eat your breakfast."

"I'm not hungry."

"Then go to your room."

The sullen child got up from the table and ran out of the room.

"What has gotten into that boy?" Bert asked, and shook his head. "Trager's a drifter."

Dana felt defensive for Jared. "That may be, but he's put in a lot of full days around here."

"You'll get no argument from me," the foreman said. "But some people just can't put down roots. Jared Trager is one of them."

Dana had heard enough. She picked up an empty plate and began filling it with food, then wrapped it up with a cloth napkin.

"So I get to eat by myself," Bert complained.

"If you're eating, you don't need company," Dana said as she headed to the door. "When you finish, I want you to check the windmill at the water pond in the north pasture today. I'd appreciate it if you'd hang around a few minutes until I got back." She didn't wait for an answer and hurried out the door. She headed to the bunkhouse, hoping to catch Jared there. She was tired of the man avoiding her. He acted as if she were trying to rope a husband. That was crazy. She'd dealt with one man who didn't want her, she didn't need another. Of course, she could get used to the way Jared Trager kissed. The way he made her feel.

Dana quickly stopped the direction of her thoughts.

Jared wasn't going to stay. So she couldn't expect anything from him but a few heart-stopping kisses. The sooner she got used to that, the better. She was determined this time that she wasn't going to let another man hurt her.

When she arrived, the sleeping quarters were empty. She placed the plate of food on a table, so he'd have it when he came in. She started to leave when she saw Jared's personal belongs on the scarred dresser. There was a popular brand of deodorant, toothpaste and a brush placed all neat and orderly, except for an envelope sticking out of the black leather shaving kit.

Was this the letter Jared had talked about? She didn't mean to pry, but seeing the name in the corner of the envelope froze her. Marshall Hastings. Seeing the name of the man she'd once loved, Dana couldn't seem to catch her breath as her heart drummed away in her chest. How did Jared know Marsh? She pulled out the folded paper. The two hand-written pages started out with "Jared…" And ended with "Your brother, Marsh."

Dana collapsed into a chair.

Jared Trager was Marsh Hastings's brother.

Jared dried off his hands and walked through the doorway. The plate of food on the table caught him by surprise, then he saw Dana. She was sitting on a chair, looking upset. His gaze went to the letter in her hand and he realized his worst nightmare had come true.

"Let me explain," he said, knowing nothing would help ease the pain he saw on her face.

"The only thing I want to know is if this is true." She held up the letter. "Is Marsh Hastings your brother?"

"He *was* my brother. He died a few weeks back." He nodded at the letter. "As you already read."

"I know. And I'm sorry," she said, sounding sad. But that quickly changed. "Why didn't you tell me who you were?"

"I don't know," he confessed. "When I had the accident, I thought I'd wait. Then I saw the trouble you were having with the ranch and I wanted to help."

"Why would you want to help me?" Her voice was heavy with sarcasm.

"Because Evan is my nephew and... Marsh asked me to make sure he was doing okay. Why didn't you ever tell Marsh about Evan?"

She was fighting tears. "He didn't want to know. If he had, he would have called me...."

Jared could understand her anger. "That doesn't change the fact that I care about the boy."

"Well, you've seen Evan and he's fine. Now, pack up and get the hell off my property."

Chapter 5

Dana marched out of the barn with her head held high, praying she could make it into the house without breaking down. She'd almost made it when she saw the familiar Chevy Suburban coming up the road. The truck pulled into the drive and Chance Randell climbed out.

He was a tall, broad-shouldered, good-looking man. Funny, Dana had known Chance most of her life. He'd always been the quiet brooding type, until he met and fell in love with Joy Spencer. Now she never saw him without a smile.

"Chance. What brings you over here?"

"Hello, Dana. Thought we could talk."

"Tell me you're not here to hound me about selling the strip of valley land. Isn't breeding the best quarter horses in West Texas enough for you?"

He grinned. "I'll save that argument for another day. Besides, I have a wife and kids to support."

"I hear congratulations are in order. Joy told me about the baby."

If possible, his grin grew wider. "Yeah, it's pretty great. That's one reason I stopped by. Joy said you might be interested in taking over managing the campground."

Dana sighed. Her friend hadn't given her much time to think about the offer. "It was your wife's idea, but I can't. With only Bert to run the place, I'm needed here."

Chance frowned. "I thought you hired a hand. Trager."

"I did, but he's leaving. He was only working temporarily while his truck was being repaired."

He looked toward the barn. "Why don't you let me talk to him? Maybe I can convince him to stay a little longer."

"No," Dana said. "Jared has made up his mind. He needs to get back to Las Vegas."

"Would you mind if I speak to him about something else?"

Dana wanted to ask him about what, but it was none of her business. Jared Trager was not her concern anymore. "Sure, he should be in the bunkhouse." She started for the house. The last thing she wanted was to see Jared again.

Jared found he didn't want to leave the Lazy S. A sadness came over him as he said goodbye to Bert. The foreman was obviously confused over the turn of events, but didn't ask questions. Jared let Bert know where to reach him in town and gave him his cell phone number.

Angry for making a mess of everything, Jared knew that Dana wasn't going to be able to handle things on her own. But, dammit, she was too stubborn to let anyone help. There was nothing he could do; she'd kicked him out on his rear end.

Jared picked up his toolbox and walked out of the barn where he found Chance Randell standing beside his Jeep. Great, this was all he needed.

"Look, I'm leaving so there's no need to run me off."

"I'm not here to chase you anywhere," Chance said, then glanced away. "In fact, I may have acted a little hasty the other night."

Jared went to the back of the Jeep and opened the hatch. He tossed in his bag, then his tools. "Doesn't matter. It was a mistake coming here. I don't know what I expected to find."

Chance pushed his hat back on his head. "Maybe a little friendlier greeting. We didn't exactly give you a Texas welcome. It's just that when our father's name is mentioned, it brings back some bad memories. The guy was a real piece of work. So you might not want to discover that he's your father, anyway."

"You're probably right." Jared started toward the driver's side door. He didn't want to deal with this. No more rejection today.

"If you're still interested in knowing the truth, I've arranged for a DNA test for you and me tomorrow morning at ten o'clock." He handed Jared a card with the lab's name and address. "Hope to see you there." Then he turned and walked off.

Jared stood quietly. Why would the Randells want to know if he was their father's bastard son? He shook his head and was opening the Jeep's door when he heard his name called out. Something tightened around his heart when he saw Evan running from the house. Damn. How was he going to say goodbye to the boy?

"Jared, don't go," the child cried. He was running so fast, he tripped and tumbled to the ground. He climbed to his feet and kept coming. Jared met him under a tree. "Don't leave," Evan cried again.

Jared caught the boy in his arms and for the first time in a long time wished he could call a place home.

"I have to, Evan. You know I have a job in Las Vegas."

The child swiped at his tears. "But I want you to stay here. Please. I'll be good."

Jared felt like a coldhearted bastard. "It's not you, Evan. Sometimes we can't do what we want." Jared looked up and noticed Dana heading toward them. "But that doesn't mean I'm going to forget you. We can write each other letters."

The boy sobbed into Jared's chest. "I don't know how to read or print very good."

"Okay, then I'll write you, and your mother can read the letters to you. And soon you'll learn how to write in school." He gripped Evan by his arms and made the boy look at him. "Now, I'll be going into town for a few days, but I promise I'll come by and see you again." He looked up to find that Dana was standing a few feet away. He could tell she wasn't happy about his plans. Too bad. He wasn't going to let the kid down. He knew how rotten that felt.

"Evan," Dana called to her son. "Why don't you go back into the house now?"

The boy glowered at his mother. "You're mean! Why are you making Jared leave?"

"Evan, that's no way to speak to your mother," Jared said, not surprised at the child's disappointment.

The boy hung his head. "Sorry…"

"Tell that to your mother."

Evan glanced at Dana and repeated the word. Then the boy shot off toward the house.

Jared didn't miss the hurt look on Dana's face. "Don't take it so hard. He'll forget about me soon."

"If you hadn't come here…"

"Look, I know I messed up," he began. "I should have told you about the trust Marsh set up for Evan." Jared went to the back of the Jeep, took out a folder from his bag and handed it to her. "I should have delivered this that first day. Inside, there's the name of the lawyer you should contact."

"Thanks," Dana said, and pulled a small piece of paper from her pocket. "Here's the wages I owe you for two weeks' work."

Jared shook his head. "No, I don't want your money."

Dana's chin came up. "I don't take charity, Jared." She pushed the check at him.

Angry, Jared snatched the piece of paper from her fingers, then proceeded to tear it up. "Think of it as a gift for Evan. After all, he is my nephew."

"Too bad you couldn't be honest about that."

"I'm sorry for that, too. But don't punish the boy for my mistake. Let me write to him."

"I don't know if that's such a good idea."

"Like it wasn't a good idea to tell him about his father," Jared accused.

"Evan's too young to understand."

"Then why has he been asking me so many questions?" He stepped closer and he saw Dana's eyes widen. He inhaled her intoxicating scent, reminding him of the kisses they'd shared. His body sprang to life and he quickly backed away. "At least don't lie to him, Dana. He'll come to hate you for it. Evan deserves to know the truth about Marsh, if not now, then sometime soon. If only to help him understand who he is."

Jared turned and walked to the vehicle, wishing with all his heart that he could stay.

After Jared got a motel room in San Angelo, he called the body shop to check the progress on his truck. The manager said the repairs would take a few more days. Great. He was stuck in town. Since he had to stay anyway, he might as well go through with the DNA test tomorrow. He'd come all this way to Texas, why not find out for sure if he was a Hastings or a Randell? Even if, in his heart, he knew the truth.

When Jared phoned Chance to tell him he'd be at the lab in the morning, he was surprised to get an invitation to come out to his ranch. Jared thought about not accepting, but curiosity got the best of him. Besides, what else did he have to do but sit around the motel room, or hang out at one of the local bars and think about Dana Shayne?

Jared followed Chance's directions to the Randell Family Horse Ranch. He turned off the highway onto the gravel road that led him through a wrought-iron archway, then to a big two-story, yellow-and-white Victorian house. The lawn, despite the drought, was a rich green with colorful flowers edging the large wraparound porch and brick walkway. Two big dogs, a chocolate and a blond Lab came running toward him, then stopped and sat down at his feet, waiting to be petted. Finishing the playful exchange with the dogs, he looked up as Joy Randell and a little girl walked out onto the porch.

She greeted him as he came up the walk. "Hello, Jared. This is our daughter, Katie."

The small child with light blond curls turned shyly and buried her head in her mother's skirt as he came closer.

"Hi, Katie," he said. "I know a friend of yours. Evan."

The girl's eyes sparkled as she looked up at him. "Eban plays with Katie. And I play with his cars."

Jared smiled. "And I bet that's fun." He turned his attention to Joy. "Thank you for inviting me."

She smiled, too. "You're welcome."

He stepped up on what was obviously a new porch floor. The tongue-and-groove oak had been left natural, with only a high gloss polyurethane coating used to protect the finish. It was a first-class job. Most of the railing had been replaced and painted a snowy white to match the house trim. Several plants hung from above, adding color to the inviting porch.

"You have a beautiful home, Mrs. Randell."

She laughed. "You should have seen it when I inherited it. Made Dana's place look like a showcase. Chance did a lot of the work himself. And please, call me Joy."

"Well, Joy, he knew what he was doing."

"That's right, you're a carpenter by trade."

He nodded as he examined the structure. "I normally work on new construction, but it's got to be satisfying to restore a place like this."

"I'm glad we took the time. And believe me, it's taken nearly three years to get to this point. There's still so much to do. It would be nice if Chance had help." Those big blue eyes lit up. "You wouldn't want to do some side work, would you?"

"I'm not staying that long."

"Oh, I thought…" She smiled again. "You know, Chance is in the mare's barn. If you want, you can go down there. I'm sure he'd love to show you around."

"I'd like that." Jared followed Joy's direction to the new white barn. It was cool inside and quiet, except for the sound of a deep baritone voice. Curious, Jared followed the soft, almost seductive tone to a stall where he found Chance talking sweetly to a very pregnant mare.

He was surprised at the gentleness the big man showed to the animal. Chance's love for this horse was evident in his voice and touch. "Does your wife know you talk to other women like this?"

Chance continued to stroke the mare's oversize stomach. "She doesn't care as long as the foal this lady produces comes out healthy and maybe even is worth some money." He glanced up. "Jared, meet Glory Girl."

Jared stepped closer to the railing and rubbed the horse's face. The chestnut with the white star on her forehead was a beauty. And friendly. She nuzzled closer.

"Well, hello beautiful," he crooned as Chance looked on. "When is she due?"

"Sometime next week. She's delivering late in the season, but her foals are well worth it." He came out of the stall and closed the gate behind him. They started to walk away and the mare let him know her irritation with a loud whinny.

Jared looked around the structure. All the stalls were freshly painted and clean. Several horses came to their gates, wanting attention.

"This is quite a place here," Jared said. "How many horses do you have?"

"Ten that I own. And another dozen that are in different stages of training. I'm alone right now, but I have two trainers and three groomers who work during the day."

"Impressive."

"It's a lot of work, too," Chance admitted. "Especially

now since our expansion with the guest ranch and camp-ground. Joy's pregnant, too."

"Congratulations." It seemed to Jared that the man had everything.

Chance smiled as he puffed out his chest. "We're both pretty happy about it."

Jared couldn't figure Chance out. Why would he care about finding out if they were related?

He looked at Jared. "Thanks for coming tonight. I have to apologize again for my behavior when you came by Hank's the other evening. After I talked it over with Cade and Travis, we all decided we'd like to find out if you're kin to us. Besides, you had no control over who your parents were, any more than we did. Believe me, Jack Randell is no prize."

"Do you have any idea where he is now?"

Chance shook his head. "Nor do I want to know. The last time Jack contacted any of us was about ten years ago when he got out of prison. He wanted money. I said no, and we never heard from him again." He shrugged. "It doesn't matter. As far as my brothers and I are con-cerned, Hank is our father. He was the one who raised us." Chance made a snorting sound. "Jack was just the sperm donor. Hank always said, you don't have to be blood to be family."

Jared knew Graham Hastings hadn't believed that. The man despised him. "Look, I want you to know that if it turns out that we're related… I don't want anything. I just need to know who I am."

Chance drew a breath and released it slowly. "That's good, because around here, we earn our place. I do have a concern, though. Dana Shayne. I don't want her hurt. Are you planning to hang around?"

Jared didn't like the third degree, but he understood it. "I have a job in Las Vegas, but I also have a commitment to my dead brother. Evan is my nephew." That was all Jared said, knowing any more of the story would have to come from her.

Chance shook his head. "I'm surprised Dana didn't run you off with a shotgun." The tone of his voice turned threatening. "I'll do worse if I find out you hurt her or her boy."

"I haven't done anything but try to help her. I know now it was wrong not to be honest with her when I first arrived, but it's not an easy thing to bring up in conversation. But Evan is my nephew and I want to make sure everything is okay with him. Since I discovered the trouble Dana is having keeping the ranch, I feel I need to hang around to make sure she and Evan will be all right."

"Dana won't like that," Chance admitted. "We've tried to help her many times. Sure, we'd like to have the land along Mustang Valley, but not to buy her out completely. She can't run the place on her own. And Bert… He's too old to handle much more."

"If the bank takes it over, where would she go? What would she do?"

Chance shrugged. "Joy asked Dana to take over managing the campground for the summer, but it's not enough to pay off the balloon payment that's due."

Jared didn't want to think about Dana and Evan losing the ranch. The Lazy S was their home. All the money in Evan's trust was tied up tightly, specifying it was only to be used for the boy's support and education.

Jared had the money in his trust, but he couldn't claim it until he was thirty-five…or married.

"What if Dana had a partner? Could she make a go

of it if she increased the size of her herd and had a few more ranch hands to help run the place? Could she make a decent living?"

"That's a question I can't answer. Several ranchers have lost out, but then others have found ways to make it work. I breed and train horses. The Randells have also gone into the tourist business. Nothing is impossible if you're willing to work at it. Why? You planning to go into cattle ranching?"

"It's a possibility. A good possibility."

Chance laughed, then sobered. "You're serious."

"Just don't say anything to Dana yet. I think I may have a way to help her, but I need to make some calls. If it all works out, then Dana can have her dream and Evan can have his legacy."

The next morning, Jared accomplished a lot. He called his lawyer, went to the bank and had a DNA blood test, all before noon.

Right now he needed to talk to Dana. They had to discuss the future before he could move forward. He pulled up in the driveway and got out of the Jeep just as Dana walked out the back door. His heart jolted at the sight of her dressed in snug-fitting jeans and a white blouse that showed off her perfect curves. Her copper hair was pulled back and braided down her back.

She came toward him. "What do you want, Trager?"

"I need to talk to you, Dana."

"We said everything we needed to say." She began to walk away.

"I think you need to listen to what I have to say. It's about the ranch."

She swung around. "What could we possibly have to discuss…and about *my* ranch?"

"I want to help you save the Lazy S."

"I can do that without you."

"You can't make the payment that's due in six weeks." Her eyes narrowed. "How did you know about that?"

"It wasn't hard to find out."

"Get off my land."

"Not until you listen to me. I want to help. You can't lose everything just because of your dislike for me. Think about Evan. I want him to have the Lazy S, too. Just give me ten minutes to explain."

She glared at him. "Why should I? You've done nothing but lie since you've come here."

"Because what I have to say just might save your and Evan's home."

"You've got ten minutes. That's it." She turned and marched up the steps and he followed.

Inside, she took him into the office, a dark paneled room with worn carpet that hadn't been replaced in years. Dana sat behind the desk. "All right, the clock has started."

No pressure at all, he thought. "It's no secret that you've had a few bad years because of the drought and you've had to sell off a lot of your herd before it was time. Now you're behind in your payments to the bank and the balloon is coming due. And the sale from your remaining herd isn't going to be enough." He studied her for a moment. "I have a solution for both of us."

Dana stared at him. "Well, don't stop now just when it's getting interesting."

"I've also talked to Mr. Janny, the lawyer in charge of Evan's trust fund. Although the fund Marsh set up is a considerable amount, Evan won't receive the bulk of the money until he's twenty-one. There will be monthly checks coming to you for his support, but Mr. Janny isn't going to give you any money toward the ranch."

"I couldn't use any of Evan's money. I want him to have that for college."

Jared nodded. "Not even to save the Lazy S for him to inherit one day?"

She swallowed hard. "That's a big risk. If I lose it, then he'll end up with nothing. At least if I sell the Mustang Valley section to the Randells, I can keep part of the ranch."

"What if I told you that I have the money you need? That I want to be your partner?"

"You've got to be crazy. Why would you want to get into the cattle business?"

"Because Evan is my nephew and I want to make sure he's taken care of." And because he hated seeing the pain in Dana's eyes. "I have money from a trust fund of my own."

"And you want to give me some of it." She shook her head as if she didn't believe any of it. "What's in this for you?"

He hesitated. This was the tricky part. "The trust is sizable. I had planned to use part of the money to buy the construction company where I work in Las Vegas. But there is a stipulation in the will…and that's where I need your help."

She frowned. "Need me? For what?"

"To marry me."

Chapter 6

"Marry you!" Dana said, unable to believe his insane suggestion. "You can't be serious."

"I'm serious all right. You're in deep financial trouble. Unless you sell some of the ranch to the Randells, you're not going to make the bank payment that's coming due."

She straightened. "I'm not selling any of my land." She hated him knowing her business. "There's some time left."

"Time for a miracle?"

She'd been praying for one. Surely this wasn't it. "I'm not desperate enough to marry you," she said, then wished she could take back the stinging words.

"You better get desperate real fast, because you're running out of time…and you could lose the ranch because of your stubbornness." He started out of the room.

Dana hurried from around the desk. "I'm not being

stubborn," she insisted. "I'm cautious." When he turned and stared at her with those hard sapphire eyes, her heart skipped a beat. Jared Trager made her crazy. "Why are you doing this?"

"Hell if I know." He looked confused and frustrated as he ran his fingers through his hair. "For Evan. That's why I'm doing it. I want him to be able to grow up here—in his home. On this ranch. He's already gotten a raw deal from Marsh."

Jared paused, seeming surprised at what he told her. He began to pace. "I'm also doing it so I don't have to wait until I'm thirty-five, roughly two more years to collect my inheritance and get my dream. To buy Burke Construction. Stan Burke wants to retire soon. He's been allowing me to buy into the business little by little. But if I had my inheritance now I could take over and purchase new equipment for the company." His gaze met hers. "You told me you could make a go of the ranch if you enlarged the herd. To do that you need money to hire more help and make some needed repairs."

"Do you know how much that's going to cost?"

"I have an idea, and I have the money to do it." He folded his arms across his chest. "Dana, Evan needs you to be his mother. You can't work twelve-fourteen hours a day and be his only parent, too."

"Are you saying that I'm not a good mother?"

"No, you're a great mother. You can have that dream—we both can have our dream, but we need each other."

"Surely there's someone else in your life that you could ask to marry you?"

He glanced away. "I'm not good at relationships. I'm doing this mainly for Evan's sake."

Dana couldn't believe it. She was actually considering his crazy scheme. The offer was so tempting. And it could be her only chance to turn the Lazy S into a successful ranch. "My dream is bigger than just raising cattle, Jared. I'd also like to breed some good saddle horses, and have a boarding stable."

So Dana was interested. Jared didn't know if he should be happy or not. "All that's a possibility."

She folded her arms across her chest. "If we decided to get married…how soon do you think—"

"As soon as possible. I don't receive the money until I have a marriage certificate."

"Of course it wouldn't be a real marriage." She gave him a questioning look. "I mean, you can't expect me—us…"

He bit back a groan. Oh, he wanted her all right, and if she were honest she'd admit she wanted him, too. The two times they'd been together diminished any doubt of that. They'd been nothing less than explosive. "To consummate the marriage," he finished for her.

She nodded as a blush colored her cheeks.

"If you're worried I'm going to jump you, I'm not. And if you want to take our relationship any further, that's up to you."

Dana released a breath. "No, that wouldn't be wise. So we're agreed that we're business partners."

"I want to have some say, but mostly I'll be a silent partner."

Her gaze met his. "I won't sign away any part of the ranch to you."

"I don't expect you to, nor do I want your land. I only want to look out for Evan's interest. He's my big concern."

"And you'll be willing to invest in the ranch with only a signed note? With no claim on the Lazy S?"

"No claim. I have no doubt that you'll do everything in your power to keep the Lazy S for your son," he said.

She started to speak and he stopped her.

"Dana, before you decide, there's something you should know. I came to San Angelo for another reason, too. It was the same reason that brought Marsh over here five years ago. He'd found an old letter that was addressed to our mother from Jack Randell. Seems they knew each other years ago. It also seems there's a chance that I could be Jack's son. I've taken a DNA test along with Chance and the results should be back soon. The outcome doesn't have anything to do with my offer—I just thought you should know."

Dana was trying to hide her shock. Jared Trager could be a Randell. She could see some resemblance, the similar build and square jaw. Those deep-set eyes were the most telling, at the same time they held so much back. "Thank you for being honest about that."

"So it's all right that we go ahead?"

She hesitated. "I have another question. How long will this marriage last?"

He shrugged. "I don't think my mother's will stipulates any time constraints. Why? Is there someone in your life?"

"No. Is there someone in yours? I mean in Las Vegas." Surely there wasn't, not with the way he'd kissed her.

"No one. But I can't stay in Texas indefinitely. Two or three months to get things going here is what I planned on. Then I need to get back to Vegas."

She suddenly realized how her son would be affected. "Oh, what about Evan? He's going to get attached to you."

"He's attached to me now."

That was the truth. Her son had barely spoken to

her since she'd sent Jared away. "I know, but it will get worse."

"Dana, I plan to stay in touch with Evan no matter what you decide about us." He took a step closer to her. He was a big man and towered over her, but she didn't feel intimidated by his size. "He's my nephew and I want to be there for him. I never had that with my father...." His voice drifted off, then his gaze met hers. "I want him to know that he can count on me."

What about her? Dana wondered. What was going to happen to her when Jared left her with a broken heart? Somehow she had to make sure she kept everything impersonal.

"If you need more time..." he began.

"No. I only need to make sure that you agree to keep this...situation strictly business. Our arrangement isn't going to be more than a marriage in name only."

"If that's what you want," he said. "I can stay in the bunkhouse."

She shook her head. "No. You can move into a bedroom upstairs. There's going to be enough questions as it is."

"Then you agree?" he asked again.

Dana drew a long breath and released it. "Agreed."

"I'll call my lawyer and let him know that there's going to be a wedding. As soon as I send him a copy of the marriage certificate my inheritance will be transferred into my account. Then I'll take care of the mortgage."

She gasped. "I can't let you pay the mortgage off."

"Might as well start with a clean slate." He quickly changed the subject. "So, you want to do this in a church, or at the courthouse?"

How could he act so nonchalant about it? Because it didn't mean anything more to him than a business deal. That's how she needed to handle it, too. This was a way to keep the Lazy S for her son. It was the only reason for agreeing to this crazy idea.

"I think the courthouse. But I have one other request. I don't want people to know the real reason we're getting married."

Jared leaned toward her, and his gaze darkened. For a moment, Dana thought he was going to kiss her. "I doubt I'll have any problem convincing people that you and I are truly married."

Two weeks later, Dana was still trying to talk herself out of this so-called marriage. As Joy helped her get ready at the courthouse, Dana was fighting with herself not to call the whole thing off.

Surprisingly, Bert hadn't tried to talk her out of this marriage. And forget Evan. He'd wanted a dad for so long, he'd been crazy about the idea of Jared taking the position. In keeping with their promise, Dana had only told one person, Joy, the real reason she and Jared were getting married today. Even after signing the legal papers to protect her and Evan from Jared making any claim on the ranch when the marriage ended, Dana knew that there was nothing to protect her heart.

Now more doubts rushed through her head. "Am I crazy, Joy?"

Her friend sat beside her on the bench. "Do you hate Jared?"

"Of course not."

"Do you think that he's being honest about wanting to help you?"

"Yes."

"Could you fall in love with him?"

Dana thought back over the past weeks. Jared had worked tirelessly, then spent extra time doing needed repairs. He'd been nothing but kind and thoughtful to Evan. What was there not to love? "Yes," she admitted. "That's what I'm afraid of."

Her friend smiled. "I know the feeling. I felt the same way about Chance. I was scared about marrying him, too. I had a baby and I needed him so much." Joy's sympathetic gaze met Dana's. "I think Jared needs you just as much. Men try to act tough, but they need love, too. I've gotten to know Jared a little better in the last week. He's quiet and distant sometimes as if he doesn't quite know where he fits in. He needs you and Evan. He needs a family."

"He has Chance, Cade and Travis. They're his family."

"Jared needs you, too, Dana."

"I'm afraid to let myself get close. He's going to leave and go back to Las Vegas."

"Then figure out a way to make him want to stay."

"I don't know how." She brushed away a tear. "The only man I've ever cared about was Marsh."

Joy patted her hand. "There's more room in your heart believe me. I felt the same way about Blake, and when he died, I never thought there would be anyone else. Then I met Chance. Just give yourself a little time. If it's meant to be, it will happen." With an understanding smile, she stood up and pulled Dana with her. "Come on, we have a wedding to get started."

Dana brushed imaginary wrinkles from the peach-colored dress Joy had loaned her. A soft sheer layered skirt hung to a princess length, making her feel feminine. The simple fitted bodice emphasized her small waist, and the neckline dipped low, exposing more cleavage than Dana ever dared before. Around her neck she wore her grandmother's cameo necklace. Her hair had been pinned up and baby's breath adorned the crown of her head.

"How do I look?"

Joy smiled. "The expression on your soon-to-be husband's face says it all."

Dana turned around and saw Jared standing across the room next to Chance. Although the DNA test hadn't come back yet, there was no doubt in her mind they were related. Tall, dark and so handsome. Jared had on a navy suit and a snowy white shirt with a striped tie. When his eyes met hers, a warm tingle rushed through her. He took a small box from Chance and started toward her. Dana swallowed back the dryness in her throat as he stopped in front of her.

"You're beautiful," he said.

"Thank you." She took a breath. "You clean up pretty nicely yourself."

He shrugged. "I did some shopping."

She had already known that because he'd taken Evan along with him. Her son had come home the other day, after spending the afternoon in town, acting as if he were hiding a big secret. Then this morning he'd come downstairs dressed in a new suit, white shirt and new shoes. Before she could even comment, he'd scurried to the bunkhouse so Jared could fix his tie. Dana hadn't planned on making such a big deal of the wedding. After all, it was only a business arrangement.

"Thank you again for Evan's suit," she said. "Although, I doubt he'll get much use out of it since he grows so fast."

"It was worth it. He wanted to look good for today.

He is my best man." He held the box out to her. "Here, this is for you."

With a puzzled look, she opened it to find a bouquet of cream- and peach-colored rosebuds. "Oh, my." She reached inside and took hold of the slender stems and raised the bouquet to her nose. "Oh, Jared, they're lovely." Dana started to say more, when the judge and his clerk came in and directed the bride and groom to stand in the middle of the room. Evan took the place on the other side of his mother, Bert next to him.

Jared had Chance as his best man. But this wasn't the small affair they'd planned. Not with the Randell family around. Although quiet, they were all in attendance. Hank and Ella, all three brothers and their wives.

Ten minutes later, the "I do's" had been exchanged and they were pronounced man and wife. Then Jared was instructed to kiss his new bride. That was one thing that they hadn't talked about: "The kiss." And maybe they should have because when Jared's mouth closed over Dana's he didn't hold anything back. He kissed her like he meant it. Full on the lips and with enthusiasm. When he released her and gave her a wink and a grin, she wanted to smash the heel of her shoe into his foot. Instead she smiled as everyone congratulated them. Then Joy and Chance invited everyone back to the Randell home for a reception.

There, Joy had outdone herself. With help from Ella, Hank Barrett's housekeeper, they had set up a banquet on the sideboard in the dining room. A white- and peach-colored, three-tiered wedding cake was center stage on top of a lace-draped table.

Dana was surprised that Joy had gone to so much

trouble. Knowing the marriage wasn't real hadn't diminished her friend's enthusiasm. But even surrounded by all the finery, Dana could not let herself believe that she and Jared would live happily ever after.

Jared had been separated from Dana when the ladies commandeered his bride. Something about opening some *personal* gifts. Just as well, he was getting weary of strange women kissing him and giving him those knowing looks.

It was a little late to have doubts about this arrangement. The one thing that bothered him was leaving Dana to face all the probing questions. But they had both known from the beginning that this was the way things would be—strictly business.

Yeah, right. And what was that kiss about? he wondered, recalling Dana's sweet taste. Dear Lord, she looked so beautiful. He'd always thought her pretty, but she had caught him off guard when he'd walked into the judge's chambers. How was he going to keep his hands to himself? Maybe he should stay parked in the bunkhouse. He closed his eyes, remembering how good she felt in his arms. How soft her skin… He took a big swallow of champagne.

"Jared," Evan called as he ran up to him. "Are you my dad now?"

Jared crouched down to the boy's level. "We talked about this before, Evan. I'm your dad's brother, so I'm your uncle." Dana and he had finally told Evan about Marsh just a few days ago.

"But you married my mom," he said.

He knew the boy was too young to understand. "How

about for a little while you call me Uncle, but then we'll see what happens."

"'Kay," he said, and ran off to a group of Randell kids.

When Jared stood, Chance came up beside him. "Getting the tough questions already?"

"You can say that," Jared said.

"I had it a little easier," Chance said. "Katie wasn't old enough to ask me questions. But I bet Evan isn't holding back."

"He wants a dad, and I can't blame him. But I don't know how to tell him I might not be around forever."

"None of us can make that kind of promise," Chance countered, then smiled. "You may be surprised how things turn out."

Jared shook his head. "I don't know what I'm doing. I've never had a good relationship with my own father."

Chance's gaze darted away. "There's probably a good reason for that." He looked back at Jared. "The results of the test came back this morning. I don't know if you'll consider it good or bad news, but you're a Randell."

Jared puffed out a breath. How did he feel? At least now he no longer owed any allegiance to Graham Hastings, the man who'd never wanted him in the first place. "I'm almost relieved. It explains so much." He looked at his half brother. "Again, I don't want you to think that I'll expect anything from you or your brothers."

Chance shook his head and grinned. "You sure are one us. You're about as stubborn as a Randell comes. As I said before, we don't give handouts. What my brothers and I would like is to get to know you, Jared. Maybe we can become friends."

Jared had always kept to himself, but found he wanted to get to know the Randells. "I'd like that."

"Just so you know, there are people around here who have a long memory when it comes to Jack Randell. He made some enemies. Some still resent us just because we're his sons. But for the most part, they know that we aren't like our father. We've been lucky. Hank took us in and raised us. He made us walk the straight and narrow before we'd gotten into too much trouble. As far as Cade, Travis and I are concerned, he's our true father."

Just then Cade approached them. "I guess Chance told you the news." He held out his hand. "Welcome to the family. I hope you're not sorry you looked us up."

"Not so far." Jared shook Cade's hand and soon Travis joined them. He, too, offered a welcome. Jared was overwhelmed by how easily the brothers invited him in. If this kept up, he might never want to leave San Angelo.

But of course, he would in the end. He just didn't fit in with family.

Around nine o'clock that night, Jared drove his new bride and son back to the Lazy S. A few days ago he had gotten his truck from the shop. Tonight the cab was quiet, with Evan and Bert both asleep in the back seat, as the soft sound of a country ballad played on the radio.

A single light at the back door greeted them as Jared pulled into the driveway. He got out of the truck, came around and opened the door for Dana.

"I'll carry Evan inside." He helped her out, then reached behind the seat to unfasten the boy from the safety seat. He got a few sleepy groans for his efforts, but Evan didn't wake up. After they said good night to Bert, Dana led the way to the house.

She opened the door and allowed Jared to go first. She followed him upstairs, into Evan's bedroom, and pulled back the covers. Jared lay the child on the cool sheets, and Dana began to strip away Evan's clothing, leaving him in his underwear. She dropped a kiss on his forehead and then she and Jared started out, but Evan called Jared back. When he leaned over the bed, Evan hugged him.

Dana turned away from the touching scene, not wanting to think about her quick decision to start a marriage that was only going to end up hurting her and her son. She walked out ahead of Jared, then together they continued down the hall past Dana's bedroom. At the end of the hall, she opened the door to the master bedroom.

"I can't sleep here, Dana. This was your parents' room."

"There isn't any other room. Besides, this is the only bed that will be big enough for you."

"Can't you move in here, and I'll sleep in your room?"

She shook her head. She'd always dreamed of sharing this room with her husband one day. "No, it's too much work for a short time. Please, Jared, let's not argue. It's just a bedroom," she said. When he nodded, she went on to say, "There are fresh sheets on the bed and towels in the bath." She pointed to the door across from her room. "I'm sorry, we'll have to share."

"That's fine." He turned his dark gaze on her, making her shiver. "I have no problem sharing."

Dana tried to stay indifferent, but that was nearly impossible. The space between them was practically electrified. She could smell the musky scent of his aftershave, mixed with a little soap. All she had to do was lean a little closer and she'd be against his hard body. As much as she tried to deny it, she couldn't stop her own desires. She had to get away from him.

"Do you need anything else?" she asked, trying to ease her rapid breathing.

"No, I think I have more than enough."

Dana nodded, afraid to say another word. She then turned and walked away. Making it safely inside her bedroom, she sank against the raised paneled door and let the tears fall. She had a right to cry, didn't she? She blamed it on exhaustion of the day. But the big factor was that this was her wedding night and she was spending it alone. When she thought about the beautiful nightgowns she'd gotten at her bridal shower, gowns she'd be the only one to see, more tears fell.

Oh, yeah, she had a right to cry.

The night had been long and sleepless, but in the morning Dana managed to drag herself out of bed. With her head pounding, she pulled on a robe and headed to the bathroom for an aspirin.

She pushed open the door and gasped as she found the room already occupied by none other than her husband.

"Oh, I—I didn't know you were in here," she stuttered, staring at the nearly naked man shaving at the sink. Well, there was a towel covering the vital parts below his waist, but his glorious chest and arms were exposed.

"Don't worry about it. I'm just finishing up." He rinsed off his face and wiped it with another towel. Dana couldn't move if her life depended on it. With his sculptured muscles along his broad chest and long arms, he was absolutely beautiful. A swirl of dark hair covered his chest, barely hiding the flat male nipples beneath.

A warm tingling sensation shot through Dana's body, causing her own nipples to ache and harden into tight buds. She bit back a groan and turned her attention to his face and was met with an intense look.

"I'll come back," she suggested.

"No need, I'm finished now." He walked forward and stopped in front of her. "It's all yours," he said as his gaze swept over her sleepwear.

Embarrassed by Jared's close scrutiny, Dana fought the need to cover herself. She'd been foolish enough to wear one of the new gowns that Joy had given her at the shower. The nearly sheer ivory-colored fabric didn't hide much.

"That's a beautiful gown," he said, desire showing in his eyes. "Did you get that yesterday?"

She pulled the robe together. "Yes, Joy bought it for me." She shrugged. "I thought I might as well wear it."

He edged past her. He was so close, they touched momentarily. "I'd say there isn't much to wear," he said. "But if you want to keep things calm around here, I suggest you not wear this pretty thing again." He tugged on the thin strap on her shoulder. "I'm only human, Dana." He stepped past her and walked down the hall, then disappeared into his bedroom.

Dana wanted to slam the bathroom door. Angry with Jared, and with herself. He was right, she shouldn't have put on the gown last night. Yet she hadn't expected to see Jared this morning. Next time she would cover herself better. Of course, he didn't need to walk around in a towel, either. But she wasn't going to tell him how that affected her.

No, the man didn't need to know how much she was beginning to care about him. Somehow, some way she had to keep her feelings hidden from him.

But how could she fool her own heart?

Chapter 7

Dana was running late because she'd decided to take a little more care with her appearance on the first full day of her marriage. She applied some makeup, even dressed in a nicer pair of jeans and a bright pink blouse. She hurried downstairs to start breakfast, but came to a halt in the kitchen doorway when she found Jared standing at the stove frying bacon.

Never had she expected to see him cooking in her kitchen. Married! Dana still had trouble believing it. She eyed the man she'd taken as her husband only yesterday. Faded jeans covered his slim waist and long legs. Her gaze traveled upward to the burgundy colored T-shirt that highlighted his perfectly sculptured back and shoulders. Her body temperature suddenly shot up.

"Mom, what are you doing?"

Dana glanced down to see her son beside her. "Oh,

nothing, sweetheart. Good morning." She smiled as Jared turned toward them both.

"Morning, sport," Jared said. Then those gorgeous blue eyes settled on her. "Morning, Dana…again."

Another shiver slithered along her spine. "Morning." She walked into the room. "You don't need to cook breakfast. That's my job."

Jared flipped and caught the spatula midair. "Says who? You work as hard as the rest of us, plus cook all the meals. I think the men in the house can manage breakfast. Isn't that right, Evan?"

"Yeah, Mom, I want to help Jared cook." He marched up to the stove. "What do I do?"

Jared took in the boy's wide questioning eyes and realized he was looking to him for guidance. Jared could remember so many times when GH had ignored him. He had no intention of letting Evan down. "How about you set the table while I finish cooking the bacon. Then we'll make some of my special pancakes."

"Oh, boy," Evan said, and hurried to the drawer, pulled out flatware and carried it to the table.

"How can I help?" Dana asked.

When Jared looked at her, hour-old memories flooded his head. A woman with hair wild from sleep, and nearly naked, walking into the bathroom. The nightgown she'd worn was so sheer he could see her rosy nipples trying to poke through the fabric. He had fought the urge to kiss away her shocked expression. He grabbed the towel from the kitchen counter and tucked it in the waistband of his jeans, hoping to hide the effect she had on him.

"Why don't you just sit down and let us men wait on you for a change?"

"Yeah, Mom, let us handle breakfast," Evan repeated

as he walked around the table, setting out the utensils at each place. Once finished, he returned to the stove. "Are we ready to make pancakes yet?"

Jared took out the griddle. "We need a few things...." He went to the refrigerator and opened the door. The cool air felt wonderful in the warm kitchen. He took out eggs and milk, then went back to the stove. "Pull up a chair, son."

Evan did as he was told and together they mixed up batter. With the boy's help the pancakes took longer and they weren't anywhere close to perfect. But Evan was so proud of his accomplishment that it warmed Jared's heart.

"Look, Mom. Look what I made." Evan climbed down, took the first stack from Jared, then carefully carried the plate to his mother.

"Oh, they look wonderful. I bet they taste good, too." Jared watched as Dana poured syrup on the stack, then took a bite. "Mmm, delicious."

The boy grinned. "She likes them."

"Well, get back over here so we can eat, too."

Evan scurried up on his chair and with Jared's help they scooped off another four as Bert walked in the door.

"Bert! We're making flapjacks for breakfast."

The foreman hung his hat on the hook by the door. "Well, *leapin' lizards,* that's my favorite kind of food."

Evan gave him a plate, then with another satisfied customer, came back to the stove. Finally they all were sitting around the table eating breakfast.

"Who taught you to cook, Jared?" Evan asked as he stuffed a forkful of pancakes into his mouth.

"After I left home, I had to learn to feed myself, and pancakes were cheap and filling."

The boy looked concerned. "Did you ever get lonely? Bein' by yourself."

Too many times to count, Jared thought. "Yeah, sometimes." He smiled. "But never hungry. Not since I learned to cook." Jared took a big bite of his food. "A man needs to know how to take care of himself."

"I can make my bed and clean my room. I can feed Sammy and brush him. Oh, and I can hammer a nail real good." He smiled with pride. "Now I can make pancakes."

"I say for a four—almost five-year-old—that's pretty good."

"I'm going to be five next month. Five more weeks. Bert and me been countin'." Evan got up from the table and went to the calendar hanging on the wall. On his tiptoes, he lifted the June sheet and pointed to the twenty-fifth of July. "That's my birthday."

"I can see that. What is it you want?" Jared asked.

Evan glanced at his mom, then lowered his head. "I want a horse, but mom says we can't afford one. We need other things."

Jared didn't know what to say. As much as he wanted to make his nephew's dream come true, he knew enough to stay out of it. "That's true. The Lazy S does need a lot of things."

"It's okay." Evan's head bobbed. "I got what I really wanted already."

"What's that?"

The child smiled. "For you to be my daddy."

Her son wanted Jared to be his father. Evan's words played over and over in Dana's head. What a great way to start off a marriage. If it were a real marriage.

Thankfully everyone finished breakfast quickly, and Bert took Evan with him to finish up the morning chores. With the dishes still on the table, Dana waited to clear the table, knowing she and Jared needed to talk.

She took a long breath and released it. "Evan seems to expect you to be his father. I don't know where he got that idea, Jared. I'll talk with him."

"Technically I am his stepfather," Jared said. "And at the least his uncle."

Dana shook her head in disbelief. She had been so careful to explain to her son that Jared would only be staying a little while. That this marriage was only temporary. "But you're not staying here, nor are we staying married. I don't want Evan to expect you to be around and end up disappointed."

"I'm not disappearing from Evan's life."

"It's not the same thing. He's only four years old. He has this notion in his head that he can make you stay."

"Okay, I'll talk with the boy."

She nodded, but knew that no matter what, someone was going to get hurt. She could handle rejection, but not Evan.

Jared didn't say anything for a long time, then finally spoke. "We need to talk about what happened this morning in the bathroom. I know it was a little awkward for you. If my being here makes you uncomfortable, I can move back to the bunkhouse."

"No," Dana said. "It's fine. I was caught off guard this morning. I haven't had another person around in a long time. If we work up a schedule that won't have us running into each other, we should be okay," she offered, feeling a little breathless whenever he looked at her.

"I have no problem with showering in the evenings."

"I have a bigger concern than our bathroom schedule."

"What?"

"The Lazy S. I just don't know where to start. I mean I know what I need and what I want to do, but...how much money is available?"

"As much as you're going to need. I contacted the estate lawyer, Russell Janny, this morning. We only need to overnight a copy of our marriage license so the trust money can be transferred into an account in San Angelo. Janny said if there's any problem at the bank to have them call him and he'll guarantee the loan payment. So how would you and Evan like to go into town this morning?"

Dana was happy and nervous at the same time. It wasn't easy for her to trust people. As soon as Jared paid off the loan she'd feel beholden to him. He would be her partner, whether he liked it or not. She bit her lips. "That would make Evan happy."

"What would make you happy, Dana?"

His eyes sparkled mischievously. He'd had that same look when she'd walked into the bathroom. She shook away the picture of the near-naked man, knowing she had to stop thinking this marriage was nothing close to a traditional one. "I'd be happy if I could get rid of the bills and get this place to pay."

"Sounds like a plan. I've been talking with Bert. He tells me that the Western Livestock Auction is in Midland this coming Tuesday. He thinks we should go and look at some stock, especially the bulls." He cocked an eyebrow. "Maybe we could look at some horses, too."

She felt her excitement build, but fought it. "It's a little soon to start thinking about raising horses, or buying Evan a large pet."

"It's your dream, Dana," he said, his voice husky. "And

I'm sure Evan wouldn't mind having a mare that you could breed, too. I mean we have six stalls available. So if you find a nice brood mare—I mean... I don't see what it would hurt to look."

She shrugged as if not caring, but her heart pounded with excitement. "I guess it wouldn't hurt—just to look."

"Good." He stood. "I'm going to talk with Bert. He says he has a lead on a couple of guys looking for work. Might as well hire them and have them finish repairing the fences before we bring in more cattle." He hesitated, then said. "I'll be back around noon, unless you need me for something."

A dozen wild thoughts ran through her head. "No, I'm fine."

He smiled. "Then let's plan on having lunch in town."

She nodded and he walked out the door.

Dana hugged herself as a warm shiver went through her. She hated herself for her weakness...her weakness for her husband. How long could she fight these feelings? More importantly, how long before he walked away? No doubt sooner or later he would, and she'd be alone again.

The following Monday, with Chance and Cade keeping an eye on the Lazy S, Dana, Evan, Bert and Jared all climbed into Jared's truck and headed to Midland for the livestock auction. Over the next two hours, Evan peppered question after question at anyone who might have answers. Jared hadn't minded; in fact he'd enjoyed spending time with the boy.

Every afternoon since he'd started the repairs, Evan had been his shadow. And Jared had put in a lot of hours in the barn. Six stalls had been practically rebuilt, and all had sturdy new gates, ready for the new residents that might take up occupancy real soon. He'd finished the corral as of yesterday so that it could be used for riding lessons.

Jared wouldn't mind if Dana found a couple of mares today. He figured she deserved to have something that she wanted, too. Maybe if she achieved her dream of raising horses, she would begin to smile again. And Dana was so pretty when she smiled.

Jared had talked to Chance about a horse for Evan. His half brother gave him some tips about what to look for in buying a good saddle horse for the boy. Jared just hoped that he could convince Dana that her son was ready.

Arriving in town, Jared stopped at one of the chain motels and got their last two rooms for the night. When they entered one of the connecting rooms, Evan scurried toward the first double bed.

Bert tossed his bag on the other bed. "The boy and I will bunk in here," he said.

Jared glanced into the other room to find a king-size bed. "Sounds good." He set his bag on the floor. He glanced at his wife and said with a quiet voice, "I asked for all doubles, but this was all they had. You want to go somewhere else?"

"No," she said, shaking her head. "It's fine. We should be able to manage for one night."

Jared nodded in agreement, but questioned his sanity. Who was he trying to convince? He watched as Dana moved around the room, putting her things away. He wondered if she'd brought the gown she'd worn the other morning in the bathroom. His body stirred to life. Oh, boy, the problems were starting already. How did he ever think he could stay totally detached from this woman?

And how the hell was he supposed to spend the night with her in the same bed and keep his hands to himself?

He needed a miracle.

They ate supper at a steak house next to the motel. Since he wasn't driving, Jared had a few more beers than his usual one glass, hoping that it would help diminish his sexual appetite. But when they returned to the motel, Dana put Evan to bed, then to give Bert some privacy, the door to the connecting room was closed, and Jared knew he was in trouble.

The silence was deafening, and at the same time, it was electrified with awareness between them. All he could think about was stripping out of his clothes and climbing into bed. No, that wasn't exactly true. He wanted her naked and with him in that bed. Damn, he had to stop the direction of his thoughts. Grabbing his bag, he went into the bathroom and took a long cool shower, then dried off and pulled on a pair of sweatpants. When he'd finally come out, he found Dana sitting on the end of the bed, gripping her nightclothes in her fisted hand.

She glanced up at him, but her gaze didn't meet his for long before she looked away. She stood and tried to move around him, but he put a hand on her arm.

"Dana, don't look at me like I'm going to jump you. Give me credit for some self-control."

She pulled out of his grasp. "Excuse me, but this kind of situation is a little strange to me. I'm not used to sharing a room, or a bed with a man. So I'm not exactly sure on how I'm supposed to act." She marched off to the bathroom and shut the door.

Inside, Dana sank against the door and released a long

breath. She knew she'd just made a big fool of herself. But how was she going to be able to get into bed with him?

Dana reached inside the shower and turned on the water, hoping the warm water would soothe away her nervousness. It was only one night. She had to keep her mind focused on the auction tomorrow. They were going to find stock for the ranch. She had to be excited about that. Jared even said she could look at horses. Dana stripped out of her jeans and blouse, then her underwear. Pinning her hair up on her head, she caught a glance of herself in the mirror. She'd always been on the thin side. Now her body was more rounded. She had long, firm legs that had a nice shape to them. Her gaze moved to her breasts. They were fuller since she'd had Evan. Her nipples had changed, too. They were darker, a deep rosy color. Her thoughts turned back to Jared again and the tips hardened into tight buds. With a groan, Dana climbed into the shower and cooled the water temperature, hoping to stop her fever.

Twenty minutes later, she came out of the bathroom wearing her usual faded nightshirt and a pair of cotton panties underneath. On the far side of the bed, Jared faced away from her. Dana went to her side, slipped into the bed and turned off the bedside light. The only illumination came through a slight opening in the drapes.

"Glad to see you made it out. I was afraid you'd drowned."

She stiffened, hoping he'd been asleep. "The water felt good."

Jared rolled onto his back. "Dana, I'm sorry about earlier. I had no right to say those things to you. Of course, you should be leery of me. You don't know me that well."

"No, you were right," she admitted, glad that it was

dark and he couldn't see her. "I had no reason to act that way toward you. You've been nothing but a gentleman."

There was a long silence, then he spoke again. "Was Marshall... Did he give you cause to be afraid?"

"No. Marshall was always nice to me." She closed her eyes trying to remember the father of her son. "Looking back now, I was the one who'd gone after him. Outside of ranch hands, who came and went, there hadn't been many men in my life. Definitely none as charming as Marshall. I was young and I wasn't exactly experienced. When he gave me a little attention, I practically threw myself at him."

"I don't think your attention was much of a hardship for my brother."

Dana didn't know if it was the dark, or Jared's soothing voice that had her admitting things she'd always kept to herself. Even from Joy. "Thank you. But if Marshall were here, he'd probably say I was a pest."

Jared rolled over toward her and propped his head in his hand. He was close, so close that Dana could feel his heat. "Don't sell yourself short, Dana. You're a beautiful woman. Marsh would have never broken his vow to Jocelyn just on a whim. You had to mean something to him."

He cupped her cheek with his hand, making her turn toward him. Then he lowered his head and touched her mouth with his. The kiss was sweet and tender and over all too quickly. Then he was gone, leaving Dana aching for more.

Dana was dreaming as she turned her face into her lover's shoulder, inhaling his intoxicating scent. Snuggling closer, she brushed her breast against his solid chest and quivered at the contact. Her smooth legs tangled with his rough ones. She stroked her hands up and down his strong arm, then traveled to his broad back.

Dana strained to get nearer and was rewarded when he shifted on top of her. She eagerly opened to him, welcoming his weight. She shivered when he placed open-mouthed kisses along her neck. A gasp escaped her lips when his caressing fingers traced along her thigh, pushing her nightshirt up higher. The sound of his husky voice reverberated against her ear, telling her how much he wanted her.

Dana wanted Jared, too. Jared! Suddenly realization of who she was with and what she was doing hit her. Her eyes shot open. Jared must have sensed her change of mood and raised his head. Neither his blue-eyed gaze nor his body was able to hide his aroused state.

He gave her a crooked smile. "This is a pleasant surprise. Guess the bed wasn't big enough after all."

Dana concentrated on slowing her breathing.

Jared looked down at her. "I guess we need to decide what to do next," he suggested, his voice low, sexy.

How was she supposed to think when his hard body was pressed against hers? She nodded.

His gaze moved to her mouth. "Should I go away, or should I just give in to temptation and kiss that inviting mouth of yours?"

Dana's heart started racing. She wanted his kiss. Oh, how she wanted his kiss. What could one hurt? She closed her eyes just as his lips touched hers.

"Mom! Jared!" Evan called out as the connecting door flew open and they both jerked apart. Jared moved off Dana as she pulled the sheet higher around her.

"Morning, sweetheart," she managed.

"Mom, Uncle Jared, aren't you going to get up?" Her

son was already dressed in his new jeans, shirt and boots. The front of his hair had been parted and combed, the back still tangled from sleep. She glanced at the clock. It was six-thirty.

Jared hauled Evan up on the bed. "Hey, sport, give your mom a few minutes. This is kind of a vacation. Not everyone gets up before the sun." He tickled the boy, glad that the distraction was cooling him off.

Evan giggled. "Stop!"

"Only if you go back into your room and give your mom fifteen minutes to get ready. Then we'll go out to breakfast at a restaurant and see if their pancakes are as good as ours."

"'Kay." He climbed off the bed. "How long is fifteen minutes?"

Jared grabbed the notepad and pencil from the night table. He wrote down a number. "When this number comes up on the clock, you can come and get us." He handed it to Evan and the boy took off. Jared got up and closed the door to give them some privacy.

He turned back to Dana. Big mistake. She looked gorgeous. All mussed up as if she'd been thoroughly loved. But not quite. He released a breath. "Why don't we just say that what happened here," he suggested, motioning to the bed, "was a slip in judgment." When he caught her hurt look, he relented a little. "I'm sorry, Dana. I didn't mean for this to happen. But a beautiful woman in a man's bed in the morning is a volatile combination."

Dana turned away. Hell, he couldn't tell her the truth. That he wanted her in his bed. He couldn't give her that kind of power over him.

She got out of bed, her short nightshirt revealing long, shapely legs. He swallowed back a groan as she walked around, gathering the clothes she was going to wear for the day.

Dana stopped and turned to look at him. "I don't see that there's a problem, since we won't be sharing a bed in the future." Her words sounded so final. Then she went into the bathroom and closed the door, leaving Jared aroused and hungry for what he could never have.

Dana Shayne Trager.

Chapter 8

Evan looked happy as they walked around the stock-yard, and Dana knew the reason. He was with Jared. The man's patience with a four-and-a-half-year-old's unending chatter bordered on sainthood. Of course, earlier in bed, Jared Trager had proven himself far from being a saint.

Dana was still trying to recover from the nearly di-sastrous mistake. She wanted to blame it on being half-asleep. She'd thought being in Jared's arms had been a dream. But the fiery touch of his hands on her, his hard body against her had been real. A surge of heat and panic rushed through her as she wondered what would have happened if Evan hadn't interrupted them.

"Land sakes, girl, are you hearin' anything I'm sayin'? I've been talkin' to myself for the last ten minutes."

"I'm sorry, Bert." She pulled the program from the back pocket of her jeans. "I guess I didn't get much sleep last night." The minute she said the words she knew what they implied. What could she say? After all, she and Jared were married—newly married.

Bert gave her a grin, then turned toward the large corral to examine the stock. That was what Dana had to do, focus on what she was here for—to stock the ranch with cattle. But one tall good-looking man kept interrupting her concentration.

When Jared and Evan caught up with them, she tried to keep her mind on business. She told Jared about the stock they'd chosen to bid on. He listened intently, then told her that the final decision was hers. It was she who had to make the decision about what was a fair price.

A little nervous, but with Jared by her side during the bidding, she bought two young bulls, along with a dozen heifers and a small herd of yearlings. Although the Lazy S Ranch had always been a mama-and-baby operation, they needed to stimulate some revenue right away.

"Yeah, Mom," Evan cheered, clapping his hands. "We got a whole bunch of calves."

Dana smiled, feeling proud of herself. "Yes, but they aren't pets."

"I know," he said. "Can we go look at the horses now?"

Dana had known this subject would come up sooner or later. She didn't blame her son. She wanted to take a glance to see what was available, too. She glanced at Jared and he winked.

"I think that's a good idea," he said.

With Bert's help earlier, Jared had already looked over the horses. He wasn't an expert, but he knew more about horses than he did cows. Still, as much as he wanted to give Evan a horse, he wasn't going to do anything to upset Dana. It was her decision to make if her son was ready for a horse.

Jared studied the stubborn set of Dana's jaw. So different from this morning when she lay in his arms, so eager for his attention. He could still feel the imprint of her soft body pressed up against him, arching into his touch. His gut tightened when he met her heated gaze. Damn, the woman had him in knots.

He took her by the arm. "Come on," he said, "let's go see some horses."

"I guess it wouldn't hurt to check out the stock," she said.

Once they arrived at the horse corral, they looked around. It was the first time all morning that Evan had been quiet. Jared realized he was very serious about his search. The boy wasn't going to pick a horse out too quickly. Jared admired the almost-five-year-old's maturity. Maybe he was ready to handle the responsibility of ownership after all.

Finally Evan singled one out. "Oh, Mom, look at that horse," he cried.

Dana turned to see her son pointing at a sweet, golden chestnut mare. She eyed the animal closely, admiring her straight back. The mare was well proportioned with no visible abnormalities. She was adorable. Her only drawback seemed to be her small size. But for what Dana wanted, she was perfect.

Then Evan pointed to another horse, a bay filly. She was a beauty with an auburn coat and black mane and tail. This one wouldn't be as easy to take home. Dana had no doubt that this pretty filly would bring a good price.

"She's a beauty, isn't she?" Jared said, coming up to the railing next to her.

"Yeah, she is," Dana agreed, feeling a tingle of heat as his arm brushed hers. "And she'll go for top dollar." Their eyes held a moment before she looked down at her program, searching over the rest of the horses up for bid. "Too expensive for me."

"You never can tell," he said as he watched Evan go with Bert to look at more horses. "Do you see anything that might work for Evan?"

Dana knew that it was useless to deny the boy. Some way, Jared was going to get her son a horse, so she wasn't going to fight it. "That chestnut mare," she said, pointing at the animal. "She looks like she'd make a good saddle horse. A little small for a full-size man, but perfect for kids."

Jared nodded. "Bert pointed her out earlier. Why don't we circle her in the program and you pick out a few more and see if we can get a good price?"

How many horses was he planning on bidding on? "How many horses do we need?"

"Enough to get you started in your business," he said.

"We can't afford it."

"We can't afford not to," he argued. "It's a business investment, Dana. There's no reason to wait. Besides, Chance mentioned he'd like to offer riding lessons to their guests, but they don't have the room or personnel. This might be your opportunity to work out a deal with the Randells, but you can't if you don't invest in good stock."

Dana knew that was all speculation. And what if she failed? "But the money…"

"I told you the money's not a problem. This is an investment and I know your riding stable is going to take off. With a little more work on the barn, we can take in boarders."

Dana couldn't help but feel excited. "I guess it wouldn't hurt to see what kind of deals we can get."

Jared smiled victoriously. They gathered up Bert and Evan, then they took their seats in the stands. As the time neared, Dana grew more nervous. She didn't want to get her hopes up, because she wasn't going to go crazy with the bidding. She had a limit on what she would spend.

When the little chestnut came up for bid, Evan jumped up. "Look, Mom, there she is. It's Goldie. I want her." He swung around to look at his mother, his expression serious. "And I don't care if other kids ride her. And I promise to feed her, brush her and keep her stall clean."

Goldie. Oh, no, he'd already named the horse. "We'll see, honey." When the auctioneer started the bidding, Dana joined in. As the price began to climb, she hesitated, then she caught the hopeful look in her son's eyes. She lifted her number in the air and held her breath until the auctioneer announced "Sold." Evan cheered and hugged her. She glanced at Jared, and he, too, looked pleased.

A few horses later, the bay filly was led into the corral. She was a beauty tossing her head back and prancing around the ring. With the amount of mumbling going on in the crowd, Dana knew that several people were interested in her. The bidding started a lot higher than Dana had expected and she wasn't going to last long. The big boys were playing, and she wasn't in their league. She tried to hold back her disappointment as she saw the beautiful animal slip from her grasp. Then suddenly Jared took the number from her and raised it when the auctioneer called for more bidding. It went higher still, and he kept up until it began to drop off. Dana remained frozen until the bidding was over and Jared was the new owner of the bay mare.

"Jared! You shouldn't have spent so much money for a saddle horse," she cried.

"I know enough about horseflesh to know an exceptional one when I see it. I have no doubt that she'll produce some great foals. You should talk to Chance about breeding her. Who's to say you can't sell a foal or two?"

"Yeah, Mom," Evan said, his head bobbing up and down. "Jared knows a lot of stuff." The boy grinned. "Now we both have horses. Can we go get Goldie now?"

"Not yet, son," Jared said. "We have more horses to see."

He couldn't be serious. "Jared, no," she said. "You've spent enough."

Jared leaned down and whispered in her ear. "You're cute when you get all bossy. But as long as we're here, we need to concentrate on buying a few good saddle horses. You need at least one more. I've told you to buy what you need."

Dana couldn't believe it. It was like her birthday and Christmas all rolled into one. Was she truly going to be able to open her stable? "Okay," she sighed, "but only one more. If you try to talk me into any more than that, I'm out of here. And remember, you still have to live with me."

Jared tried not to grin. "One more," he agreed, then glanced at Bert. "We better make it a good one."

Dana didn't trust her judgment when it came to men. She just had to put a halt to it before it all got out of control. Ever since Jared appeared in her life, she hadn't been able to control anything, especially her feelings. After this morning, she'd known she'd lost that battle, too.

Jared pulled the truck into the drive around seven that evening. He felt good. He hadn't had this much fun in a long time. He smiled as he looked at Evan in the back seat. He was awake, but barely. The kid had had a busy few days. Jared climbed out, reached into the bed of the truck and took out the bags, then headed to the house.

When Jared came back outside, he saw Chance leaving the barn. He'd stopped by to keep an eye on the place and feed the horses. "How was your trip?" he asked.

"You can tell me tomorrow," Jared said, "when the horses arrive."

Chance frowned. "Horses? You bought Evan more than one?"

"We ended up buying three. One is for Evan, the other two are Dana's. An auburn filly and a dapple gray gelding. I think you'll like the bay. She's a real beauty." He pulled the papers out of his pocket and handed them to Chance.

He looked them over, then released a soft whistle. "She cost you enough, but a classy lady usually does. She came from a good farm and has very impressive bloodlines. It seems a waste to just use her for a riding mount."

"I was thinking the same thing," Jared said. "I suggested to Dana that she might be interested in breeding her with one of your studs."

Chance pursed his lips. "Could be. I'd have to see her first."

"Sounds fair."

"When is she being delivered?"

"Tomorrow afternoon. The livestock is being shipped this weekend. I know I've asked a lot of you already, but do you think you can come by and help unload them?"

A smile tugged at his mouth. "Sure. But don't you worry. I'll get you back. I happen to know you're much better with a hammer and saw than I am."

"No problem," Jared told him. "Say, why don't you bring Joy and Katie with you? We'll barbecue some steaks." Whoa, since when did he do family gatherings?

"Maybe you should check with Dana before you go handing out invitations."

"Ask me what?" The wooden screen door slammed as Dana walked out onto the porch where she found Chance and Jared. They looked so much alike that she wondered why she'd never seen the resemblance before.

"Chance is going to help us unload the livestock on Saturday afternoon. So I invited him and Joy to stay for supper. I thought we'd barbecue."

Dana had never been a couple before. How was she supposed to act? "That sounds...nice."

"Well, you know me," Chance began, "I'll go anywhere for a free meal, but you better call Joy and work out the details."

Chance said goodbye and drove off in his truck. Jared climbed the steps to the porch. "I guess I should have asked you first."

Dana looked up at him. "About what?"

"Inviting people over to the house without talking to you first," he said, tipping his hat back. Funny, lately Dana rarely saw him without her daddy's old worn Stetson. It fit him perfectly. Jared seemed to fit in here perfectly.

He frowned. "If it bothers you we can make it another time."

She shook her head. "No, a barbecue is a good idea. Besides, you know Joy is my friend. I owe her so many meals, I've lost count." Dana smiled. "It should be fun." She turned to go into the house, pushing any foolish thoughts out of her head.

"Dana," Jared called, and she looked back. "I had a great time today. I've never been to a cattle auction."

Why did he have to go and say that? She needed to put space between them. Last night had been dangerous. "And costly," she said.

He laughed. "That, too. But well worth it."

"Yes, I suppose it was."

The deep sound of his laughter sent her pulse racing. If only she could be as playful, but she knew she couldn't without getting hurt when he left.

He sensed her mood change. "What is it, Dana?"

She shook her head.

He came closer. "If it's about what happened in the motel room…"

"No. You're right. This marriage isn't permanent. We can't start something that…"

He moved closer. "I'm only thinking about you, Dana. I don't want you hurt, and I'd hate myself if I caused you any pain. I'm here to help you and Evan, but I can't stay. It's not me. I just don't do family very well."

Dana knew Jared was mistaken. In just a short time he had developed a relationship with his brothers and he'd been a father to her son.

Maybe she should try to convince him that he fit into her family perfectly…. For Evan's sake, of course.

On Saturday, there was all kinds of excitement at the Lazy S Ranch. More than there had been in years, Dana reflected. The cattle trucks pulled in around one o'clock that afternoon and not only was Chance waiting, but his brothers, Cade and Travis, were there to help her and Jared.

It took them just thirty minutes to unload the livestock. The two bulls were corralled in a temporary pen until the brothers were ready to drive the herd out to pasture.

Dana fed the men lunch, then did up the dishes before she changed to go with them. She walked into the barn wearing jeans, chaps and boots, ready for the ride. Yet she couldn't help but detour down the center aisle to where the three new boarders, particularly the bay filly, took up residence. She opened the gate slowly so as not to spook the young horse, Sweet Brandy. Dana wanted to pinch herself. How did she get lucky enough to own this beauty?

"Easy, girl, I only want to give you some attention." The filly backed away, but stopped as Dana's soft voice began to soothe her. Then Dana took hold of the animal's cloth halter and began to stoke her. "How was your night?" Dana glanced around the stall. It was clean. She smiled, knowing the new ranch hand, Owen, must have been up early. At twenty, he was a hard worker and loved horses. Too bad Dana would lose him when he went back to college in the fall.

The filly nudged against her. "So you like this, huh?" The horse bobbed her head up and down and Dana laughed.

Jared was walking Scout out of the stall when he heard Dana's voice. Her soft, throaty tones sounded like a lover's caress, drawing him to Sweet Brandy's stall. She was stroking the filly and not paying any attention to him. Not since their trip to Midland had he been able to get close to her. Avoidance was the best solution for both of them, but that didn't change the fact that he wanted her. Desire shot though him as his gaze wandered over her shapely bottom and long, slender legs covered in snug jeans. That rich auburn hair was tied back in a braid. His fingers itched to be tangled in the wild strands.

He groaned, causing Dana to turn around. "Jared."

"Hey," he said, and forced a smile. "I see she's won you over, too."

"She did that the second she pranced into the ring." Dana came out of the bay's stall. "Thank you for buying her."

"Like I said, she's a great investment." He shut and locked the gate. "In a few years you'll be able to breed her." He took hold of Scout's reins and started walking.

"Give me a few minutes and I'll be ready to leave." She went into the tack room and came out carrying a saddle and headed toward her mount, a gelding roan named Rex.

She began to saddle her horse. "There's no need for you to come," he said. "We have plenty of help with Owen, Chance, Cade and Travis. And there's Bert, too. What about Evan?"

She paused. "Joy's agreed to watch him. So you're going to have more help with me along. I still run this place. This is my ranch."

Jared tied Scout to the railing and went into the stall. He took the bridle from her and made her look at him. "I'm not trying to take anything away from you, Dana. I only want to make things easier for you. I thought you might want to stay home today."

She folded her arms across her chest. "Well, you thought wrong."

Jared knew he hadn't handled it right. "I know that now. I should have talked it over with you." He watched her blink away tears and before he could talk himself out of it, he placed an arm across her shoulders and drew her to him. "I'm sorry, Dana." The feel of her softness against him caused his body to stir immediately. Damn, she felt good. A flood of memories of their trip to Midland came into his mind, reminding him of how close they'd gotten, how they'd nearly made love. He'd come home vowing to stay away from her. And he'd managed all week. He'd showered at night, stayed out in the barn until as late as possible. The only time they had been together was at mealtime.

"I'll try not to overstep again," he said, and pulled back. Her gaze rose to his as his hand moved down her arm and gripped her hand. "Do you think you can forgive me?"

She blinked, but it didn't erase the passion in the emerald depths. "Just don't let it happen again," she said in a soft throaty tone. And all he could think about was a naked Dana against crumpled sheets.

His grip tightened. "I'll try."

"See that you do," she said weakly.

His resistance was faltering. Leaning down, his lips touched hers, then he chanced another nibble and another. With each one of Dana's breathy gasps, his reserve faltered, then disappeared altogether and he covered her mouth completely. He pulled her against him, tilting her back and deepened the kiss. Coaxing her lips apart, he tasted her again and again.

Her arms went around his neck, fingers combed through his nape, causing his hat to fall to the ground, forgotten.

It wasn't until he heard the sound of the men's laughter that he pulled back, but didn't release her.

"Hey, you'll have to save that for later," Chance called out. "We need to ride out before the sun roasts us."

Feeling the heat rise in her face, Dana buried her head

into Jared's chest. How could she let this happen? Still trembling from the kiss, she couldn't look at Jared.

He had other ideas. "Dana," he said, cupping her chin and raising her head. "We better go. I'll saddle your horse."

She stopped him. "I don't really need to go. I could use the time to bake a few pies for the barbecue."

He grinned. "Now, I'm not going to argue with you on that one. I just want you to know that I'm not trying to exclude you. I just want to make things easier."

Little by little he was stealing her heart. "Thank you."

"You're welcome." He picked up his hat and started to leave, then stopped. "I'm sorry that Chance caught us, but I'm not sorry that I kissed you." He tugged on his hat, then led Scout out to the corral.

Dana somehow made her way back to the house and found Joy at the kitchen table, drinking her tea. "I thought you were going with the guys to move the new herd."

"I changed my mind."

Joy raised an eyebrow. "By the looks of you, I'd say one carpenter-cowboy may be changing it for you."

Dana's hand went to her hair and realized half her braid was pulled out. She could still taste him on her lips, too. She had no willpower when it came to the man. With a groan, she sank into a chair. "I'm in big trouble."

Joy smiled. "Why is that?"

"Because I'm starting to care about Jared."

"And why is this bad?"

"Because he doesn't feel the same about me, and besides, he'll be leaving soon." *And I'll be alone again,* she cried silently.

"Maybe he doesn't want to leave. He does have family here. Not just Evan, but Chance, Cade and Travis."

Dana shook her head. "He tells me all the time that he has a life in Las Vegas. That's where he's buying a company."

Joy reached across the table and patted Dana's hand. "I think Jared is fighting the feelings he has for you. He could change his mind about leaving. I remember Chance after we first were married. Oh, how he fought to stay away from me. I knew he only married me to get my land, and I needed his protection so I wouldn't lose Katie to my in-laws. But when I realized that I didn't want our marriage to be in name only, I decided I had to take matters into my own hands and let him know how I felt."

Dana was definitely interested. "How did you do that?"

"I seduced him," Joy said proudly. "A bad storm helped out. A tree branch broke the window in my bedroom, and I saw my opportunity and went for it. I went to his bed and persuaded him to share it with me." Her friend looked at Dana. "First, you have to admit that you love Jared. Do you?"

Dana didn't want to say the words out loud, but staying silent didn't change the fact. "Yes, I do," she sighed.

"Then it's simple. Let Jared know how you feel. Show him no mercy and go after him."

Chapter 9

Go after him.

Dana spent the morning preparing food for the barbe-cue, but her thoughts kept wandering back to her friend's words. This was crazy. She'd tried going after a man once, and look what had happened. She was left alone with a broken heart. A slow smile spread across her face. Not completely alone. She couldn't imagine her life with-out Evan. He was the joy of her life.

She sobered. Gone was that young, foolish girl. A mother now, she also had the responsibility of running the ranch. She couldn't take that kind of risk again. It was best to leave things as they were—to stick to their agreement—marriage in name only. She'd rather have Jared as Evan's uncle and her friend, than to drive him off completely by trying to hold him here. And besides, who said Jared was even interested in her? They'd only shared a few kisses. Surely a man like Jared would prefer a more sophisticated woman.

"Dana, the oven timer went off," Joy said.

The buzzing sound grew louder. "Oh, what?" Dana finally looked up.

"Your pies are ready."

Dana flushed as she went to the oven and opened the door to find two apple pies, the fillings bubbling through the slits in the golden brown crusts. With oven mitts, she lifted them out, placing them onto the cooling rack as a spicy cinnamon fragrance filled the room.

Just then the back door opened and Chance and Jared walked in. Dusty and dirty from the trail ride, they hung their hats on the hook and went to the sink. Jared pulled two glasses from the cupboard and handed one to Chance to fill. They drank thirstily, leaning against the counter. Both men were broad-shouldered and muscular, but slim-waisted and long-legged. And both Randells were wickedly handsome. In just the short weeks that Jared had been at the ranch, he'd come to look as much like a rancher as Chance did, who'd been born to it.

"You two look beat," Joy said.

"It's hot as blazes out there," Chance said as his wife came up to him. Ignoring the dirt, she kissed her husband as Chance placed his hand on her slightly rounded stomach. "But it was a great workout for my cutters. Dang, you should have seen Owen handle Roughneck. That kid is a natural on a horse."

"Good, but he's only here for the summer." Dana looked at Jared to find that his gaze was on her. She felt her skin warm and wished he'd greet her a little more affectionately. Of course, they didn't need to put on a show for the other couple, even if Chance had caught them kissing in the barn.

"Did things go okay?" Dana asked him.

Jared nodded. "The herd is happily grazing in the north section."

"Good." She turned to Chance. "Where are Travis and Cade?"

"They've already headed home," Chance said, then looked back at Jared. "Hey, you'd be wise to give your wife another big kiss. Take a look at the counter and see what's coolin'."

Jared glanced in the direction Chance pointed at, then at Dana and smiled. "I knew I had a good reason for you to stay here." He came toward her and Dana stiffened as he leaned down and brushed his mouth against hers. She was quite disappointed when he pulled away.

"Thanks for the pies," Jared whispered as their eyes met.

His pulse raced as it had most of the morning. Funny, he'd been the one to convince her to stay home, and then wished she'd been with them. He couldn't resist her any longer and drew her close, even happier when she didn't pull away.

"Dana, you'd be proud of Jared today," Chance announced. "He did good for a *city* boy."

"Thanks." Jared accepted the good-natured ribbing. "But I've spent time on a ranch."

Chance barked with laughter. "A fancy dude ranch isn't my idea of hard work."

He frowned. "A few years back I worked for a large operation outside of Denver. So I've spent my time in a saddle."

"But you'll probably have a few sore places tonight. Just have Dana rub on a little ointment."

Jared tried to keep it light, but the thought of Dana's hands on him had his body reacting. "Not a bad idea."

"Okay, guys," Joy broke in. "I think you both need to clean up and start the grill for some of that good Texas beef."

The sound of footsteps on the stairs told them the kids were close. Evan ran into the room, Katie close on his heels. The little girl ran to her daddy.

"Uncle Jared, you're back." Evan's eyes lit up as he ran to him. "Can you take me riding on Goldie?"

Jared crouched down. "Evan, we've talked about this. Your mother has to check out your new horse first."

The boy lowered his eyes. "Oh, I forgot." He looked up at his mother. "Mom, is it time to eat yet? I'm hungry."

The room broke into laughter. "I guess it's unanimous," Jared said. "Give me ten minutes to shower and we'll get this party started. Chance, you're welcome to use the bathroom downstairs."

His half brother shook his head. "My things are in the bunkhouse, I'll just use the shower there."

Jared nodded. They'd been strangers a month ago. Now they were becoming friends. "Thanks for today, Chance. I really appreciate it."

"That's what family is for."

It was funny, the steaks were the easy part of the meal. Dana watched through the kitchen window as Jared and Chance stood by the grill, long-neck bottles of beer in their hands, talking about the exploits of the morning's cattle drive.

But the kids playing in the yard weren't to be ignored.

Before long, Jared and Chance put down their drinks and took turns tossing the children the ball, praising every time one of them made a catch, encouraging them when they didn't. The laughter was contagious.

"That's the sweetest sound," Joy said.

"What?"

"A child's laughter," her friend said. "It's so innocent, so carefree. There's nothing like it in the world. That's one of the reasons I fell in love with Chance. The way he was with Katie. They say that kids and animals are great judges of character." She nodded to Jared as he bent down, showing Evan how to grip a plastic baseball.

Something tightened around Dana's heart. What's not to love? The man gave her son so much attention and affection.

"They're crazy about each other," Joy added.

Dana looked away. "Jared *is* Evan's uncle."

"It's possible that the man wants to be more."

Dana shut her eyes a moment. She couldn't let herself dream that dream. "I just have to take it day by day."

The men finally got the steaks and the kids' hot dogs grilled. Bert and Owen begged off and took their food back to the bunkhouse to kick back and watch television. So it was the two couples sitting at the table, with the two kids happily at a little table of their own. Jared had worked most of the week finishing a small patio area next to the house. He hadn't had time to make the cover, but an oversize umbrella shaded everyone from the late-afternoon sun.

Jared sat back, enjoying the company of the people around him. He couldn't remember ever having a Hastings family barbecue. Funny, he'd only known Chance,

Joy, Dana and Evan for such a short but they were more family than he'd ever known. There were times, like today, when he wanted to fit in. And he would miss this when he left.

He stole a glance at Dana and recalled the kiss they'd shared in the barn. There were a lot of other things he would miss. Like seeing Dana the first thing in the morning with her eyes still hooded from sleep, and her hair hanging loose....

Dana got up to tend to the children. His attention went to the white shorts she had on. The day was a hot one and it was getting hotter by the minute. He shifted in his seat as his gaze examined her rounded bottom and long legs. Her sandals exposed small narrow feet, with dots of pink polish on each toe. She wore a tank top that highlighted her trim arms with enough muscle to show she was in shape. Ranching was hard work, and Dana didn't slack on her duties. She worked just as hard as the rest. He wished she didn't have to. The consolation was that she loved the ranch. He had to admit that he, too, was enjoying the time he spent on the Lazy S. And the time he had with Evan and Dana.

Chance patted his flat stomach. "That apple pie was top-grade choice." He winked. "Dana, as long as you have pie, you can ask me for help anytime."

Dana smiled. "So that's Joy's secret way to get you to do things."

Chance grinned at his wife. "Let's just say it's one of the ways."

Jared watched the couple exchange an intimate look. It was almost if everybody else around had disappeared. They were so unaware of anyone but each other. Damn, he envied that.

Dana's eyes locked with his and heat surged through him. He thought about how much he wanted to kiss her again. Right now, right here. He knew it was more than he had a right to, but he couldn't help it.

Dana was taking longer than usual putting Evan down for the night. And of course the child wasn't cooperating.

"But I'm not tired," he argued. "I want to stay up. Please…" He stopped and yawned.

"How about a story?" she asked.

"I want Uncle Jared to read to me," he demanded.

"I'm sorry, but he's busy. I can read to you." She started to pull out his favorite book, *Mike Mulligan and His Steam Shovel.*

"That's a baby book." Evan pouted.

"Hey, partner, you giving your mother a bad time?"

They both looked to the doorway where Jared stood. "Uncle Jared, Mom says you're too busy to read to me."

"Well, I did have some chores to take care of, but I'm finished now." He pushed away from the doorway and walked into the room. "Maybe I can take over for your mom."

"Yeah, you can read me a story."

Dana gladly gave him the book. Their hands touched, sending electrical shock waves through her. Dana turned and kissed Evan good-night, then went downstairs and outside. The mess from the barbecue had been cleaned up and the chairs put away. Jared had been busy.

A cool breeze caught Dana's hair and brushed strands against her face. She pushed them back and released a long breath, trying to banish Joy's words from her head.

Let Jared know how you feel.

She thought about Jared's touch…how his kiss made

her skin tingle. Her body was wound tight, and aching for something she knew could hurt her. It had been so long since a man had wanted her. Having Jared around just made her more aware of that fact. She knew that he wasn't going to be here for much longer, so why was she wasting precious time?

"Dana…"

Dana turned around when she heard Jared's voice. He didn't say any more as he moved across the deck and stopped in front of her. Silently he cupped her jaw, leaned down and pressed his mouth against hers. The kiss was soft and achingly tender, and she wanted it to go on and on.

"Jared…" She didn't realize she'd spoken his name until he broke the kiss.

"What is it, darlin'?" He smiled. "Tell me what you want."

Her heart raced so fast she didn't think she had the breath to speak. "You…"

She barely got the words out before his mouth was back on hers in a searing kiss. His tongue moved into her mouth, dueling with hers, asking for more. His hands caressed her back, then moved to her breasts. She gasped when his fingers teased her nipple through her T-shirt.

"You want me to stop?"

"No, oh no," she whispered.

Jared had reached his limit. He wasn't going to walk away this time; he couldn't. He started to take Dana into the house when he heard his name again. This time it was a male voice.

He broke off the kiss, but cradled Dana against him. He turned to see an embarrassed Owen at the edge of the yard. "I'm sorry to disturb you, Jared, but I need to talk with you."

Jared looked at Dana. "Why don't you go inside and I'll see what Owen wants?"

Dana nodded and left as Jared walked toward the ranch hand. "What is it?"

"Bert would be angry if he knew I'd come to get you…."

"Come and get me? Why? What's wrong with Bert?"

"I think he's hurt. He slipped and fell."

Jared took off toward the bunkhouse. He kept his gait at a quick efficient walk, trying not to worry Owen. What had the old man tried to do? Too much probably.

Inside the long room, he found Bert sitting at the table. "Hey, Bert. I hear you took a fall."

The older man glared at young Owen standing in the doorway. "Looks like someone has a big mouth. I told the boy not to disturb you and Dana." Bert absently rubbed his arthritic knee.

"Owen was just worried."

"No need. I've fallen before."

Jared didn't want to overstep his boundaries. "You want me to call your doctor?"

The foreman gave him an incredulous look. "And he's just gonna tell me what I already know, that my knee isn't worth the powder to blow it up." He turned away. "Said I need to have one of those fancy surgeries."

Jared wondered if Dana knew about this. "Maybe he can give you something for the pain."

"I have a box full of painkillers. Makes my head fuzzy. I can't work like that."

"Why don't you take one to help you sleep tonight? The effects should be worn off by morning."

They finally got Bert to agree, and after one pill, Jared helped him into bed, promising himself that he'd talk with the doctor in the morning.

On the way back to the house, Jared's thoughts returned to Dana. Damn, it had been nearly an hour since he'd told her that he would be right back. He closed his eyes momentarily, recalling how close they'd come... Maybe it was better this way. He would only hurt Dana in the end.

He went into the house, shut off all the lights and went upstairs. Dana's bedroom door was closed and no light shone under the door. Pulling his shirt from the waistband of his jeans, he walked to his room and went inside. There was a soft glow from the lamp beside the bed and he froze when he discovered Dana sitting on top of the blanket. She was wearing a sheer gown and her hair was lying wild against her shoulders.

He began to tremble. "Dana..."

She smiled. "Hi." Her greeting was breathy.

"What are you doing here?"

She rose and walked toward him. "I'm waiting for you," she whispered. "What took you so long?"

"Just a little problem Bert needed help with."

"Is everything okay?"

"It is now."

She raised her arms and placed them around his neck. "Good. Then you don't have to leave again."

Her breath whispered against his mouth and she kissed him. He remained motionless, trying to hide his torment. She pulled back to look up at him.

"And Evan's asleep so I don't have to leave, either. Unless you don't want me here," she said.

Jared closed his eyes as desire ripped through him.

Of course he wanted her here. He wanted her so badly, he hurt. But he said, "Maybe this isn't such a good idea. I mean now that…we've had a chance to think about…" She raised up and pressed her body into his, then her hands moved over his chest. He couldn't take any more. "Dana…"

She stopped and looked up at him, her green eyes dilated, her face flushed, her mouth so tempting. His body instantly grew hard.

"Are you saying you don't want me?" she asked.

"No," he breathed. "But I don't want you to have any regrets later."

Her finger touched his mouth to stop his words. "I don't want to think about anything but you right now." She drew a ragged breath. "Jared, I want to be your wife…for as long as we have together."

She took hold of his hand and led him toward the bed. In the dim light, Dana stood before him. Her fingers were shaking as she slowly reached for the gown straps and slid them off her shoulders. Jared's breathing stopped as he watched the feathery fabric leisurely float to the floor.

"I want you to make love to me."

Dana's heart drummed in her ears as the seconds passed. She found herself wanting to cover herself as Jared just stared at her. She knew she wasn't a raving beauty. She was more muscular than the average woman. Maybe her body wasn't as perfect as those he'd been used to.

Unable to stand Jared's apparent lack of interest any longer, she grabbed for her gown. "Sorry, I won't bother you again."

"No, Dana, wait." He reached for her. "Don't ever

doubt that I want you. But I'm trying to be noble here and you're making it damn difficult."

"You want me?"

"More than my next breath," he admitted and swept her into his arms.

In a single motion he claimed her lips; his tongue plunged inside. She eagerly accepted the invitation and tasted him, too. Skimming his hands over her shoulders, then down her back, he cupped her bottom as he drew her closer. She moaned softly as so many feelings rushed through her, thrilling and frightening her at the same time.

Jared's chest heaved. "Dana, this is your last chance to change your mind."

Her only comment was her hands going to his shirt and stripping it off his shoulders. "I think you have too many clothes on." Once the shirt was disposed of, she went to his belt and removed it. Then she paused and placed a few kisses against his chest.

Seconds later, his boots and jeans joined his shirt on the floor. He jerked back the blanket and laid Dana down on the cool sheets, then stretched out beside her. She'd never been like this with a man before. They were both exposed, but she realized she trusted Jared and felt safe with him.

With one long finger, he traced the curve of her breasts. "Perfect."

She returned the favor and trailed her finger over his chest, toying with his hard nipple. She was delighted when he made a low guttural sound of pleasure.

Jared was losing control fast as he closed his eyes under the assault of Dana's hands and mouth.

He pushed her on her back and rose over her. "It's my

turn," he said as he let his fingertips whisper over her breasts, causing her to moan. Her nipples hardened instantly. "You like that?" He leaned down and circled one tight bud with his tongue, then teased it with his finger.

"Yes..." she breathed, arching her back, so he would repeat the pleasure.

Jared smiled. Dana might have been the one to entice him into bed, but he doubted there had been a man in her life since Marsh. It took everything he had in him, but he needed to go slow with her. Protect her.

Protection.

He grabbed his jeans off the floor and pulled a condom out of his wallet. Once he prepared himself, he came back to her.

"Look at me, Dana." She did. "What we're doing is crazy, but I want you too much to stop." Brushing her legs apart, he moved over her. He grasped her hands and laced his fingers with hers.

"I've wanted you from the first moment I saw you." He stared into her green eyes, knowing she was the most dangerous kind of woman. She was sexy as hell, but wanted more from a man than just a brief mating.

Jared's breathing grew ragged as he leaned down and nipped at her mouth, then down her neck to her breasts again. She whimpered and rotated her body against his, causing him to lose control. His hand moved down between her legs. Feeling her wetness, he slowly pressed into her sweet body.

Dana wanted Jared so badly she couldn't think straight and didn't bother to try. He filled her so completely, nothing had ever felt so wonderful.

He moved agonizingly slow. "Please," Dana cried, knowing she could never get enough of him.

"You want more?" he whispered against her lips.

"Oh, yes." Dana writhed beneath him, then locked her legs around his hips to let him know that she wanted all he had to give. Jared didn't disappoint her. With each stroke, he coaxed her until her body tightened in pleasure and finally her shuddering release tossed them both over the edge. With one last groan, Jared collapsed on top of her, then rolled away, pulling her to his side.

Only their rapid breathing interrupted the silence as Jared felt the damp weight of Dana against him. He was still trying to recover from their lovemaking, but doubted he ever would.

Damn, he had to have been crazy to let this happen. It was going to be hard enough to walk away as it was, now it was nearly impossible. She made him dream of things he couldn't have.

Jared got out of bed and grabbed his clothes. "I'll be right back." He took a trip to the bathroom, then returned dressed in jeans. He stood just inside the door, afraid that he wouldn't be able to leave if he got too close.

"Dana, maybe we acted a little rash here. I should spend the night in the bunkhouse."

Dana sat up, exposing her naked body to him. "Why?"

He sucked in a long breath. How could he want her again so soon?

She leaned against the pillow, but refused to cover her sweet little body. "Are you saying that you don't want to come back into bed…with me?"

He raked his fingers through his hair. "You know that's not true, Dana."

"Prove it."

Dana didn't live in the real world. "You know I'm going to be leaving soon."

Wrapped in a sheet, she climbed out of bed and crossed the room. "You're not leaving tonight, are you?"

He fought to keep from backing away. "No, not tonight."

Dana gave him a slow, sexy smile. "Then come back to bed." She reached for his hand. "I don't want to sleep alone."

Jared resisted with his last ounce of strength. "If I do, I'll make love to you again."

"That's perfect, because I want you to. Unless you're not in the mood."

He didn't answer her question, just swung her up in his arms and carried her back to bed.

Damn, he was going to be tired in the morning, but he was looking forward to it.

Chapter 10

The bright sunlight streamed through the window, across the bed and right into Dana's eyes. She rolled away, wanting to go back to sleep, but there was no escaping the sun's glare. Which was strange since her room faced the west. Suddenly, memories of last night flooded her head. She gasped and sat up, grabbing the sheet to cover her nakedness.

Naked!

Dana glanced around and realized she was in her parents' bed—no, Jared's bed. Alone. The clock read eight twenty-five. Oh, no, she'd slept through breakfast. Wrapping the sheet around her, she ran to her bedroom. After grabbing some clean clothes, she went to shower.

Why hadn't Jared wakened her this morning? Her thoughts turned to last night and her body warmed in remembrance. Jared had made love to her two more times.

Neither one of them had thought much about sleep until he curled up behind her somewhere around 2:00 am.

Now, it was almost nine. Dana, dressed in jeans and a red blouse, headed downstairs. A little nervous, she realized she didn't know exactly how to behave. How would Jared act toward her? Suddenly she didn't feel as brave as she had just twelve hours ago when she'd lured him to bed. Seeing the empty kitchen, she was happy for the temporary reprieve, but finding the stack of dirty dishes in the sink didn't feel that great.

Deciding she couldn't hide out all day, Dana walked out the back door and headed to the barn. Once inside the cool interior, she started down the center aisle, passing the newly built stalls. That was when she heard Jared's voice. Her breath quickened at the memory of his lovemaking and the familiar, deep-throated tone with which he relayed his need and encouragement to her. The man not only had bedroom eyes, but a voice to match. She hung back until he finished his instructions to Owen, taking the opportunity to check on Sweet Brandy.

Dana went inside the stall. "Well, how are you this morning, Miss Brandy?" she crooned as she stroked the horse's face. Brandy shifted closer. "You want some attention, don't you?"

"Don't we all?"

Dana turned to find Jared at the gate. "Hi," she said. He looked wonderful, wearing faded jeans, a chambray shirt and an old Stetson. Heat rushed to her face as she thought about how he looked without those clothes. She glanced away.

"Good morning," he greeted her.

She forced a smile to cover her nervousness. "I almost missed the morning part. Why didn't you wake me?"

"I did," he said, his smile spreading. "You told me to go away."

Dana couldn't imagine ever telling him to go away. Her body tingled, making her aware that she still wanted him. "I shouldn't have slept so late," she said. "There's work to be done."

Jared shrugged. "Isn't that the reason we hired Owen? So you didn't have so much to do."

"Still, the day starts at sun up."

"I think after last night you need some rest."

Jared watched a blush spread over her face as she avoided his gaze. Did she regret last night? He cursed himself. No matter how much he'd wanted her—still wanted her—he should have been the one to walk away from the temptation.

"Look, Dana. About last night… I don't want you to think that I expect…or take for granted that…"

Suddenly Dana's back straightened as anger flashed in her emerald eyes. "I told you before, Jared. The last thing a woman wants is to hear a man apologize, especially after they made love. And I sure as hell don't need your pity." She tried to push past him, when he stopped her.

"You think that's what I'm doing?" he asked. "You think I made love to you *three* times last night because I felt sorry for you?" He bit back a curse. "I'm fighting everything in me not to pick you up and carry you back to that bed right now."

With a gasp, her eyes rounded.

"Yeah, I want you, all right," he said. "Just like I wanted you this morning. It was hell leaving that warm bed, leaving your sexy, naked body." His voice lowered. "When all I wanted to do was to make love to you again."

"But I thought… I didn't want you to think that you had to—"

Jared pulled her against him, his hands cupping her face. "I think it's time I shut you up before you get yourself into any more trouble." His mouth captured hers in a hungry kiss. He parted her lips and drove his tongue inside to taste her intoxicating sweetness. She whimpered as her body sank against him.

He broke off the kiss, knowing he had to keep his head. "Woman, you're going to get us into trouble."

She smiled. "I've been told that before." She wrapped her arms around his waist. "So what are you going to do with me?"

He groaned, then moved her back. "I think the only safe thing is to keep you at a safe distance."

She pouted. "That's no fun." She started to go to him again when Evan came racing down the aisle.

"Mom, you woke up."

"Yes, I did." Dana bent down and hugged her son. Her fingers combed Evan's unruly hair. It had a crooked part in the front and his curls were slicked down with hair gel. No doubt Evan's handiwork.

"Uncle Jared said you were tired from cooking yesterday."

She glanced at the man who had caused her fatigue. He gave her a wicked grin, stealing her heart all over again. "I guess I was. What have you been doing all morning?"

"I've been taking care of Bert. His knee hurts. So I've been reading him my books."

Dana knew that Evan had memorized his favorite stories. "That's nice of you." Dana shot a look at Jared. "What's wrong with Bert?"

"He fell last night. I guess his knee has been giving

him trouble for a while now. I told him to stay off it until I get him to the doctor."

"Why didn't you tell me last night?"

Jared looked down at the boy. "Evan, why don't you go get Goldie's halter from the tack room? Then we'll see if Owen can exercise her."

"Oh, boy." Evan cheered and scurried off.

Jared's attention turned back to Dana. "I didn't tell you because Bert asked me not to. He knew you would worry."

"Of course I'd worry. He's family."

"I was going to tell you this morning, but I had enough to deal with trying to get Bert to agree to go to the doctor. I'm taking him in to see an orthopedic specialist to-morrow."

Dana couldn't believe that Bert had agreed to this. She had been trying for months. "He's letting you take him in," she said. She started off toward the bunkhouse, but Jared caught up with her.

"Let him be, Dana. Bert doesn't want a woman feeling sorry for him."

"But it's my job…."

"And I'm your husband," he said, then stepped closer. "Unless you don't want my help."

Dana felt the familiar heat of his body and she wanted to melt into him. She'd had to handle things for so long on her own. It would be so easy to give in, but how long would he be around for her? "I guess I don't have a problem with you helping out."

Jared smiled. "Now, did that hurt so much?" His mouth brushed over hers and she moaned, rising up on her toes for more. He pulled back, his gaze never leaving her. "You want more?"

"Yes…"

"You're a greedy woman." He leaned down and took another nibble, causing more incredible sensations. "I guess I'll just have to work harder tonight at satisfying you."

She blinked, unable to hide her reaction.

He stared at her. "Will you have a problem with sharing my bed?"

A shiver went through her. "No," she breathed.

"Good," he said, then lowered his head again and captured her mouth in a bone-melting kiss.

The next day, Dana went outside to greet Jared and Bert as they returned from the doctor. The older man didn't look happy.

"Well, isn't anyone going to tell me what happened?" she asked, staring at the two sullen men.

Jared let Bert talk. "They want to do surgery and replace my knee with a plastic one." He looked at Jared. "I told you before we went that's what they wanted to do. Do you know how much that costs? Too much." He turned around and limped off.

Dana couldn't hide her concern. "There's nothing else they can do?"

"It's the best option. There's medication, but Bert says it makes him drowsy. Says he'll handle the pain."

"How much is the operation?"

"Medicare will take care of most of it, but you know there are always costs." He paced. "I have money for the surgery. All I need to do is figure a way to get him to take it."

Her love for Jared was growing in leaps and bounds. "Bert's a proud man and I love him like a father. He was the only one who helped me after my own father died. Oh, Jared, we've got to help him."

He drew her into his arms. "Somehow I'll convince him to have the surgery."

"Thank you," she whispered. "I don't know how I can ever repay you."

"There's no need. Like you said, Bert is family."

Just then Dana saw a familiar truck pull into the drive. Chance Randell. "I didn't know Chance was coming by today."

"I called him. He's going to help me with some ideas on designing the new horse corral. If you're going to teach riding I thought you might like some special features."

When did these plans come about? she wondered. "And where is this corral going to be?"

"Just on the other side of the barn. It'll be out of the way, but close enough to where the horses are stabled. If you want, you can talk with Chance."

Dana watched as Jared's half brother got out of the truck. She was glad that the two were getting along so well. Deep down she'd hoped that their growing relationship would be another tie to keep Jared in Texas. Secretly she wished she could be enough to make him stay.

"You two can talk now," Dana said, "but invite Chance for lunch and we'll discuss things in detail then."

Jared leaned down and placed a quick kiss on her mouth. "See you later." With a sexy wink, he walked off.

Feeling giddy, Dana went back into the house and busied herself preparing lunch. Since she had the time, she put together a green salad and made egg salad for sandwiches. For an extra treat, she put a peach cobbler into the oven. After setting the table, she started to go get the men when the phone rang.

"Lazy S Ranch," she said into the receiver.

"Hello. I'm looking for Jared Trager," an unfamiliar voice said.

"He's here, but outside," Dana said. "May I take a message or have him call you back?"

"Yes, please. I'm Nate Peterson from Burke Construction. It's urgent that I speak to him."

Dana copied down the phone number Mr. Peterson gave her, then headed out to the corral. She walked through the barn, worried that the "urgent" message would take Jared away from her and Evan. But she had to give it to him. If he was going to stay, he had to make that decision on his own.

She found Jared and Chance standing in the newly mowed area that Jared had cleared just days ago. Coming up behind them, she was about to speak when something Chance was saying stopped her.

"Dana owns a real sweet section in Mustang Valley. You could add some cabins and Dana could move her stable of riding horses over, too. It would make money for all of us."

Jared was surprised at Chance's offer. So, Chance wanted to include him in the Randell business, the Mustang Valley Guest Ranch. Jared knew that it could possibly be the best investment to help supplement the Lazy S. Before he could respond, he caught movement out of the corner of his eyes. He turned to find Dana standing behind him. By the look on her face, she had already heard Chance's ideas.

"Dana, I didn't think you were going to come out."

"It's a good thing I did, or you might have decided to

give away all the Shayne land." She shoved a piece of paper at him. "There's an urgent call from Las Vegas, a Nate Peterson." She turned and marched off.

Jared glanced at Chance. "I think you need to explain things to her."

Chance raised his hands in surrender. "I doubt she's ready to listen. She still thinks I want her land."

"Then you're going to have to convince her otherwise."

"You deal with Dana," Chance said. "I've been around long enough to know that whatever I say to her now isn't going to matter." He strolled off toward his truck.

Jared didn't want to argue with Dana, but he had to confront her and he had a feeling she wouldn't make it easy for him. He hurried inside to find her in the kitchen. "Whatever you're thinking, stop. I'm not hooked up with the Randells to get you to sell."

"You couldn't anyway. I own the Lazy S."

"I know that," he said, trying to control his anger. "Believe me, I was as surprised as you were when Chance offered me—offered us—the opportunity to be a part of the Randell corporation. He said his brothers only asked us to come in because I'm family. And there is no selling of any land. Just a chance to be a part of the Mustang Valley Guest Ranch. And since everyone contributes with their own unique skills, Chance was hoping you would want to bring in the riding stables."

Jared watched a speechless Dana mull over the idea. "Don't let your stubbornness stop you from making a good investment." He walked out of the room and into the study, still stinging that Dana didn't believe him. The past weeks together, they'd shared the work, the meals... and a bed. Everything but the most important: trust.

He picked up the phone and dialed Burke Construction. He'd been checking in twice a week, Mondays and Fridays. Thanks to his sexy wife it was Tuesday and he hadn't thought a thing about the construction company.

The phone rang twice before it was answered. "Burke Construction," Nate said.

"Nate. It's Jared."

"Hey, man, sorry to have to do this, but I got some bad news. Stan had a heart attack last night."

Jared closed his eyes. Stan. His mentor and friend. All he could think about was how much the man wanted to retire and spend time with his grandkids. "Is he all right?"

"He survived, but he's going to need surgery. So I need you here."

Jared turned to the doorway and found Dana standing there. She didn't look angry, just beautiful, and he couldn't help but remember last night in bed with her curled up against him. So trusting. He didn't deserve that trust because he was going to break her heart.

"I'll be there as soon as possible."

Dana could only watch as Jared packed his bag. He'd had very little in the way of clothes, at least until he had bought boots and more jeans. It still hadn't taken him long to gather it all together. The one thing he didn't pack was the navy blue suit he'd bought for their wedding. That gave her a glimmer of hope.

Her nervousness grew. "How long will you be gone?"

"Not sure," he answered. "Stan will be in the hospital until after his open-heart surgery. At least two weeks."

He turned around and studied her. "I'll be honest with you, Dana. I doubt he'll be bouncing back. That leaves me to run Burke Construction. And right now, we have several projects and completion dates to meet."

So you can leave Evan and me without a thought, she wanted to scream at him. "I understand. And I'm sorry about your friend. Evan and I will manage all right," she lied, knowing their relationship was over. Worse, she had to explain to Evan that Jared was leaving. "Just do me one favor and don't leave without talking with Evan."

Jarred crossed the room. "You really think I'd do that? You think it isn't killing me to leave that boy…to leave you? I told you from the first, Dana. I'm not cut out to be a family, but that doesn't mean that I don't care about you and Evan."

That was the problem—he cared too damn much. He cared more than he should for the woman whom he'd started to share a bed with.

Her emerald eyes looked pleadingly at him. He couldn't resist and he pulled her into his arms. "God, Dana. I don't have a choice. I have to go to Las Vegas."

"I know." A tear slid down her cheek and Jared brushed it away. "I just wish—"

He didn't want to hear her words. He was so torn that he couldn't weaken his resolve. He let his mouth coax hers into submission, letting her know of his desire for her, his want, but mostly his need. All too soon, he broke off the kiss and grabbed his bag off the bed and walked down the hall to Evan's room.

The boy was sitting at his desk and coloring. Jared stood there for a while, just trying to absorb the boy, wanting to keep the picture.

"Evan," he called.

The boy turned and smiled, then climbed off the chair and hurried to him. "Uncle Jared, look what I drew." He handed him a picture. Jared examined it closely. It looked like a horse and three stick people.

"That's us," Evan said. "You, me, Mom and Goldie. We are a family."

Family. Jared had hated the word when it came to the Hastings. He'd never felt a part; now it was different. "It's very nice." He started to hand it back.

"No, I drew it for you," Evan insisted. "You keep it."

"I will." He looked at the boy. "Evan, I came in here because I have to tell you something. You know I have a construction business in Las Vegas."

The child nodded.

"Well, my boss got sick and I need to go there and help them finish the building."

He watched Evan's face drop. "But that's far away. I don't want you to go."

"It can't be helped, son."

"I don't care. I want you to stay here," he cried, and threw himself into Jared's arms and sobbed.

Jared hugged the boy to him, feeling like crying himself. "Hey, sport. I'll be back in a few weeks. By then you'll be riding Goldie like a champ."

The boy pulled back, wiping the tears off his face. "Will you come back and build me the fort you promised for my birthday?"

That was only two weeks away, Jared doubted that he could get things straightened out by then. And he didn't want to make the kid any false promises. "I'll try, son. If I can't be here, I'll call you."

Evan didn't like it, but he nodded. "'Kay."

"And you can call me." He went to the desk and wrote down the series of numbers to his cell phone. "If you need me, call."

The boy nodded, then hugged him. "I love you, Jared."

"I love you, too, Evan." He turned to find Dana standing in the doorway. Without a word, he moved past her and hurried down the steps.

Dana fought to rush after Jared and beg him to stay. What good would it do? He was determined to go. The pain was worse than anything she'd ever felt before.

She knew he had to go. After hearing the back door slam, she hurried downstairs.

Outside, Jared loaded his tools in the bed of his truck. After he finished the task, he went to the bunkhouse. Probably to say goodbye to Bert. A few minutes later, he came out and stood on the stoop and gazed out toward the pasture. It was as if he was taking a final look at the Lazy S. He turned toward the porch and paused. Dana's heart pounded, praying he'd come to her and promise that he would return. That he cared and wanted their marriage to be a real one.

Instead, he waved and climbed into his truck and drove off down the road, kicking up dust in his wake. Dana felt a tear run down her face and she brushed it off as he disappeared from view.

She knew in her heart that Jared Trager wasn't coming back.

Chapter 11

Jared had been gone five miserable days and six long, lonely nights. Worse, there hadn't been a word from him. Not even a quick phone call to tell her he'd made it to Las Vegas. Nothing.

Dana wasn't surprised. Jared had been honest with her. From the first, he'd told her that he didn't want anything permanent, that their so-called marriage was only temporary. Well, dammit, why did he have to treat her so special—be so loving? Why did he promise Evan that he'd always be there for him when he knew it was a lie? Wanting to protect her son, she'd made every excuse possible so Evan wouldn't know his uncle Jared had deserted him, that another man had walked away. Another man who didn't love her enough to stay.

From the kitchen, Dana heard a vehicle pull into the drive. She tried to hold back hope that it might be Jared as she went to the back door, but was disappointed to find it was Chance Randell coming up the walk.

"Afternoon, Dana." Her neighbor tipped his hat as he climbed the steps. "You think I could have a word with you?"

Dana didn't feel like discussing business today or any day, but her solitude was worse.

"Come inside, it's cooler." She held open the wooden screen door, then led the way into the kitchen. She poured them both some iced tea as Chance pulled out a chair and straddled it.

She handed him the tea and he took a long, thirsty drink. "Thanks. That hit the spot. I've been working my cutters all morning."

She took a seat across from him. "What did you want to talk to me about?"

"First, I need to set the record straight," he began. "The day I came to help Jared with the horse corral, he had no idea I was going to suggest he join the Mustang Valley corporation."

Dana already knew that. "Well, it doesn't matter anymore because Jared is gone."

Chance frowned. "I know he's in Vegas, but he's coming back."

Hope sprang eternal. "Did he tell you that?"

"Not exactly, more like…he'd be gone a while."

Dana wasn't convinced, not after the argument they had. And not when he had the lure of Las Vegas and his dream. Besides, if Jared planned to come back, wouldn't he have called her?

"Well, I doubt it now, since our arrangement was never meant to be permanent." Her cheeks reddened in embarrassment. "Jared was only helping us get back on our feet and we're doing fine."

"I think Joy and I started out saying the same thing," Chance commented, trying to hide a smile.

"No, this is different. Jared's life is in Las Vegas."

Chance frowned. "He's also made a life here. I don't think he's the type of man to leave you high and dry. You're his wife and Evan is his nephew."

That didn't seem to matter to Jared, Dana thought, swallowing back her emotions. "Like I said, we're managing."

"Is that so?" Chance watched her closely. "If you weren't, would you ask a neighbor for help?"

"It's hard for me—" she straightened "—to take charity."

"We neighbors call it a helping hand. Not too long ago there were some people around here who didn't want anything to do with a Randell. That's hard on a man's pride. My brothers and I know what it's like to feel like a charity case. I'd never do that to anyone."

Dana saw the flash of pain in his eyes. She'd been too young back then to know all about the Randell story. She could only imagine what those young boys had to go through, no one wanting them, having to live down their father's sins.

"Back to that day, my offer to Jared was strictly a business deal," Chance began again. "Joy made me see it was a mistake not to approach you both. I'm sorry, Dana. I should have included you, too, in my idea."

Dana was surprised. "What idea?"

"Mustang Valley Guest Ranch needs a riding stable. Right now we don't have the horses or the room to board the number of mounts our guests need. We also want to include your section of land in the guest ranch. Thought you might also think about adding some cabins on your property."

He drew a breath and released it. "The only reason I approached Jared is that you and I hadn't had the best relationship over the past few years. I hope we can clear up this misunderstanding. Believe me, Dana, the Randells don't need any more land. Your strip of the valley land is yours. We only want to make sure it's protected along with the mustangs. That's the legacy that Hank wants to leave to us and future generations.

"So now I'm coming to you directly with the same offer—we want you to add your section of land to ours. Join our corporation and build your riding stable closer to the valley."

She couldn't believe what Chance was offering her. "But what if Jared doesn't return?"

Chance pursed his lips. "I don't know Jared that well, but what I do know is that he cares about you and Evan. But he's a Randell and he's going to be stubborn about admitting his feelings, so it might take a while for him to work it out." Chance grew serious. "Jared wasn't as lucky as the rest of us Randells. We had Hank to love us and keep us headed in the right direction. Jared's been pretty much alone most of his life and he might think that's all he deserves."

"But he has Evan…and me now."

Chance smiled. "I think he knows that, but as Joy would say, it takes a man a little longer to admit that he needs a good woman to share his life. So let Jared work some things out on his own. Then he'll be back. I bet my top quarter horse on it." Chance got up and placed his glass in the sink. "Take a few days and think over my offer—"

"I don't need time," Dana said, too excited to sit any longer. "I want to do it. At least the part about providing the saddle horses for the guest ranch." She didn't stop there. "Would you have a problem with me having my own students? Giving lessons to people other than your guests? I was thinking it would be easier for me if I keep all my mounts in one stable." She couldn't believe she was considering this.

Chance looked thoughtful. "It'll be your business. We just need your services for our guests who want to ride. As long as you take care of the ranch guests, you can give riding lessons to anyone else who wants them. I'll give you a few days to think about it and then I'll call you. In the meantime, if you have any problems with anything let me know."

"I will." Dana nodded, surprisingly not minding Chance's offer of help.

Chance stopped at the back door. "By the way, there was an older man who stopped by the house this morning, asking for directions to your ranch. A stranger. Definitely not from around here. I wasn't crazy about him asking questions about you and Evan. Not to worry, I didn't tell him anything and sent him on his way."

Who would be looking for her? She felt Chance's concern. "Who was he?"

"Said his name was Graham Hastings."

Dana's breath caught in her throat. She gasped.

Chance returned to her side. "Do you know who he is?"

"He's Evan's grandfather. He wants to take my son away."

* * *

Jared rested his head on his folded arms on top of the desk, trying to catch a nap. He'd only managed a few hours a night in the past ten days. He'd been working around the clock with three shifts trying to get the project done on time.

The good thing was they were going to make the deadline. But as soon as they finished this job, Burke Construction had another project about to start. Luckily he had a crackerjack crew that could handle the heavy load. Jared only wished he could. He remembered a time when he'd loved the continuous work. Not anymore. Maybe he was getting old.

Jared leaned back in his chair and thought about the auburn-haired woman who'd been a constant reminder of the life he'd only gotten a glimpse of. The short time he had with her had been like a dream. Maybe it was good he'd been called away, because it would have ended soon anyway. He'd already gone too far when he started sharing his bed with Dana. He muffled a groan, remembering the closeness they'd shared for just a few weeks. What man wouldn't get addicted to having a sexy, willing woman next to him in bed? His body stirred to life at the memory of the feel of Dana's hands on him.

The trailer door swung open and Jared sat up. Nate walked in. "Hey, Trager, there's a guy out here says he's family."

It had better not be Graham. "What's his name?"

"Randell."

Jared shot out of his chair just as Chance came through the door. Had something happened at the ranch? "Chance, what are you doing here? Is there a problem with Dana and Evan? Bert?"

"They're all okay. I'm here to talk some sense into you. And yes, there are problems. But they'd be solved if you were back in Texas where you belong." He looked around the small, messy construction trailer. "How can you stand this cramped space?"

"I don't usually work here," Jared said. "I work out at the site." He pointed to the two-story framed structure outside the door.

Chance shook his head. "Still the same thing. There's too damn many people and cars in this town. How do you handle it?"

Jared leaned a hip on the edge of the desk and folded his arms. Even though he had only been gone a short time, he'd missed his brother's strong opinion. "I guess you get used to it."

"Why would you want to?"

Jared thought about it for a moment. The only thing he came up with was he'd never had a choice before. He had always gone where there was work. "Because the money is here."

"There's more in life than money, Jared. It took me a while to realize that, too. I guess you could say it was luck when Jack Randell ditched us kids and Hank took us in. Hank Barrett taught us that love of family was what mattered." Chance studied Jared for a long time. "How long is it going to take for you to realize that you belong in West Texas with your family?"

Those were sweet words to Jared's ears, but he was still afraid to dream. "I'm not like you, Cade and Travis. I don't have roots. I don't have a Hank to ground me."

"You have us. Your brothers. You have Dana…and Evan."

Something around Jared's heart tightened when he pictured Evan. He knew the boy needed him, and he wanted to be there for him. "I planned to call Evan on his birthday."

"My, aren't you generous? So much effort. I thought you promised your brother Marsh that you'd look after his son."

"I did. And I will. I just can't right now."

"Well, that's just too damn bad," Chance huffed. "Kids can't wait until we have the time for them. Before you know it, they're grown and they resent the hell out of you because you didn't give a damn about them."

"I have responsibilities here."

Chance shook his head. "With that attitude maybe it would have been better if you had never stopped at the Lazy S."

Jared had nothing to say that would answer that. He was hurting too bad. It wasn't that he didn't want Dana. He ached for her. He wanted to be the father that Evan deserved, but what if he failed at the job? What kind of example had he had?

"I'm not father material."

"If you're thinking you're like your old man, forget it. I've seen you with Evan. You love that kid and you love Dana."

Chance's words rung in his ears. He didn't want to think about feelings. All he knew was that he hadn't wanted to hurt Dana or Evan. But it looked like he had.

"I guess I wasted my time coming here." Chance walked toward the door, then stopped and looked over his shoulder at Jared. "Just think about one thing. Think about another man in Dana's life—another man touching her, making love to her... Another man being a father to Evan."

Jared clenched his fists, trying desperately to control his anger. Damn, but he wanted to hit something or someone.

Chance cocked an eyebrow. "Eats at your gut, doesn't it? Good." He jerked open the door. "One more thing. Remember when I said there was a problem? Graham Hastings is in San Angelo. He's been asking about his grandson."

Jared stood up. "He hasn't gotten to him, has he?"

"No, not yet."

"Dammit, Chance, if he gets anywhere near the boy..."

Chance glared. "Then you better do something to protect your son."

When the door closed, Jared started after Chance, but stopped. Maybe he should call Graham. No, he wouldn't give the old man the satisfaction.

Jared began to pace. He had to keep his head. First, he couldn't run out on the job here. Stan had just gotten home from the hospital and Burke Construction was in the process of becoming Jared's obligation. But at the moment, his own responsibilities to the company were the last thing he cared about. His family was being threatened and thanks to him, Dana and Evan were all alone. Wasn't his main responsibility to his family?

Jared raked his hair with agitated fingers. She had to hate him. He'd let her down just like Marsh had. How could he go back to her and make her believe? He stopped. God. He loved Dana. His chest constricted as he closed his eyes and saw her pretty face. The freckles across her nose, her sparkling green eyes that seem to look right through to his soul. Her gentle touch that erased the years of loneliness. The sweet body she'd given so freely that he thought he'd die from the pleasure.

And in return, she asked nothing from him. Well, she had stolen something. His heart.

All at once the walls of the trailer seemed to be closing in on him. How could he have been so wrong? This wasn't the life he wanted. He knew now what he truly wanted. His family. Nothing else mattered but Dana and Evan.

He only prayed they still wanted him.

It was nearly midnight when Dana carried her glass of iced tea outside to the porch. She was dressed for bed, but far from sleepy. She hoped some quiet time alone would cure her insomnia. And tonight of all nights she needed her rest for the busy day tomorrow.

It was Evan's birthday and she had planned a party. It was going to be a small one, but thanks to Joy and the other Randells, Evan was going to have his special day.

Once seated on the padded glider, Dana tucked her bare feet under her as the crickets chirped through the silence. She took a sip of her tea and inhaled the scent of roses from the trellis next to the porch. She closed her eyes, wishing she could perk up—for her son's sake.

It had been two weeks and she had to face facts. Jared wasn't coming back. So she had to move on, and if she did, Evan would have to, as well. Tears burned her eyes as the familiar ache invaded her chest. She was trying, but so far nothing seemed to work. Nothing filled the big void in her life…in her son's life. As much as she wanted to despise Jared, she hadn't been able to summon the energy.

Brushing away the moisture from her cheeks, she looked up when she heard a vehicle coming down the road.

She tensed. Of course, Bert and Owen were in the bunkhouse so she wasn't alone. Her big concern was who would drop by at this hour, unless it was an emergency. The glare of the headlights blinded her momentarily as the truck swung into the drive. When Dana caught a flash of black, her pulse started racing. It was a Chevy extended cab. Jared's.

She froze as the vehicle finally came to a stop and her husband climbed out. With the help of the moonlight, her starved gaze moved over him as he started up the walk. His long legs were clad in jeans and a dark T-shirt molded itself to his broad chest and wide shoulders. The sound of his boots on the wooden steps kept in rhythm with the loud pounding of her heart. Finally he reached the porch and her.

Dana nervously twisted her mussed braid as she glanced down at her gown and robe. Lord, she wasn't even dressed.

"Hello, Dana. I'm glad you're up," Jared said as he walked across to her.

She didn't want to see him like this. He could at least have given a girl some warning. She finally found her voice. "What are you doing here?"

"I need to talk with you," he said.

She refused to hang around and let him break her heart all over again. No way. She stood up and caught sight of Owen as he came across the yard.

"Is everything okay, Dana?" the ranch hand called to her.

Before she could say anything, Jared spoke up. "Hey,

Owen, it's just me. I drove all night to get here. Sorry I woke you."

"No problem. Good to have you home, Jared." Owen turned and walked away. Dana wanted to call him back, but it was better that he leave. This was a job she had to do.

She faced Jared. "If you need to pick up the rest of your things, be quick, and don't wake up Evan. I don't want you getting his hopes up. And don't worry about the loan money. If it's the last thing I do, I'll pay you back every cent." She started past him when he gripped her arm.

"I said, I need to talk to you, Dana, and it has nothing to do with money."

She raised her eyes to his. A bad idea, she realized as her throat tightened in longing.

"I made a lot of mistakes," he began. "But I never meant to hurt you and Evan."

"Would you stop?" She jerked away. "I don't need your pity, Jared Trager. I learned a long time ago to take care of myself. Not to depend on anyone. Evan and I managed just fine before you came. We'll make it just fine after you leave." She marched toward the door, fighting tears, praying she could get inside before she broke down.

"I won't be so lucky, Dana," he said softly. "I won't make it."

She paused, afraid to hope.

A little shaky, Jared took that walk toward her. "I thought everything I wanted was in Las Vegas. I was wrong. It wasn't until I was without you and Evan that I realized how lonely my life had been." He made a move to touch her. It nearly killed him to pull back. "Dana, I want to come back…and see if we can make our marriage work."

She turned around. Her green eyes glistened with tears and he hated that he caused it. "How can we do that, when you never wanted the responsibility of a family?"

She wasn't making this easy. "A man can change his mind. He can finally discover what's important. Maybe it took me longer than most, but I want to try…with you."

"For how long, Jared? How long before you get restless and want to leave again?"

"I'm never going to leave you."

She shook her head. "Yeah, I've heard that before."

Jared pulled her to him. "You haven't heard it from me," he breathed against her face. "So I'm telling you now. I want to be here with you—for you and Evan. I want to make a life for us."

She turned away. "I can't do that, Jared," she whispered, and he could hear the pain in her voice. "I can't risk you hurting Evan again. You broke his heart when you left."

"I know, and no one is sorrier than I am. Just give me a chance to make it up to him…to you."

"Until you decide it's time to move on. No, Jared, I can't. I can't." She rushed into the house and closed the door. The click of the lock sounded so final to Jared.

Dejected, he turned and walked down the steps. So he'd been too late. She wouldn't take him back and he didn't blame her. He headed to the truck.

"So you just givin' up?" a voice called out. "I never took you for a quitter."

Jared shot a look at the edge of the yard and discovered Bert standing there. He had on jeans and an undershirt.

"She won't take me back."

The old man shook his head as he limped over to him. Bert leaned against the bed of the truck. "So you're just goin' to tuck your tail between your legs and head for the hills."

"Well, what do you suggest I do?"

The man shrugged. "First, you have to find a way to cool her off just so she'll listen to your apology. You have to get on her good side."

"I'll take any side as long as I can talk to her."

The old foreman smacked his hand against his leg. "That's what I want to hear, son. Now, what's that girl's one weakness?" he asked, then raised a hand in warning. "Be careful. You fail this one, and I'll throw you off the place myself."

Jared found himself smiling. "Evan."

He nodded. "Now, you convince Dana how much the boy means to you. How much you want all of you to be a family. Guaranteed, you get the child on your side, then you'll soon have the mother."

"You think so?"

"The fact that the girl loves you something fierce doesn't hurt."

"Dana loves me?"

Bert nodded again. "And I wouldn't be wastin' my time with you if I didn't think you loved them both more than your own life. You couldn't help it if you were a little slow on discovering that part," he murmured.

"I *do* love Dana."

"Tell her, not me. And you better spend your time figuring out a plan to convince her."

Jared was already way ahead of him. "I think I have just the thing. Would you mind if I stayed in the bunkhouse tonight? I have a lot work to do by morning."

"Maybe, if you tell me what you're gonna do."

Jared grabbed his duffel bag and toolbox from the truck bed and started off to the bunkhouse. "Gladly, but you and Owen have to help me with Evan's surprise."

Chapter 12

The next morning came too soon as far as Dana was concerned, but she didn't waste any time. She had too much to do for Evan's birthday party. Six children would be coming. Four were Randells—toddlers Elisa Mae, Katie Rose, James Henry and also ten-year-old Brandon. Evan also had invited two friends, Matt and Michael, from his Sunday school class.

Then there were the adults: Chance and Joy, Abby and Cade, Josie and Travis Randell. Even Ella and Hank were coming. Except for Bert and Owen, Dana would be the only person who wasn't part of a couple.

She turned her thoughts to last night and Jared's return. Today could have been so different, if only she'd asked him to stay. Her heart ached at the thought of him not being in her life. It shocked her how much she'd come to rely on him. How much she'd come to love him.

Last night she'd wanted desperately to call him back, to fall into his arms, but in the long run both she and Evan would only be hurt. She couldn't let Jared back into their lives only to have him leave again. And she would do anything to protect her son from any more pain and disappointment.

Dana went downstairs to the kitchen where she found Evan dressed and waiting for her. By the expression on his face, he didn't look like he was ready for a big party today.

"Hello, sweetheart. How's the birthday boy?"

Evan shrugged. "I'm okay."

"What would you like for your special birthday breakfast?"

Another shrug. "I'm not hungry."

She pulled out a chair and sat down next to him. "You know what happens to a birthday boy who doesn't smile? He gets tickled!" She went for his ribs and realized that he had tears in his eyes.

She stopped. "Evan, tell me what's wrong."

"He promised, Mom. Jared promised he'd be here for my birthday." The child began to sob against her shoulder.

She hugged him to her, fighting her own tears. "I know, honey. I'm sorry. But sometimes things can't be helped." She felt guilty that she'd been the one to send Jared away. But in the long run, she'd had to do what was best for all of them. "There'll be lots of other people coming today. All the Randells and their kids. And Chance is going to bring his horse, Roughneck, and show you all his tricks. There'll be games and presents. Oh, and Bert and I have a real big present for you."

The child raised his head and wiped his tears away. "I don't care. I only want Uncle Jared."

So did she. "It's pretty big and way cool."

That caught his interest. "How big?"

"So big, I couldn't bring it into the house. We've been hiding it in the barn." Dana had been tickled when Bert found a secondhand children's saddle. He'd spent weeks cleaning and repairing the tack until it looked new. "How about we go out there right now and have a look?" she asked.

When he nodded, she said, "You go ahead and find Bert, I'll be right out."

"'Kay," Evan said and took off.

As soon as the door slammed, Dana's own tears fell. "Damn you, Jared Trager. Why did you ever have to come here? Why did you ever have to let us love you?"

Suddenly Evan called out. "Mom! Come outside. Hurry!"

Dana rushed to the door as her son ran up on the porch. "Evan? What's the matter?"

"He's back," he cried, waving for her to follow him. He scurried down the steps and ran to the side of the house.

"Evan, wait." Dana hurried after him around the corner of the house and stopped suddenly when she spotted what Evan was pointing at. Jared Trager up on a ladder wielding a paintbrush over the faded wood siding. By the looks of the large glossy white section painted, he'd been at it for a while.

"Hi, Uncle Jared," Evan called out as he waved.

"Hey, it's the birthday boy."

"I'm five today."

"I know," Jared said as he laid his paintbrush across

the bucket and wiped his hands on the rag hanging from his pocket.

Dana couldn't take her eyes off the man as he slowly descended the twelve-foot ladder. He wore only jeans and his work boots, his bare chest glistening in the morning sun. Her pulse started as she recalled a few other mornings, with him lying next to her.... She shook away the thought.

"What are you doing here?" she asked, trying to work up some anger.

Jared placed his hands on his hips. "I realized I have a lot of things around here that I need to finish."

Dana didn't want him finishing anything. "You've already done enough. Don't you need to get back to Las Vegas, to your construction company?"

"There's no hurry." His gaze locked with hers, and she had trouble breathing. "I don't break promises." He turned to Evan. "And I came back for your birthday."

Evan's eyes widened. "You're coming to my party?"

Jared smiled. "Wouldn't miss it. And I brought you a special present."

"You got me a present?"

Jared nodded. "Maybe if you ask your mother she'll let you open it now."

Both Jared and Evan looked at her. What choice did she have? The man wasn't playing fair. "I guess one wouldn't hurt."

"Oh, boy." Evan cheered.

"It's over there on the deck." Jared pointed and they both watched as the child ran off.

Dana glared at Jared. "I don't know what you're trying to pull, but I don't like it. Not when my son could end up hurt."

Jared knew he still had a lot of convincing to do. "I'm not going to hurt Evan. I love the boy. I'm trying to tell you that you both matter to me. I want a life with you and Evan."

"Don't, Jared." She stopped him. "We went over this last night. You don't want to stay here." Tears formed in her eyes. "Sooner or later you'll leave us. Please, give him your present and make an excuse and leave."

She turned away and Jared stuffed his hands into his pockets to keep from pulling her into his arms.

"I don't think it's Evan that you're worried about, Dana. I think it's you who are afraid. You care about me, or you would have never come to my bed and let me make love to you."

When she didn't respond, he gripped her arm and made her look at him. "And if you don't think what we have is special, or that I don't love you more than my next breath, then I guess I *am* wasting my time." He released her and started toward Evan. He took a deep breath trying to hang on to his control. He needed to keep it together for the boy's sake.

Jared grabbed his shirt off the deck and slipped it on. This wasn't working out the way he'd hoped. Although it felt as if his heart had been ripped from his chest, he plastered a smile on his face and watched Evan rip the paper off his birthday gift then lifted the lid to reveal a miniature tool belt.

"Wow." Evan held it up. "It's just like yours."

"It sure is," Jared said. "I had it made specially for you."

The boy hugged him. "Thanks, Uncle Jared."

"You're welcome," he managed, swallowing the rush of emotions. He took the belt from the boy and draped it around his narrow waist. "Now, there are some tools that go in here, but I'll put those in when we're working on something. You have to promise not to use them unless I'm with you."

"I promise." He smiled. "Look, Mom, it's cool."

"It sure is." Dana smiled. "Evan, I need to talk with Bert. Will you stay here with Jared a few minutes?"

Dana turned and hurried off to the barn, barely making it inside before she fell apart. She ended up in Sweet Brandy's stall, taking her solace from the affectionate filly.

"I take it you didn't accept Jared's offer?"

Dana looked up to see Bert. "What are you talking about?"

"Your husband is out there and you're in here crying your eyes out."

"I'm not crying and Jared was never really my husband." Dana turned away so she didn't have to look Bert in the eye.

"Girl, you know better than to lie. You two may have gotten married for different reasons, but there for a while I hadn't seen you so happy in a long time. And that man is the cause of it. He's the cause of your son's happiness, too."

"But he's leaving us."

"How do you know that? Didn't he say that he loved you and the boy?"

She nodded. "Words are easy. He left us just like Marshall did."

The old man limped to the stall gate and opened it. "There's one difference. Jared came back. Sweetheart, you can't make him keep paying for his brother's sins. If I've ever seen anyone who needs a family, that man does."

Dana was afraid to hope. "He'll always be pulled back to Las Vegas. He has his business there."

Bert frowned, emphasizing the lines on his face. "He didn't tell you?"

"Tell me what?"

"Jared backed out of the deal. He didn't buy the company."

Dana gasped. "But it's what he wanted. It was his dream."

The foreman pushed his hat back. "Funny thing about dreams... They aren't very important if you don't have someone to share them with. Jared's been looking for a place to belong. His dream is a family."

Another flood of tears threatened as Dana realized the risk Jared took to come to her. And she'd pushed him away. Made him think she didn't want him.

"Oh, Bert," she gasped, and the filly flinched. "I've been so wrong, I have to tell him...." Dana stepped out of the stall.

Bert grinned and waved. "You go on, girl, I'll handle Sweet Brandy."

Dana ran out of the barn and across the yard. Breathing hard, she rounded the house but didn't see Jared or Evan. Then she heard laughter and located the two in a grove of trees next to a stack of lumber.

She slowed her pace as she came up to them. Her son saw her first. "Look, Mom." He held out a piece of paper. "It's a fort. Uncle Jared and me are gonna build it. Together."

Jared stared into her eyes. "If it's okay with your mother."

Dana wanted to rush into his arms. Thank him for loving her son, praying he still loved her. "It's fine with me."

"Yippee! I'm gonna go and show Bert and Owen my tool belt!" Evan started off toward the barn.

Dana let her son go, her gaze never leaving Jared's face. Suddenly she was trembling, wanting him to reassure her. But how could she ask him to put himself on the line again, when she'd kept pushing him away?

"You sold your business?"

He looked surprised, then nodded. "I realized it wasn't what I really wanted."

"But it was your dream."

He shrugged. "Dreams change."

"What's your dreams now?"

"I don't think you want to hear them."

She came closer, so close she felt his heat and inhaled the familiar intoxicating scent of him. "I do," she breathed. "I wasn't ready to listen yesterday, but I am now."

"All right. I want a family. Kids." He glanced around. "I want a place like this." His eyes met hers. "Most of all, I want you and Evan in my life."

Excitement poured through her. "Did you mean what you said earlier?"

Jared knew exactly what Dana was asking. "Yes, Dana, I meant every word. I love you."

When she gasped, he enfolded her in his arms and drew her against him. "I can't live without you," he continued. "You've gotten into my heart. *You* are my heart. You and Evan."

"Oh, Jared, I love you, too. So much." She closed her eyes, momentarily. "I was afraid that—"

He stopped her words when his mouth captured hers in a hungry kiss that he hoped relayed his gratitude for her trust and love. They clung to each other like a life-line, barely controlling their desire.

"Tell me again," he asked as he cupped her face.

"I love you."

He closed his eyes and pressed his forehead against hers. "Ah, Dana, I love you so much. I thought if I went back to Las Vegas I could forget you and Evan. It only made me realize what an empty life that I truly had there."

"But you wanted to buy the construction company." She still couldn't believe it.

"It didn't mean as much to me as you and Evan."

"Oh, Jared, but you loved it."

"I love being a carpenter. And I think I'll have plenty of that to do around here. I'm going to make the Lazy S a showplace again. And after that I don't think I'll have trouble finding work around San Angelo." Jared held Dana to him, loving the feel of her body against his. "If you're worried about me being able to support you, don't. I still have plenty in my trust fund."

"I never cared about your money."

He gave her a wink. "I know, you had designs on my body."

She laughed, but it quickly died. "I've been so lonely since you've been gone."

He pulled her closer to him. "Not as lonely as I've been. I missed your body tucked up against mine. I miss the soft sounds you make when I touch you…love you. Oh, yes, I've definitely been away from you too long." His mouth closed over hers in another hungry kiss.

They broke apart when they heard the sound of a car coming up the road. A long, black town car. Dread washed over him.

"Who is it, Jared?"

"Graham Hastings." He wished he could erase the worry in her eyes. "You stay here, Dana. I'll handle it."

He walked to the car just as a white-haired man climbed out. Jared stood in front of his father, blocking his path. "What are you doing here?"

"Did you think I wouldn't find out about my grandson?" Graham said. "I plan to be a part of his life."

Not if Jared could help it. "Marsh didn't even want you to know about Evan, let alone have you in his life. Neither do I. I'm his stepfather and I plan to adopt him."

"I can give him so much more than you can."

Jared's fists clenched. "It always comes down to the money, doesn't it, GH? Evan doesn't need your money. He needs a father who will be there for him. And I will. So you can leave now."

"You really are a bastard." Graham reached into his pocket, pulled out a photograph and handed it to Jared. "But you're not Jack Randell's only one. It seems he's spread his seed all over the West. There are two more out there."

Jared fought to show a reaction. "Why is it so important?"

"Years ago I hired a private investigator to find out about your mother's…indiscretion with Randell. Couldn't have him showing up and trying to get money. It seemed I never had to worry. Jack Randell didn't want any of his…kids."

Jared didn't want to hear anymore. "Well, you've said your piece, so you can leave now. I'm Evan's stepfather and if possible I'll do everything to keep you away from him."

Just then Evan came out of the barn. Graham's attention darted to the boy and Jared thought he saw longing in the old man's eyes. Then it disappeared and Graham climbed back into the car and drove off.

Dana rushed to Jared. "Don't worry," he assured her. "He's not going to take Evan away. I promise." He kissed her.

"Yuck, you guys are kissing."

Jared tucked the photo into his pocket. "You have a problem with me kissing your mom?"

Evan shook his head. "No, 'cause she's happy when you kiss her." He came closer. "Are you gonna live here and be my dad?"

Jared crouched down. "Yes, I'm going to live here. And if it's okay I'd like to be your dad."

Evan glanced at his mother, then at Jared. "You love us?"

"Yes, I love you and your mother very much."

Evan threw himself at Jared. "I love you, too, Dad."

There was no other feeling in the world like a child's loving arms. For the first time ever, Jared knew he'd found what he'd been looking for.

Suddenly a caravan of cars moved down the road. "Looks like the party is about to start," Jared said.

"Oh, no," Dana cried as the Randells began filing out of the cars. "I have so much to do before I'm ready."

Jared pulled his wife back into his arms. "Don't worry. We're all family." He sure liked the sound of that.

Epilogue

Dana loved her life.

She sat atop Scout, looking down at Mustang Valley. A herd of wild ponies were contentedly grazing in the high grass, not paying one bit of attention to the many tourists who'd ridden along the ridge to see them.

Just two weeks ago, Chance and Jared had finished the horse corral a short distance away, so as not to disturb the natural look of the valley. In the mornings, Dana took ranch guests on trail rides, then afternoons were reserved for her own group and private lessons. Her business was booming.

Things weren't stopping there. Over the winter, Jared would be building six cabins on their part of the valley. By next spring they should be ready for guests. That wasn't all. Chance had agreed to breed one of his studs with her bay, Sweet Brandy. And Dana already had people interested in the future foal. Right now, she had Lazy S's roundup in a few weeks, but she wasn't worried about finding help. The entire Randell family had already volunteered.

Dana couldn't believe the summer was nearly over, and on Monday, Evan would start kindergarten. That was the reason for the picnic in the valley. Everyone rode in on horseback, including Evan on Goldie, for one last party for all the kids.

One big family. And the Randells included Jared as a part of it, along with her and Evan. And that family just kept on growing. Dana touched her stomach. In so many ways.

She climbed down from her horse and walked to the stream.

"What are you smiling about?"

She turned to find that Jared had ridden up. He jumped down and sauntered toward her. Over the last months on the ranch, Jared had taken to his new life as if he'd always lived here, dressed in his Wrangler jeans and light-blue Western shirt, along with his slow easy gait and even the tilt to his Stetson. Her breath quickened just looking at him.

"Hello, cowboy," she said. "I'm just counting my blessings. I have so many."

"We both have." He came up behind her, wrapped his arms around her middle and together they watched as the kids rode by on the other side of the stream.

Evan sat straight in the saddle, riding behind his new cousin, Brandon. Owen was keeping a keen eye on them both. The young ranch hand had decided to stay and go to college in San Angelo so he'd be able to work part-time at the Lazy S.

Hank Barrett brought up the rear of the group as he rode alongside little Katie Rose on her pony. Recovering from knee surgery, Bert wasn't able to ride yet. He still walked with a cane, but that didn't slow him down. He was in charge of grilling the hot dogs for the kids up at the cabin on the ridge.

"Life can't be any more perfect than this," Dana breathed, feeling so safe and loved in her husband's arms.

When Jared didn't respond, Dana looked over her shoulder and saw the faraway look in his eyes. She knew what had been bothering him. Graham Hastings's revelation about the existence of more Randell brothers. "Are you second-guessing your decision?"

"Yeah, I just hope I did the right thing by sending that photograph off to the Gentrys."

"How could you not?" she asked. "Don't they have a right to know who their father is? What they choose to do with it is their business."

He nodded. "I guess. I just feel bad because I haven't said anything to the others." He shook his head. "Two more brothers. Twins."

"And you will tell Chance and the others, if and when you hear from the Gentrys."

"Of course," Jared agreed, then leaned down and kissed her briefly. Too briefly, as far as Dana was concerned. She loved being with family, but wished they had some alone time right now. Not that she and Jared hadn't sneaked off to the valley before and made love.

"This is a special place," he said, breaking into her thoughts. "I felt it the first time I ever rode in here. Chance said that he and his brothers felt they were misfits just like the mustangs."

"Do you feel like a misfit?"

"Not any longer." He hugged her. "I found everything that I've ever wanted right here. You and Evan are my family."

Dana couldn't contain her excitement any longer and turned in his arms. "I hope you don't mind expanding our family." She reached up and placed a kiss on his lips. "I'm pregnant."

Jared couldn't hide his shock. A flood of feelings rushed through him as he moved his hand over his wife's flat stomach. There was a new life inside. His child. "Oh, God, Dana." He kissed her, kissed her again and again. "Are you sure?"

She nodded. "As of this morning."

"A baby," he breathed. His eyes met her beautiful green gaze. "I love you, Dana Shayne Trager. So much." His mouth closed over hers, wanting to tell her what words couldn't relay. That he'd finally found peace and love. And the one place he'd been searching for. A place where he belonged.

* * * * *

WYATT'S READY-MADE
FAMILY

To the family newlyweds:

John and Annie Davenport

Alissa and Tim Rawlins

Daniel and Nora Powell

May this be the beginning of wonderful lives together.

Chapter 1

Why hadn't she gotten the lock fixed?

Maura Wells huddled with her young children in the upstairs hallway, her hearing honed in on an intruder scavenging around downstairs in the house. Oh, God, why doesn't he just leave? There was nothing down there worth stealing.

The slamming of another door pierced the silence. Jeff and Kelly jumped and she hugged them tighter. Then the sound of the intruder's booted steps passed by the staircase. She held her breath, trying to control her shaking. At the same time praying he wasn't coming up. She closed her eyes and the image of outraged Darren formed in the blackness. Her heart hammered in her chest. Could he have found her...so soon? Her lawyer had assured her...

Maura drew several breaths, listening as the unwelcome guest went into the kitchen, then began opening cupboards. It was just like her ex-husband to make her suffer—make her wait for her punishment.

She'd always known someday he would come after her. Well, she wasn't just going to stand here helpless. No more. If she'd learned anything at the shelter, it was that she couldn't let Darren make her a prisoner again, in her own home. But living in the country meant she couldn't expect a quick response from the police. At least she'd had the presence of mind to call her neighbor, Cade. He was on his way. But how long would it take for him to get here?

"Mommy, I'm scared," her daughter whispered. "Make the bad man go away."

"I will, honey." Fighting her own fears, Maura pushed the kids into her bedroom. "You two wait in here. I'm going to make him go away. Don't come downstairs no matter what. Promise?"

With nods from both her six-year-old son and her three-year-old daughter, Maura closed them inside her bedroom, then crept cautiously to the hall closet and took out an old rifle that had been left behind before she'd moved in. She suspected it wouldn't shoot, not that she could pull the trigger anyway, but she wasn't going to let the intruder know that.

Maura started down the stairs. With each step, she struggled to slow her breathing. A small table lamp was on, casing a soft glow over the large sparsely furnished living room. Most everything in the house had been given to her secondhand, except the black duffel bag beside the front door.

That belonged to the visitor.

She stayed back in the shadows, knowing that if it was

her ex-husband, there would be no reasoning with him, but she would do anything she had to do to keep him away from her kids. She listened at the sound of cupboard doors being opened and closed. Then the sound of boots on the bare floors told her he was coming toward her. Here was her chance to catch him by surprise.

The huge shadow appeared, too big to be Darren. A strange relief ran through Maura, then she realized she faced a different kind of danger. He was a thief, maybe worse. She pointed the rifle at him. "Just hold it right there, mister."

"What the hell?" The man stopped at the entrance of the room.

Maura bit back a gasp as she took in the tall, handsome stranger. He was dressed in a Western shirt and jeans with a big silver buckle on his belt. He had midnight-black hair long enough to brush against his collar. His eyes were a brilliant blue hooded by dark brows.

"Raise your hands," she said, fighting to keep the quiver out of her voice, and her hands steady.

To say the least, Wyatt Gentry was surprised to find this pretty interloper in his house. By her state of dress, the long nightgown and her mussed, honey-blond hair, she'd been awakened from sleep. And she looked sexy as all get out. So she was the reason the inside of the house had looked so neat…so welcoming. Too bad the woman holding the rifle didn't.

He sure-as-hell didn't want to talk to anyone holding a weapon at him. "I'm not here to cause any harm, ma'am."

"Then you shouldn't have broken into my home in the first place."

Her home? "Why don't you put the rifle down and we'll talk about it?"

"No! We'll just wait until the sheriff gets here." Her chocolate-brown eyes widened as she waved the rifle toward the sofa. "Go and sit down."

Wyatt started to walk across the polished hardwood floor, but decided he didn't like this situation at all. And he needed to do something about it. Now. He swung around, grabbed the barrel of the rifle and jerked it from her hands. What he didn't expect was for her to fight him like a sharp-clawed cat. Her small size didn't diminish her strength as she pushed him off balance, but he took her with him when she refused to let go of the rifle. They ended up on the floor. When he finally got leverage, he rolled her over beneath him, then straddled her. She still didn't give up the fight, causing her shapely body to rub against his, reminding him that she was nearly naked and very much a woman. The friction between them was like a jolt of electricity.

"Will you stop fighting me so we can talk about this?" he asked when suddenly something hit him from behind.

"You leave my mother alone," a youngster said as a small fist plummeted him. Hard. Wyatt reach back and pulled a boy off him as he stood up.

"Hey, kid. I'm not going to hurt anyone." He held the small flailing body away from him. He glanced at the woman as she scurried from the floor to the little girl crying on the stairs.

"Please, release my son and just take what you want," the woman pleaded. "I have a little money in my purse. Just don't hurt us."

Seeing the fear in the woman's eyes, Wyatt hurried to reassure her that he wasn't going to harm her or her family. "I'm not going to hurt anyone," he insisted and tossed the rifle on the sofa. He doubted it would fire anyway. "And I don't want your money. I'm only here because I own this house and property. I have a key."

Shock turned to puzzlement on the woman's pretty face. "You bought this ranch?"

He nodded. "As of three o'clock this afternoon when I signed the papers."

"Jeffrey, stop!" she commanded her still struggling son. "The man isn't going to hurt us."

The boy finally stopped fighting, but continued his threatening stare as he was lowered to the floor and backed away toward his mother.

Wyatt straightened. "I'm Wyatt Gentry. Sorry, I had no idea anyone was living in this house."

"I'm Maura Wells, my daughter, Kelly and son, Jeff. We've been staying here for a while…"

"A while. You're renting the place?"

Her incredible dark brown eyes rounded before she glanced away. "I had an agreement with the owner—previous owner. But since you're here now we should leave."

Wyatt had no idea he would be greeted by a full house. Why hadn't the lawyer told him about the renters? How could he toss this woman and her kids out in the middle of the night? And where was her husband? He glanced at her ringless left hand.

"There's no need for you to leave—" he began.

Just then the front door burst open and a tall man rushed in and headed straight for Wyatt. He grabbed a handful of his shirt. "If you laid one hand on any of them you're going to be sorry—"

"No, Cade, please, don't," Maura said as she stepped

between them, then reached for the man's arm. "It's okay. This is Wyatt Gentry. He just bought the place."

Cade released him. "You bought this ranch?"

Wyatt nodded. "As of today when I signed the papers." He went to the duffel bag, pulled out the property title and handed it to him.

Cade glanced over the legal agreement. "Well, I'll be damned." He looked at Wyatt as a ruddy color covered his cheeks. "I guess I owe you an apology," he said and gave him back the documents. "I'm Cade Randell. We had no idea the property had sold."

A strange feeling came over Wyatt as he stared at Cade Randell. This was not how he'd planned to meet his half brother. He glanced away, fighting to stay focused on the problem at hand.

Cade Randell turned to the woman. "Maura, why don't you pack your things and you and the kids come home with me?"

Wyatt stepped in. "Like I was telling Mrs. Wells," Wyatt began, "there's no need to leave in the middle of the night. Besides, I'm not going to toss out renters."

Maura spoke up. "I'm not exactly renting...this house," she said timidly. "Cade got permission for me to live here until the place was sold. I guess that's right now."

So Cade Randell had once again been her champion. Was something going on between these two?

"It was like this," Cade said, "I know the owner, Ben Roscoe, and he agreed to let Maura and her kids stay here for a while. I guess when he went on vacation, he neglected to explain the situation to his lawyer." Cade exchanged another glance with Maura. "It's just that this old place has been up for sale for over four years. No one thought it would be a problem for Maura to take the job of house-sitter."

Wyatt had had a long day, a long week with his drive from Arizona, not counting the endless arguments he'd had with his brother, Dylan, about him purchasing the once-Randell property. Now it was nearly midnight and he was exhausted.

"Why don't we hash this out tomorrow?" he suggested. "I can get a motel room and stay there tonight. And we can discuss the living arrangements in the morning."

He studied Maura Wells carefully. Why would a woman and her two kids be living in a deserted house? He didn't like the scenario he came up with.

"Mr. Gentry, I can't make you leave your own house."

Wyatt took another look at her. Not a good idea. She had big brown eyes and fair, flawless skin. Her silky hair was the color of honey. When his body took notice of her attractiveness, he forced his gaze away and glanced around the room.

"Listen," he began, "I was told to expect to have to spend a lot of time cleaning to make this place livable so I wasn't planning on moving in tonight anyway." He placed his black cowboy hat on his head. "I'll stop by in the morning." He picked up his duffel bag and headed out the door.

Maura was thrown by the stranger's kindness. But that didn't change the fact that she and the kids would be homeless in the morning. That meant she would need to find another place to live. Easier said than done. She didn't have the kind of money it would take to relocate and to pay rent.

"I still say you should come home and stay with Abby and me," Cade suggested.

Maura ignored the suggestion and turned to her son. "Jeff, take your sister back upstairs to bed. You can put her in my room." She kissed Kelly, then her son. "Go, Kelly, I'll be up soon."

"Promise?" her daughter asked.

"I promise. You're safe now."

After they both hurried up the steps, Maura turned back to Cade. "I can't come home with you. You already have a houseful with Brandon and Henry James. I won't intrude any more. I'll think of something."

"I have a foreman's cottage you could use. Not exactly in the best shape, but we could fix it up."

Maura had been lucky to find people like Abby and Cade Randell. Between her job and the house, they had helped her so much. She'd never be able to repay them. "I think you know I'm not afraid of hard work. But let's talk about this in the morning. Sorry to bring you out so late." She turned him toward the door. "Now, go home to your family."

Maura finally got Cade to leave. She started to turn off the light, but decided she'd leave it on just for tonight. She climbed the steps, realizing she'd done what she'd promised herself she wouldn't do. She had gotten attached to this house, knowing full well that she couldn't stay forever. But two months had been too short a time. She wanted to hate Wyatt Gentry, but she found she couldn't. Instead, surprisingly, she was looking forward to his return tomorrow, especially since that meant her departure.

Wyatt had been up since dawn, but he doubted Maura Wells had. So he hung around the motel café trying to come up with a solution for all of them. There weren't any answers, especially if the woman and her kids couldn't afford rent for another house.

About seven-thirty, he pulled his truck up in front of the once white, two-story house. Home sweet home. His first ever. He raised an eyebrow at the peeling paint, the sagging porch, the weed-infested yard and flower beds.

It was all his.

No more trailer, no more campgrounds and traveling around. Wyatt was finally putting down roots. He had his dream, his own ranch. Best of all, none of it had Earl Keys's name on it to remind him that he and Dylan were never wanted, they just came along as excess baggage with their mother. Twenty years ago, Sally Gentry had married a man who promised to take care of her and her twin sons. She believed that Keys was the answer to their prayers until they discovered that he only wanted them to help work his rough-stock business.

No more. He'd worked for years riding in rodeos and working for rough-stock contractors. Now, the Rocking R was his. He belonged here, and never again would he feel like a hired hand. If he was going to work his fingers to the bone it would be because this land was his.

He chuckled. He hadn't come to Texas to buy land but to find his real father. After getting a letter from a man named Jared Trager, telling him about Jack Randell, Wyatt headed to San Angelo. That was how he ended up at the Rocking R. Although the place had been deserted by the Randells, fate had practically handed him the home he'd longed for, and at a price he couldn't pass up. All that was left for him was to move in.

But first he had to evict the squatters. Wyatt climbed out of the cab and walked up the rickety steps and around the rotted wood on the porch, making a mental note to replace them first thing. He knocked on the door and within seconds heard the scurrying of shoes on the floors. The door jerked open and the boy, Jeff, appeared.

"Oh, it's you." The kid looked grim.

"Is your mother around? I told her that I'd be back this morning."

The kid opened his mouth and yelled, "Mom!" Then he ran off leaving the door ajar.

Wyatt took a step inside and closed the door behind him. He heard a commotion upstairs and the cry of a child. A few minutes later the small girl slowly descended the stairs. She was wearing bright-pink shorts, a white T-shirt and canvas shoes, her blond curls were in a ponytail tied with a pink ribbon. There were tears in her eyes and she was making a hiccuping sound.

Wyatt wondered if she were hurt. Feeling a little awkward, he went to her. "What's the matter?"

Kelly stopped on the third step from the bottom. "Mommy's mad with me." Her tiny fists rubbed her eyes.

Wyatt squatted down. "And just why is that?"

"'Cause I got into her makeup and I'm not s'pose to. I want to be pretty like Mommy."

Wyatt had to bite his lip to keep from smiling. He figured Maura Wells didn't need to wear any makeup for that. She was already a natural beauty. "You're just as pretty with your curls." He gave a tug on the ponytail.

She giggled. "What's your name?"

"Wyatt."

She studied him closely. "Are you a mean man?"

He shook his head. "I hope not."

"Jeff says you're going to throw us out." The girl's lower lips quivered as if she were going to cry again.

Wyatt suddenly felt like the meanest man on earth.

Before he could say any more Maura Wells appeared at the top of the stairs. "Kelly Ann Wells, did you brush your teeth?"

The girl swung around and looked up at her mother. "I forgot."

"Well, you better get to it. We have to leave soon." The girl hurried up the steps, past her mother and ran down the hall. Maura descended the steps. She was dressed in a flowery skirt and a white cotton T-shirt and wore strappy sandals on her slender feet. Her golden-yellow hair was curled under just brushing her shoulders. No. She definitely didn't need makeup to enhance her beauty.

"I'm sorry, Mr. Gentry. Mornings around here are a little hectic." Before he could answer a horn sounded and she called out, "Jeff, the bus is here."

Within seconds the boy came tearing through the house. He grabbed a backpack and a lunch sack off the table by the door. "Bye, Mom." He threw Wyatt a stony glance and ran out the door.

Peaceful silence. "Sorry, like I was saying the mornings are a little busy. Would you like some coffee?"

"That would be nice," Wyatt said and followed her into the kitchen.

On the way Wyatt took the opportunity of daylight to look around. The rooms obviously needed paint, but everything was clean and neat. Maura Wells had taken care of the place. In the kitchen, she pulled down two mugs from the knotty pine cupboard, then poured the brew from a coffeemaker. "Please, sit down."

Wyatt watched as she moved around the old-fashioned kitchen. He didn't take Maura to be much older than her late twenties. She was small, maybe a little on the thin side, but she didn't lack curves. He watched the sway of her hips under her skirt.

"I'm sure you want to move in as soon as possible," she said as she sat down at the table and motioned for him to do also. "I'm sorry if we created a problem."

"Not a big deal."

She sighed. "We can be out…today."

Wyatt looked out the window and saw the sorry-looking station wagon parked by the back door. The woman definitely didn't have much. Where was her husband? He looked back at her. "Do you have a place to go? I mean, I didn't give you much notice."

"We're not your concern, Mr. Gentry."

Then why did he feel as if they were? "Please, call me Wyatt."

She nodded. "Wyatt. We'll probably stay with Cade and Abby Randell for a few days. If it's okay, I'll have to leave my furniture here temporarily, until I find another place." Why did he feel like such a rat? He couldn't do this. "Huh…that's what I wanted to talk to you about. I was wondering if you could do me a favor?"

She nodded. "Of course."

"There's so much work to do around the place. I was thinking there's no reason why you and the kids couldn't stay in the house." He rushed on seeing her start to protest. "You'd be a big help to me with decorating the inside. And you could take your time finding another place to live."

"Oh, Wyatt," she gasped. Her breathy tone caused his stomach to tighten. "I can't do that. Where would you live?"

"I thought I'd move into the Rocking R's foreman's

cottage while I was doing the work. I don't need much room."

Maura couldn't believe it. She could stay. But for how long? She didn't care. Right now, she couldn't afford to go anywhere. There wasn't enough money in her emergency fund to rent a house. She didn't even *have* an emergency fund. Besides, she hated to pack up Jeff and Kelly again. "But how would I be helping?"

"I know zilch about decorating. I'm a bachelor. Spent a lot of my life living out of a single-wide trailer with my mom and brother." *While my stepfather shouted orders from back at his ranch,* he added silently. "I don't know anything about colors and styles and I can see how well you've taken care of the place."

"How much rent would you want?"

He shook his head. "I don't want any rent, but if you could include me at mealtimes, I'd be grateful."

"That doesn't quite seem fair. Us living here and you in the cottage."

"I was planning to move into the cottage anyway while I did the work, so the house will be empty if you and the kids move out."

Maura knew he was probably lying, but bless him, he was trying to help her. She never wanted to be beholden to a man again. It had taken her a long time to stand on her own and not be afraid. But the truth was, she had to think about the kids, keeping a roof over their heads. They loved it here. How could she uproot them again? Besides, she had nowhere to go but back to the shelter once she wore out her welcome at Abby and Cade's. At least, Wyatt Gentry was offering her time to figure out where to go.

"I appreciate your offer, but I feel that if I'm going to stay I need to do something more."

"What is that?"

"I'll not only cook your meals, but do your laundry, too."

When he started to argue, she stopped him with her raised hand. "Take it or leave it, Mr. Gentry."

A slow smile came over his handsome face and a strange feeling erupted in her stomach. "Lady, you got yourself a deal."

Chapter 2

Maura ended up running late for work. But she couldn't just walk out on Wyatt Gentry. After all he was going to be her landlord. She was both excited and relieved that they could come to terms so she and the kids could stay…for a while.

She pulled her car into the parking lot of the Mustang Valley Guest Ranch Center, and escorted Kelly through the doors of the bright red-and-blue building of the employee's day care. Since summer had ended and the seasonal workers were gone until next spring, there were only four other children there.

The Little Pony Day Care had been a lifesaver for Maura. She had very few skills for today's job market and could never have made enough money to be able to afford someone to watch Jeff and Kelly, let alone a licensed day care. But Maura had been offered the free service along with her job. Best of all, Kelly loved staying here.

"Give me a kiss, sweetie," she said to Kelly.

Her daughter puckered up and kissed her. Not long ago, Kelly wouldn't willingly leave Maura's side. Now, she was a happy, independent child.

After last night, Maura was afraid her daughter might revert into her former shell, but she relaxed when Kelly ran over to her friend, Emily, and began to play. So Wyatt Gentry's surprise arrival hadn't caused the child any lasting problems. Maura wished the same was true for herself. She now had a man practically living in the house, and he'd be sitting at her dinner table every night.

"Bye, Mommy. I love you."

"I love you, too, pumpkin."

With a wave goodbye, Maura hurried out the door and across the complex to the strip mall that included a general store and the cabin check-in and rental area for the guest ranch. There was also a souvenir shop, a video arcade, the Mustang Western Clothing Store, then came Abby's Treasures that carried nice collectibles and freshwater pearls from the local Concho River. And last in line was the flower shop.

Maura unlocked the front door to the Yellow Rose. She stepped inside and a wonderful floral fragrance engulfed her, causing her to smile. She loved working with the flowers, loved to arrange bouquets for the ranch guests. And if that weren't enough, she was lucky to work for a wonderful family like the Randells, especially Abby. With virtually no experience, Abby had taken a chance on Maura and given her a job. The few things she had known about flowers had come from Carl Perry, her parents' gardener.

A lonely, only child, Maura used to follow Carl around the estate. The poor man answered every question she'd ever asked and taught her everything about flowers, from pruning to fertilizing. Her mother had always insisted there be fresh bouquets in the house daily. What Grace Howell hadn't known or cared about was that Maura was the one doing the floral arrangements. But her parents hadn't noticed much about their daughter until she'd married Darren Wells. And then they'd disowned her completely.

Maura pushed the bad memories from her head and thought about how lucky she was. She had Jeff and Kelly with her, and even received a salary for what she loved to do. Thanks to Abby's encouragement, for the past few months, she had created special bouquets for the guest cabins, and just recently, Maura had been approached to do a local wedding in San Angelo. And she had appointments to talk with prospective brides about doing two more. The Yellow Rose's business was growing and it was more than Maura could handle by herself. She needed to hire an assistant.

Maura put her purse away in the small office. Grabbing the rose-monogrammed apron off the hook, she tied it around her waist. She went to open the shutters, turned the Closed sign to Open, then picked up the fax with the list of today's bouquets. There was an asterisk beside the cabin number of the bridal suite and the name of the couple who would be arriving this afternoon. Maura smiled. Her favorites were the newlywed arrangements. She went down the list of the four other cabins that would be occupied by three o'clock. She needed to get busy.

Maura started toward the work area when the bell over the door sounded. She turned around expecting to find a customer, but instead Abby Randell rushed through the door.

"I didn't think you'd ever get here," Abby said, her green eyes sparkling.

At thirty, the beautiful woman wore her auburn hair short with the ends flipped up. A pair of hoop earrings hung from the tips of her earlobes. Tall and slender, she was dressed in tailored navy slacks and an ecru crepe blouse. Abby was the mother of two young boys, Brandon and James.

"Sorry I was late, but I needed to talk with Wyatt Gentry."

"I know. I wanted to come by the house, but I had an appointment with an artist this morning. He's agreed to let me sell his paintings at Abby's Treasures. Forget about that." She waved her slender hand. "Look, Maura, you and the kids can move in with us. Cade and Travis will come by later and help get your things. Don't worry, we'll find you another place. It was a crazy idea to put you in the old Randell house, but at the time it seemed the best and fastest solution."

Maura tried to interrupt her friend, but she couldn't get a word in. Finally Abby ran out of steam. "Really, there's no need," Maura said. "I'm going to stay where I am."

"What?"

"Wyatt Gentry insisted we continue living in the house…for now."

Abby crossed her arms. "And just where is this… Mr. Gentry going to live?"

"In the foreman's cottage," Maura announced. "At least while he finishes the repairs to the outside of the house."

"Why would he let you stay?"

Maura was puzzled herself. "I'm not exactly sure."

Abby studied her for a while. "And you're okay with this?"

What choice did she have? "He seems like a nice man." She also had to admit that Wyatt Gentry was a very handsome man. That was, if she paid attention to those things. "And he's giving me time to find another place to live."

"Then we'll go looking for another place as soon as possible."

Maura reached for her friend's hand. "Look, Abby, I need this time. I haven't had a chance to save much money." She turned back to the work area.

Abby followed her. "Then Cade and I will loan it to you."

Maura shook her head as she pulled open the cooler's glass door, stepped just inside and picked up the canister of fresh-cut roses that had been picked up by Abby earlier that morning.

"No. I can't take any more from you, Abby. Both you and Cade have done so much for us already. Really, we'll be fine. Thanks to Mr. Gentry, I have a little breathing space. This morning we worked out an arrangement. He's not going to charge me rent, and all he wants in return is some decorating help and…meals."

Silently, she watched as Abby studied her. This woman was more than her employer, she was her friend. They'd met few months ago at a women's shelter in San Angelo, where Abby was a volunteer. Maura had come seeking refuge from her abusive ex-husband. Even though Darren had been sent to jail for robbery, he'd threatened to punish her because she had been the one who turned him in to the police. After leaving Dallas, she'd moved around until her money ran out, then ended up at the shelter's door.

It had been Abby Randell who counseled her, who'd helped her feel good about herself. During the hours they talked and cried together, Abby confided to Maura about her abusive first husband and how long it had taken her to leave the man. Now, she was happily married to Cade Randell, the man she'd always loved and the father of her two sons.

Maura reached for the flower clippers. Starting with the roses, she handled them with great care as she began to trim, then added wire to each long stem. She placed the first rose in the crystal vase, deciding she would go with all white, representing purity and innocence, for the bridal suite. Maybe tomorrow, she would move onto the passionate bloodred roses. Suddenly her thoughts turned to the dark-haired man who'd burst into her life. Why didn't she feel threatened by him?

"You say you're going to help him decorate the house. Does he have a family?" Abby asked.

"He's a bachelor. And he spoke of a brother."

A long pause. "And you're cooking his meals for him?"

"Yes, and I'm also doing his laundry." She rushed on, "That was my idea."

"And I'm not sure if it was a good one."

Maura understood that Abby was just being protective. They both knew how hard it was to trust anyone, or not to worry about falling for the same type of man and end up in the same brutal situation.

"Just promise me that if you feel you don't like this arrangement, you'll come to me for help," Abby insisted.

"I promise, I will," she said. "Besides, it's only going to be for a month, or so. By then, I'll have another place."

"And you always have a place to stay with us," Abby added.

Tears rushed to Maura's eyes. Never in her life had anyone cared about her like Abby and her family. "And I thank you for that. You've always been there for me, you also taught me to stand on my own and realize my inner strength. And I think it's about time I did." Later that day, Maura drove home with Jeff and Kelly in tow. Her son's school bus had let him off at the day care where he spent the past two hours with his sister until Maura closed the shop.

Now, Jeff had time to finish his homework while Maura fixed dinner. She was a little worried. Darren had complained a lot about her lack of culinary skills. Not that they could afford much more than ground beef.

Taking the grocery bag out of the car, Maura started up the walk toward the house. The kids had stopped at the door, but they weren't waiting for her. They watched as Wyatt Gentry pulled rotten floorboards from the porch.

She wasn't as disturbed about the condition of the floorboards as much as she was with Wyatt's lack of clothing. Shirtless, beads of sweat covered his bronze skin, clinging to his broad shoulders and chest. He turned around, tipped his black baseball cap and smiled. Her entire body grew warm, and a warm blush covered her face.

"Hello, Maura," he said in that low husky tone. "I hope you don't mind, but I figured this was a good place to start the repair. I'd hate for one of you to fall and hurt yourselves."

"We're not stupid," Jeff growled. "We don't walk in holes." With a glare, he stomped into the house, letting the screen door slam in his wake.

Maura started to apologize for her son's behavior when Kelly sat down on the step and announced, "My brother's scared of you."

"Kelly!" Maura was mortified at her child's openness.

"He is?" Wyatt asked as he grabbed his shirt from the railing and slipped it on. "I guess that's because I came into the house last night."

Kelly nodded. "But I'm not scared of you."

"You aren't?" Wyatt asked, studying the child.

The girl's large brown eyes roamed over him and he felt himself holding his breath, waiting for her to make a judgment. He hadn't had much experience with kids. Just the ones who hung around the rodeo. They were more interested in his horse than him.

"Nope, 'cause your eyes don't look mean."

It was crazy but her appraisal pleased Wyatt. "Good."

"You're nice." Her ponytail danced against her shoulders. "You let us stay here. And now you're fixin' the broked porch so I don't falled down again. I got an owie. See."

Wyatt leaned down and examined the tiny red mark on her knee. "Well, Miss Kelly, I'm sure sorry about that. I'll just have to make sure that doesn't happen again."

He was rewarded with a giggle. "Can I help you fix it?"

Her mother stepped forward. "Oh, no, honey. You better come inside and stay out of Mr. Gentry's way."

Wyatt straightened and Maura Wells took a step back. Her eyes widened, causing him to freeze in place. She was frightened of him.

"I don't mind if Kelly wants to stay out here," he assured her. "I'll leave the door open and you can hear her from the kitchen." He smiled. "I wouldn't want anything to hamper your progress on dinner. May I ask what's on the menu?"

She shrugged. "It's just meat loaf and baked potatoes."

"There's nothing 'just' about home cooking, ma'am. Not when you've been eating restaurant food, or your own cooking for as long as I have."

"I hope you're not disappointed." She started up the steps. "Just send Kelly inside if she gets in your way." Maura opened the screen door and went inside. Wyatt's gaze followed the gentle sway of her hips as she walked through the house. Maura Wells did have a cute backside. He shook away the direction of his thoughts. That was as far as he could go, admiring her from afar.

Wyatt had been fitting some of the pieces together, and he didn't like how they added up. Someone had put that sadness in Maura's eyes, more than likely her ex-husband. Wyatt assumed he was an ex—if not, the man deserved to be hog-tied and hung out to dry for deserting his family, leaving them to live in a run-down house.

"Wyatt." The little girl tugged on his hand. "You gotta tell me what to do so I can help."

Wyatt already knew he'd gotten in over his head when he allowed Maura and her kids to stay in the house. He'd always been a sucker to help out. So he'd done his good deed and it wasn't putting him out that much. She'd be gone in thirty days, and out of his life.

He picked up the board he'd sawed to size earlier. "Why don't you hand me those nails, Kelly?" He pointed to the box of finishing nails.

Kelly's tiny fingers reached into the box and pulled out one. "Thank you," he told her and she rewarded him with a smile so sweet it caused his chest to tighten.

Wyatt couldn't let this idyllic moment detour him from contemplating his troubles. First of all, his new neighbors, the Randells, had no idea that he was their half brother. When would be the best opportunity to drop the bombshell? He needed to talk with the man, Jared Trager, who had sent him the information about Jack Randell being his father, before he made any announcements. Of course, Wyatt had confronted his mother when he'd gotten Trager's letter. And after more than thirty years, Sally Gentry Keys finally told him and his twin the truth.

When Wyatt first arrived in town, he'd stopped by the Lazy S, but the foreman had told him that Jared Trager and his family were out of town. So it looked like he had to wait it out a little longer.

In the meantime, there were other Randell brothers around the area. He'd met Cade already. Would one of them recognize him? Not likely. He'd always been told he looked more like his mother's family. Dylan and he were fraternal twins, and his brother was the one who resembled Jack Randell.

Wyatt pounded in the nail and Kelly handed him another. Nothing had turned out the way he'd planned. Even with Dylan urging him to let the matter go—to stay away from a man who hadn't wanted them—Wyatt still found his way to San Angelo. Not only had he come here, but he'd bought the old Randell homestead.

Did he need to belong so badly that he had to buy his old man's land? Wyatt had told himself over and over it was just a good deal—a great deal. He'd only made a ridiculously low offer and the seller accepted it. How could he not want the place?

He had wanted his own ranch for years. Unlike Dylan, he hated all the travel on the circuit and he'd always wanted to put down roots. A home. The old Randell place might not be in the best shape, but it was his. And with the money he'd saved over the years, from rodeoing and working stock, soon he'd be able to start his business as a rough-stock contractor. Over the years he'd made several contacts in the rodeo business. So once he rebuilt the ranch, repaired the corral and the stalls in the barn, he could begin. He already owned six horses now that a friend was boarding until he had the place ready. One in particular a bucking horse, Rock-a-Billy. He just needed to concentrate on his business.

His attention went to his distraction, pretty Maura Wells. Hopefully by the time he brought his stock here, she and her kids would be long gone.

"That was the best meal I've had in a long time," Wyatt said, scooting back from the table.

"Thank you," Maura said. "Would you like some coffee?"

"That would be nice," he replied, smiling at her.

Feeling a little tingle, Maura got up from the table and took two mugs out of the cupboard. After filling them, she walked back to the table. "Cream or sugar?"

"No, just black." He took a sip. "Good coffee."

"Thank you," Maura said again, then was distracted when Jeff dropped his fork on his plate.

"I got homework." He stood and started out of the room.

"Jeff, you didn't ask to be excused and I think you forgot about your plate."

"Can I be excused?" He came back to get his plate and all but tossed it into the sink.

Maura didn't want to call her son on his rude behavior, but she wasn't going to let him get away with it, either. She'd talk with him later. Jeff had had these bouts with rudeness on and off since they'd left Dallas…and his dad. Of course, he had blamed their separation on her, but she couldn't bring herself to discipline him, especially in front of a stranger.

"Mommy, I ate all my green beans. Can I be 'cused?" Kelly flashed a bright smile at Wyatt. "I want to play with my dolly. Her name is Suzy."

"That's a nice name," Wyatt said.

Again Kelly smiled. If Maura didn't know better she'd say her daughter was flirting with Wyatt Gentry. "Just remember that your bedtime is in one hour and you still need a bath."

"Can I have a bubble bath?"

Maura was too tired. "Not tonight, honey. Mommy has to do dishes."

"Why don't you go on with Kelly? I'll clean up," Wyatt suggested.

Maura shook her head. "No, I can't ask you to do them."

"You didn't ask, I offered." He got up and carried his plate to the sink. "You just need to tell where things are."

Maura got up, too. "Kelly, you go play, I'll be up in a while."

The little girl took off.

"You've worked all day, Mr. Gentry. I can't ask you to do dishes."

"And *you* have worked all day, taken care of two kids and fixed dinner. And I thought you were going to call me Wyatt."

Wyatt closed the drain in the sink and began running water, then he looked in the most obvious place for the soap, under the counter. That was where he found the small off-brand bottle of green liquid. The room might have needed paint and the pine cupboards were scarred, but everything in the house had been cleaned within an inch of its life. He squirted a generous amount of soap in the water, creating bubbles. "I guess Kelly could have helped me and played in bubbles here."

"The operative word is *play*," she said. "She'd make a mess."

Maura tried to scoot in front of the basin so he would move, but the man didn't budge at all. She wasn't comfortable standing so close to him and stepped back.

"You mean like this?" He slashed bubbles at her.

She gasped. "Mr. Gen—Wyatt!"

He cocked an eyebrow, looking far too handsome… and dangerous. A warning went off. She didn't like the feelings he created in her.

"If you don't want more of the same, I suggest you head upstairs to help your daughter. Don't worry, Maura. I can manage a few dishes. But you have a lot more to handle." He stared at her a moment, then said, "I'm not trying to pry, but in case he shows up one day, is there a Mr. Wells?"

She felt herself tense. God, no. "There is… I mean was, but he's not in our lives any longer. I'm divorced and I have full custody of the children."

"The man must have been a fool to let you and the kids go."

"He had nothing to do with it," she said. "It was my decision to leave, and it was a good decision." She felt her anger building and she took a calming breath. "If you don't mind, I *will* go upstairs and help Kelly with her bath." Maura turned and walked out, nearly running was more like it. She never had much experience with men, and definitely not men like Wyatt Gentry.

She'd be better off to stay far away.

* * *

After two bedtime stories and a back rub, Kelly finally went to sleep. Maura had gone into her son's room. Jeff was reading, and he never even looked at her, but with some coaxing, she left with a good-night kiss.

Coming down the stairs, she brushed a tear from her eye, telling herself that although Jeff hated her now, she knew she'd done the right thing leaving Darren. Her ex-husband's abuse had gotten out of control long ago. Although she'd protected the kids most of the time, she couldn't stay and watch as Jeff turned into the same type of person. All he ever saw from his father had been cruel and abusive behavior, especially to women.

Worse, Maura knew that if she stayed, Darren would someday kill her. And her kids would be left alone. So she had to do something, even if it meant turning her husband in to the police.

Maura knew it hadn't been the best thing to steal her children away in the middle of the night, but it had been her only escape, the only way she could leave Darren. After the police took him in, she grabbed everything she could put in the station wagon and got out of Dallas. The small amount of money she'd managed to save only went a little way. And what was she supposed to do for a job and a place to live? She'd gotten the help at a women's shelter in San Angelo.

Maura turned off the lamp in the living room, then walked into the kitchen. She gasped when she found Wyatt sitting at the table, reading the newspaper.

"I didn't realize you were still here."

He smiled at her. "I hope you don't mind. I'm having another cup of your good coffee." He stood and offered her a chair. "Care to join me?"

So polite, but so had been Darren…at first. "I really should get to bed."

"I know, but I only want a few minutes."

Maura made her way to the table and sat down. "Is there a problem?"

"That's what I want to know, Maura. Did I do something to upset you? I mean, if it bothers you to have me at the dinner table, I can eat in the cottage."

"No, of course not. You've been so generous letting us stay here. I mean, you could have insisted we leave."

He shook his head, blue eyes piercing into hers. "I couldn't do that." He took a breath. "I don't want to pry, Maura, but it's obvious that you've had some hard times. I don't want to make them worse. So you take your time. I promise I won't get in your way." The chair scooted against the worn floor when he stood. Then he headed out the back door.

Maura wanted to call after him, tell him the truth, but she couldn't, not yet. She still had a long way to go before she trusted a man.

Maybe never.

Chapter 3

The next morning, Wyatt rolled over on the lumpy mattress and groaned as bright sunlight came through the bare, cracked window, reminding him where he was. His new home. Unable to get back to sleep, he decided to get up. He swung his legs over the edge and rubbed his eyes. He glanced at the travel clock on the table and realized it was nearly six-thirty.

He released a long sigh, thinking about what he had to do today…and tomorrow, and the next day. He was already tired but it had nothing to do with his endless list of future chores, and more to do with his lack of sleep last night. No matter how many times he'd told himself to forget about Maura Wells, she still had managed to keep him awake. He was breaking his own rule—to never get involved with a woman with kids…again.

Memories of Amanda Burke and her son, Scott,

flooded into his head. He'd fallen hard for the pretty barrel racer. So he'd knocked himself out trying to win the kid over, too. Thanks to the example of Earl Keys, he hadn't known about being a father figure, but he'd tried his damnedest. In the end he'd lost them both when Amanda went back to her ex-husband.

Maybe that was what intrigued him about Maura. She didn't seem to want anything to do with him. From the moment they'd met, she'd acted as if he had the plague. But that hadn't stopped the attraction. He was drawn to her. Maybe it was the sadness in those big brown eyes of hers, or the fear he saw every time he got too close. At the dinner table last night, he'd felt the tension with Maura. And she couldn't get him out of the house fast enough.

Wyatt never had trouble getting female attention, not since he and Dylan had been fourteen and grown to six feet tall. They'd learned quickly how to charm the ladies. But he had outgrown conquests with the buckle bunnies at the rodeos long ago. He'd passed thirty now and wanted to put his full concentration on the ranch and start his business. He had no time or desire to get involved with someone else's problems. So he would put up with the minor inconvenience for the next month, then she and her kids would be gone.

Wyatt slipped on his jeans and walked to the small and shabby kitchen area. It needed a good cleaning, and a lot of work. He tried to close one of the cabinet doors, and it swung back open. Yesterday, he'd chased out a family of squirrels and broke up several spiderwebs. This morning he would call an exterminator and have the cottage sprayed. Probably wouldn't hurt to do the house, too. He'd just have to make sure that Maura and the kids would be gone for the day.

There was a soft knocking sound. He went to the door and found Kelly standing on the stoop. She looked cute dressed in a pair of blue shorts and white top, her hair in a neat ponytail. In her hands she had an insulated coffee mug covered securely with a tight lid.

She smiled. "Good morning, Wyatt. Mommy says you prob'bly need this." She handed him the coffee. "And breakfast is in ten minutes." Her brown eyes rounded as she shook her finger at him. "And you better not be late." The child turned around and skipped off toward the house.

Wyatt couldn't help but smile at the thought of both the daughter and the mother. So maybe he had charmed his way back into the house. He frowned. Maybe that shouldn't get him so excited.

Maura tried not to make too much of the invitation, reminding herself she was just following through with her agreement. After all, fixing the man a few meals was a great trade for a month's free rent.

There was a knock at the back door and she looked up to find Wyatt standing on the porch. Right on time. Even a little rumpled from sleep, he was a gorgeous man. Tall, with broad shoulders and a narrow waist. Seeing him yesterday without a shirt, she knew he didn't have an ounce of fat on his body. It was all muscle. Her gaze moved upward to his face to catch his grin. Another blush warmed her cheeks.

"Wyatt, come in," she said.

"Thank you, ma'am." He opened the screen door and walked in, then winked at Kelly as he hung his hat on the peg by the door.

"Have a seat." Maura turned back to the stove and the

pancakes. This was one thing she could make without fail. "Kelly, go get your brother."

The little girl scurried off, leaving them alone. Maura took a deep breath and released it, then picked up the plate of pancakes and carried them to the table. "Help yourself."

"Don't mind if I do." He stabbed into the stack, taking four.

She slid into the chair across from him. "I want to apologize for last night."

Wyatt stopped pouring syrup. "There's nothing to apologize for. I overstepped my bounds."

"You have every right to ask questions. You're letting us stay here."

He shook his head. "Listen, everyone is entitled to their secrets."

Maura didn't want to talk about her past. She wanted to move on. But she also needed to make Wyatt understand.

"My husband, Darren...we didn't...the divorce was hard on all of us, especially Jeff. With the move from Dallas to San Angelo, he's having difficulty adjusting."

Wyatt knew that Maura was leaving out a lot. Just the look on her face when she talked about her ex told him she was terrified of the man. That only meant one thing—the man had abused her. He felt himself tense. In his book there was nothing lower than a man who used his fists on a woman.

"Maura, I have only one question, then I'll drop the subject altogether. Is there a chance that your ex-husband will come here and bother you?"

"No! He doesn't know where we are," she admitted, terror in her voice. Wyatt wanted nothing more than to take her into his arms and assure her that he would take care of her.

"And as long as you and the kids are under this roof," he said, "I won't let anything happen to you."

Maura started to speak when Kelly came running into the room, crying. Soon to follow was her pleased-looking older brother.

"Mommy, Mommy, Jeff said my freckles were ugly spots."

The little girl ran to her mother. She sobbed as if her heart were broken.

Wyatt glared at the boy, who looked satisfied that he caused chaos. "You're not ugly, Kelly. You're the prettiest little girl that I know."

The girl wiped her eyes. "Really?"

"Do you know what your freckles mean?"

She shook her head causing her ponytail to swing back and forth.

"You've been kissed by the sun."

A bright smile appeared as she looked at her brother. "See, I've been kissed."

Jeff started to speak, but thought twice when he saw Wyatt's challenging look. He turned to his mother. "Mom, I want some pancakes, too."

"Please," Wyatt added.

The boy remained silent for a few seconds, then added, "Please."

Maura dished up two large cakes, then directed Kelly to her chair and put one on her plate and began to cut it up. "No, I want Wyatt to do it." Kelly smiled. "Please."

This was a new experience for him. He had never cut up a child's food. Maura nodded as she sat down. He picked up a fork and began cutting the cake into bite-size pieces.

"There you go, princess. Want some syrup?"

She smiled at him sweetly, then looked at her brother. "Wyatt called me princess." Jeff mumbled something under his breath, then continued eating his breakfast.

Maura finished her own pancakes and carried her plate to the sink. She hustled her daughter along, then upstairs to brush her teeth. Handing her son his lunch, she sent him off to find his backpack.

When she returned, she discovered Wyatt running water into the sink basin. The man didn't give up. "I told you, you don't have to do those."

"House rules," he said. "You cooked breakfast, I do the dishes."

Maura started to argue but he looked at her with those seductive blue eyes. A warm tingle pulsed through her, settling deep in her stomach and she forgot all about everything. It wasn't until the school bus honked that she realized she was staring. She rushed off to get Jeff out the door.

Wyatt watched as Maura scurried from the room. Seemed the pretty blonde was in constant motion. He couldn't help but appreciate the soft curves of her backside.

Whoa, just rein in those thoughts, buddy. She's off-limits.

Just then little Kelly came into the kitchen. She dropped her backpack on the table. "I go to school, too. But I don't hafta leave yet." She dragged a chair over to the sink. "So can I help you?"

Definitely off-limits. "That would be nice, but I don't want you to get wet."

"I can wear Mama's apron." She darted to the drawer and pulled out a colorful floral apron and tried to put in on. She went to him. "I can't do bows yet."

Wyatt dried off his hands and after only two attempts, he managed to tie the too-big apron on the child. He handed her a towel and she started drying the flatware, and placing each piece carefully on the counter.

"I help Mommy a lot," the child began. "She lets me dust."

"That's very nice of you to help your mother. And you're only three years old."

Her head bobbed up and down in agreement. "I'm going to be four on Thanksgiving. Mommy says I'm not a baby anymore. That I'm growin' up." She eyed him. "Do you have any little girls?"

Wyatt shook his head, wondering when the questions were going to stop. "No. No kids."

"You all by yourself?"

Again he nodded.

"You get scared?"

"I have a mother and my brother."

"Is he mean to you?"

Wyatt had to smile, remembering how he and Dylan had fought when they were kids. "We had fights, but not too many anymore."

"Jeff is a mean brother. He calls me a dumb girl all the time." Tears filled her eyes. "I'm not dumb."

Wyatt wiped off his hands. No sooner had he turned to the girl than more tears began to run down her angel face.

"Now, don't go cryin' on me, princess." He took the towel and dried her wet cheeks. He'd never felt so awkward and clumsy in his life as he patted her back trying to soothe her.

Maura stood in the doorway and watched the touching scene between her daughter and Wyatt Gentry. Kelly had never known the gentleness of a man. Her own father had never wanted her around. So Maura had done everything to keep out of his way. She was surprised that her daughter would seek a man's attention.

Just then Wyatt looked at her and their eyes locked. A spark of desire shot through her and she wondered what it would be like to have this man's arms around her.

Just as quickly the moment ended. "Kelly, look, your mother's here."

The child suddenly brightened. "Mommy, I'm helping Wyatt do the dishes."

"I can see that." She walked to the sink and asked her daughter, "Are you okay?"

Kelly nodded. "Jeff hurt my feelings."

"I'll talk to him after school."

Maura saw Wyatt tense. She knew her son's behavior wasn't perfect, but he'd gone through a lot in the past months. She would deal with it…later.

"It's time to leave for work."

"Okay," Kelly said as she climbed off the stool, then looked up at Wyatt. "I liked helpin' you."

"Thank you, princess. See ya after school." He waved as she started out the back door.

Maura braced herself for Wyatt's criticism for her not disciplining her son, but he didn't say a word.

"If it's okay with you," he began, "I'm going to have an exterminator out to spray the place."

"How long will we have to be out?" she asked.

"I'm hoping I can get someone out today, tomorrow at the latest. At any rate you should be able to come into the house the same evening."

How considerate. There was a kindness that showed in his eyes, along with something else that she didn't want to examine. He looked strong and dangerously masculine. Maura felt a shiver of awareness and realized she was a little breathless. "I'd appreciate that," she managed to say.

"So you won't mind if I use my key?" he asked.

"Of course not. It's your house," she said.

"No, it's *your* house for the time being. I won't come in here unless you say so." He studied her for a moment. "I realize you don't know me very well and I guess that's my fault. There's not much to tell, though. I was born Wyatt Alan Gentry thirty-one years ago, five minutes before my twin brother, Dylan." He cocked an eyebrow at her. "He claims he's the good-looking one. I've lived on a ranch outside Tucson, Arizona, all my life. My mother is Sally and my stepfather is Earl Keys. They've been a rough-stock contractor to the rodeos for years. So most of our lives were spent traveling around Arizona and California. Most of the time we lived out of a trailer."

"It must have been crowded." Maura had lived in a mansion growing up, and had been so lonely.

He tossed her one of those easy grins. "That's one of the reasons I bought this ranch. I got tired of traveling. So I plan to stay put. My goal is to board and train rodeo stock here, hoping when Dylan retires from bull riding he'll join me." He sighed. "That's about it. Unless you want some references, then you can call any rodeo grounds from Arizona through southern California. They'll vouch for the Gentrys."

Wyatt held his breath while Maura took her time studying his face. She looked so pretty in her crisp white blouse and bright flowered skirt. Her blond hair shimmered as she tugged the long strands behind her ears.

"You don't need to provide me with any references," she insisted.

"I don't want you to feel uncomfortable with me around. Like I said, I can eat in the foreman's cottage."

"I'm not uncomfortable," she said. They both knew she was lying. "And you'll eat your meals—at this table— with us. That's our arrangement."

He folded his arms across his chest and peered back at her. "What about you?" he asked. "Where you from? Your accent doesn't ring native Texan."

She shook her head. "I'm originally from the east, New York State. I've been here for nearly eight years, but we've moved a lot…" Her gaze moved around the room, anywhere but at him. "I should get to work." She pulled her car keys out of her purse and headed for the door. "Speaking of our agreement, just let me know when you want to discuss any ideas or color scheme. I could help you with the painting inside."

"I still have so much to do outside," he said. "I need to get the place repaired and painted before winter gets here. But I would like to hear some of your suggestions for the inside of the house."

She nodded. "I'll be home around five-thirty. Any suggestions on supper?"

He smiled. "Surprise me."

For the first time she returned his smile. "Oh, it will definitely be that. See you tonight." She turned and walked out.

Wyatt realized that he was looking forward to when she came home, to seeing her again.

That was not good.

* * *

Just as Maura had said, she and the kids arrived home about five-thirty as he worked tightening the hinges on the screen door.

Jeff was the first out of the car. He ran up to the porch without even a word of greeting.

Not Kelly. She jumped out of the car, smiling. "Hi, Wyatt." She took off her backpack and pulled out a piece of paper, the corners a little bent. "See what I made today? A picture. That's you." She pointed to the colorful rough stick figure on the page.

"Really? You made a picture of me?"

She nodded proudly.

"No one has ever drawn me a picture. Thank you."

She twisted her fingers together. "You're welcome."

"Where should we put this? How about on the refrigerator? That way I can see it every day when I eat."

"Okay, I can hang it up for you." With a grocery bag in her hands, Maura climbed out of the car. Wyatt knew she was shopping for extras with him there. She made her way up the steps and looked around at the progress he'd made. He'd replaced nearly a third of the porch in front of the door. He was now working on the broken railing.

"You've gotten a lot done," she said. "It's going to look nice."

Wyatt felt his body warm with her words, realizing he'd wanted her approval. "Thanks. It was a lot of work, but this old house is worth it."

"It is a wonderful house, just neglected. Except for the roof, it's new," she said. "Cade said that was the one thing I didn't have to worry about when it rained. The house had been built by his grandfather."

"So Cade Randell grew up here. Why doesn't he live here now?"

Maura brushed her hair from her face. "He told me after his mother died there weren't many good memories left. Anyway, his father went to prison and the state confiscated the property and sold it at auction for back taxes. He and his brothers had to go into foster care."

Wyatt knew little about the Randells, just a few sketchy details from Trager's letter. He tried to act nonchalant, but news about his so-called father being in prison caught him off guard. He'd known that good old Jack hadn't been a man of honor, but he never thought about him as a lawbreaker.

"So Cade and his father aren't close?" he asked.

Maura shook her head. "Abby says the man hasn't been back here in years. Just as well, if you ask any of the Randells. Of course the brothers ended up better off. That's how they connected with Hank Barrett. The man took them in and raised them on the Circle B Ranch. The Mustang Valley Guest Ranch is part of Hank's property. It also borders with Abby and Cade's ranch, and with Dana and Jared Trager's. Then there's Chance and Joy. He runs a horse breeding ranch that is on the other side of the Circle B. They run the Mustang Valley Lake and Campground. Travis and Josie live on a section of Hank's land close to the valley. Travis manages the guest ranch."

Wyatt still couldn't believe it. He had four brothers, and three of them he'd never met. "It sounds confusing."

"Their family is large." She smiled. "It must be wonderful to have so many siblings…and nieces and nephews. And there's still more coming. Joy is expecting a baby in a few months."

Wyatt wondered if he were man enough to face the

Randells. Would they accept him? Would he fit in here? He realized that as much as he loved his brother and mother, he needed to find out about his father, the missing piece of himself.

Dylan didn't have this problem. If the decision were up to Wyatt's twin, he'd forget about finding a family, and an old man who never wanted his bastard sons. His brother didn't need or want anything to do with Jack Randell.

Maura's sudden cry drew his attention. He swung around just in time to catch her as she stumbled over a piece of wood. He wrapped his arms around her slender waist and lifted her easily out of harm's way. He set her down beside the railing, but didn't step back. He couldn't. Those big brown eyes of hers locked with his, sending his pulse racing. His breathing suddenly became labored.

"You all right?" he managed to ask.

She nodded and looked down at the crushed bag clutched at her chest. "The groceries seemed to have survived. Barely."

"Good."

They continued to stand there until Maura finally spoke, "Well, I guess I should start supper."

"What's on the menu tonight?"

"Chicken," she said. "Please tell me you like chicken."

"Fried, roasted or grilled, I love chicken."

"You're an easy man to please."

He shrugged. "Some things aren't worth getting upset about. I save my anger for important things."

She started to go inside, but stopped. "Oh, speaking of the Randells, Abby and Cade and the rest of the family have invited us to a barbecue tomorrow night at the Circle B. It's sort of a welcome to San Angelo." She tilted her head a little, looking sweet and sexy at the same time. "If you don't want to go, that's okay…"

"No, I think it's time that I meet the rest of my…neighbors." Wyatt just hoped that they were ready to meet him. The next evening Wyatt drove them over in his truck, putting the kids in the roomy back seat. Maura sat in the front, feeling strange sitting next to this man. Correction. This good-looking man in his sharply pressed Wrangler jeans and starched tan Western shirt. His brown boots were polished and his tan Resistol cowboy hat sat low on his head.

He was pure cowboy.

And she had no doubt that the Randells would think about pairing her off with Wyatt. The last thing she wanted was for any of them to think he was her date. Why was it always the happily married couples that wanted you to find that perfect mate?

Well, Maura didn't want to find a man. She wasn't even looking. Besides, she wasn't foolish enough to think a man like Wyatt would give her a second look. She gazed down at her own clothes, a pair of discount store jeans and a plain red sleeveless blouse. She was pleasant looking, but certainly not exciting…and she had two kids. Most men would run in the other direction. Wyatt Gentry hadn't had a choice. She was living in his house, but soon would be leaving. But to where?

To a place Darren would never find her or the kids.

When Wyatt drove under the Circle B archway he felt himself becoming a little nervous. He was about to meet his family. And although he'd only been here a few days, it bothered him that he hadn't told Cade who he was. How would they receive him if they knew, especially now that he had purchased their former family home?

He glanced around the impressive ranch, including the pristine white outer buildings and miles of well-kept fence that penned some beautiful horseflesh. He watched as three mustang ponies galloped around the pasture. Then the large two-story house came into view.

"Well, we're here," Maura announced. "Just park over by the other trucks at the barn."

Wyatt pulled in and climbed out, allowing Jeff and Kelly to exit the cab. Maura came around carrying the cake she'd baked for tonight.

"You'll like the Randells." She smiled. "They're the best people. And Hank is a sweet man."

"Still, I'm the stranger here. And I just bought their childhood home."

"If Chance, Cade or Travis would have wanted the ranch, they could have easily bought it."

"You finally made it." A tall, beautiful woman came toward them. Smiling, she hugged Maura, then turned her attention to him. "You must be Wyatt Gentry."

"Yes, ma'am, I am." He shook her hand.

"Welcome to Texas and the Circle B. I'm Abby Randell. I hear you've already met my husband, Cade."

"Briefly."

"That's the best way to meet this family—in small doses. Oh, no, here they all come."

One by one, Abby introduced them—Chance and Joy, Travis and Josie. Then came an older man, tall, straight-backed with thick white hair and friendly hazel eyes. "And this is Hank Barrett."

The man stepped up to him. "Glad you could make it, son."

"Thank you, sir. You have quite a place here."

"Anytime you'd like, I'll show you around."

"I'll keep that in mind."

"How about tomorrow?" Hank suggested. "Come by and we'll saddle up a couple of horses and ride out." The older man frowned. "Unless you're too busy. I hear you're puttin' in a lot of work on your place."

"I think I can take a few hours off."

The group broke into laughter. But Wyatt noticed Hank was studying him...closely.

"You say you're from Arizona?"

"Tucson." Wyatt was telling the truth, but it bothered him the part he was holding back. If only Jared Trager were here.

Before Maura could protest, she was whisked off to the kitchen to help the other women. The Circle B's housekeeper, Ella, was busy arranging the carry-in food for tonight's party. The tall, older woman had been around at the ranch for years and had had a big hand in raising the boys. Chance, Cade and Travis loved her like a second mother. All the kids thought of her as their grandmother.

"That's one good-looking cowboy you brought with you," Ella whispered to Maura.

"He is?" Maura said, trying to act nonchalant. "I hadn't noticed."

"Sweetie, you'd have to be dead not to notice that man," Ella said. "I'd say he fits right in with all those other tall, dark and handsome boys out there."

Joy came up to the counter carrying a bowl of potato salad. "Well, it wouldn't be the first time," she said. "That was the way with Jared Trager. He first came here to find his deceased brother's son and ended up marrying Dana Shane from the Lazy S Ranch and adopting her son, Evan. Of course, when Jared claimed to be Jack Randell's son, it was not without resistance from Chance,

Cade and Travis. They'd even insisted on a DNA test to prove Jared was blood. Even after their rocky start, he fits into the family just fine."

Ella looked at Joy. "When are Jared and Dana supposed to get back from Las Vegas?"

"Dana called me yesterday," Joy said. "She said tomorrow at the latest. I hope so. She's doing fine with the pregnancy, but I miss her." She patted her own extended belly. Her baby was due in a few months. "She's going to be sorry she's missed everything going on around here."

"No, she's not," Abby said pointing out the window. "Because Dana and Jared just drove up."

The women dropped what they were doing and headed out the door to greet the family members who'd been gone for the past two weeks. Joy hugged Dana, then everyone took turns going after Jared, then six-year-old Evan.

"You'd think we were lost in the desert," Jared said, but eagerly accepted a kiss from Ella.

"The last I heard, Las Vegas *is* the desert. Glad to have you all back."

The men arrived by now and they shook hands. It was Cade who stepped up and introduced Wyatt.

"Jared, Dana and Evan, we want you to meet Wyatt Gentry, our new neighbor. He bought the Rocking R. Wyatt, this is our other brother number four, Jared."

Wyatt stepped up and shook Jared's hand, not missing his shocked look.

"That was fast," Jared said. "How come you never called or wrote back? How long have you been here?"

"Thought it would be better just to show up."

All the brothers exchanged glances. "You two know each other?" Cade finally asked.

"Well, sort of," Jared said. "I wrote to Wyatt and his brother, Dylan. It seems that years ago, their mother, Sally Gentry, knew… Jack."

Chapter 4

"You can't be saying what I think you're saying," Cade said, his gaze darting from Wyatt to Jared, then back again.

Jared nodded slowly. "Wyatt Gentry is our half brother," he said.

Everyone in the group grew silent as if waiting for further explanation. Wyatt felt their expectant gazes burning into him. He knew he should speak. The Randells had every right to hear about the circumstances of his birth.

But it was Jared who began. "I got the news a few months ago when Graham Hastings came to see Evan. At first, I thought that the old man was just trying to get back at me for not letting him see his grandson, but then…"

"What exactly did he tell you?" Cade demanded as he placed his hands on his hips, his brothers, Chance and Travis, flanking him. They were all waiting for an answer.

"GH didn't say much. Just that I wasn't Jack Randell's only bastard. Then he gave me a packet from a private investigator with a picture of Jack with a woman named Sally Gentry. Maybe I should have shown it to you all, but I decided it would be best to first contact Wyatt and Dylan—"

"Dylan?" Chance interrupted. "Who the hell is Dylan?"

"He's my twin brother," Wyatt answered, hearing his pulse pounding in his ears.

A mumbled curse came from Cade, then he said, "Hope you didn't come here to collect anything from your daddy," he said, sarcasm lacing in his tone. "You're sh—out of luck."

"Cade!" Abby gasped as she appeared at her husband's side. "Let Wyatt talk."

Cade raised his hands. "I don't want to hear any more about Jack Randell's sins." He turned and marched through the crowd, off toward the house.

Jared came up to Wyatt. "I think it might be a good idea to give them some time to let this news settle in."

Wyatt nodded. Never had he felt like this. All alone. Every other time, he'd had Dylan with him and they handled rejection together. They'd fought their battles side by side. Not tonight. "I'll go."

"I'm sorry," Jared said. "We'll talk soon."

"Sure," Wyatt said and strode off.

Maura watched Wyatt start off toward the truck, his shoulders squared, his head held high. He was definitely a Randell. Why hadn't she seen the resemblance? Tall, dark and with the same good looks as his brothers. One difference, he was alone.

She gathered Jeff and Kelly and followed after him.

Abby stopped her. "Maura, maybe it would be best if you and the kids stay here."

"Why?" she asked, her gaze on Wyatt as he climbed into the cab. "Wyatt Gentry is the same man he was this morning," she said. "He can't help who his parents are."

"You're right," her friend finally agreed. She hugged Maura. "Be careful. You're vulnerable…and so is he. Tell Wyatt that Cade will come around and so will his brothers. They just need some time."

Maura said goodbye and rushed her complaining kids toward Wyatt's truck. She called to him as he was backing out.

He stopped, then peered through the open window.

She picked up her pace. "You can't leave without us."

He looked surprised, then confused. "I just figured you'd want to stay."

She shook her head. "No, the kids have school tomorrow. May we get a ride back with you?"

"Are you sure?"

"I'm sure." Maura walked around to the passenger side and helped the kids inside. She climbed in the front seat and Wyatt took off down the road toward the highway.

"Mom, what about supper?" Jeff whined and crossed his arms over his chest. "Aren't we going to eat?"

"I'll fix you something when we get hom…to the house," she began. She couldn't call the ranch her home. They were going to be gone soon.

"How about I treat everyone to hamburgers, or pizza?" Wyatt suggested.

"You don't have to do that," Maura said sending her

children a stern look as they cheered for pizza. "I have food at the house."

"I know, but Kelly and Jeff had to leave their friends." He glanced away from the road to look at her, his blue eyes sad. "Let me do this, Maura."

She found she wanted to reach out to Wyatt and let him know that it didn't make any difference to her who his parents were. "I guess it's still early and we do have to eat. And pizza does sound good."

Both Kelly and Jeff cheered again, then sat quietly until they pulled into the parking lot of the Pizza Palace. Wyatt walked around the truck and helped Maura out of the cab, surprising her when he gripped her around the waist and lifted her down. His touch was strong, yet gentle and lingered even after he set her on the ground. He tossed her a wink that sent her heart racing. Then just as quickly, he turned away to assist her children.

Inside the restaurant the ringing and beeping sound of video games filled the large room along with the aroma of oregano and pepperoni. After a short discussion they decided on toppings for the pizza. Then before Maura realized what Wyatt was doing, he took some bills from the front pocket of his jeans. He held out two dollars toward Kelly.

"This is for helping me yesterday."

Her eyes rounded as she accepted the money. "Thank you, Wyatt."

He turned to Jeff and held out two more dollars between his fingers. "These are for you, Jeff…if you help watch your sister play her game and if, I can count on your help tomorrow for about an hour."

Maura watched her son stew over the decision. "What do I hafta to do tomorrow?" the boy asked.

"Help with some cleanup," Wyatt said. "And maybe if you get that finished you can swing a hammer at a few nails. And if it doesn't interfere with your other chores, I could use your help again on Saturday. I'll pay you well if you're a good helper."

Jeff looked at Maura for permission. She nodded.

"Okay," her son said, then took the offered money and went off with his sister in tow toward the change machine.

Maura and Wyatt found a booth and sat down across from each other. The high-backed seats and the hanging lamp that threw off dim light made the small space seem more intimate. She immediately felt Wyatt's formidable presence, along with his warmth, and the light scent of his aftershave wafted toward her. The man might be large, but there was a gentleness about him that didn't threaten her.

Maura's thoughts turned to her past, knowing too well how fast things could change. How tenderness could turn into accusing words, caresses into slaps and a swinging fist. She quickly shook off the bad memories of her life with Darren.

"You okay?" Wyatt's voice drew her attention.

Maura released a long breath. "Yes," she said, knowing she was no longer the same woman who'd let herself be controlled, abused. She could protect herself now and that's what she planned to do. Her eyes locked with Wyatt's mesmerizing blue ones.

He was making it difficult not to wish for things she could never have. That didn't stop her curiosity about the man. She had questions. Questions she shouldn't ask, but she couldn't help herself.

"Why did you buy the old Randell ranch?" she blurted out.

Wyatt couldn't fault Maura for her curiosity. If things were reversed, he'd be asking, too.

"I didn't start out to buy it," he said honestly. "I'd only planned to come to San Angelo and talk with Jared Trager. All my life it seems I've been looking for this missing part of me, wondering about the man who fathered me. My mother always refused to tell Dylan or me who he was. Then out of the blue, I got Jared's letter, and she had no choice but tell us about Jack Randell."

"What did she think about you coming here…looking for your father?"

Wyatt glanced toward the video game machines to make sure Jeff was helping his sister. "She wasn't crazy about the idea. Neither was Dylan. My stepfather even less." He raked his fingers through his hair. "I'm the one who needed to confront the man, ask him why he ran off from his responsibilities. Then I got here and discovered that he'd been gone for years. But I was curious about his life…his family."

"That's when you decided to buy the family ranch?"

"I never planned to buy *that* particular ranch," he said truthfully. "When I drove by and saw the For Sale sign, I only went to inquire about the property. Somehow, I ended up offering a ridiculously low price. They accepted it.

"Then that night I came in and found you and the kids at the house, and Cade appeared. How could I say…hey, I'm your long-lost, bastard brother?" Wyatt had known the word too well. He'd lived with it all his life.

Maura saw the pain in Wyatt's eyes and her heart went out to him. As much as she tried to stay uninvolved, it was too late the minute she walked away from the barbecue and climbed into his truck.

Their order number was called and Wyatt went up to get the pizza while she gathered her kids. Kelly sat next to her and she put Jeff beside Wyatt. If her son had a problem, he never voiced it. His only interest was the food.

Maura picked pepperoni off of Kelly's piece and handed it to her. Her daughter smiled. "Thanks, Wyatt, for taking us here. It's fun."

"You're welcome, princess." Wyatt turned to Jeff. "Thanks for watching your sister."

Shyly Jeff said thank you, too.

Maura was happy to see her son coming around. "What are you going to be working on tomorrow?"

"I'm going to be tearing the roof off the porch before it falls down." He glanced at Jeff. "You think you can handle loading the wheelbarrow with the old shingles? Then this weekend I'll be ready to finish nailing the porch floorboards. Maybe you can help me."

Jeff perked up. "Okay," he said, then quickly concentrated on his pizza.

Wyatt glanced across the table. "I'll be right with him all the time. I'd never do anything to put him in jeopardy."

A mother always had fears about her children getting hurt, but her son needed a positive male role model. "If you're sure he won't get in your way."

"Mom, I'm not a baby." Jeff glanced at his sister, but didn't say anything.

"No, he won't get in my way. We'll be fine," Wyatt assured her.

"I know," Maura said. But she had more than her son's physical safety to worry about. It seemed as if Jeff and Kelly were getting far too attached to Wyatt Gentry. She looked at him and her eyes locked with his. A warm sensation poured through her, making her feel things she hadn't felt in a long time.

No, it wasn't just the kids she had to worry about.

The next morning, Hank Barrett drove his truck off the highway onto the gravel road. He passed under the broken gate sign that used to read the Rocking R Ranch. He knew the place well. It was where he'd come to get Chance, Cade and Travis. Every time the young boys ran away from the Circle B, they'd end up back at their old home.

Years ago, most everyone had told him he'd be crazy to take in three hoodlums. And with that bad Randell blood, to boot. Their daddy was a low-down cattle rustler. In west Texas, there wasn't much worse than that.

But Hank knew the young boys needed him. Although they didn't want to come live at the Circle B, the courts had insisted. At fourteen, Chance was too young to look after his brothers. Children's Services had tried to separate them, but somehow they always found a way to get back together. Hank had been the only person who'd take all three of them.

He smiled. "A widowed man without a child of his own... I was doggone crazy."

Although he was lucky enough to discover his daughter, Josie, as far as he was concerned, Chance, Cade and Travis were his sons. He never regretted a day he'd had with the boys.

Now their lives had been rocked again by another of their daddy's transgressions. A second illegitimate son had surfaced—with his twin to come. The rumors in the community were bound to start up again. Not that Hank was worried. His boys were made of tough stuff. They could share their lives with another brother. They'd already come to accept Jared, included him in the family. They would come around again.

Hank stopped in front of the old house. First thing he saw was Wyatt Gentry busy tearing off old shingles from the sagging porch. Hank climbed out of his truck and went up the walk.

Without stopping his task, Gentry spoke, "If you're here to run me off, you're wasting your time." More shingles came flying to the ground.

Hank grinned. There was no doubt this man had Randell blood in his veins. "Can't a neighbor come pay a visit?"

This time Wyatt stopped and glared down at Hank. "You weren't very neighborly last night."

"And you weren't very honest," Hank countered.

They both stared at each other. Finally Wyatt spoke. "Would you like some iced tea?"

"Wouldn't turn it down," Hank said.

Wyatt climbed down the ladder. "Come inside to the kitchen." He held open the screen door and Hank walked in ahead of him. He glanced around the familiar living room. Not much had changed over the years. It needed a lot of work.

"This is a great house. It's a shame that it was neglected over the years."

"You knew Jack Randell?"

"I knew his daddy, John Randell, Sr. His family used to have quite a spread here. A real showplace. After John's death, Jack wasn't any good at running things. He married a local girl, Alice Howard. No sooner had the newlyweds settled in, Jack took off on the rodeo circuit.

He was never home and the ranch suffered. When the boy's mother got sick and died, Jack finally came back. He was lousy at managing the ranch—and worse at being a father to three small boys." Hank looked at Wyatt. "I think you already know that he was sent to prison."

Wyatt nodded and started for the kitchen. He pulled two glasses from the cupboard and filled them with tea from a pitcher in the old refrigerator. They both pulled out chairs and sat down.

"Why did you buy this place?"

"Because I've been looking for a ranch, and it was dirt cheap." Wyatt quoted the price.

"Damn! You're right," Hank said. "Ben Roscoe was giving it away."

"I heard it's been on the market for years."

Hank nodded. "Cattle ranching hasn't been that profitable lately. That's the reason we thought it would be a good idea for Maura and the kids to move in here temporarily. We were all shocked when we heard you bought the place. Thanks for letting her stay while she looks for another house."

"That's not a problem."

Hank shook his head. "She sure did do a lot of work here. Needs some paint, but it's clean as a whistle."

Wyatt finished his tea, wondering where Hank Barrett was headed with his inquiries. "Well, I think my break is over and I need to get back to work." He stood and Hank followed him and placed his empty glass in the sink.

"C'mon, I'll help," the older man started through the house. "C'mon…"

"You don't have to…"

Hank stopped. "If I help, I figure it'll take us about

an hour to finish, then we can take a ride out to Mustang Valley."

Wyatt had heard about the valley and grinned. "Sounds good."

"Well, let's get crackin', boy. The day's not going to get any cooler." The older man had his sleeves rolled up by the time they reached the porch. He glanced up and eyed the rotted wood. "Besides making it livable, what are your plans for the place?"

"I'll be boarding rodeo rough stock."

Hank grinned. "Well, that's interesting." He looked thoughtful for a minute. "Gentry. Say, your brother wouldn't be 'Devil Dylan' Gentry, the champion bull rider?"

Wyatt smiled proudly. "That's Dylan."

"Well, I'll be damned. Hey, you two wouldn't want to attend my rodeo coming up in at the end of the month? I put it on every year after roundup. All the neighbors are invited."

Hearing the word neighbors, Wyatt's hopes soared. Maybe he did belong here after all.

Maura drove the golf cart down the path to the honeymoon suite. The most secluded cabin of them all, and the most popular one. In the middle of the grove of oak trees a small creek ran just outside the cabin window. On the porch a small table was decorated with two place settings and in a few hours a nice supper would be sent down for this evening's meal. She was here now to deliver the flowers and make sure everything was ready.

She went to the back of her cart and took out the two white-and-green bouquets, one a centerpiece for the table and the other a vase for inside the cabin.

She had an hour to add the finishing touches before the honeymoon couple arrived. After unlocking the door, she walked inside the large room. The flagstone fireplace was filled with kindling, ready for a romantic fire. The overstuffed love seat and matching chairs were nearly covered with fat pillows. Partially covering the planked wood floors was an off-white shag rug that was so thick she was tempted to walk barefoot through the thick pile.

Instead, she went to the small alcove where a deep-red silk comforter covered the large canopy bed. A dozen pillows were arranged against the high, carved-wooden headboard. Numerous candles were arranged around the room.

Maura approached the bed and touched the smooth material, knowing that underneath the covers were ivory satin sheets. She wondered how the cool fabric would feel against her bare skin.

She closed her eyes and pictured herself on the bed. Surprisingly the image of a man appeared. Wyatt. He was naked to the waist, wearing only jeans. She couldn't take her gaze off him, his broad shoulders, his well-defined chest. Her breathing grew labored as he started toward her, his eyes never leaving hers. Standing in front of her, he lowered his head, his mouth so close his warm breath caressed her face. Her body grew warm and achy as her lips parted in anticipation of his kiss.

"Maura," he whispered her name.

"Oh, Wyatt," she said and reached out for him.

"Maura… Maura."

Snapping back from the wonderful reverie, she opened her eyes and gasped when she saw Wyatt standing across the room. He was fully dressed and looking confused.

"Oh—Wyatt." She straightened, she glanced away. "What are you doing here?"

Wyatt was wondering the same thing. But seeing Maura standing in this room surrounded by flowers and candlelight, he couldn't stop the daydream. Maura lying in bed waiting for her lover…for him. Desire shot through him like hot lava. Hearing his name again, he quickly reined it in.

He pulled off his hat. "I went riding with Hank Barrett. He was showing me around the valley…and I saw you come in here. I thought I'd come by and say hello." He was stumbling over his words like a teenage boy and he noticed her flushed face. "Are you all right?"

She turned away. "I'm fine. Just busy trying to get ready for the ranch's guests."

Wyatt's focus turned to the huge canopy bed and his imagination started off again. He quickly yanked his thoughts back. "So, this is the bridal suite."

"Yes. Lovely isn't it?"

Suddenly soft music came on, the lights dimmed. Oh, boy, this was all he needed. "Hey, this can really set a mood," he tried to joke. "Not that newlyweds need any help," he quipped, wondering why he didn't just shut up.

"It's nice to be romantic," Maura said as she crossed the room and began to arrange the flowers in the vase.

"Your flowers are beautiful. You did a wonderful job arranging the bouquet."

"Thank you. I like to use white, especially on the couples' first night. White stands for unity, love, respect and purity."

He found himself drawn closer, inhaling the fragrance of both the roses and her. To him, Maura's scent was more intoxicating.

"What about red roses? For passion and desire. Wouldn't a bride want her husband to feel those things, too?"

Wyatt watched excitement light her large eyes, then suddenly it faded away. That was when he knew that Maura Wells had never experienced any of the those wonderful emotions. Deep down, he wished he could be the man to show her what she'd missed.

Chapter 5

After his ride with Hank through the valley, Wyatt returned to the house to finish the job of tearing away the old porch. Hard physical work should help drive away the picture of Maura in the bridal suite from his mind.

With a shake of his head he took the sledgehammer to the railing and began swinging at the rotted wood. The ancient lumber splintered and finally gave way in surrender. Within minutes he'd collapsed the entire section. "You're a fast worker."

Wyatt turned to find Jared Trager standing in the walkway. The man looked like the rest of the Randells, tall and broad with dark hair. They all had the same easy smile, and a bit of an attitude, as if they didn't give a damn as to what people thought of them.

"Need some help?" he asked.

"I'm doing just fine on my own."

That brought another smile from Trager. "I had the same idea when I came here. I could do everything on my own. Didn't need anyone's help, especially a Randell. It took a while, but I was proven wrong."

Wyatt kept on working, but Jared wouldn't be ignored. "You need to give them some time. I don't think you would be here if you didn't want the same thing I wanted. To be accepted."

"All I wanted was to find out who my father was," Wyatt said, his voice strained as he grabbed one end of the railing and began to drag it toward the pile of scrap wood. "I've done that and I didn't like what I discovered. End of story. I'll survive…and move on."

Jared took hold of the other end of the railing and helped with the taxing load. "That's why you bought this place? So you could move on? There has to be dozens of ranches like this around the country, including Arizona." They dropped the section of porch on top of the pile with a grunt. Jared raised his hands. "I know…the price was right, but I think you wanted more when you decided to come here. I think you wanted a sense of family. A place to belong, like I said." His eyes held Wyatt's. "I was looking for the same thing when I showed up at the Lazy S and found Dana and Evan."

"Our stories are totally different," Wyatt insisted, then turned and headed back to what was left of the porch.

"Maybe, but not by much. A man named Jack Randell fathered us all, and he didn't give a damn. In spite of that, we seemed to have turned out to be decent guys. And in spite of everything else, that's a bond between all of us. Chance, Cade, Travis, you, Dylan and me. We're brothers."

Wyatt felt a tug on his heart at hearing those words,

but he tried not to show any emotion. He still had a lot to work through.

"It's going to take a while," Jared continued. "I even went through DNA testing to prove that I was a Randell. At least your mother verified Jack was your father."

"Doesn't make any difference," Wyatt said. "The Randells don't want me here."

"Give 'em a chance." Jared frowned, reminding Wyatt so much of Dylan. "It's hard for Chance, Cade and Travis to keep hearing about their father's transgressions." Jared raked his hand through his hair. "I should have been here when you arrived, if only to prepare them."

Wyatt wasn't in the mood to talk anymore. He wasn't about to beg the Randells for acceptance, either. "Doesn't make any difference now. I'm here and like it or not, I'm stayin'."

That made Jared grin. "Good. Let me know if you want any help putting the new porch on. I need to get home to supper. I have a pregnant wife who can't think about anything but food right now."

Jared started toward his black truck and Wyatt found himself calling out to him. "Saturday. I'll be working on the porch frame."

He saluted. "I'll be here as soon as I finish the morning chores. Say around eight?"

"Thanks," Wyatt called out.

"No problem. That's what family is for." Jared climbed in his truck and started off just as Maura's station wagon came up the road. She parked and the kids jumped out. They both came running toward him, Kelly stumbling and nearly falling in her excitement. Jeff made it first, but his sister was quickly at his side. Wyatt found his mood brightening, especially since Jeff had been more accepting of him.

"Hi, Wyatt," the girl said with a big smile.

"Hello, princess. How was your day?"

"We went to the library. I got books, but I can't keep them, I have to give them back. So I hafta be careful. You want to see?" She pulled them out of her backpack.

"Sure." He leaned down and examined her books, one about a lost kitten and the other a velveteen rabbit. He glanced at Jeff. The boy was dying to talk but didn't want to appear anxious.

"How was your day, Jeff?"

He shrugged. "We practiced for a fire drill and I learned how not to burn up in a fire."

"You don't say. How is that?"

The boy proceeded to drop down and roll on the ground. Maura came up the walk. "Jeffrey Wells, what are you doing in your good school clothes?"

"Uh-oh," the boy echoed.

"Sorry, Maura," Wyatt said. "It was my fault. I was just asking what they did in school today. Jeff was showing me how to stop, drop and roll in a fire."

Maura's heart rate accelerated. One look at the man, even dirty and sweaty from work, and she couldn't find her voice. Same as when he'd first come to the cabin. She could never go into the bridal suite again and not picture him there.

She pulled her gaze away and looked at her children. "Okay, you both go upstairs and change your clothes. Dinner will be ready soon." She started off and he stopped her.

"Can I vote for hamburgers?" Wyatt asked while the

kids cheered. "I happened to buy a grill today and I was wondering if we could try it out and cook some burgers."

"Oh, can we, Mom?" Kelly pleaded.

Maura didn't like to have to disappoint them. "Not tonight, kids. I don't have any ground beef."

"I also stopped at the grocery store and got some meat and buns."

Maura didn't know what to say. The man was taking over her one job—fixing his meals. She sent the kids into the house.

"Look, Wyatt. How am I supposed to fulfill my part of our agreement if you keep paying for the food?"

"If you're talking about the pizza last night, it was my fault you and the kids missed supper. And as for tonight, it's been so hot lately, I thought cooking outside would keep the house cooler."

She crossed her arms. "I won't take charity, Wyatt."

"Okay." He reached into his pocket, pulled out the grocery receipt and handed it to her. "I bought a few other things that I needed, but the cost of the meat and buns are on there. You can pay me back."

She nodded, knowing maybe she was a little over the line, but she wasn't going to be dependant on a man again. It would be so easy to rely on someone like Wyatt Gentry. He was big and strong, yet gentle and caring. She could see that every time he was with her and Jeff and Kelly. And darn it, her own pulse raced whenever he came close. But she wasn't a foolish girl any more. A sweet talking man couldn't sway her. Her breath quickened. No matter how handsome he was.

She took out her wallet, counted out the four dollars for the food and handed it to him. "Please try to understand, Wyatt. I need to pay my own way."

He nodded. "I understand. In fact, you remind me a lot of my mother. She taught her boys the same. Do an honest day's work for an honest day's pay."

Maura glanced around. "Looks like you've done more than your share today."

"The tear down is the easy part. It's cleaning up and rebuilding that's going to take the time."

"Well, don't let Jeff get in your way. I'm not sure how much of a help he'll be."

"Let me worry about him."

"Thank you for taking time with him," she said. "He hasn't had much experience with a positive role model."

"Whoa, don't make me out to be something I'm not. I just want to help the boy lose a little attitude."

She found herself smiling at his embarrassment. "Whatever, I thank you. I think I'll make some potato salad and deviled eggs. We'll make it a picnic."

He shook his head. "The way you've been feeding me, I think I better worry about my waistline."

Her gaze went to his trim waist and flat stomach. She wondered what it'd be like to open the buttons on his shirt, to run her fingers over his sweat slick skin, his taut muscles and broad shoulders. Realizing what she was doing, her gaze moved to his face. "You don't have anything to worry about."

But she sure did if she didn't stop having these wanton thoughts.

Saturday morning arrived and so did Jared. Without much discussion, the two went to work and built the frame for the new porch. Somewhere around nine o'clock, Maura came out with some iced tea for them and lemonade for Jeff, who'd been working on picking up the scraps of wood. They all sat down for a well-deserved break.

"Looks like we're making some headway," Jared said. "I'll help you finish this, but I need to be home by noon. Evan has a soccer game and I help coach the team." He nodded at Jeff as he went back to work at the edge of the yard. "I tried to talk the boy into playing, but he didn't seem interested." Jared shook his head. "It's tough being the new kid in school. I don't think he's made many friends, yet."

"I know how that feels," Wyatt offered. "With all the traveling we did as kids, our mom had to do a lot of the schooling herself. We weren't around much to make many friends. Maura said Jeff misses Dallas."

"Maybe Jeff will be ready for baseball in the spring." Jared took the last swallow of his tea. "That is, if they stay here."

Wyatt was surprised to hear that Maura was thinking about leaving San Angelo. "I didn't know she was leaving the area."

"She only planned to stay temporarily. Just to get away from her ex-husband." Jared frowned. "I shouldn't have said anything."

"It's okay. I know she has an ex out there." Wyatt thought back to the promise he'd made that he'd do whatever it took to protect her and her kids if the man ever showed up and caused trouble.

"She has a good job at the Yellow Rose, but it costs a lot to support herself and two kids." Jared gave him a sideways glance. "You've been good to let her stay here."

Wyatt told himself not to think about trying to help her, not to get involved any more than he already was. She and the kids weren't his problem, but he couldn't keep himself from asking, "I take it her ex wasn't a nice guy?"

Jared stiffened. "Don't know him, but from what I gather, the guy's a jerk. The scum had a way with his fists. Luckily, Maura got away. I think she's still afraid that he'll find her and the kids." Jared looked at him. "Again, it's great that you let them stay."

"No big deal. I hadn't planned on moving into the house at first anyway. I still have a lot of work to do. Speaking of which, we need to get back to it. It's not getting any cooler." He stood and grabbed his hammer.

In another hour the porch frame was finished and Jared headed home. Tomorrow, Wyatt planned to hang the shingles. The new railing had been milled and assembled at the local lumberyard, and was being delivered on Monday. He needed to have everything ready. That meant the porch floor had to be finished this weekend. He turned to the six-year-old working in the yard. "Hey, Jeff, you think you can help me hammer a few nails?"

His eyes rounded. "I never used a hammer before."

"Well, come up here and I'll show you."

The boy had worked like the devil all morning. To Wyatt's surprise he never complained once. He hesitated to ask him for more. Maybe he should send Jeff inside to rest, but he didn't want to disappoint him if he wanted to stay.

Thirty minutes later, Maura helped when she called them inside for lunch. After washing up, Wyatt sat down at the kitchen table to two egg salad sandwiches and left-over potato salad. The kids ate peanut-butter sandwiches.

"You didn't have to make me special sandwiches," he told Maura. "I like peanut butter." He winked at Kelly.

The girl giggled as she ate around the bread crust.

Maura came to the table. "You don't like egg salad?"

"Yes, I like egg salad very much," he stressed. "Just don't go to so much trouble for me. I'm sure you have plenty else to do."

"It's fine," she said. "That reminds me, I washed your clothes and took the basket down to the cottage."

"There was no need to," he said, recalling the condition of the cottage. "I could have taken it down myself."

He watched as Maura moved around the kitchen. She had her hair tied up in a ponytail, but nearly half the silky strands were curled around her face. She wore a pair of shorts, showing off trim calves and shapely thighs. A large white T-shirt was knotted at her tiny waist.

"You've been busy," she said. "Besides, it's part of our agreement."

Wyatt was starting to hate their agreement. He found he looked forward to her coming home every day, hearing about the kids' day at school. It seemed so natural, all of them being here. But truth was, she would be gone one day…and soon. He had to accept that.

By the next week, Wyatt had nearly completed the repairs to the house. He had finished rebuilding the porches, both front and back. Most of the peeling paint had been scraped off. Now, he was busy replacing the cracked windows and puttying the ones that were still intact.

The late September morning was another hot one. Wyatt chose to spend it on a twenty-foot ladder to work on the second story, finishing the last row of windows. Next he would prime and paint. He already bought twenty-five gallons of oil base, whisper-white for the house and forest-green for the shutters.

He smiled in amazement as he spread putty along the pane. It had been three weeks since he'd taken possession of the property. Well, maybe not exactly possession, since he shared the place with a woman and her kids. But he wouldn't have changed the last few weeks for anything.

In fact, he was going to miss Maura's special touches, and not just in the house. She'd managed to weave some hominess into the cottage, finding time to clean and organize his temporary living quarters. No use in trying to stop her, she would just insist she was paying her way. Fine. He wasn't about to argue with a stubborn female.

Correction. A beautiful, stubborn female that he was going to miss a lot.

Wyatt was just scrapping the last pane when he reached for his knife and began to slip on the ladder rung. Losing his balance, he grabbed at the window but couldn't get a good grip. With no time to think, he pushed himself away, praying he'd land on the ground and not atop the ladder. Wyatt got his wish and tumbled to the hard ground with a thud. Pain sliced through his body, especially his back and legs as every bit of air was forced from his lungs. His last thoughts were of Maura and the kids. He hated the thought of her finding him like this.

Then everything went black.

Maura returned to the house to pick up Jeff's permission slip for the field trip so she could fax it to the school. Inside the house, she found the paper on the table, right where her son had left it. She started to leave, but decided to let Wyatt know she stopped by.

She'd been surprised that she hadn't seen him. Going on a search, she went out through the kitchen and called out his name. No answer. She then walked around back and froze seeing him sprawled on the ground.

"Wyatt!" She raced to his side and she knelt down beside his motionless body. "Oh, God. Please, let him be all right," she whispered, tears already filling her eyes. She felt for his pulse and found one, then she heard him groan. "Wyatt, I'm here. Don't move."

"I don't think I can." He groaned again. "I hurt," he managed and opened his eyes when she touched his face.

"I'll take care of you." She continued to stroke his face, then realized she had to get him help. "Wyatt, I've got to go call someone, but I'll be right back."

Swallowing back her panic, Maura ran to the house. First she called for an ambulance, then Cade. He told her he'd meet her at the hospital. After hanging up, she got a blanket and a cup of ice and hurried outside.

"I'm back, Wyatt," she said, and sank down beside him.

He blinked at her, then opened those gorgeous blue eyes. This time he smiled. "I guess I zigged instead of zagged," he joked, but pain was etched on his face.

Maura saw the extension ladder laying on the ground and knew he had been working on the second story. She closed her eyes. He could have been killed, he could have a spinal injury. She sent up a silent prayer. *Please, don't let anything happen to him.*

"Here's some ice," she offered, not knowing how long he'd been lying there. Luckily he'd been in the shady side of the house. She placed an ice sliver against his lips and he drew it into his mouth.

"Where do you hurt?"

"Everywhere." His breathing was labored. "That's good. At least I can feel every part of my body."

"You shouldn't have been up there without someone to hold the ladder."

"You sound like my mother."

"Well, I am *a* mother. And when you do foolish things…" Tears flooded her eyes and ran down her face. "Darn it, Wyatt, you may have really hurt yourself."

He glanced up at her, then raised his hand to her eyes and touched a tear. "Don't cry, Maura, I'm fine. I've been hurt worse in my rodeoing days when I got tossed off broncs."

She didn't believe him. "Do you want me to call someone? Your family?"

He took her hand and gripped tight. "No. You're all I need."

She brushed away another tear. "Oh, Wyatt. I'm not sure what I can do for you."

"You're doin' fine…"

Maura touched his hair and brushed it back. She couldn't deny that this man had come to mean so much to her. More than she ever wanted to admit. She prayed that he would be all right.

He hated hospitals.

Wyatt lay on the cold metal exam table, his back hurting like hell as he waited for the doctor. Maura was outside, probably pacing. He knew he'd scared her. The look on her face, and the panic in her voice had told him that. Hell, he'd scared himself.

The pain in his back was so bad he was sweating by the time Maura had reached him. But he soon forgot the discomfort the second she put her hands on him. Her touch, her soothing voice… Maybe she revealed more than she wanted, but she cared about him.

Just then a young doctor walked in. "Well, Mr. Gentry, you didn't break anything, but it seems you twisted your ankle and have a bad back sprain." He smiled as he glanced up from the chart. "All in all, I'd say you were a lucky guy."

"Good, then I can go home."

The doctor raised his hand. "Just let me explain a few things about your care, first. I better get your wife in here. She's been so worried."

Before Wyatt could say anything to the doctor, he ushered Maura into the room. "Mrs. Gentry, I was just about to tell your husband that if he wants to go home, he'll need complete bed rest for the next five to seven days."

Wyatt could see Maura's blush at the doctor's assumption, but neither one of them said a word as the doctor reeled off his instructions.

"Wyatt, your back isn't going to heal overnight. You're going to be in pain for a while." He began writing on the chart. "So I'm prescribing some painkillers."

"I don't need any pills."

Maura looked at Wyatt sternly, then spoke, "Doctor, I'll make sure *my husband* follows your instructions, even if I have to tie him up."

With a groan Wyatt laid back on the table, trying not to think about the different kind of pain Maura was going to inflict on him.

Wyatt was actually relieved when Cade showed up to help him get home. All he needed was bed rest for the day, and he'd feel better tomorrow. Maura climbed in the back seat and they drove by the pharmacy to get the pills. When they'd reached the ranch, they helped Wyatt into the house.

"Where are you taking me?" he demanded weakly.

"Upstairs into the master bedroom," Maura said to Cade, who had Wyatt's arm over his shoulders, helping him navigate the stairs. By the time they reached the large room, Wyatt felt like he'd run a mile. He was breathing hard and unable to argue about what room they deposited him in.

Maura had pulled back the comforter and blanket, exposing flowery sheets. No doubt this was her bedroom.

"Maura, I can't take your room."

She ignored him. "I'm going downstairs to make some lunch. Cade, will you help Wyatt undress?"

As Cade nodded, she disappeared from the room.

"I'm not staying here," Wyatt insisted.

"Why not? It's your house."

"I can't take Maura's bed."

"Then you're going to have to leave under your own power," Cade challenged. "But if you know what's good for you, you'll just stop fighting and take the time to heal. From what I hear, you came pretty close to doing some real damage to yourself."

Wyatt ignored Cade as he tried to pull his shirt from the waistband of his jeans. He had zero strength. Without a word, Cade took over and did the job for him.

Once his boots and jeans were removed, Wyatt wasn't feeling good at all. His back was going into spasms. He grimaced as Cade helped him under the sheets.

Maura returned with soup and a pitcher of ice water. Without a word, she took out a pill and handed it to him.

Wyatt didn't hesitate. He wanted relief from the pain. He tossed the small pill into his mouth, then drank the entire glass of water.

The last thing he remembered were the soft sounds of Maura's voice and her touch, then he was oblivious to anything after that.

"How are you going to handle this on your own?" Abby asked from across the kitchen table. Maura's friend had come by with supper for her and the kids, then helped clean up.

"There's not much to handle. Wyatt's in bed."

"But what happens when he needs to get out of bed... when he needs to go to the bathroom? You want Cade to spend the night?"

Maura shook her head. "That's the reason I put him in my room. The bathroom is close. I can get him there. Cade has been wonderful. And both he and Jared promised to stop by tomorrow."

Abby nodded. "Okay, but don't worry about the Yellow Rose. Your new assistant, Carol, can run the shop for a few days. Luckily there isn't anything special coming up until next weekend." She stood up. "Just call if you need anything."

Maura nodded. "And Abby, thank you for giving me the time off," she said walking her friend to the door.

"Are you kidding? It's you who's brought in the business. Your arrangements are unique, Maura. Do you know we had two orders for bouquets today and both customers insisted that you do the arrangements?"

Maura was pleased, but surprised. "I could come in tomorrow for a few hours when Jared comes by."

Abby raised her hand. "Not necessary. Luckily they're both for this next weekend. The only thing I need you to do is order the flowers from the wholesale mart." A big smile appeared. "Isn't it wonderful? We're suddenly in demand."

Maura was excited, too, but she couldn't think of anything other than helping Wyatt recover. "It's nice to know we're wanted," Maura said as she walked Abby out.

She waved as the car drove off. Thank God things had quieted down. She was grateful that some of the Randell family had wanted to help, but it felt as if nearly every one of them had stopped by, dropping off food, offering to help out. And Wyatt had slept through all the commotion. Just as well. He needed sleep more than anything else.

Maura locked the doors and shut off the lights before she climbed the stairs. She found Jeff in his room. Her son had bathed and dressed in pajamas without even being told.

She went to him, took him in her arms and kissed his cheek.

"Thanks for helping out today."

He nodded. "Mom, is Wyatt going to be okay?"

She could see the fear in her son's eyes. "Sure, he's going to be fine," she assured him. "His back will be really sore for about a week." She brushed her son's hair away from his face, tickled that he hadn't pulled away from her. "And I have to thank you, Jeff. I had to come home to get your permission slip, or Wyatt wouldn't have been found for a long time."

He smiled. "Then I'm glad I missed the dumb trip. And I'm glad Wyatt is okay."

"I'm sure he'd like to hear that."

"And tomorrow after school, I'm going to finish cleaning up the yard."

She hugged him again, then walked out of the room. Next, she went looking for her daughter. Not surprising,

Kelly's bedroom was empty. Maura walked down the hall to her room. She heard Kelly's tiny voice even before she went inside. Wyatt was stretched out under the covers and Kelly was seated next to him. Her library book was open and she was pretending to read the words as she made up her own.

"And they lived happily ever after…forever and ever. The end," she said and closed the book. "You want me to read it again?"

A groggy Wyatt could barely speak. "Not tonight, princess."

Maura decided to rescue him. "It's time for this princess to go to bed," she announced as she crossed the room. "And Wyatt needs his sleep, too."

Kelly bent down and carefully kissed his rough cheek. "I'm glad you're feelin' better. Good night, Wyatt."

Maura looked at Wyatt. "I'll be right back," she promised, then took Kelly off to her room. She tucked her in for the night, promising her daughter she'd be right back to share her bed.

Maura returned to Wyatt's room to find him struggling to get up. She rushed to his side. "Whoa, you can't get out of bed."

He was shirtless and a pair of black sweats rode low on his slim hips. His hair was practically standing on end and he needed a shave. He was more appealing than ever. "I better or I'm going to embarrass myself. And I haven't had an accident in bed since I was four years old." He grimaced. "If I have to, I'll crawl to the toilet."

"How about if I help you?" She braced her feet on the floor and held out her hands. "Grab hold and I'll pull you up."

He looked unconvinced that she could get him to his feet.

"I'm stronger than I look." She gripped his hands and after a few tries she had him standing. "See, I told you." She moved to his side and placed his arm over her shoulders. "Now, slow, easy steps." They finally made it to the door.

"This is as far as you go," he said, reaching for the door frame.

She found herself blushing. "I'll wait here."

He murmured something she didn't want to decipher. After a few minutes, she heard a flush and water running, then the door opened.

Wyatt had to bite his lip, anything to try to mask his pain. He didn't want Maura to worry anymore. She needed her rest tonight. She'd already spent too much time caring for him. Not that he didn't like it, but she had too much on her plate as it was.

He was weak, but determined not to show it. She came up beside him and placed her arm around his waist.

"Lean on me."

"As if I have a choice," he groaned, feeling her delicate body against his. Damn, the pills sure didn't slow down his libido. He felt every curve and smelled her wonderful scent, making him more light-headed than any drug.

Once he was back down, she took out two more tablets and handed them to him. He took them along with a glass of water.

"Oh, that tastes good. Cooling."

Maura poured him another, then went to the windows and made sure they were opened. Though a slight breeze was coming in, it was still warm in the room. "I could bring in the fan," she offered, then went to the closet and took out a table fan. She plugged it in and immediately the air started cooling off the stifling room. "How is that?"

"Good…"

She then began to straighten the sheets.

"Maura, stop," he insisted, his mouth suddenly dry, his tongue fuzzy. The pills were working. "I'm fine."

She leaned over him to arrange his pillow. Damn, she was killing him. "Are you in a comfortable position? You want me to help…"

He shook his head.

She finally turned off the bedside light. The moonlight through the window illuminated the room enough so he could still see her. He looked up and discovered their faces were mere inches apart. Unable to resist, he raised his hand and took hold of her wrist. "Did I thank you for taking care of me?"

She nodded. "Yes, many times," she whispered, her warm breath teasing his cheek.

"Maura…you are so beautiful." He drew her hand to his face, then turned and kissed the warm palm. She gasped but didn't pull away, nor did she fight him when he reached out and drew her head down to his.

He knew this was crazy, but couldn't stop himself. For days he'd ached to kiss her… The touch of her lips was like a spark that ignited a blaze. She whimpered and he took another nibble, then another, until he grew hungry for more. And she gave it to him. He cupped the back of her head and feasted on her delicious mouth.

He was in agony, but it wasn't in his back.

Chapter 6

What was she doing?

Maura suddenly came to her senses and tore her mouth from his. Seeing the desirous look in Wyatt's eyes, she gasped and quickly stepped back from the bed.

"I have to go," she whispered, then hurried from the room.

Once inside Kelly's room, she shut the door and sank against it, trying to draw a breath. She touched her lips, still able to feel his firm mouth…his intoxicating taste. Her heart raced, not from fear or regret, but surprisingly from desire.

The experience was nothing like when Darren had come after her. Drunk and demanding, he'd taken what he wanted, leaving her… Maura closed her eyes to shut out the pain of her ex-husband's abuse and Wyatt's face appeared, along with the soothing feel of his roughened hands against her skin. She had never known that being with a man could feel like that.

Abby had told Maura how tender Cade was with her, and promised that some day she would find a man who would love her that way. At the time, Maura hadn't wanted to think about being with any man.

That was before Wyatt.

Maura walked to the bed, her body still tingling from his kiss. She scooted her daughter over slightly and climbed in the double bed, then pulled the sheet over both of them. As much as she longed for someone in her life, she couldn't let it go any further. She had her children to think about…and there was Darren. He wanted revenge and he would come after her, ruining any chance she would have for happiness.

She couldn't allow anyone to get hurt because of her, especially a man who had been nothing but kind to her and her kids. She closed her eyes, reliving Wyatt's kiss, knowing that was all she would ever have.

A memory.

A house had fallen on him, Wyatt was sure of it as the early morning sunlight came through the window and woke him. He attempted to get up, but collapsed back on the bed when his body refused to cooperate. Still groggy from the leftover effects of the pills and sleep, he finally managed to swing his feet off the bed and sit up. He fisted his hands on the edge of the mattress and tried to stand. Just then the door opened and Maura walked in.

"Wyatt!" She rushed to him and helped him up. "Couldn't you wait for me?"

"There are some things a man's gotta do on his own."

"You do a bad imitation of John Wayne."

He didn't feel like it, but he couldn't help but smile. He needed a pain pill in the worst way, but had to get his wits about him before he spent another day in a fog of drugs. Drugs that made him do crazy things, like kissing Maura. Damn, she had to think he was lower than a snake.

After finishing in the bathroom, he opened the door to find her still there, waiting for him. She was dressed in jeans that hugged her shapely legs and a blouse that tapered in at her tiny waist. His gaze moved to her face. Devoid of makeup, she looked natural and pretty and he liked that. She had yet to look at him with those big brown eyes of hers. He didn't blame her. He'd had no business manhandling her last night. He wanted to blame the drugs, but he'd known exactly what he was doing.

Finally they made it back to the bed. She released him and stepped back. "Do you need anything before I start breakfast?"

"Yes, your forgiveness," he said, then didn't know where to begin. "I was out of line last night, Maura. I had no right to kiss you. I only…meant…to thank you for all your help, but the pills made me a little crazy. I promise you don't have to worry about it happening again."

"It's okay," she said. "Just forget about it. I need to go and get your breakfast."

Maura nearly raced for the door. She didn't want to let Wyatt know what that kiss had meant to her. She was crazy to have thought that he felt the same. The man was good-looking. He could have any woman he wanted. Why would he want to get involved with someone with a hundred problems and two kids, to boot?

She found her way down to the kitchen, angry with herself for ever thinking about the man. She had to put things in perspective. Very soon, she'd be out of here, and Wyatt would be moving on with his life, his business. And someday, he'd marry a beautiful woman who didn't have a past with an ex-husband who was set on getting even.

"Mom, do I have to go to school today?"

Maura turned to find her son still wearing his pajamas. "Of course you do."

"But I need to help Wyatt," he insisted.

"Honey, Wyatt would be the first to tell you how important school is. Besides, Cade and Jared are coming by today to help out." She went to him. "But if you want, you can help when you come home. I'm not going to work today so the bus will drop you off here. After you finish your homework, you can help until supper-time."

Jeff opened his mouth to argue, but instead he smiled. "Okay. I'll do my homework on the bus." He rushed off to get ready for school as Kelly walked into the room already dressed for the day. "I wanna eat breakfast with Wyatt 'cause he's lonely."

"I think Wyatt needs a little quiet time. But I'll let you help me carry up his food. Why don't you go outside and see if you can find some pretty flowers to take him?"

Kelly shot out the door and ran past Cade Randell coming up the back steps. "Good morning," he said to Maura.

"Good morning," she greeted him and offered him a cup of coffee.

"How's the patient?" he asked as he took a seat at the table. "Any problems?"

Just that the man kisses like a dream. She shook her head. "He's quiet now, but earlier I caught him attempting to get out of bed by himself."

"Uh-oh, I was afraid of that. Do you want me to send

in the big artillery? I could have Ella over here in thirty minutes."

Maura had heard stories about the Circle B's housekeeper. "In his weakened state, drugged and disabled, I think I can handle him."

Cade smiled and it reminded her of Wyatt.

"You know, I can see a resemblance between the two of you."

His smile faded. "I know I didn't behave real well toward Wyatt when we heard the news. But you have no idea how tired we are hearing about good old Jack's exploits. I have nothing against Wyatt personally, it's just… hearing his news took a little getting used to. Maybe with this accident we'll get the chance to get to know him." He took a drink of coffee.

Maura joined him at the table. "You and your brothers are good people. Whatever you do, I know you'll be fair."

He nodded. "We try. I was looking around outside. Jared told me Wyatt was doing a lot of repairs on the place. I had no idea he'd gotten so much done."

"He starts before I leave for the day and is working until the sun goes down," she informed him. "He said he and his brother, Dylan, spent a lot of their lives living out of a trailer and traveling around with the rodeo."

"I take it that was where Jack met their mother."

She shrugged. "I think you and Wyatt should be talking about this." She got up from the table and poured another cup of coffee. "I better get him some breakfast. Here, take this up to him and get to know the man. He's your brother."

Cade took the mug along with his own. "Bossy woman. You've been hanging around Abby too much. You're beginning to sound just like her."

Maura smiled. "I take that as a compliment"

"You should, she's a helluva woman."

She couldn't help but wonder what it would be like to have a man love her like that. She knew about the history between Abby and Cade and how many long years it took them to find each other again.

Cade stopped in the doorway and looked back at her. "Since Wyatt's gotten all the prep work on the house finished and there's plenty of paint in the barn, I was thinking that maybe Chance, Travis, Jared and I might have some spare time to start painting the house."

"Oh, that's a wonderful idea," she said. "But I don't think Wyatt would ask you to do it."

A big grin appeared. "If he's drugged for the next few days, I think we might be able to get away without telling him."

For the next few days while the Randell brothers painted the house, Maura was busy playing nurse to her patient. She figured that Wyatt wasn't going to spend more than three, maybe four days in bed. The doctor ordered five, but the way things were going, she'd be lucky to keep him off his feet until the weekend. He was taking fewer of his pills and becoming more and more aware of things going on.

Maura also needed to go into the flower shop and help Carol fill some orders. Kelly would go with her and spend time at preschool. Since Cade was at the house, he promised to keep an eye on Wyatt.

For three days, the brothers had been working tirelessly on the house. They came over in the morning right after their chores, worked until about noon then returned to their own ranches.

Maura was right. By the fourth day, Wyatt was spending less and less time asleep. Finally he refused to take any more painkillers during the day, only to help him sleep at night. It wouldn't be long before he discovered what was going on.

Wyatt was sick and tired of lying around in bed. In fact, he hated it. His back still hurt, but the pain was tolerable, and he needed to get back on his feet. First on the list was a real shower. He was tired of so-called sponge baths.

He got out of bed and shuffled himself to the bathroom. After closing the door, he brushed aside the plastic shower curtain and turned the water on in the chipped, claw-foot tub, then stripped off his sweat pants. Grabbing the towel rack for support, he slowly raised his leg over the edge and managed to pull himself under the spray of warm water. He just stood there and let the water sluice over his body, invigorating him. He turned so the spray hit his lower back, making him sigh in pleasure. Who would have thought that a shower would have been his biggest turn on in months?

Well, that wasn't exactly true.

Maura Wells had been on his mind far too much. In fact he couldn't get her out of his head. The past few days, she'd missed work to take care of him. Suddenly he realized that as of this Monday she would have been here a month. That had been the agreed upon time limit. She was supposed to move out. How could he let her and the kids leave? She had nowhere to go. Besides, with her nursing duties, how could she have found the time to look for another place?

And why did she have to leave? Their arrangement wasn't so bad. The kids were happy. He was happy. Who wouldn't be happy to have a beautiful woman around?

He'd been afraid that she'd panic when he touched her, but she seemed to trust him. When he kissed her he'd seen the desire in her big brown eyes. He couldn't help but wonder if they darkened when she made love. His body stirred to life.

He groaned and dunked his head under the spray, then grabbed the shampoo and lathered his scalp just as he heard a loud knock on the door.

"Wyatt, are you all right?" Maura called to him.

Beautiful, but maybe a little annoying, too. "I'm fine," he yelled back.

The door cracked opened to the steam filled room. "Cade is here. You want me to get him to help you?"

He cursed under his breath. "I don't need help. Can't a man have some peace?"

There was a long pause, then he heard the door shut.

Damn. He quickly rinsed off, then retrieved a towel from the rack. After drying off, he wrapped it around his waist and carefully climbed out of the tub. He opened the door to find Maura sitting on the edge of the bed. She jumped up, looking strangely guilty and innocent at the same time.

"See, I made it," he said, ignoring the fact that he had on next to nothing. "All by myself."

She didn't say a word, just got up and walked out of the room.

He couldn't stand it and called her back. She stopped at the door.

"What do you want?" she asked.

"I'm sorry," he said. "I should have told you I was going to shower."

"I wouldn't have stopped you, Wyatt. I was just concerned about you getting in and out of that old tub. But I can see you did just fine." Her gaze raked over his body, and he felt the heat searing his skin as if she were touching him. "You're right, you don't need me." With those parting words, she walked out and closed the door.

He let out a breath, then found a fresh pair of sweats in the dresser and pulled them on. It seemed to take him forever and afterward he fell back on the bed exhausted. There was a knock on the door.

Maura was back. He struggled to sit up. "Come in."

Cade peered inside. "Can you handle some company?"

"Sure." He hadn't seen Cade in a few days. "But I warn you, I'm in a hell of a mood."

"Sounds like you're feeling better." Cade walked in and behind him were Jared, Chance and Travis.

"What is this, a party?" he asked.

"Just thought we could talk," Jared said as he and Cade sat in the chairs next to the bed, while Travis and Chance leaned against the dresser.

"You guys here to run me out of town?" Wyatt tried to joke.

"No, we're here to welcome you," Chance said. "As the oldest..." He cocked an eyebrow. "I am the eldest, aren't I?"

"I'm thirty-one," Wyatt stated.

Travis grinned. "Looks like I lost my place as baby of the family. You and your twin, Dylan, have that distinction now." Wyatt got a strange feeling in his gut when Cade mentioned family. But that was what they were. Family. "My mother always refused to tell us who our father was," he began. "She said it was because she discovered too late that Jack was already married."

Jared began to share his story. "My mother passed away before I ever got a chance to ask her," he added. "I got the news from an old letter of hers. When she learned she was pregnant with me, Jack Randell rebuffed her. She married another man, Graham Hastings. For years, I thought he was my father and never understood why he resented me so much. It wasn't until my brother, Marsh Hastings, died that I learned the truth."

"Maybe you two were lucky," Chance began. "We've been Randells all our lives and have paid a heavy price for our daddy's sins. There are still some people around here who will have nothing to do with us. You might find settling in West Texas wasn't such a great idea."

Wyatt saw the deep pain on Chance's face. "When I came to San Angelo, all I wanted was to know about my roots. To meet Jared. It's strange to suddenly learn you have a family and you have an opportunity to meet them. When I came by this ranch and saw the For Sale sign, I went to a real estate agent just for some information. When he saw my interest in the place, he convinced me to make a bid. I gave him a ridiculously low offer and he took it."

"You got a good deal," Chance said. "If we get rain, this is good grazing land."

"I'm going to keep rough stock," he told them.

Travis grinned and said, "Hey, I hear our brother is the one and only 'Devil Dylan' Gentry. When do we get to meet him?"

Wyatt didn't want to lie to them. "I'm not sure. Dylan's not as excited as I was knowing about his father. I may have to coax him here."

"Damn. I was hoping he'd come for the Circle B Roundup and Rodeo." Travis shrugged. "Oh, well, Hank doesn't have bull riding events anyhow."

"Dylan and I used to compete in the team calf-roping events. Until he decided that it was too tame to suit him."

Travis smiled with a faraway look in his eyes. "I bet he gets his share of the girls, too."

Chance nudged his brother. "Hey, why should you be thinking about such things when you have Josie?"

All the brothers laughed.

"My wife knows I adore her and our daughter, little Alissa Mae," Travis insisted.

Wyatt got caught up in the kidding, too. Each one of his brothers was happily married to a beautiful independent women. Despite their childhoods, they all had turned out to be completely unlike their father. Family came first. No doubt Hank Barrett had had a lot of influence on them.

"Speaking of good-looking women," Travis began. "What's it like to have your own private nurse?"

"At the moment, I don't think she's talking to me," he confessed. "I haven't been in the best mood."

"I think you better do something about that," Cade said. "Never leave a woman to brood for too long. The punishment just gets worse." He looked at Wyatt. "If you want your home happy I suggest you try and smooth things over."

Wyatt was surprised. Were they giving him the okay to pursue Maura?

Wyatt decided to talk with Maura, but she hardly ever stayed in his room long enough to carry on a conversation. He was at fault, but would she ever forgive him? Okay, so he'd been a little grouchy, as Kelly would say. How could he explain that he'd been dreaming about her, about their kiss…? Not only that, he liked having her around. She had become so much a part of his life.

The kids had, too.

Even Jeff had surprised him. Every day the boy had been cleaning up the wood scraps and sweet little Kelly sat with him in the afternoon reading to him, chatting away about her day. But when Maura came anywhere near him, she refused to say a word that wasn't necessary. He'd hurt her and now he had to try to make her understand.

That night when she came in his room, he was waiting for her.

"Maura, I'd like a word with you."

She paused at the door.

"Think you could come and sit down?" He motioned to the chair beside the bed. "I promise I won't try anything, but we need to clear the air."

She came across the room, but didn't sit down. "If it's about my leaving…"

"Yes, that's one of the subjects I had in mind."

She frowned. "I know it's the end of the month…"

"Yes it is, that's why I wanted to talk—"

"We can be moved out in a few days." She started to leave, when he reached out and grabbed her arm to stop her. She stiffened and he released her, silently cursing her ex for causing her such fear.

"Maura, please, I'm trying to tell you that I don't want you to leave."

Her mouth opened, but she didn't say anything for a long time. "You don't?"

He shook his head. "How could I, after you've devoted the past week to taking care of me? What kind of man would toss you and the kids out after all you've done?"

He raised a hand before she could speak. "Don't answer that. I know I haven't been the greatest patient. You've had to put up with a lot since my fall. If you're worried about me touching you again, you have my promise that won't happen. There is no reason why I can't continue to stay in the cottage and you and kids live here. Please, I'd like you to stay."

Maura let out a sigh of relief. She'd been afraid to even hope for a reprieve. Of course there was still the problem of money, even more how this man affected her. She had to push aside these feelings and think about her children. "But I can't afford to pay rent and I can't take your charity, either."

His voice was husky. "And I'm not giving it, Maura. I should be the one to pay you for nursing me. You didn't even go to work the first three days of this week. I owe you, Maura. Please stay… At least until you can afford to move out."

"Okay, I will," Maura agreed, all the while knowing that when the time came, it was going to be even harder to leave. She'd come to care more for Wyatt far more than she should and she had no one to blame but herself.

Later that afternoon, Wyatt made his first trip downstairs since the day of the accident. And by God, he was going to make it on his own. Slowly, and with Kelly's encouragement he maneuvered the steps.

"You can do it, Wyatt," the three-year-old cheered as he paused on the landing to catch his breath. His strength was zapped. But after he got the okay from the doctor later today, he had to get back to work.

Kelly opened the door and the fresh country air smelled wonderful. He'd been inside too long.

"Hold my hand, Wyatt," Kelly said. "I'll help you go see your surprise." The girl's eyes widened and her tiny fingers covered her mouth as if she said something wrong.

"It's okay, Kelly," her mother assured her. "Why don't you help Wyatt outside?"

Wyatt was confused, but not for long. He stepped out on the porch to find that the floor had been sanded and varnished. He glanced toward the new railing and posts. They'd been painted a glossy white. The lawn was cleaned of any of the old porch wood and mowed, showing sprigs of green along with rows of colorful flowers lining the edge of the porch.

"Look this way, Wyatt," Kelly called.

When he turned around and looked up at the two-story house, he found that the entire structure gleamed with fresh white paint and the shutters were dark green, just as he'd planned to do.

"How do you like it, Wyatt?" Jeff asked. "We all helped, even Kelly."

Somehow Wyatt found his voice. "It looks great." He glanced at Maura unable to mask his shock. "You couldn't have done this all by yourself."

She shook her head. "No, someone had to keep you in bed," she said, then called over her shoulder, "c'mon out, guys."

Just then Chance, Cade, Travis and Jared appeared from beside the house, along with their wives and numerous kids carrying a roughly painted sign that read, Welcome To West Texas.

Wyatt swallowed back the sudden tightness in his throat. He couldn't believe it. They had done all this? "Man, I don't know what to say."

"You don't have to say a thing, just offer us a drink." Cade walked up the steps. "And you also have to feed us."

Abby was right behind her husband. "Don't worry, Wyatt, we brought the food. You think you feel good enough to supervise the guys at the barbecue?"

"Sure." He was still unable to believe what the Randells had done. "Why would they do this?" he said to Maura, not realizing he'd spoken out loud.

Cade placed a gentle hand on Wyatt's shoulder. "Because we think if things were reversed, you'd come and help...a neighbor." He leaned closer. "In fact, you already did when you let Maura stay in the house. In my book that makes you an okay guy." Cade's mouth twitched. "Now, do you know how to barbecue prime Texas beef, or do I need to show you how a native does things?"

Wyatt's back was suddenly feeling much better. "Why don't you go and start up the grill, but I'll come to supervise? I just need to talk to Maura a second."

With Cade and Abby leading, the Randells headed through the house to the kitchen. Maura was about to follow with Jeff and Kelly when Wyatt called to her. She hung back, but sent the kids on.

She looked up at him expectantly. "Do you really like the house? I wasn't sure if I should let Cade and his brothers do it, but you had already bought the paint and..."

"It's great," he said. "Better than I could have hoped. It would have taken me weeks to finish. But thanks to you..." Wyatt couldn't seem to stop himself as he moved closer to her. This woman had been there for him, cared for him when he hadn't been such a nice guy.

"I'm glad you like it," she said. "Now you can concentrate on the barn and corral and bringing your stock here." She was acting shy with him again.

"Maura, look at me. Please," he found himself pleading.

She slowly raised those big bedroom eyes to him and he was lost. He tried to take a breath, but found he had trouble pulling air into his lungs. She made him forget everything he needed to think about. He had always been the practical one, now this woman drove every rational thought from his head. And yet, he didn't seem to mind one bit.

"Thank you, not just for this, but for everything." His voice lowered as did his head. "I couldn't have made it through this week if you hadn't been here to take care of me." Even when he'd been in the fog of drugs, he'd known she was at his side that first night. He recalled her touch as she helped him stand, the feel of her body against his as she helped him to the bathroom.

"I'm just happy I can pay back some of your kindness," she said.

There was laughter and the sound of loud voices in the house, but it didn't distract him. "I'm glad you're staying, Maura," he told her. "I would miss you and the kids."

She glanced away. "We'd miss you, too," she said, her voice barely a whisper.

He leaned closer, catching her familiar scent. "That's good to know." Their eyes met and he ached to close the distance and kiss her, but the promise he'd made to her lingered in the back of his mind. He couldn't break that trust. The last thing he wanted to do was scare her off. He cared about her too much to ever want to see her hurt again.

He wanted to show her how a real man could act. Someday. He backed away. Right now, he could wait until she was ready.

Chapter 7

A flash of lightning zigzagged across the dark sky, followed by a loud clap of thunder. The rumbling sound seemed to vibrate the walls, though that wasn't what had kept Wyatt awake. The past week, ever since he'd moved back into the cottage, he hadn't been able to sleep worth a damn.

He finally got up from bed and slipped on his jeans, then walked to the small living room. At the window he watched as sheets of rain poured off the rickety porch. No doubt this area needed a gully washer, but could the cottage handle the storm? He knew the main house was stable, but what about the barn and the outer buildings? He made a mental note to check things out in the morning.

His concern was still on tonight…the storm. He looked toward the house and saw a light in Maura's bedroom. Was she frightened? Were the kids? He shook his head, telling himself they weren't his to worry about. Maura had made it clear several times that she could handle things on her own. She didn't need him…or any man.

How was he supposed to turn his feelings off? They'd been more or less been cohabiting for the past six weeks. They shared breakfast and supper together daily. He knew the name of Kelly's favorite doll, Suzy, and that Jeff had a talent for drawing pictures. For a six-year-old, he was pretty good, a talent he came by naturally.

He knew Maura had tried to shield more of herself from him. There was no doubt, she was an artistic person. Her flower arrangements had showed that, along with all the other special touches she'd made around the old house. He glanced over his shoulder, even in the cottage he could feel Maura's presence. She had turned the small, dingy rooms into an inviting place. She had found an old quilt in the attic. After washing it, she spread the colorful patchwork on his bed, and arranged fresh flowers on the scarred nightstand every time she came down to clean.

Everywhere he turned there was something to remind him of Maura. He should know from past experience with Amanda that he shouldn't get involved only to have her and the kids walk out of his life. But how could he keep Maura out of his head when she was in every nook and cranny of his life…of his heart?

There was another flash of lightning, along with a gust of wind, causing the cottage to shudder under its power. Wyatt drew a breath as he listened to the rain pelting down on his fragile roof. As a rule he liked storms. This one he wished was gone. But according to the weatherman, the storm front was going to last a while. Any more of these strong winds… He looked out just in time to see a part of the porch roof lift.

"Damn. I don't need this." He ran into the bedroom, grabbed his shirt and pulled it on. When he heard a crash he hurried faster. He'd barely got his feet into his boots when he heard the sound of wood splitting. Hurrying back to the living room, he found water streaming in through a large hole in the roof that had been torn away. He grabbed a few things, and took off toward the house.

And Maura.

Maura sat on the bed trying to go over her monthly expenses. No matter what she did, she couldn't scrape together more than four hundred dollars a month for rent. She couldn't get even a one bedroom apartment that cheap, and she would still need first and last and a security deposit just to move in.

And what about utilities? She didn't have any money for them. This house already had the electricity and the water on. She paid for the phone herself, knowing she needed to be able to call for help. Just in case.

She could probably get state aid for Jeff and Kelly. Maybe she should call her mother. She shook her head. No, Grace Howell had turned her down before, not even wanting to see her own grandchildren.

A flash of lightning lit up the sky, making her more uncomfortable. She had few choices. No matter how many times she went over her finances, the bottom line never changed. The only other thing she could come up with was to ask Wyatt if she could rent the cottage. It was small but there were two bedrooms. Maybe he would let her continue to cook his meals and do his laundry for a cut in the rent. She didn't want to impose on the man any longer, but she didn't have any other options.

With another lightning flash, the lights flickered,

then went out all together. Maura froze momentarily. She hated the dark, a reminder of how she'd tried to hide from Darren, but he'd always found her. She pushed the memory from her head and quickly got out of bed and lit the candle on the dresser. Once the soft glow appeared, she went to check on the kids. Luckily they were still asleep. She went downstairs to make sure things were secure. That was when she heard the pounding on the back door. She hurried through the kitchen and found Wyatt on the porch.

"Wyatt! What happened?" She stepped back to let him enter the dark kitchen.

He dropped the bundled quilt on the table, pulled off his hat and wiped the rain from his face. "The damn roof blew off the cottage."

"Oh, no," she cried, examining him more closely. "Were you hurt?"

"No, but the place is in shambles," he said. "Looks like I'm going to have to move back in here."

Maura swallowed her dismay. "Of course you can stay the night. Then tomorrow you can fix the roof."

"It's going to take longer than a day or two. I don't have the time to put in on repairing the structure. Don't worry, I figure I can stay in the small room off the kitchen." He pointed through the doorway.

"But it's a mess in there," she said. "Boxes and junk are piled everywhere." She had put a lot of it there herself.

"Then I guess I'll just have to clean it out," he said. "I'll buy a new bed and it'll be fine."

Although the room was dark, Wyatt could see Maura's discomfort. "Is there something wrong?"

"It's just that with all of us living here…it's not right. I think the kids and I should leave."

"And go where?" he asked.

"That's not your worry. We shouldn't have stayed here this long anyway."

She started to walk away and Wyatt stopped her. "Maura what's the real reason? Surely you're not afraid that I'll try something..."

She glanced away. "No. No, but people will talk..."

"Then let them. Besides, I stayed here when I hurt my back. In *your* bed."

"But that was different. You were injured."

He released a long breath. "Other than sleeping in the barn, I don't have a choice, Maura."

She still didn't look convinced. "How long before the roof can be repaired?"

"It's not going to be a simple job. The structure has damage. But the repairs are going to have to wait. My stock will be arriving in a few days."

This time she sighed. Where were she and the kids going to live now? "But...you don't understand."

"I guess I don't, Maura," he said. He was too tired to think about it tonight and a little hurt that she was so resistant to letting him stay. "I'll sleep on the sofa, unless you object to that, too." Not waiting for her answer, he marched into the dark living room and spread the quilt on the sofa.

She followed him. "I'm sorry, Wyatt. It's not fair to keep you out of your own home. It's just that I don't want the kids to get any ideas."

He turned around to find Maura standing there in her long cotton gown, the candle casting a soft glow over her face. She looked much the same as she had the night he first arrived, the same night he'd first been aroused by her.

"What kind of ideas?"

"I don't want them to think that you'll always be a part of their lives," she confessed. "I also don't want them to think that you're a live-in boyfriend. I was married to their father, and he was the only man in our lives... until you."

Wyatt stepped closer. "You don't want people to think you're giving me special favors...in lieu of rent."

Even in the dim candlelight, he could see her blush.

He wanted so badly to pull her into his arms. "Maura, please believe me, I would never ask you... I care about you and the kids too much. But with this situation, I can't see there's any other answer. If you're worried about what people will think, tell 'em...that we're... engaged."

She gasped. "Oh, Wyatt. No!"

For some reason her reaction hurt. "Why? Jack Randell's bastard son isn't good enough?"

She looked as if he'd slapped her. "How could you think that? It's just that the kids would begin to get used to you being around all the time. And since we're leaving..."

He moved closer. "Why do you have to go, Maura? Why can't you stay here?"

"Because, this is your house, and you need to move in. The kids and I will just crowd you."

He raised an eyebrow. "Have I complained?"

"No, but it still isn't right."

His gaze met hers. "What if I wanted you to stay?"

Her breath caught. "But you can't want me..."

The hell he couldn't. He released a frustrated breath. "Ah, Maura, don't you know how special you are? How beautiful? Any man would be thrilled to have you in his life." He took the candle from her hand and set it on the coffee table, then reached out and cupped her cheek. He felt her tremble. "I don't know what your ex did to you, but not every man is cruel." She started to pull away, but he wouldn't let her. He bent his head, then paused before his mouth touched hers. She sucked in her breath. "Maura, let me show you how a man should treat a woman."

"Wyatt…" She breathed his name as her eyes closed.

Slowly, he drew her into his arms. "I would never hurt you, Maura. Never…"

The first kiss was gentle, then he pulled back, then dipped his head again and nibbled gently on her lower lip. "You taste good," he whispered, trying to slow his own fervor. It was difficult. "Ever since that first time I kissed you, I wanted to again and again."

Her gaze met his. He could see desire in those incredible whiskey-colored eyes of hers, but she wasn't ready to believe him. He didn't blame her. Trust came hard for him, too. He needed to take things slow, for the both of them. But right now, he wasn't exactly thinking rationally. Not when Maura was tempting him.

"Put your hands on me, Maura. Touch me."

His shirt hung open and he was still wet from the rain. When her warm fingers raked across his flesh he nearly came apart. He groaned and placed his hands over hers. "Woman, you do unbelievable things to me."

"Really?" She sounded surprised.

"Really," he repeated, right before he captured her mouth in another kiss. When she didn't resist, he ran his tongue over the seam of her lips. With a soft whimper, she opened for him and allowed him inside to taste her again. By the time he finally broke off the kiss, they were both breathing hard.

He smiled, despite his agony. "That was nice."

"Nice," she repeated, then surprised him when she raised up on her toes and pressed her mouth to his. He couldn't resist the invitation to intensify the kiss. This time she kissed him back, mimicking everything he did to her. When he reached out to touch her breasts, she gasped.

A lightning flash illuminated the room momentarily. "I want you, Maura."

"Wyatt…" She whispered his name when suddenly the sound of a child's cry filled the room.

She jerked back. "Kelly." Grabbing the candle, Maura hurried upstairs and Wyatt followed her.

They reached the bedroom to find the tiny girl sitting up in bed sobbing.

"I'm scared, Mommy," Kelly cried. "I'm scared a bad man is coming to get me."

"Shh, baby," her mother soothed her, wrapping her arms around her child. "You're okay now."

"I'm here, too, princess," Wyatt said as he moved to the bed. "And I'm not going to let anything bad happen to you."

Wyatt looked down at Maura holding her child. Something tightened around his heart and he knew that he'd kill anyone who would ever try to hurt them.

Wyatt woke up early the next morning to bright sunlight and found last night's storm had left a lot of damage in its wake. He went out to examine the destruction. The newly painted house had held up very well, but he'd lost a few trees and the cottage had sustained a lot of damage. The repairs were going to take a lot more time and money than he wanted to spend at the moment.

He needed to focus his energy on other things. He had two days to get the barn and corrals ready for the horses, Rock-a-Billy and Stormy Weather. His friend, Bud Wilks, was also bringing along a few other horses that he told Wyatt were promising. Since Bud was going to be his manager, Wyatt trusted his judgement on the stock. He couldn't help but be excited about how things were moving forward, but at the moment bucking horses were the last thing on his mind.

Maura was the first.

What would have happened last night if Kelly hadn't woken up? Would Maura have let him make love to her? Deep down, he knew she wasn't ready. Maybe she'd never be ready to let him into her life. He knew that she'd been abused by her husband. Maybe she would never let another man get close again. She had kissed him back. Did he want to go to the next step? He had to be damn sure that he wanted it all. Maura Wells wasn't the kind of woman a man took to bed and just walked away from.

Wyatt wasn't sure about love. He'd been hurt before and decided that a permanent relationship might not be in the cards for him. All he knew was that he wanted Maura here, in his life.

Kelly pushed open the screen door and stepped out to the porch. The little pixie was so cute dressed in a little red skirt and white shirt. Maura wasn't the only female in the house who had stolen his heart.

"Hi, Wyatt." She smiled shyly. "Mom says that breakfast is ready."

"It is?" he said walking toward her. "What are we having this morning?"

"Mommy's fixin' me pancakes 'cause I got scared last night."

He sat down on the edge of the porch. "I know. Did you have a bad dream?"

She nodded. Tears filled her beautiful eyes. "Don't let the bad man get me, Wyatt, please."

He took her in his arms. "Shh, princess. I promise, I'll never let anyone hurt you."

Kelly's tiny arms circled his neck. "Good. You know what?"

"What?"

"I wish we can stay here forever and ever. So I don't hafta be scared anymore."

Wyatt choked back an angry comment. What kind of father had Maura's ex been? "I'm not sure your mother will go for that idea."

"You could marry Mommy."

Whoa. How was he going to answer that one? Think quick. "How can I marry your mother when I'm plannin' to marry you?"

She giggled. "But I'm a little girl."

"Then I'll just wait until you grow up."

Maura called for her daughter and Kelly got up and headed inside. Wyatt sat for a while. Marriage. Not just to take a wife, but if he wanted Maura, he had a ready-made family.

He thought about his own mother, raising him and Dylan without any help from the man who'd fathered them. Who didn't want them. Growing up, Wyatt had always felt there was part of him missing, never knowing exactly who he was. Now that he learned about Randell, he didn't feel any better. His chest tightened. Maybe that's the reason he seemed to relate to Jeff and Kelly.

All kids need a father who cares.

Realizing the direction of his thoughts, he shook away

the crazy notion. What the hell did he know about being someone's daddy?

Wyatt stood and went into the kitchen and found Maura at the stove. She was dressed for work in a dark skirt and a fitted white cotton top. Her blond hair was pulled away from her face and held with clips. She looked tired. She probably hadn't gotten any more sleep than he had.

She finally glanced at him and his pulse rate sped up. He smiled. "Good morning."

"Good morning," she said. "Was there any more damage from the storm?"

He shook his head and sat down in his usual seat at the table. "Just the cottage and a few trees."

Maura handed him a mug of coffee. "Pancakes all right?"

"They're my favorite." He winked at Kelly who was already eating. Jeff walked into the room and sat down.

"How did you sleep, Jeff?" Wyatt asked. "Did the storm wake you?"

"No, I wasn't scared." he insisted a little too quickly.

"I sure was," Wyatt admitted. "When the roof blew off the cottage and I came running to the house."

"Wyatt's gonna live with us," Kelly said. She pointed toward the utility room. "He's sleeping in there."

Jeff jerked his attention back to Wyatt. "Are you staying here for good? Do we have to leave?"

Wyatt shook his head seeing the boy's panic. "No, you don't have to leave. I just need a place to sleep until the cottage gets repaired. Maybe we can work on it together. What do ya say, Jeff?"

He shrugged. "Maybe." He turned to his mother. "You sure we're not leaving?"

She peered at Wyatt for a moment. "You know we can't stay here permanently." She sighed. "I'm going to look for apartments after work."

"But Mom, I want to live here," Kelly said. "My room is pretty and Wyatt says we can stay."

"Kelly, finish your breakfast."

"I don't want any more," she said and lowered her head.

"Then go upstairs and brush your teeth. Jeff, you, too."

The boy started to speak, then changed his mind. "C'mon, Kelly. I'll help you," he said and took his sister's hand and they left the kitchen.

When had Maura made the decision to leave? Wyatt wondered. "Why are you doing this to the kids?" Wyatt asked. To me? "I told you that you can stay here as long as you need."

"And I told you that I can't keep taking your charity."

"It's not charity, dammit! You work harder than two people around here. Can't we share this large house?"

"Can't you see that it's only going to be harder when I have to go? And I was planning to leave. I'd decided to ask you about renting the cottage, but as of now it looks like I can't do that." She got up from the table and turned away from him.

Wyatt got up, too. "Maura, please. I care about you and the kids. Is it because I kissed you last night?"

"That was a mistake," she said, then moved across the room. "I don't want you to think that just because I'm handy I'll go to bed with you."

"And you honestly believe that I would take advantage of you like that? In the past few weeks, have I tried to take advantage of our situation? I thought that kiss was mutual. I thought you wanted it as much as I did. I guess I read your signals wrong." He stood behind her, but kept his hands to himself.

"Believe me, Maura. I would never intentionally do anything to hurt you or the kids." He stared at her stiff back, knowing he wasn't getting through to her. "Ah, hell, think what you want." He started for the back door, then stopped. "Just don't mistake me for your ex-husband."

Two days later, Maura was going stir crazy. She hadn't seen Wyatt since the scene in the kitchen. She knew she might have been a little unfair to him. He was right; he wasn't anything remotely like Darren. But that was just it. What if Darren *did* find her? Knowing her ex-husband, he wouldn't stop until he got what he wanted: revenge. How could she let someone as kind and wonderful as Wyatt into the mess she'd made of her life?

But she couldn't stay away from him any longer. With her children spending the day with Abby and her kids, she went in search of him. Not finding him at the cottage, she wandered down to the barn. Inside, she saw that each stall had been cleaned out and lined with fresh straw.

She walked down the center aisle, following the sound of a country and western song coming from the tack room. The door was open and she found the place to be neat and clean. A scarred desk was along one wall on top was a phone and several folders were stacked and orderly. Another wall was a cot where Wyatt sat busy polishing one of the bridles that hung on the wall.

Dressed in faded jeans and a chambray shirt, he looked wonderful. Her stomach began to flutter. Oh, how she'd missed him.

He looked up, no doubt surprised to see her. "Maura, is something wrong?" He got up from the bunk.

She shook her head, biting at her lip. "Oh, Wyatt, this is where you've been sleeping. I feel so awful."

Wyatt went to her, still having trouble believing that she came to him. "It's all right, Maura. It hasn't been so bad. I've cleaned up the place pretty good," he said, recalling the late hours he spent on the room when he couldn't sleep.

"I'm sorry," she said, her eyes sad. "Please, come back to the house. You belong there."

He wanted that more than anything. "No, because if I do, you'll leave. And I don't want you to leave."

"I don't want to leave...either." A lone tear found its way down her cheek. "I was scarred, Wyatt." She swiped at the moisture on her face. "There are things...you don't know about my life."

"No, I don't," he confirmed, "but I figure when you're ready you'll tell me."

"I don't know if I'll ever be able to."

"That's okay, too." He brushed a wayward curl from her face, aching to take her in his arms. "I'm not going anywhere." He just realized that he was making a commitment to her.

"Will you move back to the house?"

"Why should I?"

"Because I don't care what people say. I want you to."

Wyatt grinned. "That's all I wanted to hear." He sobered. "I don't want you to feel uncomfortable with me around."

Being uncomfortable wasn't what Maura was worried about. She didn't need to get involved with this man, for his sake more than hers. But she couldn't seem to stop the feelings he created in her. "I won't be uncomfortable," she fibbed. "But I think we shouldn't… I mean we can't let what happened the other night happen again."

He cocked an eyebrow. "Are you talking about the kiss?"

She nodded.

"The kiss that we both enjoyed, and I might add seemed to take a lot of pleasure in."

"Wyatt, please! I have children who could be watching."

"Dammit, woman. I happen to like kissing you."

She sucked in a breath as a shiver ran through her. She did, too. No, she couldn't let anything more happen.

Wyatt stepped closer. "Okay, but how about one last kiss?" he asked in a low husky voice as he lowered his head. He paused just inches from her.

The sound of a throat being cleared caused them both to turn to the door and found Hank Barrett standing in the doorway.

"Hank," Maura said as heat flooded her face. "I didn't know you were coming by."

"I apologize for disturbing you." Hank's grin widened.

Wyatt refused to let Maura leave his side. "What can I do for you, Hank?"

"Well, first of all, there seems to be a caravan of trucks coming up your driveway."

"So they finally made it," Wyatt said, then took off. Once outside the barn he spotted Bud's green truck and horse trailer. Behind him was his friend, Dusty Adams, with another truck and trailer.

Wyatt went to greet Bud. "Hey, welcome to Texas. Have any trouble getting here?"

"Thanks. We hit some bad weather that slowed us down a little. I think we should get these fellas unloaded."

"Sure. Let's put them in the corral so they can get some exercise." Wyatt followed Bud to the trailer and they dropped the gate. He walked up the ramp and unhooked the lead rope to the bay horse and backed him out. Bud followed with the buckskin. Wyatt stopped when he noticed Hank's interest in the spirited animals.

"Hank, meet Stormy Weather, and this guy is Rock-a-Billy. These two are some of the best bucking broncs around." He patted the animal on his neck. "I especially have high hopes for this guy. Could be a contender for horse of the year."

Hank ran his hand over the hind quarters as the horse danced sideways. "How do you feel about trying him out locally?"

"Where would that be?"

"At the Annual Circle B Rodeo."

Chapter 8

Two days later, Wyatt stood at the pasture fence and watched his horses graze. They seemed to be getting used to their new home, but they weren't going to be lazing around the ranch for long. Eventually, they'd be making money for him. He'd already signed contracts for two local rodeos for the early spring. Next month, they were headed to southern Arizona, then on to California for bigger events. He was still small time, but hopefully that would change when word of Stormy Weather and Rock-a-Billy got around.

There was no doubt in Wyatt's mind that in a few months, his two broncs would make a name for him. He'd been on the rodeo circuit all his life and he'd learned a few things about good stock. The one and only good thing about Earl Keys, the gruff old man had taught him the business. And in his gut, Wyatt knew these horses had what it took.

A cloud of dust kicked up in the distance and alerted Wyatt that someone was headed for the ranch. Hank Barrett's truck pulled up next to the barn and he climbed out. With his posture erect, the large man tugged on his Stetson, then started his long sure strides toward Wyatt. Hank didn't look anywhere near his age.

"Good morning," the older rancher said.

"Good morning." Wyatt returned. "You're out early."

"I hope you don't mind. I forget that not everyone is up with the sun."

"I was up. I have stock to feed now."

Hank squinted against the bright sun as he looked around. "This place is shapin' up real good. If I didn't know better, I'd swear your granddad, John Randell, was still runnin' things. All you need is a few hundred head of good Texas steers."

Wyatt laughed. "I'm not a rancher, Hank."

"Well, your grandpa John was a helluva one. He was also a good friend of mine." Hank sobered. "It's a shame his son, Jack, didn't inherit a few of his qualities."

"Does anyone know where he is?"

The lines around Hank's hazel eyes deepened as he squinted into the sun. "Jack Randell isn't exactly welcome in these parts. There's a few people who still believe that a cattle rustler should be strung up. That might not be the news you want to hear, but you had to know that your daddy's character was…questionable. He was married when he was with your mother."

"Yeah, but kids always have silly notions about turning their old man into a hero." Wyatt couldn't believe he was spilling his guts.

"None of us are perfect, son. I did the best I could with the boys. If you're looking for a hero, like I said, your granddaddy was quite a man."

Wyatt was amazed how easily Hank had ac- cepted him.

Hank gave him a questioning look. "Something wrong?"

Wyatt shook his head. "It's just that since I've arrived here, you've treated me so fairly. You don't seem to think I have some ulterior motive."

The older rancher turned to the pasture, rested his arms across the top fence railing and looked out at the horses. "I'm not as trusting as you might think. When Jared showed up here, I did some checking. Jared showed me the private investigator's report on you and Dylan. I was curious about you buying this place, but you were right. The price was too good to pass up." He tossed a glance toward Wyatt. "My concern has always been the same. I don't want Chance, Cade and Travis hurt. They've gone through hell because of Jack."

Wyatt found he truly envied his half brothers to have this man's love. "They consider you their father."

Emotion showed in Hank's eyes. "And I love them as if they were my own. I've always said you don't have to be blood to be family. About a year ago I discovered that I had fathered a child years ago, a daughter. After her mother died, Josie came to the ranch to find me." He smiled. "She's married to Travis."

"It must be nice to have a large family."

"There's nothing stopping you from having the same," Hank said. He nodded toward the house. "I know there's one pretty filly that's already caught your eye."

Wyatt was confused about how he felt about Maura.

"A ready-made family might be a little more than I can take on."

Hank shrugged. "I'd call it a bonus. That's how Chance got Katie Rose and Travis got Elissa Mae. Kids don't ask for blood tests from their parents, just love and being there for them."

"How does a man know if he can handle the job?"

"How hard is it to give to a boy who already idolizes you and a little girl who's crazy about you?"

Wyatt couldn't think of anything to say.

"And Maura has had enough pain to last a lifetime. She needs a gentle touch and a man who is willing to love her. But I guess if you're not up to the task, there'll be someone who'll be willing to give her what she needs."

Wyatt stiffened, hating the possibility. He didn't want another man kissing her, making love to her.

Just then Maura walked out the back door with Kelly. She was headed to work. That meant that she'd be gone all day. She waved and helped Kelly into the car, then drove off.

"This place must get pretty lonely with no one around all day. Just think about the nights once Maura and the kids leave."

"I know what you're trying to do, Hank," Wyatt said. And dammit, it was working.

"Just stating some facts," Hank assured him. "I came over to see if you'll let me contract your stock for the Circle B Rodeo."

"You haven't gotten your rough-stock supplier yet?"

"We've had some problems, so I told them to forget it." He sighed. "I know it's a small time rodeo, Wyatt, but I thought maybe you'd want to show off your new broncs."

"Sounds good. And I'll do it with one condition—that you stop playing matchmaker."

"Oh, I don't have to play anything." The man grinned. "You're already a goner. You just haven't admitted it yet."

"Mom, you're not listening to me," Jeff insisted.

"What, honey?" Maura broke out of her reverie. "Did you say something?

"You need to sign my printing homework."

She took the pencil from Jeff and wrote her name on the space available. "I'm sorry, I must be tired."

"That's okay. I know you work hard."

Maura was happy that her son thought so. But the real reason she had been so absentminded was Wyatt. Her gaze had been glued to the back door, wondering when he was going to come in for the night. It seemed he'd been spending more and more time away from the house. She understood he had animals to care for, but that didn't change the fact that she missed him, especially after Jeff and Kelly went to bed.

And she was alone.

Not that she didn't have enough work to keep her busy with cooking and the kids. She needed to concentrate on her general business assignments and help Jeff with his schoolwork, not think about a rodeo cowboy.

Suddenly the screen door opened, Wyatt walked in and placed his hat on a nearby hook. Maura's breath caught as her hungry gaze moved over him. He was in dirty, worn jeans and a shirt that had been torn and there was a day's growth of whiskers covering his square jaw. He looked wonderful.

"Sorry, I didn't mean to disturb you," he said. "I'll just

wash up and get out of your hair." He went to the sink and began washing his hands.

Jeff got up from the chair. "I finished my words. See?"

Wyatt smiled. "Hey, that's pretty good." He grabbed the towel off the rack and wiped his hands.

"Now, will you let me see the bulls?" the boy asked.

Wyatt hung up the towel. "How about tomorrow after you get home?"

Jeff frowned. "But it's dark then."

"Then you'll have to wait until Saturday," Maura said.

Wyatt saw the boy's disappointment, but there wasn't much he could do. "Sorry, Jeff, I guess that's how it has to be. But I'll have another surprise for you and your sister by then."

The boy's eyes lit up, reminding Wyatt of Maura. "What?"

"If I tell you, it won't be a surprise, will it?"

"But Saturday is two days away."

"Maybe you better get to bed so it'll come faster," his mother said and waved him toward the door. "I'll be up shortly."

Jeff smiled at Wyatt. "Night." He hurried off.

Wyatt turned to Maura, but she quickly glanced away and busied herself putting Jeff's homework in his backpack.

"Maura, are you worried about having the bulls here?"

"I'm not crazy about them, but it's your business."

"I've made sure they're in the best reinforced pens and the pasture is secured, too. They aren't going to get out. Besides, if they aren't hassled they're pretty mild."

She gave him an incredulous look. "Even I'm not that naive."

"Maura, it's safe. I've taken every precaution. Believe

me, for what I paid for them, I don't want those bulls out any more than you do."

Wyatt had built the bulls' pen way behind the barn to keep them out of view of the house. With Bud here to care for the stock until he left for the circuit at the beginning of the year, Wyatt had help getting more things done around the ranch. First on the list was to repair the cottage, then maybe build a bunkhouse so he could hire on help. And Wyatt had been thinking a lot about Hank's idea of raising cattle.

Maura finally nodded. "I guess you're right," she admitted, then glanced away.

"Is there something else bothering you?" She hadn't really looked at him since the day in the barn when he'd nearly kissed her. That was seven long days ago.

"I went to the paint store today and picked out some color chips for the living room and dining room walls. They're in your room," she said.

"Good, I'll have a look, but I'm going to leave the choosing up to you. So what else is bothering you?"

"I know you've been busy, but I was wondering if I've done something to make you angry."

Not angry, but frustrated as hell. He leaned against the old sink to keep from pulling her into his arms and showing her how badly he wanted her.

"No, you didn't do anything wrong," he said. "I've just been busy with the stock." The distraction still hadn't kept him from thinking about her. But he had to be fair to Maura. She needed a man who was ready to give her a commitment. He wasn't sure he was that man. He'd been down that road and ended up getting burned. But dammit, that didn't stop him from wanting her.

"Maura, I care about you…"

She raised those brown eyes to his and he had to swallow the sudden dryness in his throat. "But I don't think either of us are ready for something long-term."

He watched as she bit down on her lower lip, and he remembered how sweet she tasted. He held on to his resolve and kept his distance.

"Of course you're right," she agreed. "And I have children to think about." She went to the table and picked up the clutter. "I need to go check on Jeff and Kelly." Books hugged against her chest like a shield, she faced him "So... I guess I'll see you in the morning. Good night."

An empty feeling came over Wyatt as he watched Maura walk out of the room. No matter how much he cared for her, he had to let her go. He wasn't ready to risk his heart again, but he knew deep down that it was already too late. Maura Wells had already stolen it.

Saturday morning an excited Jeff and Kelly were out of bed at dawn. Maura had overslept and when she reached the kitchen, Wyatt had already started breakfast for Bud and the kids.

She hugged her robe tighter. "I'm sorry. I guess I forgot to set my alarm." She walked to the stove and tried to take over for Wyatt. He nudged her away.

"Why don't you let me handle it this morning?"

"Yeah, Mom," Kelly chimed in. "We're going to make breakfast. Scrambled eggs and bacon."

"It's a cowboy's breakfast," Jeff added.

Wyatt winked at her. "Here, have some coffee." He handed her a mug. "Why don't you go and take some time for yourself? We have things under control here."

She glanced down at robe. "Do I look that bad?"

He turned her around, back to where she'd come from.

"No, you look too good," he whispered against her ear, causing little shivers along her skin. "Now go and change, and I'll have a surprise for you when you get back."

After breakfast and with the kitchen cleaned in record time, Wyatt and Bud asked for ten minutes before she brought the kids down to the barn. Both Jeff and Kelly were going crazy by the time Maura told them it was time to go.

Jeff cheered as he banged open the screen door and ran out to the porch, then stopped and came back to help his sister.

Maura could feel her own excitement as she hurried to keep up. At the barn door, Maura called out. "Wyatt, we're here," she said, recalling that she hadn't been inside since the day she'd asked Wyatt to move back into the house. That was ten days ago.

Wyatt came toward them. "You guys ready?"

"Yes!" Jeff called.

"Oh, yes, Wyatt," Kelly said as she jumped up and down.

"Okay, Bud bring out Sandy."

The slightly built cowboy with the easy smile walked out of the shadows leading a caramel-colored pony with a bleached-blond mane and tail. She was saddled and ready to take riders.

Neither Jeff and Kelly could contain their excitement. Maura wasn't sure what to do as she looked at Wyatt.

"This is Sandy," he said, "She's from the Circle B. Hank said she hasn't been ridden much lately and he thinks she needed a couple of kids to spend time with."

"So she's used to kids?" Maura asked, nodding toward the small animal.

"She's as gentle as an old dog." He rubbed the pony's neck, then showed Kelly and Jeff how to pet her.

"See, Mom, Sandy likes me," Kelly said and demonstrated by rubbing the animal's face.

"Here, feed her some sugar," Wyatt gave each child one cube and demonstrated how to feed the pony.

"Mom, can we ride her?" Jeff asked.

Wyatt cocked an eyebrow as if asking for her okay. She knew in her heart that he'd never put her children in danger. It sometimes amazed her how much she trusted him.

"I think it will be all right, if Wyatt walks with you around the corral."

"That's what I planned," he promised.

"Ladies first." Wyatt lifted Kelly onto the saddle and put her feet into the stirrups, then started to lead the pony out of the barn. As he passed Maura, he leaned down and said, "Don't go wandering off, I have plans for you later."

Another tingle shot through Maura as she took her son's hand and walked to the corral fence. They climbed onto the top railing. She watched the kids' excitement as Wyatt took turns with them both. Maura's trust grew and she allowed Jeff to take the pony's reins and go on his own, as long as Wyatt was there beside the animal.

"Mommy, look," Kelly cried and she pointed to the barn.

Over her shoulder, Maura turned and saw Bud come out leading another horse. This time it was a big, black stallion.

"Wyatt, is that your horse Raven?" Jeff asked.

"That's him." Wyatt grinned proudly. "He got here yesterday while you were at school."

How did the kids know about Wyatt's horse? The realization made Maura feel a little left out.

Wyatt had Jeff climb down off the pony, then he am-
bled over and swapped animals with Bud. Both children
sat with her on the railing. "Wyatt, make him do his
tricks," Jeff called out.

They watched as Wyatt took the animal to the center
of the arena. "What do you say, Raven? You want to do
some tricks for Maura, Jeff and Kelly?"

The horse began moving his head up and down, making the kids laugh. Then Wyatt placed his booted foot
into the stirrup and easily swung into the saddle. With
a cocky grin that would leave any woman weak-kneed,
Wyatt adjusted his hat, then tugged on the reins and the
horse spun around in a circle. When he moved the reins
to the other side and the horse reversed directions. Jeff
and Kelly clapped their hands. Raven had only begun.
He reared back, kicking dust up. Then the magnificent
animal rose on his hind legs, peddling his front legs in
the air. The kids went crazy and Maura was captivated
with the performance. But her interest was focused on
the cowboy seated on the powerful animal.

Wyatt enjoyed watching the kids having a good time.
He realized, too, how much he'd missed having Raven
around this past month. Finally he had found a permanent home for both of them.

"Do some more tricks, Wyatt," Kelly cried.

Wyatt decided that Maura had been missing out on
all the fun. He walked the horse to the railing. "Oh, I
think it's time that your mother had a chance to ride."
He reached over and wrapped his arm around Maura's
waist, plucking her from the railing and onto the horse.

She gasped. "Wyatt, no, I can't."

"Just relax," he said as he held her slender body in front of his. "Now, swing your leg over the saddle. That's it," he coaxed. "Just sit down in front of me." He gave her the saddle and he slipped onto the rump of the horse. "Wyatt, you're crazy!" she exclaimed.

He wrapped his arms around her rib cage, just under her breasts and his body stirred instantly. Yeah, he was crazy. He certainly wasn't listening to his common sense. But no matter how hard he tried to stay away, he was drawn to her. Was that so bad? Was it so bad that he wanted her, he wanted to touch her...to hold her? He looked at the Jeff and Kelly sitting on the fence and felt a strange protectiveness toward them. Was this how it felt to have a real family? If so, he liked it. A lot.

"Why don't we do a little showing off for Jeff and Kelly?"

"I want to get down," she said tensely.

"Maura, you have to know that I would never let anything happen to you," he whispered against her ear, inhaling the clean scent of her hair, feeling her softness against him.

Maura looked over her shoulder, her dark eyes sensual, yet trusting. "I know," she said and didn't pull back. She was so close all he had to do was move mere inches and he could kiss that tempting mouth of hers. Realizing what he was thinking, he straightened and patted the horse's neck.

"Hey, Raven here is a sweet guy. Aren't you, buddy?"

The animal raised his head up and whinnied loudly. Everyone laughed, including Maura. Finally she relaxed back against him.

Then she smiled, sending his pulse pounding loudly in his ears. "Okay, cowboy, take me for a ride," she said.

"My pleasure, ma'am," he said, taking the reins and moving closer to her, cuddling her against his chest. Oh, he was enjoying this.

"This is fun."

"It's more fun if you take the reins." He demonstrated how to hold the leather straps. "Now, you're in control."

"What do I do?"

"Raven responds to both touch and voice commands. If you move the reins right or left he'll go in that direction. Make a clicking sound with your tongue and he walks. Kick your heels into his side and he'll take off. Tug on the reins and he'll stop."

"So you just have to know what gear to put him in," Maura said, trying to hide a smile.

Wyatt was dumbfounded hearing Maura's joke. And he wondered how long it had been since she took time to enjoy herself. He poked her in the ribs and discovered she was ticklish and had a contagious laugh.

"You should do that more often."

"What's that?" She laughed again. "Ride a horse?"

"That, too, but I meant laugh." He tugged his hat lower and watched her go through the routine. She seemed pretty pleased with herself once she had circled the corral on her own.

"Pretty good for a greenhorn."

She sucked in a breath. "I'd say it's *very* good for my first time on a horse."

"Yeah, Mom, you're great," Jeff said.

"Hey, Maura," Bud called to her, holding the pony's reins. "Is it okay if I let the kids help me brush down Sandy?"

"I guess it's okay," she said. "Jeff, watch your sister,

and Kelly, stay with Jeff." Both children nodded and followed Bud and the small horse into the barn.

"You don't have to worry, Bud'll take care of them."

She released a sigh. "It's just that they've never been around animals."

"You lived in the city all your life?"

"Yes, and the kids, too. They've never even had a dog."

"I take it your husband didn't like animals." Wyatt felt Maura stiffen. "Hey, I'm not trying to pry, just making conversation."

"No, Darren didn't like animals…or kids."

Raven shifted and Wyatt set him walking again. "Maybe it's better for all of you that he's out of your life."

"I wish that were true," she mumbled.

He stopped the horse in the shade beside the barn. "Maura, I know that you haven't talked much about your marriage, and I'm not going to ask anything about the past. But I have to know, would you ever consider going back to him?"

Her eyes grew large and filled with tears. "Never! I'll do anything to keep him away from the kids."

"Ssh…" Wyatt wrapped his arms around her and pulled her trembling body against his chest. "I won't let him hurt you, Maura. Never again," he promised.

"You don't know him, Wyatt, or what he's capable of doing."

"I know as long as I'm around, he's never going to hurt you or the kids." God, he ached to get his hands on this guy.

Maura's gaze locked with his. "You can't make a promise like that, Wyatt. Darren *will* come after me. He swore he would, so I can't stay in one place too long. It would be better if I moved on."

Wyatt felt a panic like never before experienced, not even when Amanda left him. "You can't run away."

"It is if it's the only way I can survive. I have my children to think about."

"Then don't leave. I can protect you here. Bud's going to help me repair the cottage. It should only take a few weeks and then you and the kids can move in."

He watched her eyes light up. "I thought you said you weren't going to do the work just yet."

"If it keeps you safe and here, I'll do about anything. So I'll rent it to you. Just stay, Maura."

"But—I—"

"Just listen a minute. I'm not asking you to jump into anything. Just spend some time with you."

She hesitated for another second. "I'd like that," she finally said.

He released a breath. "Okay, how about the Circle B Rodeo?"

"What about it?"

"How about if I ask you to go…as my date?"

Chapter 9

Hank stood next to the corral and watched as the men finished setting up the stock pens for the day's events. He'd been up since 4:00 a.m. making sure everything was ready, and Chance, Cade and Travis had worked until well after midnight last night.

Funny, the Circle B Rodeo had started out as a way to get the boys involved in something and over the last twenty years it had grown into a full-fledged rodeo. Although all the events were for amateurs, more and more of the local ranch hands entered each year and over three hundred people were expected to attend today. Just the thought of all those people to feed made Hank tired, but he loved putting on this rodeo. At sixty-six, he had considered retiring, handing the reins over to the boys to continue the tradition. He sighed. But he wasn't ready to let it go just yet.

Hearing his name called, Hank turned to see Ella hurrying toward him. She was dressed in her usual jeans and Western blouse. Her gray hair was cut short and combed away from her heart-shaped face. Nearly sixty, she was a handsome woman with expressive eyes. It had taken him awhile but he'd learned to read her moods, and stayed out of her way when she got out of sorts.

For the past twenty-five years she had run the house like a drill sergeant, but he'd never questioned her love for Chance, Cade and Travis. She'd raised those boys as if they were her own, and treated the grandkids the same. The woman had been around for so long he couldn't imagine the place without her. "Hank, I need some of the men to help set up tables." She placed her hands on her hips. "Those high-school kids Chance hired never showed this morning. And I don't want any of the ladies to lift heavy things."

"I don't, either," he said. "They should be concentrating on the food."

She shook her head, fighting a smile, as she glanced at his waistline. He knew it drove her crazy that he never put on any weight. "Is that all you ever think about? Food?" she demanded.

"On a day like today, I get to sample heaven. Did Claire Watson bring her cheesy potatoes?"

Ella huffed. "Of course. That woman would do anything to catch herself a man."

Hank knew that was true, and he steered clear of widow Watson, but not of her potatoes. "What's wrong with trying to please a man?" he asked.

"A woman can please a man without having to cook for him."

He shrugged. "What else does a man my age have to think about, but food?"

"If I got to tell you, Hank Barrett, maybe you are too old." She winked at him, then turned and sauntered off.

A strange feeling came over him. "What the devil is the woman takin' about?" he mumbled to himself. He pushed aside the thought and looked up to see Wyatt Gentry's truck pull up beside the barn.

Wyatt climbed down from the truck cab then helped Jeff out of the back seat. Before he let the boy go, he made him promise not to hang around the rodeo pens unless he was with an adult. Jeff agreed, then took off to find his friends.

Wyatt had delivered the rough stock early this morning when none of the neighbors were around. This would be his first return to the Circle B since his identity became public knowledge. There would probably be some who'd question him about his relationship to the Randells.

He walked to the rear of the truck and dropped the tailgate to help unload the boxes of food Maura had spent all last night preparing for the barbecue. She and Kelly came up beside him. Looking at him with those big brown eyes, Maura smiled. "It's going to be all right, Wyatt."

"What's going to be all right?"

"You're worried about today," she said. "Your bucking broncs will be great. And of course some people will probably ask questions about Jack, but your brothers will be there."

He'd never thought himself easy to read, but he didn't seem to be able to hide anything from Maura. "How did you know it was bothering me?"

She smiled in that warm way of hers and his body

temperature shot up. "You've been frowning since you got into the truck."

"Maybe I was just squinting because of the sun."

"Maybe," she agreed as Kelly tugged on her arm.

"Mommy, I want to go play with Katie."

"Okay, honey, but you have to stay in the play area. There are too many people and trucks around."

"I will, I promise." She drew an X over her heart, then took off toward the fenced area sectioned off for the younger kids, with adults taking turns supervising the kids.

"She'll be okay," Wyatt said.

"I know." She looked toward the house. "I guess I should take my potato salad and green bean casserole inside."

He stopped her when she went to reach for the box. "Maura, now it's your turn. Tell me what's bothering you?"

"Nothing's bothering me," she claimed, but they both knew she was lying.

His eyes held hers. "I think you're concerned about what people are going to say about us living together."

He'd liked staying in the house these past weeks, being with Maura and the kids. Although he hadn't touched her, he desperately wanted to. Even knowing he could be headed for heartbreak again, he still wanted a chance to see where it could lead.

"There's nothing we can do about that, Wyatt."

"Well, you could tell them that you and kids are going to rent the cottage." He didn't like the idea of them crowded into that tiny place, but he'd do just about anything to keep her close by.

She finally smiled briefly. "But people will see us together and just assume that we…"

He leaned closer. "I can't help it that when you look at me it turns me every way but loose."

She blushed. "Maybe I should stop looking at you."

"Or stop worrying about what people think."

"Look who's talking. Hold your head up, Wyatt Gentry, you have nothing to be ashamed of. You are a good man."

"Then trust me. You stay in the house where there's more room and I'll move out to the cottage."

"Oh, Wyatt, I can't let you do that."

"What if the circumstances were different?"

Her eyes widened. "What do you mean?"

Yeah, what did he mean? Before he could come up with something, Chance called to him.

Wyatt excused himself, walked a few feet away to speak with Chance. By the time he got back, Maura was already carrying one of the boxes into the house. He grabbed another and followed her.

Once inside the large Circle B kitchen he paused and watched dozens of women chatting while busily preparing the food. Being the new guy in the area, he didn't know any of them, but Maura was greeted warmly by the neighbors. Then Ella noticed his presence.

"Well, ladies, will you look at what has wandered in," the housekeeper declared. "He's a handsome devil just like his brothers, wouldn't you say? How are you doin', Wyatt?"

"Fine, thank you," he said as he deposited his box on the counter. He started off when Ella called to him again.

"I hear you're supplying the rough stock today."

"Yeah, I hope no one is disappointed."

Another woman waved her hand in the air. "Hey, today is all for fun. The men just want bragging rights for the next year. We only pray no one gets hurt."

Maura smiled as she walked by. "I told you so," she said and headed out the door.

He followed her outside and back to the truck to get more cartons.

She walked briskly to the truck. "Wyatt, you better go check the horses. I can carry the rest of the food in."

With a quick glance around, he could see things were getting busy. "I'm fine. Bud is handling the stock, but I'll need to get over to the pens and help soon. I wanted to talk with you first." He took Maura by the arm and pulled her toward the large oak tree next to where his truck was parked. It was the best he could do for privacy. He looked at her and suddenly his mouth went dry. She was so pretty, dressed in her Wrangler jeans and bright pink Western blouse. She even had on boots.

"You make a mighty pretty cowgirl," he said.

"Thank you. Most of these things are Abby's. The boots." She patted her black Stetson. "And hat."

"They look good on you."

Her smile brightened. "Thank you. I admit, I'm excited about today. I've never been to a rodeo." Her big dark eyes raised to his. "I can't wait to see you ride."

He shook his head. "I hope you're not disappointed. It's been a while since I've ridden in a rodeo. Dylan's the true star in the family."

"I bet you're good, too, and I'll be rooting for you."

His chest suddenly swelled. "Every cowboy wants a girl to cheer him on. Will you be my girl…for today?"

She blinked. "Look, Wyatt, I know you brought me today, but there are so many people—women…beautiful women here. If you happen to see someone that you want to spend time with…"

"I don't care about other woman, Maura, I care about you."

Maura's eyes widened and he kissed the end of her nose.

"Besides, with all the guys around," he said, "I don't want any of them coming on to you. I don't want you dancing with anyone else, or…kissing anyone else." He reached for her, pulled her against him just before his mouth captured hers. She whimpered, but not in protest, and raised her hands to his shoulders and parted her lips, allowing him to deepen the kiss. By the time he broke away, he had trouble drawing air into his lungs.

"That's so you'll only be thinking about me today."

Wyatt marched off, hoping that the kiss had dazed her as much as it had him. Because he didn't know how else to get through to her that he cared about her…a lot.

Two hours later, Maura was sitting in the bleachers next to Abby, Jeff and Kelly, waiting for the festivities to start.

"So what's it like living with Wyatt?" Abby whispered.

Maura tensed, wondering if anyone else heard her friend's question. "I'm not living *with* him, just in the same house."

Abby smiled. "It's kind of nice, isn't it?"

Maura wanted to deny it, wanted to say she hated having a man in the house, but she couldn't. In the beginning the last thing she'd wanted was a man in her life. Now, she looked forward to seeing Wyatt every morning, and every evening, when she returned from work.

In fact, she'd been getting up earlier in hopes of running into him before he went out to feed the stock.

Maura glanced at her kids who were busy watching the rodeo clowns. "I thought you were worried about me trusting him too easily."

"That was before I got to know him," Abby admitted. "Besides, Chance, Cade and Travis like him. They're great judges of character. And I see how he treats you, the way he looks at you. The man is smitten."

Maura smiled to herself. "To answer your question, yes, it is nice," she said. "And Wyatt is nothing like Darren. He's good to me and to the kids. Is that what you want to hear?"

"So are things getting serious between you two?" Abby asked.

Maura refused to think about the future. She wasn't going to get her hopes up. How could she expect Wyatt to take on her problems?

"No, nothing is getting serious. I'm just living in his house and when the cottage is repaired, he's renting it to me."

Abby folded her arms over her chest. "Well, then, I guess I was mistaken when I saw Wyatt kissing you under the tree earlier."

Maura felt heat flame her face. "Okay, we kissed. But it's not going any further."

"Why not? I mean, if you have feelings for the guy, who's to say you couldn't make a life with him? You *are* divorced."

"You know it's not that simple, Abby. Darren swore he'd find me."

"Then tell Wyatt about the threats." She lowered her

voice. "If he cares about you as much as I think he does, he won't let anything happen to you and the kids."

Maura wanted to trust in the future, but would Wyatt hang around if things got too complicated?

Crazy.

That was the only word Wyatt could think of as he climbed the outside railing of the chute where a snorting and kicking Rock-a-Billy was penned. The animal was not happy. Wyatt's old injuries began to ache. He'd never forgotten what a bucking horse could do to a body.

Too late now.

Hearing his name being announced as the next rider, Wyatt got into position. With his legs braced on either side of the railing, he hovered over the animal and slid his rosin-covered glove under the rigging. He shoved his black cowboy hat farther down on his head, then lowered his body onto the bronc. With his nod the gate swung open, causing the crowd to cheer as the horse charged out into the arena.

Billy lowered his head and immediately went into a fast spin, but Wyatt had expected it. When the bronc reared up in a high kick, he felt his entire body jar painfully. Spin and kick. When Billy bucked the second time Wyatt managed to stay on. By the third time, he wasn't so lucky and he landed at an odd angle and was unable to regain his balance. The next buck pitched him high in the air and this time he hit the hard ground.

The buzzer sounded.

Wyatt's survival skills took over. He scrambled to his feet and hurried out of the way of the wayward horse. Out of breath, he made it through the gate and confronted a grinning Chance.

"Hey, that was a damn good ride," Chance said. "And that's one helluva bucking horse you got there."

Wyatt tried to hide the pain in his body and smile. "You think so?" He brushed the dirt from his pants and chaps.

"Man, I don't know anyone who could stay on that animal. But we'll know for sure later on."

Wyatt glanced up in the stands to see Maura coming down the steps toward him.

"Wyatt, are you hurt?"

Not wanting to be in the crowded area, he took her hand and pulled her away from the stands. "No, I'm fine," he said, pleased about her concern.

"Maybe you shouldn't have ridden so soon after your accident."

"The doctor said it was okay," he assured her.

"You're not going to ride again, are you?"

"I doubt it. I didn't last out the eight seconds."

Her gaze moved over him again. "Are you sure that you didn't get hurt?"

"I'll feel a lot better if you'd give me a kiss." He cupped her face between his hands. "It'll help me forget about the pain." Then he lowered his head and touched his mouth to hers, gently, sweetly. He pulled away and smiled. "Oh, darlin', I'm feeling better already."

Maura was feeling pretty good, too. Too good to think about what people would think. Too good to worry about any problems that would stop them from being together. She wanted to be with Wyatt, wanted to feel free to get to know him…to see where it would lead.

"Wyatt, you were great," Jeff said as he ran up to him.

He stepped back from Maura. "Thanks, Jeff, but I'm afraid I'm a little out of practice."

Jeff looked toward the ground. "I wish I could do that," he mumbled.

Wyatt glanced at Maura, then back to the boy. "Well, why don't we sign you up for the kids rodeo?"

Maura felt panic. "Oh, no. Jeff's too young to be on a horse."

"Maura, the kids ride sheep and they wear helmets for protection. I'll be right there with Jeff." His gaze connected with hers. "I won't let anything happen to him."

After having seen this man with her children, Maura knew he spoke the truth. "And I trust you," she said, then turned to her son. "Jeff, listen to Wyatt and do exactly what he tells you."

"I will, Mom," he promised, then hugged her. "I'm gonna win, because Wyatt will teach me." He took Wyatt's hand. "C'mon, we got to go so I can practice."

With a big grin, Wyatt winked at Maura. "I guess I'll catch up with you later. Save a spot for me at the barbecue."

"I will." Maura wanted to go with them, but she'd promised to help with the food. She glanced at her watch just as Abby was coming down the bleachers with her two-year-old son, James, and Kelly.

"One kiss, I'll believe you're just friends. A second kiss, there's no way. The man is crazy for you. And I think you're crazy for him, too."

"I'm still not jumping into anything," Maura swore, but that didn't mean she could stop her growing feelings for Wyatt.

She doubted anything would stop that.

The afternoon had turned out to be so much fun. When Ella had found out that Jeff was riding in the children's rodeo, she sent Maura on her way. She arrived just in time to catch her son's attempt at bareback riding. He lasted a few seconds on the animal before he fell off. Seeing her son lying facedown in the dirt, she wanted to go to him, but Wyatt beat her there. He helped Jeff up and brushed him off as the crowd cheered. For his efforts he won a ribbon and a straw cowboy hat with the Circle B Rodeo band.

Maura had seen so many changes in her children in the past few months, especially in Jeff. He no longer had a bad attitude and wasn't causing problems at school anymore. Most importantly, he no longer asked about going back to Dallas and his father.

Now Maura had another problem. Everything out of her son's mouth was Wyatt this, or Wyatt that. She couldn't help being concerned, but she was selfish enough not to want to give up this time she and the kids had with Wyatt, either. It could all end, though. Darren would never allow her to be with anyone else.

But Darren wasn't going to spoil their good time. Not today. At the picnic area, she and Kelly found a table under a shade tree, making sure there was plenty of room for everyone, including Abby, Cade and their children.

Maura was standing in the food line when Wyatt came up behind her and whispered, "Hey there, beautiful. You want to share a picnic with me?"

She glanced over her shoulder at him. To say he was good-looking didn't begin to cover it. He was a rodeo cowboy and fit right into today's events. He was self-assured and had an easy smile. He shouldn't have worried about people accepting him. He attracted everyone's attention, especially the women.

Females of every age were nearly drooling over him,

dressed in his fitted Wrangler jeans stacked over his fancy tooled boots and a starched, royal-blue Western shirt. Including herself.

"Oh, but I promised to eat with the cowboy who brought me." She looked around, enjoying their playful game. "Maybe you've seen him. He's tall and skinny, a little bowlegged." She began to laugh when he poked her ribs.

"I'm not bowlegged."

"And you're not skinny, either." A warm blush flooded her cheeks.

He leaned closer. "So you've been giving me the once-over, huh?"

Heat surged through her and she tried to pull away from his intoxicating scent. She was acting like a teenager. "Not that you haven't noticed that every other woman has, too."

Wyatt refused to let her sidestep his question. "But all I care about is you." He grew serious and whispered, "I can't wait until the dancing starts and I can hold you in my arms."

Maura's pulse raced, so did her uneasiness. "I don't know if we should stay that late. I mean, the kids will be pretty tired by then."

"We'll see," he said. "We'll see."

They continued through the line and piled their plates with as much food as they could handle. Back at the table, Maura assisted Kelly and Wyatt brought Jeff a plate. She'd never before realized how much Wyatt had helped her and the easiness they shared together. Maura didn't miss Abby's eagle eye watching from the end of the table.

Kelly took a bite of her hot dog. "Wyatt, I told Katie Rose that Rock-a-Billy is the prettiest horse at the rodeo.

She said that her daddy's horse is the prettiest." She gave him a pouty look.

"Katie's daddy raises horses for show," Wyatt said. "My horses are for the rodeo." He smiled at her. "I'm glad you think Billy is pretty, but he's not a riding horse. He's trained to buck and kick, so you have to promise me that you won't try to ever get close to him."

"I promise," she said. "But I think Raven is a nice horsey."

"But still too big for you," Maura said. "Stick with Sandy."

Cade sat down next to his wife. "You know, Wyatt, Jared and Dana have some good saddle horses, if you're interested in more riding stock. He gives family discounts."

"Maybe I'll look into it."

"And for your information, you can get from the Rocking R to Mustang Valley by horseback. That is, if you want to ride that far." Cade smiled. "Of course, it's well worth it when you get there. Abby and I ride there all the time." He winked at his wife. "It's nice to get away by ourselves, isn't it, honey?"

Kelly refused to be denied attention. "I can ride a pony. Wyatt teached me."

Abby spoke up from the end of the table. "You know, Kelly, we have a pony at our ranch." The woman's green eyes lit up. "Oh, I have an idea, Maura, why don't you let Kelly and Jeff come spend the night so all the kids can go riding in the morning?" She was obviously delighted at her great idea.

"Oh, Mommy, can we go?" Kelly begged.

Her son joined in. "Yeah, Mom, please, I want to go, too."

"Abby, I can't ask you to take on all these kids tonight. You have to be exhausted after today."

"No, really. It's fine." Abby nudged her husband as he ate. "Isn't it fine with us, Cade?"

"Huh? Oh, sure. The more the merrier."

She smiled. "See, now you two can have a free night, even stay late at the dance, or…go home."

Maura was too embarrassed to look at Wyatt, but she admitted to herself it sounded like a wonderful idea.

Wyatt stood on the side of the patio as the band began to play their first song. Maura still hadn't shown up. He was beginning to think that she was hiding from him. Had he come on too strong and scared her off?

Chance came up to him and handed him a beer. "So, how are you liking the festivities so far?"

"It's great. Hank puts on a great rodeo." Wyatt had been surprised at how well organized and professional it was.

Chance took a long pull from his bottle. "Your horses were a great addition to the competition today. Usually we don't have such high caliber stock for our amateur riders. As you could see, not many of us could stay on long."

"I didn't do much better."

"Yeah, but I bet Dylan 'the Devil' Gentry could. What do you think the chances are that he might stop by next year?"

Wyatt hated to disillusion the Randells about Dylan. "I'd like that, too, but it's going to take a lot to convince my brother. He's still upset about me buying the Randell ranch." Wyatt left out the fact that Dylan hadn't returned his calls.

"He'll get over it."

"Maybe. But it didn't sit well with your family at first that I bought the Rocking R."

Chance smiled. "We're over it. My brothers and I didn't want any part of the ranch, so it seems fitting now that you have it, especially since you're bringing the place back to how it used to be. Which leads me into another proposition. How do you feel about helping out with the Mustang Valley Guest Ranch?"

Wyatt jerked his head to Chance. "Help out how?"

Chance shrugged. "We're not sure exactly. You have some prim grazing land on the Rocking R. And at the guest ranch we get a lot of requests for cattle drives. Why not run a small yearling herd and have people pay you to round them up?"

Wyatt was caught off guard by the offer.

"Maybe you could stop by for a family meeting and work out some of the details. If you're interested…"

Before Wyatt had a chance to speak, they both looked up at Maura, who was coming across the patio. She had changed her clothes. Now, she was wearing a denim skirt and white top covered by a suede vest. Her hair was pulled on top of her head with stands of curls dancing around her face.

"Whoa, Maura sure looks pretty," Chance said. "I guess we'll be continuing this conversation later." With that he walked off.

Wyatt barely noticed Chance's departure. His gaze was on Maura as she walked to him.

"Hi," she said nervously.

"Hi, yourself, beautiful," he said and reached for her hand and led her to the dance floor. He took her in his arms and began the two-step. She stumbled, then with his encouragement, she caught on to the rhythm.

"You're a good dancer," he said, wanting to pull her closer.

"I should be, since my mother had me taking lessons since I was three years old. It never made me the prima ballerina that she'd hope for. I never seemed to fulfill any of Mother's expectations."

Wyatt didn't miss the sadness in her voice. The music ended and a slow song began. He drew Maura close and inhaled her sweetness along with the wonderful feeling of her soft curves against him. Heaven.

"Where do your parents live?"

"The east. New York state."

"Why didn't you go back there after your divorce?"

She raised her head from his shoulder. The pain reflected in her eyes told him more than her words. "They didn't want me…or the children cluttering up their lives." Her voice softened. "They haven't had anything to do with me since I married Darren."

"Maura, I'm sorry." Wyatt tightened his hold as they moved to the Garth Brooks song, "To Make You Feel My Love."

"I guess we can't choose our families," he said, feeling the softness of her breasts brush against his chest as they moved to the sultry ballad. "But you have the Randells…and me."

She lifted her head again. "Wyatt, I don't want you to feel that you're responsible—"

He placed a finger against her lips. "Don't tell me how to feel, Maura. I know you don't trust men easily and… if I'm coming on too strong, or if I'm speaking out of turn, I'll back away. The last thing I want to do is hurt you, I swear."

She swallowed. "I believe you. It's just there is so much you don't know about my situation."

He danced her toward the corner of the patio, then took her hand and walked to a dark, secluded part of the yard. "Do you trust me, Maura?"

She nodded slowly.

"Do you believe that I care about you and the kids?"

She nodded again and he released a long breath. "Good."

He pulled her into his arms and kissed her. He groaned when she gripped the front of his shirt and held on as she returned his passion. When Wyatt heard people's voice and laughter, he broke off the kiss and pressed his forehead against her. "I think this place is getting too crowded. I want to be alone with you in the worst way."

He felt her trembling in his arms. "I want that, too." she admitted. Wyatt took her hand and they headed across the patio. Maura didn't have to worry about the children because Abby and Cade had already headed home for the kids' sleepover.

Hours earlier, Bud had loaded the horses into the trailer and taken them back to the Rocking R. All that was left was saying good-night to Hank. They caught up with him along with Chance and Travis and talked a few minutes, then excused themselves and said they'd be leaving.

Silently they walked to the truck. They reached the cab driver's side door and Wyatt lifted Maura in his arms and placed her inside, then slid in next to her.

"Don't move, I don't want you too far away. In fact, I plan to keep you close to me all night."

His gaze met hers in the dark truck, only the moonlight outlined her silhouette. He could feel her tremble. Was she still afraid of him?

"Maura, I want you to know how much I want you. But I'd never force you into anything." He started to move away.

"No, Wyatt, don't leave me." She took hold of his shirt to stop him. "I want to be with you tonight, too."

Chapter 10

The twenty minute ride to the Rocking R Ranch seemed to take forever. All the while Wyatt kept his hand locked with Maura's until he pulled the truck up next to the back door. Without a word, he unbuckled her safety belt, took her in his arms and kissed her deeply. When he finally tore his mouth away, he drew in needed air. Never in his life had he wanted anyone as much as he wanted Maura.

"Let's go inside," he said, then opened the door and climbed down from the cab. He helped her out and kept her close to his side as they made their way up the porch steps and into the dark kitchen. A tiny light was on over the stove, throwing the room in shadows, but it was enough so he could see her, see the longing in her eyes.

"I had a good time today," he said, suddenly feeling as nervous as an adolescent boy. He released another breath and drew her against him. "God, Maura, I don't want to leave you. Just tell me you feel the same."

"I don't want this night to end, either," she admitted as she rested her head against his chest. The feel of her soft curves awakened every nerve ending in his body.

Go slow, he warned himself.

But his pulse sped up. When he murmured her name into her hair as he stroked his hand down her back, Maura moved against him restlessly. Her fingers knotted in his shirt front and she turned her face up to his. He felt her breath feather across his cheek, adding fuel to his desire. She raised up on her toes and her lips brushed his. When she pressed her mouth to his, Wyatt forgot his resolve and kissed her.

She whimpered, straining closer to him as he deepened the kiss. Her lips yielded to him. Parted. He dipped his tongue inside, teasing hers into an erotic dance. Suddenly his mind forgot all reason as his body grew warm with need.

His hands roamed over her soft body, bringing her so close she couldn't help but feel his desire. He couldn't get enough of her. He cupped her breasts through her T-shirt, gently squeezing the luscious weight in his hands.

"Oh, Wyatt," she breathed as her hands went to the snaps on his shirt. Once they were opened, she reached inside and caressed his chest. Her touch nearly drove him crazy.

His breathing was ragged. "I want you, Maura, so much."

"I want you, too."

That was all he needed to hear. He swung her up into his arms and carried her to his bedroom off the kitchen. There, he set her down next to the large bed, sliding her along his front, then taking her mouth in another hungry kiss. He moved away and flicked on the small light next to the bed in the sparsely furnished room.

She looked so fragile and shy. "Oh, Maura, if you're not ready… I'll understand."

"No, I want you Wyatt…so much. It's just… I haven't been with anyone else…"

Wyatt cupped her face between his hands, feeling her tremble.

"Not to worry, darlin'. You give me pleasure just looking at you." He touched her hair. "Tonight, I want to fulfill your desires."

Wyatt's promise stole Maura's breath away. And the last thing she wanted to do was pass out before she experienced loving this man. Even if they could never have a future together, she wanted to pretend, just for a while, that it was possible.

"Make love to me, Wyatt," she murmured.

Wyatt stood back, striped off his shirt, then removed his boots and belt. He left on his jeans and returned to her.

He reached out. "May I," he said in a husky voice, "do the honors?"

Unable to find her voice, Maura nodded and he slipped off her vest, then sat her down on the bed and removed her boots. Next came her skirt and top, leaving her in only a bra and panties. She fought not to cover herself, not to let years of abusive conditioning make her feel unattractive. But not tonight. All she had to do was look into Wyatt's eyes, and he told her without words how much he desired her.

"So beautiful." He kissed her and pressed her backward until she rested on the mattress. His mouth left hers and rained kisses along her neck to her chest. He unfastened her bra, baring her breasts to his gaze, but then paused, as if waiting for her to make the next move. For the first time in a long time, Maura wanted a man's hands on her, wanted him to make her feel like a woman.

"Wyatt…touch me," she pleaded.

Wyatt savored Maura's gasp when he cupped her full breast in his hand then he lowered his head and took her nipple into his mouth. She cried out, sinking her fingers into his scalp. He grew more aroused knowing what he was doing to her.

He looked in her eyes as his hand moved over her stomach to the rim of her panties. "Maura, I'm going to stroke and kiss every inch of you…"

She reached up and placed a kiss on his lips, then began to move down to his chest, using her mouth to drive him closer to the edge. "Make love to me."

"Hold that thought." Wyatt groaned, and moved off the bed. He began stripping off his jeans, only thinking about loving Maura. Then suddenly he heard a loud pounding on the back door, then Bud calling his name.

"What the hell? I'll be right back." He walked out, closing the door behind him.

Maura sat up and hugged the sheet against her body on hearing the muffled voices.

Within seconds, Wyatt came back. "Somehow Billy and Stormy got loose and Bud and I have to go after them." He sat in the chair and began pulling on his boots.

She tried to mask her disappointment. "Oh, Wyatt. How did it happen?"

Grabbing his shirt off the floor, he put it on as he walked to the bed. "Bud's not sure, but if we don't chase them down…"

"Of course."

He leaned down and kissed her. "We're not finished here," he whispered. "So don't you go changing your mind, darlin', 'cause I'm going to love you like you've never been loved before. I want you waiting right here—in this bed."

She could only nod. He kissed her again, sending more warm shivers through her. Then he left.

Maura collapsed back on the pillow with a smile. "I'll be here, Wyatt. I love you…" she whispered in the empty room as she snuggled into the soft mattress. She closed her eyes a moment, maybe even dosed off when she heard a noise. Maybe he'd forgotten something.

"Wyatt…" she called.

No answer. She sat up in bed as a strange feeling came over her. Something was wrong. She got up and grabbed one of Wyatt's shirts from the top of the dresser and slipped it on. She'd no sooner finished with the buttons when the door swung open and a figure appeared in the doorway. Panic filled her.

She gasped. "Wyatt…"

"Sorry, bitch, but your lover is long gone."

Maura's lungs refused to work as she watched Darren Wells stroll into the bedroom. At five foot eight and with his stocky build, he outweighed her by a good fifty pounds. He had dirty blond hair that was too long, and his body odor nearly gagged her.

From years of conditioning and knowing his brutality, she automatically backed away. "What are you doing here?" Her heart hammered against her ribs as she gripped the edge of the dresser.

"Ah, Maura, is that any way to greet your husband?"

"You aren't my husband," she said, trying to sound in

control. She prayed Wyatt would appear any second, but now knew that probably wouldn't happen.

He grinned at her, making her stomach clench. "You thought you were rid of me, huh?"

"How did you get...out of jail?"

"Got myself a hotshot lawyer who found a loophole. Seems that the Dallas police didn't follow procedure when they arrested me." His voice turned angry. "And you didn't waste any time finding yourself a lover, did you?"

"What did you do to Wyatt?" Maura demanded. Why hadn't the D.A. called her? she wondered wildly, looking around for a way to escape.

"Let's just say he'll be chasing horses for a long time." He looked around the room. "You have a nice setup here. Too bad you aren't going to be able to stay and enjoy it. Get dressed, bitch. We're going to get the brats and get the hell out of here."

"No, leave the children out of this."

"Can't do that," he told her. "It's the only way I'll keep you in line."

She couldn't go through this again. "I'm not going with you."

He walked toward her, then pulled a gun from the belt of his trousers. "You are, unless you don't want your lover to live."

Maura gasped, then caught her skirt as Darren threw it at her. She dressed as fast as her trembling hands would allow, all the time trying to come up with a plan to get away—and keep Wyatt safe.

"C'mon, quit stalling." Darren grabbed her by her arm and pain shot through her.

Memories of her old life flooded back, but she couldn't

let him get control again. She also knew that her ex-husband was going to make her pay for her betrayal, for calling the police on him. She had no doubt that he would hurt her, maybe even kill her. Thank God that Jeff and Kelly were safe with Abby and Cade. She would make sure they stayed that way.

Darren hauled her through the dark house and out the front door. She didn't see a vehicle, but realized that he wouldn't be so stupid as to drive up to the door.

"How did you find out where I was?"

He jerked her along beside him toward the road to the highway. "Simple. Remember that nosy old biddy who lived downstairs, the one who was always calling the police on me? Well, I phoned her and said I was from the D.A.'s office and needed your new address for the file."

He stopped abruptly and she ran into his sweaty body, his sour beer breath nearly made her gag. "Don't you know that you can never get away from me?" His mouth crushed against hers. As never before, she found the strength to fight him. She pummelled her fists into his chest until she broke free. She began to run, praying she could hide in the dark.

She didn't get to the high bushes before he tackled her to the ground, driving the air from her lungs. He pinned her as he smacked her face. She hit him back, scratching and clawing at him. She didn't know how long they struggled before she felt his weight being lifted off of her.

Wyatt! She watched as the two men fought, then Darren rolled away and pulled out his gun. She heard the sound of the hammer being cocked.

"No, Darren, don't!" Maura cried as he aimed the weapon at Wyatt. "I'll go with you, just don't hurt him!"

"Maura, no," Wyatt growled.

Before anything happened, the shrill sound of the sheriff's siren filled the silence. Wyatt caught Darren off guard and lunged at him. The gun went flying. Then Wyatt rammed his fist into Darren's jaw and he dropped to the ground, unconscious.

Wyatt hurried to Maura's side and wrapped his arms around her as the patrol car skidded to a stop, flooding the area with its headlights. The lean built sheriff and a young looking deputy sprang out of the doors with their guns drawn.

"Raise your hands," he demanded.

Wyatt did as he was told. "Sheriff, I'm Wyatt Gentry. I made the 911 call," he said and nodded to the ground. "This is Darren Wells, he tried to kidnap Maura...and held a gun on us both."

The deputy held Darren down and handcuffed him as the sheriff retrieved the gun, then returned to them. "Are you okay?" he asked Maura. "Do you need to go to the hospital?"

"No, I'm fine," she said. "He didn't hurt me."

Wyatt knew she was lying. Her face showed the end result of Darren's fist. "You sure you don't want a doctor to check you out?"

She shook her head. "What about you?"

"I'm fine," he said. "I'm just glad I got here in time."

"It was Darren who let the horses out," she told him.

"I figured something was wrong when I found that the fence had been cut. I called the sheriff thinking someone was stealing the horses. I didn't know Darren was behind it until I came to see if you were safe."

"What about Stormy and Billy?"

"I sent Bud to retrieve them and I came back to make sure you were okay."

"Now that the police are here, maybe you should go and help him."

He shook his head. "I'm not leaving you, Maura." He slipped his arm around her, but she pulled back.

"I'm fine, Wyatt. I just want to see my children." Tears flooded her eyes. "I need to know that they're safe."

Wyatt pulled the cell phone from his pocket. "Here, call Abby and make sure."

Maura took the phone and walked a few feet away to make the call. Wyatt wanted to stay with her, but she seemed to want to be alone so he took the opportunity to talk to the sheriff. "You have to keep Wells locked up. Look what he did to her face."

"I don't see it as a problem. We ran a check on Wells as we drove out here. Seems he's been ID'd for an armed robbery in Dallas. If we're lucky that will be enough to put him away for a long time. But I'm gonna need a statement from Mrs. Wells on the assault, which will add to the charges."

"They're no longer married," he snapped, then realizing how possessive he'd become of Maura. "Sorry, it's been a rough night. Could she come in tomorrow morning?"

"No problem. We have plenty to hold him." The sheriff went back to the car and drove off.

Maura returned to Wyatt and handed him the phone. "Jeff and Kelly are asleep, but I need to see them. Please, can you take me there?"

"Sure. I can run you by for a while."

"No, Wyatt, I'm not coming back here. I'll be staying with Abby and Cade." She couldn't meet his eyes. "I'm not sure what's going to happen after that."

Wyatt's gut tightened. "Maura… I care about you. I thought that you and I have something between us."

She looked at him. "Right now I have to concern myself with my children and surviving. I can't drag you into my mess of a life."

He stepped closer. "What if I want to be there, to help you?"

She shook her head. "I have to help myself." This time she met his gaze. "Please, Wyatt, try to understand. I have nothing to give you." She swung around and hurried off toward the house.

Wyatt just stood there, feeling as if his heart had been ripped from his chest. She was wrong. Maura had everything to give him, everything that mattered to him.

It had been one week since Darren Wells had shown up at the Rocking R Ranch. One week since Maura had moved out, since he had last seen Jeff and Kelly. And he missed them like hell.

He should be spending his time on the business. Bud was at a rodeo in New Mexico. Wyatt had no desire to go along, even though he was going stir crazy. He saddled Raven and headed out, following the directions Cade had given him, he rode off. The stallion pranced, eager to run. Wyatt finally let him loose and they took off across the open pasture.

Twenty minutes later Wyatt slowed Raven when they reached the group of trees at the edge of Mustang Valley. He'd been here once before and remembered the place's peacefulness and beauty. At the crest of the rise, he looked down at the trees lining the creek. Off in the distance he could see the shadows of the cabins partially hidden in the shrubs. On the other side, in the hills, he spotted a large structure. The two-story home was all natural-stained wood and the back side was nearly all glass. Travis and Josie's home. He turned his attention back to the pasture and he found the herd of mustangs in the high grass.

Silently, he climbed off Raven and led the horse to the water's edge. They both took a drink, careful not to disturb the serene atmosphere. He watched in fascination as two mustang studs began to whinny and nip at each other. Before long, the two were all out fighting over the buckskin mare. Finally the dominate male ran the younger one off. So engrossed in the action, Wyatt didn't hear Hank come up behind him.

"It's still survival of the fittest," the rancher said. "And it's as old as time, males fighting over a female." He studied Wyatt. "I thought maybe you'd be doing the same."

Wyatt frowned. "She won't see me."

"Maura thinks she's doing the noble thing, saving you from all the trouble in her life. Plus, she's just plain scared."

Wyatt clenched his fists. "She didn't make the mess to begin with. That bastard of an ex-husband did that all on his own."

"Maybe you need to convince her of that."

He wished he had the chance. "How can I when she doesn't want to see me?"

Hank cocked an eyebrow. "Well, she may have said that, but I know for a fact she isn't happy these days. The kids aren't in much better shape." He pushed his hat back. "But, son, in good conscience I can't allow you to go over there if your intentions aren't honorable."

Marriage. It had been all he'd thought about since Maura left him. Being alone these past days he realized the home he'd always wanted meant nothing if he couldn't share it with Maura. "I want to give her everything she's never had, a home for her and Jeff and Kelly. Yes, I love her."

The older rancher gave him a sly smile. "Now those three words may just change her mind, if she knows that you want it to be permanent between you. That is what you're talkin' about, isn't it?"

Wyatt nodded. "Yeah, I guess it is."

Hank nodded in approval. "Then she better be the one you're tellin'. Women need to hear it all spelled out. You know, with pretty flowers and all the fancy words."

Wyatt wasn't good with words, but he refused to let Maura walk out of his life, not without a fight. "Do you happen to know where Maura might be today?"

"Sure do. When I left Cade and Abby's place just a while ago, she was sittin' on the porch looking pretty, and mighty lonely." Hank pointed toward the west. "If you head up the rise, you'll have no trouble finding the way. The trail will take you right there."

"Thanks." Wyatt swung up onto Raven's back, tugged on the reins and shot off in the direction of the Rocking R. This was the first time in a week he felt a glimmer of hope.

Chapter 11

Maura sat on the porch and watched Kelly and Katie Rose play with their dolls off in a corner. It was a cool autumn day and Maura had the day off from the Yellow Rose. In a way she wished she could work. At least it kept her busy so she wouldn't have so much time to think about how much she missed Wyatt…and remember. Remember how it felt to have him hold her, to kiss her. She closed her eyes recalling the night they'd nearly made love.

"Thinking about a certain sexy cowboy who lives up the road?"

Maura's eyes shot open to find Abby sitting in the chair next to hers.

"No," she lied. "I have too many other things on my mind, like my future and finding a place to live. We've imposed on you enough."

"Our house has plenty of room," Abby insisted. "Besides, Cade told you that you can move into the foreman's house." She took Maura's hand. "You don't have to run anymore, Maura. Darren is going to prison, and with the armed robbery charge, he's not getting out for a long time. Texas has tough laws. So you and the kids can have a life, a good life. Don't waste any more time on your ex."

"It's thanks to you, Abby. You and your family took us in when I had nowhere else to go."

She smiled. "Everyone needs help now and then. You've paid me back many times. You've made the Yellow Rose prosper with your creative designs. But you need to think about yourself, think about the man you love."

Maura wished she could give into her feelings. "Who says I love him?"

Her friend raised an eyebrow. "You're denying it?"

Maura knew it was useless. "Sometimes love isn't enough. How can I ask another man to take on a family, plus all my baggage? Jeff or Kelly might have problems because of their father's abuse. I'm still in counseling."

"So am I. And because sometimes love is the only thing that gets you through. Besides, life has no guarantees," Abby stressed. "If I hadn't taken a chance and let Cade back into my life, I wouldn't be with the man I love. And Brandon wouldn't have his daddy. I definitely wouldn't have Jamie."

Maura wanted so badly to believe Abby, but the fear was still with her. Besides, Wyatt hadn't made any indication that he wanted her…forever. "If he wants me, why hasn't he come?"

"As I recall, you asked him for some time."

Maura started to speak when she spotted a horse and

rider coming through the pasture toward the house. She immediately recognized the large black stallion and the man. Her heart raced. It was Wyatt.

Wyatt slowed Raven as he approached the large ranch house. Nerves had his pulse pounding in his ears. He touched the brim of his hat at the two women seated on the porch, but before he could get any closer, little Kelly came running down the steps to greet him. He climbed off his horse and swung the child up in his arms.

"Wyatt! Wyatt! You came!"

"Yes, I did.

She pouted. "I missed you." Then her voice lowered to a whisper. "Jeff and me want to live at your house, but Mama says we can't." Her eyes teared up. "Can you tell her it's okay?"

Wyatt glanced toward the porch to see that Cade had joined the ladies on the porch. He hadn't planned on a crowd. "I'll do my best."

Suddenly Jeff came tearing out of the barn. "Wyatt, you're here!" the boy cried.

"How you been doin', partner? You being good for your mother?"

Jeff nodded. "I got an A on my printing, too."

Kelly wasn't going to be left out. "I've been good, too. And I drawed you lots of pictures."

"Why didn't you come for us?" Jeff asked. "Don't you care about us?"

"I care a lot about you and your sister," Wyatt tried to assure them. He tugged on Kelly's blond ponytail, then looked over his shoulder to see Maura watching them.

"Do you love us?" Kelly asked. "Do you love Mama?"

Wyatt couldn't find his voice and nodded.

"Then marry Mom," Jeff said.

These kids didn't mess around. He decided maybe he should plead his case to them before he faced Maura. He set Kelly down.

"Come on, you two," he said as he tugged Raven by the reins and all of them walked the short distance to the water trough. As the horse drank Wyatt turned to the children.

"Yes, I want to marry your mother. And I want to be your dad, too." He watched as two pairs of eyes widened.

"Can we live with you forever?" Kelly gasped.

He nodded.

"Oh, boy!" the girl cheered and Wyatt quickly touched his finger to her lips to quiet her. She lowered her voice. "I want you to be my daddy."

"You love us?" Jeff asked.

Wyatt swallowed as placed his hand on Jeff's shoulder. "Yeah, I love you." He saw the child's hesitant look. "Jeff, I can't promise you that I won't get angry with you and your sister, but I'll never raise a hand to either of you." Wyatt thought about his own stepfather's abusive behavior. He'd never treat any child that way.

"I know you won't," Jeff said so confidently. "Will you teach me to play baseball? And can I ride Raven when I'm older?"

Wyatt had trouble speaking. "I'd planned on it."

Kelly spoke up, "And will you read me stories at night?"

"It will be my pleasure, princess. Now, you two need to give me some time with your mother…alone. I'd like to take her back to the ranch so we can talk. So I can tell her how much I care about her. Is that all right?"

They both nodded enthusiastically.

"I can watch Kelly," Jeff offered. "We'll be good for Abby."

"Great, son, because I'm going to need all the help I can get." He patted the boy's shoulder. "Remember, it's a surprise."

Kelly cupped her mouth and whispered, "Give Mommy kisses. She likes kisses." Then she ran off with her brother.

Wyatt smiled. At least he had the kids on his side. "I'll do my best," he promised, recalling the feel of Maura's mouth under his. He sucked in a breath to curb the direction of his thoughts, then led Raven toward the porch.

"Hello, Maura, Abby, Cade. Maura, do you think I can talk with you a minute? Alone."

She hesitated, then came down the steps. He couldn't help but notice the weight she'd lost and the dark circles under her eyes, those big, beautiful eyes. At least there were no remaining traces of bruises.

"How are you doing?"

"I'm fine," she said.

"Good." He felt awkward and glanced off to where the kids were playing on the tire swing that hung on the huge oak.

"Kelly and Jeff seem to be doing well," she said. "I hate to think of what would have happened if they'd been at the house when…"

"But they weren't," Wyatt stressed. "They were safe and they'll be safe from now on."

He took a step closer, aching to touch her, to take her in his arms. To hold her and erase her pain, her fears. Instead, he asked. "When are you and the kids moving back to the house?"

She didn't say anything for several seconds. "I don't

think that's such a good idea. I mean, I can't keep imposing on you indefinitely."

"You weren't imposing, Maura, not then and not now," he said. "I want you to come back...to give us a chance."

A hundred times Maura had thought about the night they'd nearly made love. The night Wyatt gave her a glimpse of paradise. She loved this man beyond belief, but...she also needed to learn to rely on herself. No matter how wonderful Wyatt might be, she wasn't ready to trust another man.

"Come back with me to the ranch now. Just to talk," he coaxed.

Looking into those mesmerizing blue eyes of his, Maura felt her resolve slipping. No. She straightened. "I can't now, Wyatt. Maybe after the kids and I get settled."

"When will that be? Never? That's a cop out and you know it. But if you think that's all there is between us, I can't change that."

Maura wasn't frightened of Wyatt's anger, just disappointed when he took hold of the reins and climbed on Raven. He was giving up.

"I can't force you, Maura, but I won't hang around where I'm not wanted, either." The horse shifted sideways. "Just let me know where you want the rest of your things sent." With one last look, he kicked the horse's sides and took off. Maura ached to go after him. She loved him, but knew she couldn't give him what he needed. So all she could do was watch as he rode past the corral and out across the open field.

Suddenly her attention changed when she caught a small figure running after the horse and rider. It was Jeff. Maura watched as the six-year-old yelled and waved frantically to Wyatt. When the rider didn't stop, Jeff changed direction and cut through the fenced pasture. Maura's heart went to her throat and she started after her son.

Wyatt heard someone calling him and glanced over his shoulder to find Jeff racing through the field waving at him. He slowed his horse, then swung him around to go back to the boy. Suddenly Jeff tripped and fell to the ground, but he didn't get up. Wyatt felt panic and kicked Raven's side and they shot off. The horse jumped the low fence, making his way through the grass to the injured boy. Then Raven whinnied and reared up in distress.

"Whoa, boy." Alerted to danger, Wyatt patted the animal's neck. Jeff was about twenty feet away where he'd fallen and hit a rock. The large rock seemed to be home to a Texas rattler, who now was about five feet from the boy's still body.

Wyatt swallowed back the bile in his throat and slowly climbed off the horse. He could see that the child's head was bleeding, but worse, he was coming to. With Jeff's whimper, the snake sounded his rattle.

"Jeff," Wyatt spoke in a quiet, soothing voice. "Don't move, partner. I know you're hurt, but you have to pretend to be asleep. Trust me, I won't let anything happen to you."

Maura was running as fast as she could to keep up with Cade. When they reached Wyatt, she saw her son lying motionless on the ground.

"Jeff," she cried with what little breath she had left.

Wyatt held up his hand to stop them. Cade grabbed her to keep her from going any closer. A rattling sound alerted Maura to a snake dangerously near Jeff. "Oh, God," she gasped.

Cade held her back. "Maura, let Wyatt handle it."

"Please, Wyatt, help him," she begged, feeling help-less. "Please…"

"I will." Wyatt backed up slowly to Raven, then opened the flap on his saddlebag. He took out a knife and pulled the long blade from its sheath. Maura's heart pounded as she could only watch Wyatt release a breath and take aim. With a skilled flick of the wrist, the blade went sailing through the air and impaled the snake to the earth. Then there was only silence.

No sooner had Cade released her than she took off to her son. Wyatt was already there, checking for injuries. "Hey, partner," he said. "You did good." He ran his hands over Jeff's limbs as Maura knelt beside her son.

"Oh, Jeff," she said, fighting tears. "Are you hurt?"

"My head." He grimaced, then said to her, "Did you see Wyatt, Mom? He killed the snake."

"You did a good job, partner," Wyatt said, as he looked into the boy's eyes, checking the pupils. "You did exactly what I told you and stayed quiet."

"'Cause I knew you'd save me." Jeff tried to sit up. "Can I see the snake?"

Cade got off his cell phone. "I'll save it for later, Jeff. We need to get you checked out." He looked at Wyatt. "Good job with the knife."

Wyatt shrugged. "I've had a little practice."

Just then Cade's ranch foreman, Charlie, drove up in the truck. Wyatt relinquished Raven to Charlie's care, lifted Jeff into the back seat beside Maura, then climbed in the front beside Cade and they all headed to the emer-gency room.

An hour later, the doctor had examined Jeff and di-agnosed with a slight concussion. He'd put a bandage on the cut on his head and told Maura to periodically check his pupils for the next twenty-four hours, then bring him back tomorrow. When she brought Jeff out to the waiting room she found Wyatt still there. Tears welled in her eyes. He hadn't left them.

Wyatt looked down at Jeff. "Looks like the doctor is sending you home."

"Yeah, but I have a concussion. I have to stay awake all night."

Wyatt smiled and Maura realized how hungry she'd been to see it, even if it wasn't directed at her. "Well, maybe you should lay in bed anyway," Wyatt said. "Just to rest."

Jeff nodded then hugged him. "Thanks for saving me, Wyatt."

"Any time, partner," he said putting his arms around Jeff. It dawned on her that she'd never once seen Darren hug his son.

"Well, I've got to get back to the ranch." Wyatt stood and looked at Cade. "Bud's waiting outside for me. Would it be all right to leave Raven at your place until the morning?"

"No problem," Cade said.

Wyatt knelt down in front of Jeff. "You take it easy for the next few days, but that doesn't mean you have to give your mom a bad time."

"I'll be good," he said, then leaned closer to Wyatt. "Are you going to talk to Mom about...you know?"

"I don't think now is the right time," he said.

Jeff looked disappointed. "But you will, right?"

He hugged the boy. "Yeah, I will," he promised.

Wyatt stood and nodded to Maura, then headed for the door. Before exiting, he turned around and their eyes met and she ached to call him back. Then it hit her that he was giving her what she wanted. Wyatt was walking out of her life…forever.

Cade came up to her. "You ready to go?

Afraid to speak, she could only nod.

Cade lifted Jeff in his arms, then placed an arm across her shoulders. They arrived at the car and put the boy in the back. Cade walked her around to the passenger side, but before she got in, she asked, "Am I doing the right thing with Wyatt?"

He pulled off his hat and ran a hand through his hair. "Only you can answer that, Maura" he said. "If you're worried that he'll be like your ex, don't be. We Randells talk big, but we don't have a mean bone in our bodies, unless you mess with our family. Then we'll fight you until our last breath." He glanced at Jeff in the back seat of the truck. "I saw that fierce look in Wyatt's eyes when your boy was lying on the ground. There was no doubt that the man would have gone after that rattler bare handed to protect him. Jeff knew it, too." Cade blinked several times. "Wyatt is definitely a Randell. And I mean that in a good way. My brothers and I are the new generation. We don't walk out on those we love."

Maura smiled despite her pain.

Cade went on to say, "I believe Wyatt came to San Angelo for one reason—to find family. I think he got more than he bargained for. He's crazy about you and your kids."

The back window came down and Jeff leaned out. "Yeah, Mom. Wyatt loves us. He said so."

Maura's chest tightened at her son's words. How she wanted to hear those words from Wyatt. "I'm so confused."

"We're talking about how you feel, Maura," Cade said.

"And if you're not ready…" He leaned toward her. "But ask yourself this, why do you so easily trust the man with your child…but not your heart?"

Chapter 12

Two days later, Maura sat on the edge of the cold, metal chair inside the jail's visitors' room. Her palms were sweating, her pulse pounding in her ears as she watched the guard escort in Darren Wells. Looking at the heavy-set man with greasy blond hair, she couldn't imagine ever loving him. A long time ago she had, before he started abusing her. She shut her eyes to blank out the bad memories, wanting only to remember that he was the father of her children.

One thing was for sure, she wasn't going to allow him to control her life. Not anymore.

"Well, well, if it isn't my loving wife." Darren sat down across from her at the table, only a high Plexiglas partition separating them.

"I'm no longer your wife. Our divorce was final months ago."

"That'll change," he assured her. "I'll be getting out of here."

Maura's breathing stopped, but she tried not to react. "You're not getting out of here any time soon," she insisted. "I talked to the D.A. about pressing charges of kidnapping and abuse. Between that and the robbery, you'll be in prison for years."

He leaned forward and gave her a threatening look that used to have her trembling. She wasn't trembling now.

"If you know what's good for you, Maura, you better not do that."

She met his gaze defiantly. "No, I should have done it years ago. I should have protected my children from you, protected myself from you. I'm a person, Darren." She sat up straighter, feeling her strength grow. "You had no right to lay a hand on me. I'm here to tell you that you never will again."

"You better watch it, bitch," he growled. "You don't know when I'll come and get you."

She didn't even flinch at his threat, that in itself made her smile. "Well, I'll be waiting. I'm not afraid of you, Darren. You can't hurt me anymore."

He leaned back in his chair. "So you're going to rely on lover boy?"

"No, I'm relying on myself. I'm stronger now. You're never going to control me again." She stood, seeing his surprised expression. "If you have any decency left, you'll do what's right for your children and relinquish your claim to them. Give Jeff and Kelly a chance at a life." She turned and walked out of the room, feeling as if she could breath again.

She was finally free. She could do anything. Have anything. She laughed, then it died away. All she'd ever wanted just might be out of her reach. Or was it? Maybe the man she loved would be willing to give her a second chance.

Maura pulled her car by the back door at the Rocking R Ranch. When she glanced up at the beautiful white house, her heart ached, remembering when she'd first came here to live. She loved the house back then, she still loved it. But the man who lived inside was who she wanted. She only had to convince him to hear her out.

Before she'd left to come here, Cade had encouraged her to speak her mind, tell Wyatt how she felt. Make him understand how much she cared about him and that she needed him in her life. So did her children. Jeff and Kelly told her not to come back without Wyatt. Maura took a calming breath and picked up the special floral bouquet from the seat and got out of the car.

At the back door, she knocked, but hearing no answer, she stepped into the kitchen and called for Wyatt. There was no reply, just the sound of music. The first thing Maura noticed was the smell of paint, then saw that the walls were a new bright yellow. Not only that, the knotty pine cabinets had been refinished and stained, and white tile had replaced the old battered countertops. She looked down at the floor to see that was also new.

Maura's curiosity took her into the dining room to find it had also been transformed during her two-week absence. The once empty space had been painted the "luscious moss" color she'd chosen and there was a long oak table and six high-back chairs. She ran her fingers along the antique sideboard in awe.

What had Wyatt done?

The music grew louder and Maura followed the voice

of Tim McGraw into the living room. She peeked her head around the corner to find Wyatt in the middle of room, busy pushing a roller over the prepped walls. Her gaze moved over his paint-spattered jeans and a once-white T-shirt that hugged his broad shoulders and chest. As if he sensed her presence, he turned and looked at her.

Her breath caught as his gaze moved over her. She tingled from head to toe, praying that he wouldn't reject her. His mouth tugged at a smile which gave her encouragement. "Hello, Wyatt."

"Maura. What are you doing here?"

Wyatt knew immediately he'd said the wrong thing. He set down the roller and wiped off his hands. The last thing he wanted to do was make her feel unwelcome, especially when he'd been praying she'd want to see him. "I mean, I didn't know you were coming by." He gestured around. "As you can see, the place is a mess."

"It looks nice. I hardly recognize the kitchen."

"Yeah, I had someone come in and redo the cabinets and counters. Do you like them?" He was rambling like a teenager.

"Yes, they did a wonderful job."

Wyatt watched her move around the room. She looked good, damn good. She had on a pair of dark pleated slacks showing off her tiny waist. A snowy white blouse made her look businesslike, yet feminine. Her soft blond hair was curled up on the ends and draped behind her small ears. A strand clung to her cheek, and he had to fight to keep from brushing it away. He glanced at the flowers in her hands.

"Who are the flowers for?"

"Oh…ah…they're for you." She held out the bouquet to him. "I wanted to thank you for helping Jeff."

"You don't have to thank me, Maura. I would never let anything happen to him."

"I know." Tears welled in her eyes. "Without you, I don't want to think about what could have happened."

He shook his head. "Then don't. Jeff is fine." He wanted more than her gratitude.

Wyatt took the colorful flowers and walked into the kitchen. She followed him. He opened the cupboard and found a glass vase. At the sink, he added water and set the assortment of flowers inside, then carried it to the table.

"These are really nice. I've never gotten flowers before," he said, seeing that Maura looked as if she were about to bolt out the door. He couldn't let her do that. "Is it true that each flower has some special meaning?"

She shrugged. "I guess."

"Come on, Maura. Surely you know what kind of flowers to suggest…say for someone who wants something for their mother, brother, or sister…or their lover…" He held her gaze, refusing to let her look away. "Did you pick certain flowers because the bouquet was for me?"

She managed a nod. "The daffodils stand for respect," she began, pointing to each flower. "The blue hyacinth, for kindness, and the pussy willows are for friendship."

"What about the roses, Maura?" he asked, hoping she was trying to tell him of her feelings. "What do they stand for?" There were white, pink, yellow, and red roses. Their fragrance made him light-headed, but not as much as Maura's presence.

"The yellow rose stands for friendship." She came to the table and touched each flower, then moved to the next one. "The pink for grace and beauty." Her fingers trembled as she stroked each petal. "The white is for unity, and worthiness."

"You're worthy of anyone, Maura," he said.

Maura looked up at Wyatt and swallowed back the dryness in her throat. It was now or never. If she wanted this man, she had to be the one to take the chance. His blue eyes locked with hers as her heart pounded in her chest. Then she pulled the red rose and ivy from the bouquet and held it out to Wyatt. "The red is for passion and…love."

"What else does it mean, Maura?"

"Trust. It stands for trust. And I trust you…"

Wyatt took the flower from her and placed it on the table. He lowered his head and touched his lips to hers, then pulled back. "You know what else it means?"

She nodded, but remained silent.

So he spoke, "It means… I love you, Maura. I love you."

"Oh, Wyatt…" Maura's twined her arms around his neck. "I love you, too," she whispered, just before she pulled his mouth down to meet hers in a searing kiss.

Wyatt finally broke off the kiss. "Tell me again." he said.

"I love you." Tears flooded her eyes. "I love you. I'm sorry that I didn't trust you—"

He stopped her words. "No, I didn't give you enough time. Just because I knew immediately how much I wanted you didn't mean you were feeling the same."

She laughed through her tears. "How can you say that when I nearly blurted out the words the night we were together…the night we almost made love? Then Darren showed—"

"No, Maura, you don't need to bring up what happened."

She kissed his fingers and removed them. "It's okay,

Wyatt. I don't need you to protect me from Darren. I went to see him, and I told him that he wasn't going to control my life anymore."

He cocked an eyebrow. "You went to the jail?"

"I wanted to come to you with no ghosts from the past. No fears. I didn't want my past stopping us from having a future together." Her eyes met his. "That is, if you still want me."

He pulled her against him. "I haven't stopped wanting you from the first night I saw you waving that rifle at me. When I offered you and the kids the place to live, believe me, it was purely selfish on my part. I wanted you more than any woman I'd ever known. I want to take away all your sadness, Maura. Erase every bad memory in your past, and make it all perfect."

She smiled at him. "That's nice to know."

"Then marry me, Maura Wells. Let me take care of you and the kids."

When she shook her head and he felt his gut knot in agony. "No, Wyatt. If I'm going to be your wife, I want to be an equal partner in our marriage. We'll take care of each other."

He broke out into a grin. "I wouldn't have it any other way. I love you being independent, but not so much that you don't need me."

"Oh, I need you, Wyatt. I just don't want to use you as my crutch. I want to be your wife more than anything, but I'd like to keep working." Her eyes locked with his. "I want to have your child."

He swallowed several times trying to hold his emotions in check over her words. "Oh, Maura. I came here to San Angelo, looking for my father, wondering why he never wanted me. All my life, my stepfather told me that

I wasn't good enough to be his son. So I was going to show him. I was sure that all I needed was my own ranch to be happy." He cupped her face in his hands. "Then I found you and Jeff and Kelly. It wasn't until you walked out that I realized this place isn't a home without…love."

He lowered his head and captured her mouth. He parted her lips, then dipped his tongue inside to taste her, to savor her. He wrapped his arms around her body and pulled her closer, letting her know his desire.

They finally broke apart. "You want to start working on the baby now?" He was halfway teasing.

"Don't tempt me," Maura said. "But I think we better go tell Jeff and Kelly the news. You know, it isn't easy being parents."

"I know, but we can give them the one important thing. We're going to stand together and give them a lot of love."

She moved closer. "Maybe you could start with convincing their mother."

Wyatt lowered his head to hers. "My pleasure."

Epilogue

Seated atop Raven, Wyatt led the riders down the steep rise and into the valley below. He looked over his shoulder to see his new wife of three months on her mare, Trudi. Next came Kelly on Sandy, then Jeff followed up the rear on his small mare, Tawny, a present for his seventh birthday and a report card that had straight A's.

"We can have our picnic beside the creek," Wyatt suggested, then climbed off Raven, helping Maura and Kelly. Jeff was already off his mount and smiling. The boy was a natural rider.

"Can we see the ponies?" Kelly begged.

"If they come to the valley," Wyatt said. "Sometimes when people are here they're shy about coming around."

The girl sat down on the blanket Maura had spread on the grass. "I'll be real quiet," she whispered.

"Why don't you two sit here and eat your sandwiches

and watch for them," Maura said. "I want to talk to your dad."

Wyatt got a thrill being called by his new title. He still couldn't believe that Darren Wells signed away his rights to the children. So the man had some decency and Wyatt had two wonderful kids.

Maura took hold of her husband's hand and took him off toward a group of trees and away from the ears of the children. It had been wonderful being a family, but they also cherished their time alone. That was mostly late at night after Jeff and Kelly had gone to sleep. Wyatt would take her into the newly decorated bedroom and he'd make love to her, so tenderly that it would bring tears to her eyes. He'd made the bad years disappear, and the loneliness a thing of the past. Every day she counted her blessings that she and the children found him.

Wyatt sat down at the base of the tree and seated Maura between his legs. They faced the valley, appreciating the beautiful scenery. "How much time do you think we have before they interrupt us?" he teased her, then placed a kiss against her temple.

Maura tipped her head back to look at him. "Not much, I suspect. But don't worry, that will change. There will come a day when they'll want to deny knowing us."

Wyatt slapped his chest, looking heartbroken. "Not my Kelly. She'd never deny me. I'm just worried about how to keep the boys away from her. She's going to be just as gorgeous as her mother."

Maura was touched. "You make me feel beautiful," she told him.

"And you make me feel…needy." He nuzzled her neck crossing his arms under her breasts as he whispered in her ear, "You think the kids will fall asleep so I can make love to my wife? Maybe I can convince you it's time to have a baby."

Maura sucked in a breath, feeling a tingle race through her body. They'd talked about waiting, but she wanted Wyatt's child more than her next breath. "You wouldn't have to work too hard talking me into that."

His piercing blue eyes met hers. "Really?"

"Oh, Wyatt. Of course I want *your* child…so much."

She watched the emotions play across his handsome face. "I love you," he whispered then placed a tender kiss on her lips.

Maura reached up and took a teasing nibble from his tempting mouth. "I hope you feel the same when I get out of bed in the middle of the night for my cravings," she said.

"I wouldn't mind at all," he promised her. "I like spoiling my lady. How about I bring you back here later and show you how much?"

With a groan, Maura turned in his arms as his mouth captured hers. This time the kiss was heated by passion and need. No doubt in her mind that making a baby with Wyatt was going to be a most enjoyable experience.

Wyatt couldn't believe how his life had changed since coming to Texas. He thought that buying the ranch would be the home he'd always longed for, thinking that a structure would stop his loneliness. He soon realized that without Maura and kids, his life wasn't complete.

Wyatt also had his extended family, the Randells, and now he was a partner in Mustang Valley Guest Ranch. He had agreed to run a herd of cattle for roundups, something else to offer the ranch guests. Hank Barrett had given him a start with two bulls and a dozen heifers. By next year they would have cattle on the Rocking R just like in the day of their grandfather, John Randell. He finally had roots and a family.

The kids' voices drew his attention and he saw a lone rider coming down the rise. It was Cade. "Forget about coming back here, this place has too much traffic."

Wyatt stood, taking Maura's hand as they walked back. "Cade. What are you doing here? I thought you were in Dallas."

"Got back this morning," his half brother said. "Wyatt, I just got a call from your mother, Sally. I hate to bring you bad news, but it seems your brother, Dylan, had a bull-riding accident."

Wyatt's heart stopped. "Is he alive?"

"Yes, but I won't lie to you. It's serious."

Maura touched his arm. "You have to go to him, Wyatt. Then when he's well enough, bring him home. We'll help him get through this together."

Wyatt hugged Maura to him. She was his strength… his life. This was what he'd always longed for. Now, if he could only convince Dylan how important family was, too.

* * * * *

SPECIAL EXCERPT FROM

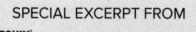

HARLEQUIN®

SPECIAL EDITION

Mackenzie Wallace is back and wants excitement with her old crush. She hopes there's still some bad boy lurking beneath the single father's upright exterior. Dan Adams isn't the boy he was—but secrets from his past might still manage to keep them apart.

Read on for a sneak preview of the next book in the Gallant Lake Stories series, Her Homecoming Wish, *by Jo McNally.*

"There's an open bottle of very expensive scotch on the counter, just waiting for someone to enjoy it." She laughed again, softly this time. "And I'd *really* like to hear the story of how Danger Dan turned into a lawman."

Dan grimaced. He hated that stupid nickname Ryan had made up, even if he *had* earned it back then. Especially coming from Mack.

"Is your husband waiting upstairs?" Dan wasn't sure where that question came from, but, to be fair, all Mack had ever talked about was leaving Gallant Lake, having a big wedding and a bigger house. The girl had goals, and from what he'd heard, she'd reached every one of them.

"I don't have a husband anymore." She brushed past him and headed toward the counter. "So are you joining me or not?"

Dan glanced at his watch, not sure how to digest that information. "I'm off duty in fifteen minutes."

Her long hair swung back and forth as she walked ahead of him. So did her hips. *Damn.*

"And you're all about following the rules now? You really have changed, haven't you? Pity. I guess I'm drinking my first glass alone. You'll just have to catch up."

He frowned. Mackenzie had been strong-willed, but never sassy. Never the type to sneak into her father's store alone for an after-hours drink. Not the type to taunt him. Not the type to break the rules.

Looked like he wasn't the only one who'd changed since high school.

Don't miss
Her Homecoming Wish *by Jo McNally,*
available February 2020 wherever
Harlequin® Special Edition books and ebooks are sold.

Harlequin.com

*When Jed Dalloway started over, ranching a
mountain plot for his recluse boss is what saved him.
So when hometown girl April Reed offers a deal
to develop the land, Jed tells her no sale.
But his heart doesn't get the message…*

*Read on for a sneak preview of
the next book in* New York Times *bestselling author
Allison Leigh's Return to the Double C miniseries,*
A Promise to Keep.

"Don't look at me like that, April."

She raised her gaze to his. "Like what?"

His fingers tightened in her hair and her mouth ran dry. She swallowed. Moistened her lips.

She wasn't sure if she moved first. Or if it was him.

But then his mouth was on hers and like everything else about him, she felt engulfed by an inferno. Or maybe the burning was coming from inside her.

There was no way to know.

No reason to care.

Her hands slid up the granite chest, behind his neck, where his skin felt even hotter beneath her fingertips, and slipped through his thick hair, which was not hot, but instead felt cool and unexpectedly silky.

His arm around her tightened, his hand pressing her closer while his kiss deepened. Consuming. Exhilarating.

Her head was whirling, sounds roaring.

It was only a kiss.

But she was melting.

She was flying.

And then she realized the sounds weren't just inside her head.

Someone was laying on a horn.

She jerked back, her gaze skittering over Jed's as they both turned to peer through the curtain of white light shining over them.

"Mind getting at least one of these vehicles out of the way?" The shout was male and obviously amused.

"Oh for cryin'—" She exhaled. "That's my uncle Matthew," she told Jed, pushing him away. "And I'm sorry to say, but we are probably never going to live this down."

Don't miss
A Promise to Keep *by Allison Leigh,*
available March 2020 wherever
Harlequin Special Edition books and ebooks are sold.

Harlequin.com